The Italian

by

Gary W. Hixon

For Mary Hixon

'It's either one thing or it's your mother.'

Sigmund Freud

Chapter One

The world is full of stupid people, is what my father said to me. It was the second sentence, along with telling me that he was dying. What he'd meant by it was that he was pleased to not have long left in the world surrounded by those stupid people. He might have said, *Son, I am dying, but don't worry about me, I'm more than ready to go.* But he didn't say that because that would have been too undemanding and genteel, and my father was not such a man as to announce something like *I am dying* without a tinge of spitefulness and arrogance.

When he said the first bit, the *I am dying* bit, I recall emitting a stifled whimper. I knew that he'd been unwell for some time and that my half-sister had given up a great deal of her time and had neglected her normal routine to convey him to one hospital appointment after another, but the revelation that his condition was now beyond repair had actually come as a shock to me. And stifled whimpers are but one of the sounds people make when they've been given a shock. At least I didn't scream out, *oh, for the love of God, no,* and start crying in front of him. A stifled whimper, or maybe it was a desperately sad sigh, was just about the right reaction to his news.

I think I'd lowered my head and placed my hand on top of his when my reaction came out, but he'd pulled his hand from beneath mine and immediately uttered his follow-up sentence as though my gesture had compelled him to say it. Was his sentiment directed at me? Was I one of the *stupid people* he'd been referring to? Had he felt compelled to tell me that I was moments after telling me that he was going to die soon as though he knew he would not get another opportunity to say it and could not go peacefully from his life until he had? If that were so, then it was the opposite of what he ought to have said – what most people would expect to hear at such a moment – but then my father was that sort of man. He always did the opposite of what convention dictated was appropriate. He'd spent his whole life upsetting people by giving them the unabridged truth with eloquent but caustic words that were always waiting on the tip of his tongue for their chance to offend.

In that sense, my father was a two-fold type of man. People either loved him or hated him. His circle loved him. The people at his chess club loved him. My half-sister practically worshiped him, and I'm almost certain that when he'd told her his news – before he'd told me, obviously – he wouldn't have followed it up with *the world is full of stupid people* or pulled his hand away so instinctively. It would have been, I'm sure, a tender, lamentable, desperately sad moment for both of them. My half-sister loved him. I hated him.

The world is full of stupid people seemed to me a very strange thing for an eminent psychiatrist to say, given that those *stupid* people, deluded people, anxious people, people who were perhaps lost in a fog, lonely people, heartbroken people, people who'd been 'wired wrongly', people who loved too easily, people who couldn't love at all, people who loved themselves too much, people who got angry at stupid things, people who never got angry at anything and allowed people who did to do stupid things to them, *people*, had allowed my father to make a name for himself.

Stupid people had paid for his Edwardian terraced house on a street in the town of Henley-Upon-Thames – with its porticoed entrance, beautiful original features and a garden that almost backed onto perhaps the most famous river in the world (if it wasn't for the allotments which he'd always resented and loathed their attendees for stubbornly blocking his access) and had financed the villa in Le Marche, Italy, on the outskirts of Porto Sant'Elpidio, which almost had a sea view. Le Marche because Tuscany, Umbria, etcetera, were full of tourists and, you guessed, stupid people. A villa, incidentally, which my half-sister and her lanky, gormless, bald-too-young husband were never away from, but a place where I was never encouraged, nor ever wanted to go.

Come to think of it, my brother-in-law, or half-brother-in-law, or quartered brother-in-law – I was never sure – was probably the stupidest person I'd ever met. He seemed to be a bit too quiet and always let my half-sister do the talking for both of them, as though they were one person split into two parts, and whenever he did raise the courage to speak, his words were always followed by a nervous chuckle that always reminded me of a dog choking. And come to think of it, Sant'Elpidio was full of stupid people too. His gardener, or maintenance man, for instance, who tended to the property all year round – even when my half-sister or my father were not there – could not read or write. But my father seemed to like – or tolerate – both my bald, quartered brother-in-law and the short, thickset Italian much more than he ever seemed to like me.

I suppose, thinking back, for him, it was merely a question of perspective, and even though someone could not read or write his own name or speak freely from his own mind without sounding like a choking dog – nervous and always loitering – as long as they tended to the olive grove, or kept his beloved daughter moderately happy, they were rendered not *stupid* but necessary.

haps that was the nub of our relationship, for the
a better word: I was not necessary. I was an
ence. I was just there. I existed, which meant
that he had to acknowledge me. Always there, at the most
inconvenient moment imaginable, at the point when he'd
almost forgotten, when he could at last be free to be whom
he wanted to be. But there was I, reminding him of my
mother, whom he'd adored, deified almost, but who had
never loved him back half as much. There was I, always,
to remind him of what he'd lost. There was I, pricking his
skin with a needle, and whenever he turned to see what
had caused him so much discomfort, there I was to remind
him of what he could have been. There was I to remind
him of her, and so every time he looked at me, his heart
broke all over again. So it became better for him to not
look at all.

Or perhaps he did not like me because I was forever
asking him for money? I only ever called him or visited
the house in Henley when I wanted to extort him of his
money for one too-good-to-be-true business opportunity
after another. I looked at him and all I saw was pound
notes and little else, as if I were a parasite sucking
everything out of him. Well, that was his interpretation of
our relationship, and it has always angered me.
Particularly when he'd taken latterly to greeting my phone
calls – or in person on his doorstep on the rare occasion
when I summonsed the energy to visit – by saying, 'I
haven't got any money'! *Oh, it's you, what do you want?*
Or something like *I suppose you'd better come in*, would
have been preferable to his inane announcement that he
was cash-strapped when obviously he wasn't.

His declaration of poverty, though, was not what
made me angry. It was the simplistic assumption that I
wanted anything from him at all; that it was impossible

8

for me to call him to enquire how everyone was or knock on his door so that I could confirm to myself that he was alright without me having an ulterior motive, that riled me every time he said it. This was a man who was one of the foremost psychoanalysts of the late twentieth century who had spent his entire career – and had made his fortune from – studying people to get to the nub of what was troubling them, yet could not be bothered to try and understand his own relationship with his only son, or why I would have the need to call on him in the first place, like a mistreated dog that kept going back to its master again and again, time after time. It was just, well, lazy. It was careless, in the sense that he just couldn't care less.

His greeting, or rather his snarly put-down, was something that he obviously became fond of saying, and it always left me bereft of anything to counter it with. There seemed to be no answering it, so in the end, I resigned myself to just sighing resignedly. On one occasion when I visited, I dared myself to believe that he wasn't going to say it at all. There I was, standing on his doorstep, and in the pause, he looked at me and I thought that he was poised to say something else. Something fatherly; an avowal of affection or anything that wasn't *that* that would have made me stop hating him, because that's all it would have taken. It turned out that he'd merely swallowed some bitter liquid spit from his pipe and was giving himself the time to recover from the taste without letting his discomfort show. Once he'd exhaled the stale smoke and removed the offending item from his mouth, he said it with gusto and reclaimed enthusiasm. So, I said nothing, as usual, and side-stepped past him without an invitation to enter the house.

I always wanted to counter his *I haven't got any money left* with, 'What the hell did my mother do to you

9

to make you hate me? Is it because I'm the spitting image of her?' Or even better: 'Where the fuck is my mother anyway? What happened to her?' Oh yes, either of those would have reduced him to nothing or made him throw me out once and for all. But, for reasons I can't explain, I never said either of those things. A good psychoanalyst would get to the bottom of why I never asked him those questions, if only I knew one.

And yet, and yet – I couldn't entirely blame him for his oh-so-low opinion of me. There was a semblance of truth to it that I'd always rebuked myself for. I was angry with myself for providing him with the ammunition to fire right back at me, although at the time I considered it absolutely necessary. I asked him for money on three occasions over a fifteen-year period. The first time was a piffling amount, a couple of grand, which was like pocket change to him, which he reluctantly agreed to give me but dressed it up as a loan even though both of us knew that not a penny of it would ever be paid back, not even nominally. The second was a little bit more, but not an earth-shattering amount. The third time was forty-five thousand. I remember his face when I asked for it, a mixture of contemptuous gloom and enlightened opportunity. An opportunity to never let me live it down whether he'd agree to the 'loan' or not. For that amount, he needed time to think about it and to consult his accountant. Weeks that were like purgatory. Days without end when I must have checked my phone a thousand times in case I'd missed his call that would provide the answer. He never called.

During those weeks, my father had become unwell with a pain in his abdomen that overpowered him and laid him low. I remember the phone call from my sister to inform me that he had been taken into hospital for exploratory tests. I recall that her tone had been different. Not the usual contrite, malicious quality to her voice that usually requested that I stay away from one family function or another because my presence would be unsettling for her *pappa* (an Italian thing that was a joke between them that I was never privy to, but hey-ho) but much more mellow and empathetic towards me, as though she knew – had some kind of daughterly sixth sense – that he would not, could not, overcome this latest bout of ill-health. Empathetic in the sense that, as his only other child, I had a right to know too. It was a problem shared, though not halved, but doubled, to make it real at last in her mind, as though she needed someone else's sadness and shock to bounce straight back at her and slap her across the face and say *pull yourself together, you stupid bitch*! It was a strained and very strange conversation between siblings, or half-siblings, during which there was almost a connection. Almost, but not quite. A phone conversation, even if the two participants are in neighbouring rooms, is always a conversation from a distance, wherein the tone of someone's voice is always open to misinterpretation. She may well have been speaking kindly to me, longing for me to connect to her, but it was hard to tell and, in any case, I knew her too well. She was my father's daughter. She possessed most of his traits, so any kind of connection was always unlikely. But who knows, maybe it was me?

The hardest part about having asked him for that amount of money was that it meant that I couldn't randomly call him up to enquire about his condition – what the prognosis was and what the pattern of his treatment was likely to be – without him assuming that I was really ringing him to chase his money. That conclusion in his suspicious mind was inevitable, so during those weeks I wished that I had never asked him.

I could have begun any conversation with him by declaring, 'Listen, I don't want that money anymore, but thank you for considering it,' then proceeded to ask him how he was feeling and when he was next due in hospital, or whether he needed me to go with him, even though he'd have scoffed and told me that his daughter was taking him but thank you. I could have done that, but the fact was I really needed that money, whether he was ill or not, or whether I'd cared that he was alright or not.

A business opportunity really had presented itself that surely wasn't too-good-to-be-true this time. The forty-five grand would act as a booster to the money I already had saved up, so if I'd sensed that the opportunity was too-good-to-be-true then I wouldn't have risked my own cash along with his. So I didn't contact him at all during that period, and thinking about it now, my inaction and inattentiveness must have appeared as proof positive that he had been right about me all along; that I was a bad penny, a rotten apple, a cuckoo in the nest, a parasite on the back of a pedigree dog that lived with a pristinely normal Disney-type family. A *wrong un* who they were lumbered with.

Like mother, like son.

Then out of the blue, he rang me instead and told me matter-of-factly that he was going to 'gift' me the forty-five thousand, and instead of it being a loan, he wanted me to have it, *gratis* (adjective: given or done for nothing). That's when I knew that he was going to die. Whilst he was explaining that the money was going to be transferred into my bank account the following morning, I realised that he was a dead man walking on his last legs, a spent force, a steam train that had run out of, well, steam, and about to just stop on its tracks, where it would rest as a reminder to a bygone age, a glorious age, halfway between an upcoming tunnel and a viaduct already crossed. Done for. The end. A whole six months before he'd actually told me that he was dying, and when he'd announced that the world was full of stupid people, and when I'd attempted sadness and remorse and had issued some kind of weird whimper, I knew that he was dying.

The forty-five grand was guilt money. It had to have been. The whole gesture, the whole course of that conversation wherein he'd announced happily that he was going to 'gift' me the money, with no need to think any further about it or would have to obtain permission from his accountant in London, was almost a confession. A confession to being a failure as a father to his only son.

That forty-five grand was akin to a medieval lord paying a priest or a monk to absolve his sins: or a rich bishop financing the construction of a great cathedral so that purgatory could be avoided. Purgatory must be avoided at all cost. Forty-five thousand pounds that was like a spit in the ocean compared to what he'd 'gifted' my sister throughout her adult life. Oh, I knew that to be a fact. My sister was an 'Earth-mother' type, all hairs, and big breasts, smocks instead of dresses. She had given him two grandchildren, two boys called Arthur, after the mythological king (I suppose) and Martin, after him, whom she considered the king of everything. Arthur and Martin; they always sounded ridiculous. Little shits.

Arthur was the eldest and was actually quite a nice boy, and I'd always assumed that his name was my sister's attempt at breaking free from my father, but not succeeding to, so that the next son was duly named after the man himself but maybe by then it was too late and the damage was done. She had never properly worked a job. Why should she, after all? She was an 'Earth mother' who existed only to taxi him from one meeting to another, one drinks reception after another, to take her children to school and then be there to pick them up again and to prepare their meals, to take them to *Pappa* on a Saturday morning: like a limp medieval queen tendering to the heirs of everything.

As for my bald-too young brother-in-law, or quartered brother-in-law (oh, it doesn't matter), he was a teacher of English Literature (GCSE's) at a college in Slough and not a great earner at all. Slough, that town that exists across the river from Eton, where everything else exists beneath vaulted ceilings that had been paid for by men with guilt on their minds. Oh, I *loved* the fact that he taught in Slough. Not because I thought of the joy and fulfilment he must have obtained by explaining Austin or the Brontës, Shakespeare, Chaucer, Dickens, Larkin (ironically) to a class full of the children of immigrants from Pakistan or India or Iraq or the Caribbean or even Langley or the Britwell Estate, but because I knew that he taught three miles away from Eton College and that that's where my father would have told his colleagues, associates, etcetera, where he taught English Literature because it was so close that it was almost true. And so did my sister, probably. For all I know, maybe that's where my father actually thought that his son-in-law taught Shakespeare, having been told that by his daughter, and only Arthur and Martin and I were privy to the truth, never to be told in fear of that *disappointment*.

Thirty grand, maybe thirty-five. Definitely no more than that for a teacher of GCSEs at a college in Slough. Yet my sister and her bald-too-young husband with their two kids lived in a genuinely nice, semi-detached house in Marlow-Upon-Thames with lawns at the front and the back, parking, outbuildings, barely three miles downriver from my father, where the average price of a house was six hundred thousand pounds for a semi. There isn't a bank or a building society in the land that would lend that amount to a teacher of GCSEs in Slough!

It doesn't take a genius, does it?

Forty-five thousand? It never came close to the amount of money that could allay his guilt for the way he'd treated me. It was pocket change to him. But at the time, it had kept me quiet, pacified, in that moment when he knew that he was dying. In that moment – during that phone call – it had been enough. It had allowed me to purchase a ten-year lease on a restaurant in Windsor train station, from where I would unfurl my great plan to ply the tourists from the US or China or Iraq with good, old-fashioned English fish and chips that would make me my fortune.

But that was then, and this is now. That was 2019 when the world had been normal, and the wheel had spun on and on. This is 2020, and everything has changed, and the wheel has been broken, and I am stranded in a house in Henley-upon-Thames with my father, whilst my half-sister is stranded in Le Marche, Italy, with her two sons, her bald-too-young husband but not the illiterate gardener too, sadly.

Chapter Two

A traditional, upmarket, British fish and chip restaurant stationed in the biggest tourist trap in the country (outside of London) was one of my better ideas. I've had many business ideas in my time that I don't wish to dwell upon anymore, but that one was like a eureka moment: a lightbulb on top of my head waiting to ping at any moment.

And when it happened, I was standing on the concourse of Windsor train station looking at an empty premises next to a coffee shop that had a 'lease this building' sign hanging above the boarded-up doorway. The kind of tatty blue, triangular sign that I'd seen so often on a closed down public house or on a street corner shop or on the edge of town that I'd always thought: *yeah, right, who the hell would want it*? But not this time. Even though I couldn't peer through the windows to see inside because they were boarded up too, my heart suddenly started to pulsate. It was then that I knew how Newton or Einstein or Steve Jobs must have felt when they'd had their own 'lightbulb' moments. Okay, so my idea wasn't going to change the world or alter how people live or explain the meaning of everything. But it was going to give some of the tens of thousands of international tourists who got dropped off in that town every day of the year, whatever the weather, the thrill of tasting traditional British fayre that I knew they'd be prepared to pay an exorbitant price for.

I knew Windsor well. I had been there hundreds of times – many hundreds of times – so many times that the actual number was rendered academic. To even begin to reckon on how many times exactly was just as ridiculous as asking an eighty-year-old man who had lived in the same house all his life how many times he had crossed the threshold of his front door. Pointless! The point being that it was just as familiar to me as my hometown and would have been my hometown had the price of a house not been eighty thousand pounds above the average for my area, all because of its position on the river and its huge, fairy-tale castle in the middle of it. I loved the place; every street and alleyway; every cobblestone on the narrow streets in the old town next to the castle; the crooked houses in the old town that were like something out of a Dickens novel. I even loved the snobbishness of the place, the way the people who lived there had aspired to do so all their lives and had worked and worked to finally achieve it. Or that the people who had been born and bred there and were connected firmly to it, would be unnerved, startled a little by the way the whole world wanted to visit their small town. I loved the inconsistency and absurdity of that small town being quintessentially English but populated by people from every nation in the world. Most of all, as I stood on the concourse of the old railway station looking at that shuttered-up building, I loved that fact that the day-trippers from London had eight hours to kill and a wedge of money to spend.

The fact that my father had always hated Windsor only helped elevate my admiration for the place. Oh, he appreciated its history and connections to royalty, but after that, he considered it a ghastly tourist trap, no better than Blackpool or Disneyland. To me, it was like Wonderland, and just like Alice had been tempted to 'drink me' when she stumbled across that little bottle at the beginning of her adventure, my message – just as unavoidable and irresistible – said *lease me* in big white letters. But my message had a phone number attached to it.

Windsor train station was no longer a place where trains departed from or terminated at. That is to say, not the station I am talking about. Nowadays, if you arrived at Windsor on a train from London, you would alight at a modern station close to the river across from Eton.

The old Victorian station, that magnificent wrought iron and steel creation with its vaulted roof that covered its vast space, reaffirming all that complicated and ingenious Victorian design which had always aroused me to think about a Dickens novel again whenever I saw it, had been turned into a high-class, elegant shopping and eating centre in the 1990s. It was a temple to the beautiful bourgeois, the kind of people my father called *new money* even though he was one of the newest – his own father had been an engineer for British Rail – and to where the tourists were lured so as to lighten them from their burdensome pound notes. It was packed with boutique fashion shops where an appointment to enter was helpful; independent retailers selling everything from hand-carved wooden chess sets to hand-weaved tapestries depicting Greek gods, King Arthur and peculiarly an array of cats; restaurants serving tapas, Vietnamese, and everything in-between where people sat and ate beneath that vaulted roof and for the uninitiated to this new religion of middle-class Englishness seemed too intimidating to walk in and request a table.

There were no high-street chain stores here, not even the coffee shops which had otherwise infiltrated every town centre shopping precinct in the country. There were coffee shops, of course, but tasteful ones with authentic, Italian baristas (supposedly) and where the process of preparing a cortado was pure theatre, and if you requested a latte, you would almost be thrown out. And bars, lots and lots of bars, where the beautiful people would meet during lunch or after work for cocktails and strong Italian beer and where the cocktail waiters were the high priests of this new temple to desire and ambition. They tended to the ever-burning flame of the good life.

As I stood at the entrance looking down the concourse at the beautiful people mulling around and wondering where to drink coffee or whether to eat Thai food or buy a chess set that they'd never play with, I listened to their collective noises which was like a Gregorian chant. I did wonder what they would make of my *John Bull's Traditional British Fish and Chips* establishment opening up and joining their little world. I wondered whether any of them would frequent it. It was a fleeting concern, however, for when I looked back down the high street, I'd seen an umbrella – just an umbrella – being held aloft, and I knew that following closely behind it were approximately forty or fifty tourists that had alighted from their tour coach. So, who needed the beautiful people and who cared what they'd think?

That thought was fleeting too because at that moment, my idea was precisely that: just an idea. And besides, the cost of the lease in that location would be extortionately high. But what if Alice had never drunk from that little bottle? What if she'd had more sense and walked away? Then she would never have known, would she? If I'd walked away, if I hadn't rung that number, if I'd had more sense than she did, then I would never have known, and I would still be absorbedly in love with Windsor.

The woman in the agency who answered my call was able to give me the particulars of the lease straight away without having to consult a colleague or bring up the file from her computer, as though it was the only listing on her books; as though this boarded-up building was her life's work and the reason she got up every morning was through the desire to offload it and then ring her customer and tell them: *some sucker has taken it! I know, can you believe it?* But she was very professional in her delivery and had curtailed her excitement well enough to suck me in further even though, unbeknownst to her, she really hadn't needed to once I ascertained the cost of the lease, which turned out to be surprisingly reasonable (I dare say cheap) for that location in that town. I should have smelt a rat then and there on that concourse during the telephone conversation. I should have followed up my gasp of excitement with: 'what's wrong with the place?' But I didn't. My only thought was *I can afford it. I've got over half of the money already and I can borrow the rest from the old man. If he refuses, I'll be able to get my hands on it somehow, surely.* The woman who I had been talking to was young, under thirty, I'd assumed. There was no reason for this assumption other than the fact that anyone over thirty would have, by that age, developed some kind of conscience.

As the telephone conversation developed from an initial enquiry – a pig-in-a-poke kind of question – into something more substantial, when I'd actually registered my interest, my excitement gave way to nervousness with the realisation that my big idea was affordable and doable. After all, the dream is always better than the reality. The young woman almost apologised as she told me that it was only a ten-year lease but that didn't matter to me. Ten years was more than enough time for me to make good money. Ten years of endless tourists begging to be relieved of their pound notes. Yes, ten years was long enough to prove to myself and to the old man and to everybody else that I was capable of achieving something. So I made an appointment to get inside.

"What do you intend to do with the place?" the agent asked while showing me around the premises.

"Traditional British fish and chips and other traditional British fayre," I proudly told her.

"What a great idea," she'd feigned, which was nice of her, and the comment greatly bolstered my ambition. "The tourists will love it."

And the beautiful people will probably lynch me! I thought without actually replying, just smiling at her in an attempt to be cagey and not too keen.

Inside the boarded-up building with the lights on, I could clearly see that it had been a restaurant business before. "The fixtures and fittings are included, I presume?"

"If you want them to be," she replied.

The wooden tables were in tatty condition, but a few of them were good, and the rest of them would scrub up nicely enough. Besides, I could always use linen tablecloths to give the place an air of 'fine dining', which the other eateries further down in the railway station didn't do, so my place would have the edge in that regard. The kitchen was kitted out well enough to get started quickly too, and even though everything seemed to be coated in a film of old grease and dirt, it would all clean up with a bit of effort and application.

"Everything works, I presume?" I presumed quite a lot during that viewing.

"You'd have to get everything tested for fire regulatory purposes." She was very professional. But she didn't actually answer my question. She was very competent. She was a credit to her profession since she did not say anything that would incriminate herself or her agency and give me a pretext for complaint and compensation once I'd signed for the lease and discovered, to my cost and despair, that nothing actually worked. I recall trying to light the oven when she backed away and shielded her face with her arms. I thought it was a bit of an overreaction and put it down to her unfamiliarity with a working kitchen. But nothing happened, not even the slightest spark, which worried me until she informed me that the gas meter had been removed by the gas board once the previous tenant had absconded owing them four thousand pounds in unpaid bills, which strangely, hadn't worried me at all.

The whole process from that initial telephone conversation on the concourse of the old railway station to getting the keys and the place being mine (well, at least for ten years) took only three weeks, since my fawning visit to my father when I'd asked him for the rest of the money, had turned out to be surprisingly easy. Maybe he had some kind of foresight and knew what would happen to me, and he was looking forward to watching the show since there was little else he could do while ill? That was in March of 2019, which seems like ages ago now. The world is indeed full of stupid people. But what if it wasn't? What then, in a world void of people willing to take a risk or of people who dreamed big and longed for something else? Would the world move forward at all without the stupid people? Without the dreamers, would there be any kind of advancement for humankind at all? I recall how excited I'd been when I got the keys. The game was afoot; the world was my oyster; the Chinese were about to sample the subtle texture and taste of mushy peas. My adventure was beginning and would be filled with just as many ridiculous characters as Alice's had been.

Correction: I believe that I've been referring to my half-sister as my 'sister'. I'm surprised to have made that fundamental mistake since the distinction has been firmly drilled into the both of us from childhood. The difference was important to my father who, when referring to her in a conversation with me, had always done so in the third person as 'your half-sister, Jane'. *Your half-sister has prepared for me a lovely beef stroganoff; your half-sister and her husband are in Italy.* Your half-sister this and your half-sister that. Very rarely did he refer to her by her name. Once, he even referred to my nephew as *your half-sister's eldest son* when commenting on the little brat's proficiency at the piano. Was he even my nephew at all then? Was *she* even related to me? Were any of them? It was always hard to know if they were since my father had always studiously created the chasm by using that simple four-letter word. I'm not sure if he did the same thing to Jane when referring to me, but I assume he did; otherwise, what would be the point of it?

But if he did, then it never seemed to have the same destructive effect on her that it did on me. Or maybe she never thought that it was an unusual use of a word or the necessity of the distinction because he'd always used it to the extent that it had become normal language during our childhood? Or she'd simply shrugged it off with the resolve to think about me as her brother, not as her *half-brother*. Or she'd had more strength and resolve than to let such a simple word crush her every time it was used. If the world is full of stupid people, then she is one of them for never wondering why he had the need to form the distinction.

I was four when she was born, so it's not as though there's a vast age gulf between us. We were brought up together in the same house. The woman who had given birth to her also fed and clothed and nurtured me and held my hand across a busy road, etcetera. Perhaps that's precisely why my father's vocabulary never affected her: because she was brought up by both of her natural parents and thus, always had a sense of superiority over me since I was an interloper or worse, a parasite who ought to be thankful that he's allowed to live with them. So that in the end, she was just like him. Thank God my stepmother was her own woman; otherwise, I probably would have begged and begged to have been adopted out or put into care if it had only been those two.

I was three when my mother left my father. They say that what you never had, you never miss, but I missed her every day. I thought about her every day, and in my thoughts, she was always beautiful, even though I don't actually know what she looked like other than the fact that she looked like me, or I looked like her. It was hard to know the truth since there was inevitably some of my father in my appearance, but thankfully not his nose, which was gargantuan. My half-sister used to have a penchant for tugging on it playfully when she was a child, and he would always make a noise like a steam train whistle to make her laugh, so she'd do it over and over again until I wanted nothing more than for that steam train to crash into a rockslide. Maybe she did it throughout adulthood too for all I know. Was that how they'd parted company each time she visited the house? By her tugging on his nose and by him blowing like a steam train, then each of them collapsing into fits of giggles once he'd been placated and she'd been reassured by the tenderness of it? *Hahaha, Jane. Much love to Michael and the boys* as she walked away from the house. Pair of idiots. Pair of stupid persons.

But I digress.

Chapter Three

"We're gonna make a fucking fortune!"

"Correction, *I am* going to make a fucking fortune, and I'm going to pay you to work for me. The amount you requested, which is considerable. And if I do make a fucking fortune, then you know me well enough to know that I'd see you alright."

His name was Luigi, and he was my friend. His excited comment was his opening gambit when I showed him around my restaurant for the first time. If my father had ever met him, he would have either loved him because he was authentically Italian, or he would have been appalled by him because he'd consider him one of the 'stupid people' that so irritated him (an assessment that I would have found hard to disprove, frankly).

Luigi *was* stupid; so authentically, over-the-top Italian that he made the baristas in the coffee shop next door look like floppy haired Eton schoolboys. He was short and round and if it wasn't for his full head of jet black, reclaimed hair – quite an achievement for a man in his early sixties – he would have been a Mussolini doppelganger. He was so grotesquely Italian that he was almost a caricature of every old Italian man you've ever evoked in your minds-eye. He was their John Bull, their Uncle Sam. He was customarily in a foul mood, and he gesticulated with his arms and hands; foul-mouthed, forthright, and occasionally outright aggressive. He was a difficult man to know, much less like. But I *did* like him because when he wasn't those things, he was sensitive, vulnerable, kind, and occasionally as insightful as an Italian Confucius. When one day he'd turned to me and said, 'Hey, man, I love you like you are my brother', I knew that I would like him, or at least have a reason to think about him fondly, for the rest of my life. *Brother*, not *half-brother*. None of that nonsense with this guy. You either *got him* or you didn't. You were either in or you were out, and he didn't really care which it was.

I first met him during what I call my 'downtime'. Not downtime like overworked, professional people know it to be when they spend quality time with their families and go on long country walks or ride their bicycles through parks or gather together at mealtimes to discuss the whys and wherefores of their respective glistening lives, but rather a time when I was genuinely *down*. Not fully buoyant and not yet completely sunk but sinking, nevertheless. On the way down into the abyss of inconsequentiality, regardless of how hard I tried to float and keep my head above the waterline.

It was during a long(ish) term relationship with a woman whom my father had actually quite liked, called Fiona, a nurse from Maidenhead, whom the old goat had almost instructed me to try and keep hold of because she was as good a person to marry as I could expect. It had been another *don't screw this up like you've screwed everything else up* conversation, which we had many of. I think that's why I stayed with her for as long as I did, because I didn't want to invoke his condemnation, another one to add to the others, but the truth is that for a large portion of our time together, she just got on my nerves. Fiona was academic; I was not. To be academic is to be focused and studious, whereas I have always been more fleeting and very easily distracted by what was happening elsewhere, as though my body rested upon marbles instead of feet. But Fiona was, is, a decent woman, and whenever she tried to be beautiful, she *was*

27

beautiful. And it's true that during those four years when I was with her as her partner, I'd obtained many more invitations to the house at Henley than the years before or after her; when my sister would abduct Fiona and whisk her away into the kitchen or the garden, probably to discover information about me on my father's behalf. 'Is he drinking too much? Is he looking after you? Does he treat you well?'

But my sister would never have asked such questions as 'does he make you laugh? Do you laugh together? When he walks into the room, do you swoon like a pen swan? Does he make your heart pulsate as though it's about to burst free? Do you understand his need to disappear from time to time? Do you recognise that he is lost, and he lives his life in the constant, overwhelming belief that one day someone will find him? Is that someone you, Fiona? Is it?' No, she wouldn't have said any of those things because she hadn't known any of those things, or if she had, didn't care. Nor did she tell her 'He has serious *mother* issues because his mother abandoned him when he was three years old, so now he believes that everyone he ever gets close to will abandon him too, whereas those people who he is not close to are ever-present, constant, obdurate, and once you understand that, you will understand everything.' But I can't blame her for not telling Fiona any of that, because neither did I.

Sorry, sorry, *half-sister*, not *sister*. It won't happen again, I promise.

But I did tell Luigi. I don't know why, and I don't recall when. All I know is that, at some point, I'd told him everything about my grandiose, cantankerous, vicious father, who was a psychiatrist but who hated me, the Earth mother half-sister and her bald-too-young husband, and their little shits; my step-mother Sandy, who I adored and wished above all else that she had actually given birth to me; the villa at Porto Sant'Elpidio, which had pricked his attention, and where my only memory of my actual mother was formed, wherein she was smiling, and golden, and just as elusive and temporary as God. When he'd had to break free from my onslaught and had gone to the bar, then brought me back another glass of pecorino and said, 'Hey, man, you know I love you like a brother,' and then I knew that I was bound to this crazy Italian for the rest of my life, like Frodo Baggins was to Gollum.

I'd gotten a job as a waiter at the Sun Inn at Hurley, a village close to where I lived. It had been just a bog-standard village pub in the fifties, sixties, seventies and eighties, but when the greatest chef in the history of the world bought it in the nineties, he turned it into the kind of establishment that forced all the hoity-toity, preposterously rich – and by the process of evolution, the pinnacle of creation – from London and from the big houses in the towns on its outskirts, to travel and to taste the food created by the greatest chef in the history of the world (although by then he was already in L.A).

The Sun Inn became something else entirely. Luigi was assigned to me as my 'buddy'. That meant that it was his responsibility to train me how to serve food and wine to the *pinnacle of creation*. He was easily the most obscure, impatient, hard-line teacher I'd ever had, but I wasn't deterred or intimidated by him at all since I had seen the glint in his eye that suggested that he savoured other people's apprehension like a fine, full-bodied red rioja, so I resolved not to give him the satisfaction. A resolve, at that time, I didn't know I had left in me. Once he realised that I wasn't some spotty-faced boy working his first job and that I wasn't going to be overrun by his aggression and frustration at being 'buddied' up with someone else yet again; that I was a full-grown man who had simply found himself in an awkward position and needed the job in order to pull himself up off his knees, a mutual respect that has been there ever since formed between us.

Drink is what did it for me. Fiona had quickly established my drinking as the reason why the relationship ended, and it formed the basis of her explanation to my father (I still cannot fathom why she'd felt obliged to). I maintained that I had been sober when I met her and a drinker when I left her, so read into that what you will.

When I had my eureka moment on the concourse of Windsor train station, and once I ascertained that I could afford the lease, I knew straight away that I wanted Luigi to join me on my adventure. He was a career waiter in the way only Italians, Frenchmen, and Spaniards can think of it as being any kind of vocation at all. For the English, waiting on tables was merely a stopgap, a fill-in to earn money whilst they waited for greater things to happen to them. That was how I approached my position at the Sun Inn, not realising at the time that four years later it would lead me to becoming a restaurateur in my own right: the top honcho, the self-made man, the cash-cow who paid the wages, and the biggest idiot in the northern hemisphere.

He was everything you would want from an Italian waiter. He could turn it on when he needed to, and I often wondered whether all the boldness and swagger was just a performance or whether it came naturally to him. It was certainly hard to believe that he could turn from being the very essence of a Sicilian godfather into the most endearing, meticulous, reliable maître d' you could ever conjure up. But then again, I suppose anyone can turn into anything when they're being paid to do so. Whenever the door went, it was *Good evening, signor, nice to see you again* even though he had never set eyes on him before in his life. And even though the guests knew they had never frequented that establishment before, they loved him for saying it nonetheless, especially when they had brought a friend or two along, who also recoiled in their admiration. *Signor, you taste that wine for me, tell me what you think, whilst I take the beautiful signorina's coat* and whilst kissing her hand, they'd suddenly adored every inch of him whether he was being chauvinistic or not. The signorina may very well have been the most powerful woman in London, who in her day job beckoned to her attention hundreds of men, but right then, she would soften like putty in his hands like a groupie at a rock concert. It was quite a performance and quite a show. It never failed to impress me or them.

During the quiet periods when the door did not 'go', Luigi filled the pauses by channelling the *raconteur* in him by recounting tales of his life as a career waiter; when on the QE2 he used to have a woman waiting for him in every port – and when I looked at him and wondered, *Jesus, what must they have been like*? Or when he'd owned a restaurant in Leeds, Pavarotti had demanded that the place was emptied so that he and his entourage could eat pasta and pizza in privacy without the ever-present glare of admirers (he'd been performing at the West Yorkshire Playhouse in the eighties, apparently), when that great man, and copious eater, had insisted that Luigi and everyone else should call him *maestro* all evening. Or when he'd gotten Prince Charles pissed in the nineties when he'd called into his restaurant in Middlesbrough for something to eat whilst *Lady Di* had been on duty elsewhere, opening a new wing of the James Cook University Hospital and he'd spiked his drinks. No wonder they'd had to get divorced. It turns out that it had nothing whatsoever to do with Camilla. They had merely encountered Luigi, that's all it was. Prince Charles must have been sober when he'd met him but a lousy drunk when he'd left him.

I often wondered how true it all was. I began to doubt him when I was told about the three years he'd spent in Dubai when the sheiks would frequent his establishment just so they could drink strong liquor in secrecy, knowing that their Maitra d' was the soul of discretion and easily paid off like any Sicilian don worth his salt would be.

But the thing about liars is that a good liar has got to have a good memory, so that they can keep a track on their tall tales, even elaborate on them when the occasion arises and not to trip themselves up and expose the fraud. Because fraud does not have to be physical. It does not need to be *they've cleaned out my bank* account. It is mostly verbal, imaginary, illusionary. The most common form of fraud is boasting. The most generic form of fraud is *look at me, look at what I've done.* And yet, and yet, can it be fraud when at the same time it is self-preservation, dignity? Luigi was a terrible liar, to his eternal credit, so that on other occasions when the door had not 'gone', he'd been more melancholic and self-reproachful, and he'd confessed to me about being bankrupted three times and that was why he was working as a career waiter at the Sun Inn at Hurley, Berkshire. But I've always hoped that the bit about Pavarotti and Prince Charles was true and knowing Luigi, it probably is. After all, God loves a trier. Even though nobody else does.

Thinking back to that morning on the concourse at Windsor train station, it hadn't occurred to me how a thickset, authentically Italian, career waiter – who'd been around the world on the QE2, who'd closed his restaurant for Pavarotti, who'd gotten Prince Charles, and the sheiks, drunk – would transfer his skills to selling fish and chips? *Mushy peas or garden peas, signor?* Or whether his deep-seated Italian accent would ever – even if it had been coerced out of his mouth by the greatest vocal coach in the West End – be able to pronounce the word haddock when it'd always sounded like *hachhh*, as though he was clearing his throat. *Cod or hachhh, signor?* When that poor, bemused customer would poke his head above his laminated menu and dare to ask *cod or what …?* Or that when the Chinese or Japanese tourists would ask him what mushy peas were, he would reply, exasperatedly – most likely thinking about the time he'd closed his restaurant for Pavarotti or when he'd gotten Prince Charles drunk or of any halcyon day that he'd ever known – he would reply, 'They're garden peas that have been fucking trodden on'! When I'd tried to chastise him for being rude, for having allowed the Italian in him to rise to the surface, and when he'd retorted, 'Is this what I've been fucking brought down to', and I'd found it hard to argue with him.

"We're going to need a chef," I'd said to him as I showed him around my empty premises.

"You haven't even got a fucking chef?" was his second gambit.

"I haven't got anyone, Luigi, apart from you."

As Luigi had lifted the corner of a linen tablecloth to see what was beneath it, and whilst I cringed with shame because I knew what was beneath it and hoped that my friend didn't notice, it was clear that Luigi had taken my comment as it was intended: a lament for my failure to acquire anyone in the way of 'staff'. But as the words had fallen out of my mouth to cover the distance between us, I wasn't convinced that that's all I'd meant at all. It was just a thought, a flash through my mind like a gadfly, in one way then out the other. That's what thoughts are: biting insects that fly in through your ear to arouse a sluggish brain; to sting people once inside and whip them into a fury, all in the service of truth, then fly out of the other ear. Thoughts are fleeting, temporary, and as elusive as God. They are the moments before a memory, they are the visions of the future, they are the sting that provokes in the stung a wince from pain, or a sudden waft of cold air on a burning mind that rouses a moment of comfort. Some enter in and trample all over, staying longer than necessary and stinging every available surface in a person's mind, finding their way into every crease and crevice; others enter in to repair the damage, to apply a dab of camomile lotion onto the sting; but the most ephemeral are the ones that barely have the courage to enter in at all, but once they've summoned the courage to, tiptoe around in there and hardly touch the surface as they search pensively for the exit.

It had been just a thought, like a flash of electricity through my brain. It had been like awakening after a bad night's sleep to find that the dawn had brought with it the reality of my life. It had been like a sting. Was Luigi – that little, plump, bad tempered, Mussolini doppelganger – really the only other person in my life who meant anything to me? Right then, as we'd stood together in my empty, cold restaurant, as we'd discussed the future and the merits of using linen table coverings in a sphere where every other restaurateur had turned *ultra-modern* with booths of reclaimed wood, it seemed to be the case.

"Anyway, you don't need a chef. You're going to be serving fish and chips, so all you need is someone who can fry. I can fry. You could fry. My mama's fucking Pomeranian could probably fry!"

"But I want this place to be so much more than fish and chips, Luigi," I'd answered. "I want the menu to offer the very best in British cuisine." I'd been empathic with my response, gilding my words with ambition and purpose, but I didn't convince Luigi.

"Like frog in the ditch!"

"Toad in the hole," I corrected him. "Yes, like that. But done well with the finest ingredients and prepared by a chef who cares about what's going onto a plate and across the pass!"

"Then why have you called it 'John Bull's Fish and fucking Chips?'"

"To get the tourists in."

"Precisely, for fish and chips!"

I sighed deeply. "You don't understand, Luigi. OK, the name might be wrong, but we can change that." We couldn't. As we were speaking, the sign guy was outside on the concourse punctuating our conversation with the sound of his drill, probably beseeching the fury and condescension of the 'Italian' baristas, boutique-keepers and the beautiful rich from further down who were standing watching as a 'Googled' image of John Bull, resplendent in his union jack waistcoat and pork-pie hat, was being fixed to the wall. "There's a gap in the market for good old-fashioned, British food done well and with a twist!"

"There's a gap because no fucker wants it!" he bellowed.

"You're wrong. There *has* to be a market for it."
There'd better be, I thought. But then, you know what
thought did. It stung you on the nose.

"You're gonna need a chef," Luigi concluded after
sighing for much longer than I had and with much more
consternation on his mind.

"I know," I replied, happy that the conversation was
back at the point where it had begun.

He took his phone out of his over-sized jacket
pocket. It seemed strange how an Italian man – who
almost by definition should be the epitome of style – was
wearing a jacket that was obviously two sizes too big for
him as though he had bought it from a charity shop for
Italians in distress. "I'll ring Rocco!" he announced before
proceeding with a phone conversation in Italian that I had
not been privy to with a man named Rocco, who I had
never heard the slightest mention of. For a while it seemed
that the two men were arguing. Luigi's free arm was
gesticulating wildly and looked likely to fly from its
socket at any moment. Later, however, Luigi was
laughing and evidently saying something tender and
wonderful when his arm was drawn back into the hulk of
his body and the palm of his hand touched his forehead.

"Ah, grazie, grazie, Rocco. Ci Vediamo!" Luigi
ended the call and slipped his phone back into his pocket.
"Rocco will be here on Thursday!"

"Who the hell is Rocco?" I gasped. Everything was
moving too quickly for my sensibilities.

"He is the greatest chef you will ever meet! Rocco
can cook anything, and he has, all around the world.
Rocco has cooked for the director of the FBI (yes, that
one), he has cooked for royalty, for presidents, for the best
there is. Rocco has cooked for the fucking pope! And your

luck is in, my brother, because Rocco has just been sacked from the Grand Hotel in Brighton!"

The concern must have shown on my face because Luigi moved quickly, almost lunging at me, to allay my fears. He knew that he had to; otherwise, his friend Rocco would have had a wasted trip from Brighton.

"He was not sacked because of the quality of his cooking," Luigi assured me, ardently. "No way, my brother. He is a genius. But he's also a dirty bastard."

That addition did him no better. "Dirty as in he keeps a dirty kitchen or dirty as in personal hygiene wise?"

"Dirty as in Thailand wise!" Luigi answered quickly. Then he started to chuckle. "Rocco, he likes to go to Thailand twice a year, capisci? I don't judge him. Every man needs his release. Every man has his, how you say … preferenze!" I nodded. "For me it is big breasts." He laughed again and nudged my shoulder, playfully. "Hey, my first wife, you know how I met her?" I shook my head; of course, I didn't. "In Leeds, she was coming down the staircase from the mezzanine level of my restaurant as I was about to go up. She was a vision of beauty … the Earth's mother … a mermaid, but no man ever looked at her fish tail, capisci?" He laughed one more time. "I said to her, 'Mama Mia, look at them bad boys!' Now, one of two things was going to happen. She was either going to slap me across the face, or she was going to marry me." Another laugh until his face had fallen still as his memory of that woman had soured with the circumstances surrounding how the relationship had ended. Not so well, I guessed, but I didn't say anything. Then he became animated again with the resolve to put that woman out of his mind. "And you, you like women who wipe your nose for you just like your mama should have done! And Rocco? God only knows. But I don't judge anyone."

Hang on a minute. Just a cotton-picking minute. What vibe had I been giving off for Luigi to have said something like that? For him to have assumed that my preference was for women who were like a mother-figure? He'd never even met Fiona or any of the women who I'd been involved with and there had been many – too many. What had I said during our short association with one another for him to have formed that hypothesis? It hadn't mattered what I'd said. What had mattered was that Luigi had turned out to be the greatest psychoanalyst in the history of the world. Much better than my father had ever been, who couldn't even analyse himself. And yet my father was a rich man with a big house in Henley and a villa in Italy, whereas Luigi was a career waiter.

Yet, it had been just a quip; an off-the-cuff remark during a conversation wherein I'd gotten off lightly compared to his chauvinistic penchant for breasts and his dubious friend's penchant for God knows what. Just a wisecrack that he'd thought nothing of, but it had pierced my armour as though we had been on the battlefield. Had my disguise been that bad all along? A disguise that I had worn all of my life. Was it so easy to see through it after all? Because with that simple comment which he had thought nothing further of, he had stripped me bare and analysed me to within an inch of my life. So, it was Luigi who ought to have had the big house in Henley, the villa in Italy, and all the renown and prestige that being a 'great' man brings along with it, and my father should have been serving fish and chips to the Chinese, Japanese, Canadians and Americans. *Mushy peas or garden peas, sir/madam?*

For we all wear a disguise in one form or another. A *brave face*, a *bull-dog spirit* just like old John Bull or Uncle Sam, etcetera. Yet, behind the disguise, the façade of normalness, the veneer of what one thinks may be acceptable to everyone else, there lies a million thoughts that sting the mind like gadflies. And with each sting there is a memory that brings regret and sorrow. And the sting digs deep, or at least it should. Unless, unless I wasn't like everyone else. Maybe some people are fated to feel the sensation of the sting of the gadfly, whereas others aren't. Were the people who did feel it the *stupid people* that my father had referred to, or the people who didn't? It was hard to tell. All I knew was with that simple, throw-away remark in a conversation where I'd actually appeared to be the *normal* one, compared to that petulant little Italian with *women* issues and his perverted friend, the penny had finally dropped; the nail had been hit squarely on the head. Was he right? Did I have a penchant for women who would 'mother' me? You'd better believe it. Because I was a man whose mother had up and left when I was three years of age. Of course, I had. How could I not have? It doesn't really take a psychiatrist to work it out. I don't know why I hadn't realised it before that Monday morning in an empty restaurant whilst the noise of the sign being screwed to the wall outside resounded all around.

"They sacked him because he likes to go to Thailand?" I followed up, shaking off that moment of self-analysis (and gladly so).

Luigi laughed again. He liked to laugh. His disguise had always been better than mine. "No, Lewis, of course not. That would be illegal." He came closer again. "Whilst he was showing a waitress … someone whom he'd thought was his friend ... a photograph on his phone of the hotel he used to work at on the Amalfi Coast, he swiped just a little bit too far, and what he'd actually shown her was a photograph of one of his ... how you say ... ladyboys!"

"Well, that's precisely how you would say it," I said.

"The bitch reported him to the manager, who is duty bound to take him down the line, and who sacked him. Rocco is a very unfortunate man."

"Aren't we all?" I said. And actually, my concern had been allayed.

"But Rocco is the greatest chef you will ever meet. And a great singer too."

"A singer?"

"As he cooks, he sings," Luigi replied whilst making a gesture with his hands as though he was tossing pasta with a wooden spatula and fork. "Puccini or Verdi ... opera ... anything." He looked towards the kitchen, which was visible from the dining space. "And here we have an open kitchen, Lewis," he said, excitedly. "He will sing, and he will lean over the pass and get everyone in the restaurant to sing along with him as he cooks their meals!"

A singing chef, I thought immediately. *They'll be queuing up the street to get in.*

I was going to make a *fucking* fortune.

Chapter Four

Whenever my father called me on my mobile, I was always a little bit shocked that he even knew my number. I had a mobile phone like everyone else for maybe eighteen or nineteen years, right from the get-go when it ceased to be the size of a house brick and had evolved into something that was, well, actually mobile. From a dinky little thing with a flip-top screen through to the most up-to-date smartphone with enough technology in it to ascertain the meaning of life. I kept hold of the same number for twelve of those eighteen or nineteen years, yet my father only ever contacted me via said mobile on *three* occasions. The old man, incidentally, never owned a mobile phone despite my half-sister's insistence that he should get one, particularly since my stepmother had passed on and he'd been wandering around the big house at Henley on his own. She must have imagined a frail old man shaking and twitching in darkness and solitude when she hadn't been there, but I never had that image of him.

The second time my father rang me on my mobile was a full eight years after the first, and I remember being ashamed and a little bit sad by how seeing his name displayed on my phone screen had shocked me just as it had that first time. A heart-shuddering shock that caused me to back away from wherever I was standing at the time into a corner, as though by dialling my number, it somehow granted him an all-seeing eye that would determine where I was, what I was doing, and what drunken state I may, or may not, have been in. It was the same kind of jolt through my body as a thump from behind or hearing a knock on the door in the middle of the night.

The purpose of my father's second phone call was to inform me – hesitantly and unconvinced – that he'd decided to 'gift' me the forty-five grand and when I discovered that he was dying. I recall being relieved that I answered his call, as my first instinct was to throw the mobile phone across the room, not to destroy it but to just get it out of my hands, as though it was the ring of power and I was Frodo Baggins, and I was wary of it suddenly. But really, I think that I'd had too many glasses of wine, and I had been worried that my response to him would be slurred, and he'd detect that I'd drank too many wines; enough for him to withdraw his kind, gracious, barbed, stuttering offer to help me. When answering his call, I corrected myself just in time (like any good drunk can) and I got away undetected. It was the most ill-fated call I'd ever taken because now I know what happened to his forty-five grand and the remnants of my money too. Now I know how much I loathe Windsor, despite it once being my dream. Now I know how much I loathe people who once had been my friends. Little things in life make a big difference, like stepping onto the wrong train and meeting the greatest person who turns your life full way; or deciding to turn left instead of right, then hearing the howls of despair and the screams from the people who had decided to turn right and, consequently, ploughed into by a bus that did not have the time or the space to stop in time. I still would have found out that he was dying if I hadn't taken that call. Some things in a human life do not hang on a moment of fate; they are appointed and therefore find their way through life naturally, like how water always finds its course, through a desert, say, or over rocks in a wooded valley, or in my case: through the light fittings in the ceiling just as a man from Chicago was about to put a fleshy, plump prawn into his mouth, and his wife had gasped in horror and abruptly stood upright and summonsed *the manager*!

The third time my father called my mobile, it didn't come as a shock to me at all. It was not perceived as a thump in the back or a knock on the door at midnight. It was expected, predictable, and an inconvenience. On this occasion, I was out on my daily trip to the supermarket for 'essentials' when he called my number from his death bed to instruct me to buy him the finest bottle of Italian Limoncello that I could find in one of those bourgeois 'supermarkets' (by that stage of his life he had completely forgotten that his own father had been an engineer for British Rail) because he fancied one, that's all. I hoped, as I recall, that the 'essential worker' on the checkouts would not question the definition of *essential* as her or him had checked me out. But more of that later …

… because I want to talk to you about the first time my father called me. Because I think it's important. Because unlike the couple from Chicago or that bottle of supermarket Limoncello or whether or not that poor prawn ever got eaten or whether the checkout operative on Henley High Street considered my purchase essential or not, I think it is relevant. It has something to add. Because this occasion when my father called my mobile for the first time ever, has stayed in my mind … where I was, what I was doing … for far too long.

And it's time it went!

It's curious how the human mind can retain the most inane, inconsequential things; how it stores them away like it's duty-bound by its code to keep them safely out of the way until the time comes when it deems them to be necessary again. Simple things: occurrences, moments, words spoken to another or heard from another that even at the time were by their very nature ordinary, mundane, idle, but are captured in the mind's hard drive, imprisoned there, fated to wait for that moment when reality turns up with a saw hidden in a cake to free them. So the human mind – I mean when it's at full throttle, it's gears and cogs oiled and primed and working effortlessly together as though they are really one part of an elaborate invention; fire in its boiler and full steam ahead; the human mind, unsurpassable in its complexity, its ambitions of grandeur, it's necessity and therefore its longevity, its durability, its range and its ambition; in the way that it computes emotion, grief, unbridled joy, despair, success and failure and so on and so on, and treats each one the same, to be stored away in its own memory file – is either the greatest object in the natural world with more gigabytes than the men or women who'd created the world's very first mobile phone could ever imagine was possible …

… or it's an overrated, overthought, cumbersome relic of a time when such a thing as a *memory* was considered important, valuable and worth preserving. A grand old steam train careering off a Swiss mountain bridge or a NASA computer with the ability to send a probe to Mars (if only the Russians hadn't interfered and inserted their damn virus that sent it crashing into the dust so it could never dig into the Martian soil for signs of life).

Hard to know which.

I am not, by any measure, what you would call an *intelligent* man. I don't have letters after my name, I didn't go to Harvard or Oxbridge, or in my father's case the UCL, for five years when he studied philosophy and psychology and where he honed and perfected his trick of being able to look into someone's eyes and could instantly repair their tortured soul (if this were a text message, I have qualified that last remark with a "LOL" or a "*hahaha*" or half a dozen crying faces). I'm not, however, unintelligent either. I am not one of the *stupid people* that so riled my father. I know things. I see things. Maybe not as clearly as him but then it would appear that no-one ever could. I am always willing to learn from anybody with an instinct to teach. I yearn for new experiences.

But I have to admit that my highest level of academic qualification is GCSE. Eight of them, in fact. And top grades in English and history I might add. I did stay on at school with every intention of extending my academic career through university, but I flunked my A-Levels so that was that. I'd like to say that my father was furious and disheartened, but the truth was that he didn't really care. In fact, I presented him with an opportunity since for the next five or so years he was able to point to me as an example of what happens to someone when they don't study diligently and pursue a course to academic success, and my half-sister never missed his point and always made him happy and smug with her assurances that she would not fail and let him down like I had.

If I had gone to university, I would have undoubtedly studied history. Probably not at Cambridge or Oxford of the UCL but somewhere provincial and local. Reading, more than likely. But history, undoubtedly, because it has always fascinated me how things, moments, sometimes obscure and negligeable that happened a long time ago, that at the time seemed like nothing, have the power to affect the world and its ways and what people do or feel or think about in the present. Like a stone that is tossed into a millpond by someone who could not have cared less. So, the stone hitting the surface of the water is the moment, and the ever-increasing circles until the water breaks against the earth bank becomes the effect of it. The ripple effect of history that has always fascinated me. Who knows why?

I did consider buckling down and getting good A-level results and then going to university, but it would have been somewhere as far away from the house at Henley as I could possibly get; somewhere in the north of England, maybe even Scotland, but somewhere that could be considered 'away' from them all. Just to be able to start again in adulthood, as though I were baptised into a cult that promised to cleanse the soul and the memory of an unhappy, stagnant existence. A new world stepping forwards to liberate the old. A world where there was no mother or father, certainly no half-sisters or half anything, where I could be an orphan if I had chosen to be, deny my association with my father like Saint Peter denied knowing Jesus. A brave renewal in a different dimension and when people asked me who my parents are and what they do – an inevitable effect of history, one of the ripples – I would say to them 'I haven't got any parents'. But it wouldn't have sounded weird. I would have answered that inevitable question by saying that but in such a way that gave my interrogator the impression that I did not wish to explain rather than coming across as some strange, aloof extra-terrestrial being that had been dumped on the planet Earth.

I may have even changed my name by deed-poll and become someone else entirely, by law so to speak. A proper renewal. Almost a rebirth. An immaculate birth, a miracle, that would not require the presence of a mother or a father. There was a time in the nineties when American children were at liberty to 'divorce' their parents in court if they deemed them to be inadequate; stupid people; flawed; not fit for purpose; the kind of people my father made fortunes from. The presiding judge always took those children seriously. It was a thing for a short time. It doesn't happen nowadays but it felt like that at the time. It had felt like I should do something like that and going to university a long, long way from Henley would have presented me with a similar opportunity. The opportunity to stand in front of a sympathetic judge and renounce my parents, my upbringing, my beginning, everything, and be given the chance to begin again.

That had been for a good three or four months whilst I studied for my A-levels, my intention. It was my design for the rest of my life, a blueprint of immaculate precision. The reason why it didn't come to pass, why the blueprint was destined to remain on paper, was because of the dog my father bought. For my eighteenth birthday, he brought it into the house. He carried it in a blanket: a tiny, golden ball. It wasn't my birthday present since he presented it to my half-sister first, who'd been so excited by the sight of it and had screamed so loudly that the poor little thing shit itself, and my father's anger had boiled over. Then, believing it was in trouble, it jumped into my arms. In that moment, I protected it. And when the little golden ball looked into my eyes, I knew that it hated both my father for bringing it into that house and my half-sister for being so over-excited and loud. In that moment, I just *got* that dog. I fell in love with that dog.

And that was my father's intention all along. He gleamed with satisfaction whenever I went to my room and the dog followed me up the stairs to lay in the well beneath my desk; when it lay on the bottom of my bed whilst I slept; the way it ran to me whenever I came back into the house; the way it greeted me as if it were trying to say *thank God you're back, they're all fucking idiots*! Apart from my stepmother, whom he liked because she let it out onto the back garden, and when my father wasn't

47

aware, boiled him some chicken so that he may taste something different from time to time.

It was no coincidence that on the occasion of my eighteenth birthday, the moment when I legally became an adult – the dawn of my manhood (and for my father: D-day) that the dog arrived in the house. The dog was meant to be a distraction. And it worked. What a clever man to even think of such a thing. The way I fell for that dog, and the way the dog became my responsibility, was the fruition of his master plan. It gave him the prospect of saying to me: 'You cannot come with us to Sant'Elpidio, Lewis, because someone has to stay behind to look after the dog. You're a man now, Lewis, so step up to your responsibilities'. And it worked every time. There was no way the dog was ever going to be placed in kennels for a fortnight or a month or however long they went for. Whenever my stepmother suggested it (so that Lewis can come too), I always objected because I knew that the rejection would kill it, and my father always agreed with my contention. And off they went, the three of them, time after time, leaving me with the dog in the big house. What a clever man, my father. I was seventeen the last time I went to the villa at Sant'Elpidio, Le Marche, Italy. By the time the dog died – which broke my heart – there were other distractions to keep me away.

Here I go again, off on one of my tangents, babbling on about flunked A-levels and a dog that broke my heart when it died, when I should really be getting to the point by now. I really, really should be telling you about the first time my father called me on my mobile phone, yet here I am rambling on about things that don't matter. Most things don't matter, after all. It's just what I do. I always take the longest route when I'm telling a story. You'll get used to me. Or not, in which case, you've probably already stopped listening to me. You'll have turned your face away from me, a little embarrassed and trying to be as graceful as you can while plotting your escape. Just another person who is plotting their escape whilst they feign interest.

It's a strange word: *tangent*. It's the kind of word that, when said repeatedly, sounds as though it isn't a word at all. It sounds made up or as though it ought to be peeled and eaten or jumped on and ridden to who knows where. It sounds like an alleyway, as in *ginnel* or *snicket*. A long, narrow alleyway, a *tangent*, with darkness and threat at one end and at the other, daylight and freedom and … relax. And whichever end you are walking towards depends upon your frame of mind at the time.

So, really, I don't care that I ramble from time to time. I will make no apologies for taking the longest route when I tell a story. Otherwise, what is the point of telling a story? And if you're still listening to me at this juncture, neither do you. Come to think of it, what is the point of being alive without being permitted to wander from time to time? Without being able to glance to the side to look away from what you had been considering: something mundane, to see something quite different? Something wonderful.

Consequences is another strange word that, when said repeatedly, sounds like nonsense. It sounds a lot like *consecrated*. Consequence is the darkness at one end of the passageway, and consecrated is the light at the other. Isn't language a fascinating thing? Aren't words wonderful? The sheer overabundance of them. Words that mean one thing and words that mean the opposite. Words. A word. Just a word. Words articulate everything that awaits within a human mind, unrehearsed but ready to go.

Words give life to a memory. Words give life to everything. Just a word. What is a memory without words? It's nothing. It's non-existent. It's a whim. But when you put words to a memory, rehearsed and articulated, that memory ceases to be a memory. Words, when chosen well, bring the memory back from the brink. The memory becomes real again, as though it isn't a memory at all, but a thought that is right here, right now. Words can do that. Once words become actual voice, a human voice, words that are spoken; once a noise coming out of an animal's mouth makes complete and utter sense to another of the same species, then words become … they become … I don't know what they become … but they bring memories back from the brink of inconsequentiality.

Now, there's a big word. *Inconsequentiality.* Everything that ever happens to a man, or a woman, has *consequences.* Every little inconsequential thing that happens, that at the time was nothing, grows and grows into something else entirely. An occurrence, a happening, an incident, however tedious at the time, must by its code, become something else entirely. It must, by its code, by its reason for existing, become something else. As a gadfly must grow, from its safe and warm cocoon, to ultimately leave and break free from its cocoon so that it can sting us all.

Do you remember the time you pulled me up off my knees? I hope you do; otherwise, what's the point of me even speaking? I remember. I remember your hand extending down towards me. I remember needing your hand to help me onto my feet because I did not have the strength to pull myself upright. I remember being grateful and thinking that when someone is on their knees, that's

50

all they need: a hand extending down to them. It happened to be you, but in all honesty, it doesn't matter who it is, as long as someone is there to do it. It might even be a stranger. But as long as somebody is there – somebody who, when a person finds themselves on their knees, is there to act as a sign that reads: *you're not alone*, then that is enough.

Undoubtedly, words bring memories back from the brink. They resurrect a moment. *Do you remember the time …?* And suddenly you do, and it ceases to be a memory. It's all made real and perceptible again as though you were living that whole, solitary moment once again, and the rest of your life is rendered inconsequential. Your real life, the real world in that moment, becomes senseless and ridiculous until the moment of remembrance, and how you felt about it becomes a memory in itself, and so on, and so on; the ever-increasing ripples spreading out across that millpond, and the moment they break upon the bank is the moment when a man suddenly finds himself on his knees; helpless and adrift.

From the age of eight, I went to the villa at Sant'Elpidio every year for a month in September, encroaching upon October, when the heat wasn't too oppressive. From the age of seventeen, I never went back. I never liked it there. My half-sister and my stepmother adored the place, but I never did even though it was more mine than theirs; more connected to me than it could ever be to them like an imaginary umbilical cord that was tied around my neck: connecting that damn place to me no matter where in the world I happened to be. But they loved it, so all was well. Apart from the fact that I never really enjoyed September and the first week of October

51

until I was eighteen – legally an adult – and when those weeks revealed themselves in their true, gloomy, English glory, and my dog pounded around my legs at the slightest encouragement, and when he ate boiled chicken every day, I have no memories of that villa in the sun next to the sea.

Apart from one.

The day my mother left me was an unusually cold, grey, dank day, and even though it was an Italian day, it may as well have been a November day in England. Or so I recall. Actually, I have no idea what the weather was like on that day or what part of the year it was. But I remember that she wore a scarf around her neck, presumably to keep off the chill. I think it was red. Her lips were red too. Not red like blood but red like a blood orange. That is to say, vibrantly red containing no threat whatsoever. Not like blood contains a threat. It was the opposite shade of red to the colour of blood.

I remember sitting in a chair that was far too big for me, and my legs didn't even reach the edge of it. I remember watching a skinny man who wasn't my father trimming a tree with his sheers and singing songs in Italian. I hope it was a Cyprus tree because they've always given me a thrill. Cyprus trees, you see, can't grow in the damp English climate.

I recall that she had black hair that was like threads of jet tied tightly to her head. I recall that her face was beautiful. But it doesn't matter if it weren't because I knew instinctively that I belonged to her like a toy, so it wouldn't have mattered if she had the face of a bull. I just knew that I belonged to her, was connected to her, that she was my sanctuary and my salvation, and so long as she was around, I would be safe. That's what I recall when she came up to me whilst I was sunken in that seat watching a man who was not my father trimming a tree. I recall that I was safe and that there was no threat whatsoever and that there never could be as long as she was around. I recall that her eyes had been green, not green like the tree had been green, but a green like the tree was exhausted and wilted by the sun. Red and green should never be seen.

I recall tears when she brought her face to mine, and suddenly I felt a little less safe. Instead, I felt uneasy in my extra big seat when the sound of the man's singing was a little less jolly. In fact, as I recall, he stopped singing altogether, and he'd started watching what she did. Watching, as she brought her face close to mine, and in my recollection, when I held out my arms, she didn't gather me up like I expected her to. Instead, she simply kissed me with her blood-orange lips. And then she whispered in my ear – whispered so that no-one else could hear her – *How long is forever? Sometimes, just one second.* Which I now know is a quote from *Alice in Wonderland*, but at the time, they were just words that didn't mean anything at all. I remember her smiling and nodding at the man as she walked away and that he politely, delicately, genuinely, smiled back at her. I recall that she had a scarf around her neck, jet-black hair that was tied tightly to her head, blood-orange-coloured lips, tree-green eyes, and was clutching hold of a small bag that I now know contained everything that she held dear … except for her favourite toy. I recall that after she quoted Lewis Carrol, she wished me a happy birthday before walking away, captured in the sunlight and then she disappeared.

I recall, as I hollered and kicked, a man who was my father had appeared in front of me. He gathered me up in his arms, and together we had walked back towards the house. I don't recall him saying anything to me.

Wait a minute … wait just a cotton-picking minute! She walked into the sunlight on a grey, dank Italian day? How in the world could she have done that?

But she had, as I recall. But now I'm not so sure. Now I'm not so sure that a memory is a true facsimile of what actually happened. So perhaps memories are condemned to fall off the edge? Perhaps memories aren't the truth. Perhaps the here and now is all there is, all we are left with, after all? Or that memories are destined to become myth, and myths are something else entirely. They are a half-truth, just a pigment. Not to be trusted. I recall a lesson at a primary school in Henley-Upon-Thames when I'd fallen hook, line, and sinker in love with history. My teacher had sat us all around her and had proceeded to tell us the story of the Minotaur and how Theseus had to find his way through that beast's labyrinth. And there he found it dwelling at the maze's centre: half man and half bull and when Theseus had blazoned his trail with string, he'd be able to find his way out again. I loved it.

Until, whilst studying ancient history for an A-level, my tutor explained that in the Minoan culture, men had been ordained as a man only once they had partaken a ritual that demanded them to jump over and beyond a live bull – a creature that was venerated in the Minoan culture as being a thing of extraordinary strength and durability. If a boy could survive that, then he would rise on the other side of the bull a man. My tutor had stripped back a story that I loved to leave only the bare bones. He explained, quite expertly, that the myth of a half man, half bull, came from that Minoan practice of young men

54

jumping over bulls. That Minos, the king, had lived in a palace that had been so over complicatedly designed that it resembled a labyrinth to anyone unfamiliar with it. And that the author of the myth had recalled the whole preposterous ritual of boys being coerced to run and jump over raging bulls quite differently from everybody else. Until a memory had become a myth in the telling.

God-damn you, memories. Better to have none than to see them disgraced. Yes, much better to have no recall whatsoever than to be forced to live in the here and now, much like those boys had been forced to leap over a raging bull just to prove something to everybody else – something that they didn't even need to prove to themselves.

So maybe her hair hadn't been the colour of jet, tied tightly to her head. Maybe her lips weren't the colour of a blood orange, but of blood, with all the threat involved. Maybe I wasn't as safe as I recall, and her tears, her sadness, was the only true facsimile of what had actually happened on that day, and the rest – the image of that woman that I have retained in my mind ever since, the safe sanctuary of her embrace – is all just a myth? Anyway, it doesn't really matter since that memory of her face, tear-stained or otherwise, on that cold, dank Italian day is all I have left of her. It's the only embrace she can afford me now. Negligeable sanctuary, but better than nothing. But at least I know what her name is. Apart from that, I don't know anything about her or whether she ever actually existed at all except in my mind as a vague and consoling memory. All I have is a domineering sense that I belong to her, that I am connected to her, and her to me, as though the umbilical cord was never cut. That's all I have. Not enough, I know. But then, I never asked my father anything about her, so it's my own fault because I always had a sense that questions would not be welcome and would not get answered. He moved on, so must I.

Incidentally, one of the other A-levels I flunked was English Literature. I opted for it because I always liked words and stories, and since my father never told me a story, true or fictional, I always had to make them up and tell them to myself to fill the void and pass the endless days of childhood. This will sound strange, but as I was growing up, I always had a sense that someone was narrating the story of my life. I don't know who, and it was not necessarily my mother, but that someone, somewhere, was narrating and knew what was going to happen next. God, perhaps it was God who was narrating, but I doubt it. It was probably just my own voice in my head that had accompanied me through childhood when I would stay silent and absorb myself in my own imaginary world. They must have considered me a very strange child, my father and stepmother. Strange that I never required or sought out their affection or attention. Strange that I was happy and content in my solitude. Strange that the long, narrow garden at the back of the house at Henley that would have backed onto the River Thames if it weren't for those damn allotments was my true sanctuary, where I always felt truly at peace in my own world.

When our teacher set us an assignment that required us all to write an essay about our favourite book – the reasons why it was our favourite, what we liked about the characters, a description of the narrative (first person or third person), etcetera, I realised that I hadn't actually read one from beginning to end. Just because I enjoyed stories and words as a child does not necessarily mean that I was a bookworm. I never needed to read books because I had my own private narrator whispering their stories in my

56

ear. So, I scoured my father's bookshelves in his study whilst he was at work and picked out a work of fiction that looked thin and manageable. This was before Google and cut and paste, so I actually had to read it. It was *Alice's Adventures in Wonderland* by Lewis Carrol. It was a very strange book for my father to have on his bookshelves, squashed in-between Freud and Thorndike, but the next book along had been Colleen McCullough's *The Thorn Birds*, so that was at least something. That book, incidentally, looked interesting but was just too damn thick, and I didn't have the time. So, I read *Alice in Wonderland* when I discovered that what my mother had said to me, as – I now know – she was preparing to leave me, *How long is forever? Sometimes it is just a moment,* is a quote from that book. And it had pricked my interest to read some more, right on to the end and then I wondered whether I'd actually read it before as a child and had forgotten all about it? Or whether my mother had actually said those words to me at all, and it had all been just a part of the myth because I had, in actual fact, already read the book?

My homework turned out to be much less an essay than simple, one sentence answers to my teacher's bullet points. *The narrative:* written in the third person; *favourite character:* Tweedle Dee and Tweedle Dum because they're funny; *the reason you like this book:* because it's all a little bit creepy and nothing seems to make sense. I got a 'D' for that assignment, and that's when I realised that an academic life was not the life for me. But once I had read that book, it's position between Freud and Thorndike was precisely where it ought to be, I realised.

Looking back, my homework should have been awarded a 'U', as in unqualified. It must have been my comment 'nothing seems to make sense' that saved it, since my teacher must have read it as well and then been assured that I had. But at least he hadn't written his usual comment of: *you need to stop rambling, Lewis, and get to the point.*

So, I will, finally.

The first time my father called me on my mobile phone was on the twelfth of September, two thousand and sixteen, five-fifty PM (to be precise), while I was in the wine cellar of the Sun Inn at Hurley searching desperately for a particular bottle of dessert wine because my customer was a very demanding shithead from the city via a shithole in County Durham, I figured out. I remember feeling my mobile vibrate against my leg and being thankful for having had the sense to turn off the volume because we were supposed to leave our phones in our lockers because the management didn't like the impression of a phone being in a tight trouser pocket. I took the phone out of my pocket only because I knew I wouldn't get caught in the wine cellar. When I saw *Henley* displayed on the screen as the identity of the incoming call, I panicked all of a sudden and answered it.

"It's your father, Lewis."

"I know, what's the matter? What's happened?" Because I knew that something must have happened. Perhaps my half-sister had fallen into the river and drowned? Oh, wait, the garden did not reach the river because of those damn allotments, but you get my point.

"Nothing is the matter. I merely wanted to wish you a happy birthday, that's all. Where are you?"

"I'm at work," I stuttered, still in too much shock.

"That's a pity on your birthday. I thought perhaps you would have taken the day off?"

"No."

"Is it busy?"

"Very busy. I'm searching for a bottle Chateau Rieussec, actually, but can't find one."

"Luckily for your customer."

"But not for me. Is everything alright?" I detected that nothing was alright and that the whole conversation wasn't making any sense.

"Of course. I just wanted to wish you a happy birthday, that's all."

"Thank you."

"I hope you've managed to have a nice day?"

"Well, you know, all work and that."

Then a pause so long that all eternity could have been poured into it.

"Have you heard from your mother?" he asked, almost longingly, almost too ashamed of himself for having asked.

And that was the moment I understood the purpose of the phone call. I ended our conversation by throwing my mobile across the wine cellar until it smashed against the wall above a cask of ale called Perpetual Motion, ironically. And when I sunk to my knees and the world around me collapsed inwards – because I realised that my mother actually did exist and that she must still be alive. More than that because I realised that it must have been thirty years since my mother left me on that chair in the garden at Sant'Elpidio because I had been three years old. And that phone call had been on the occasion of my thirty-third birthday.

"Are you alright, Lewis?" she asked me, finding me on my knees.

My words were incoherent when I spoke, garbled noises between gasps of shock. "How dare he?" I answered. "How dare he speak of that woman to me?"

Chapter Five

And since we're talking about Tweedle Dee and Tweedle Dum, Rocco was two weeks late, leaving me to wonder whether he was real or not, whilst my restaurant was rendered unopened, a forgotten memento, an undelivered promise. If he did turn out to be real, then at least I knew that I had a chef, and at last, off we could go on another adventure, far better than that Alice's; and if he wasn't real, then I knew, for as long as I lived, to never trust another living, *real* person again.

But he was real, so that was that, whether he was two weeks late or not. And it turned out that Rocco was a doppelganger of Gandhi! Not Gandhi in a suit, who'd been a student of law at the University College London, but the Gandhi in your imagination, the authentic Gandhi, dressed in a loincloth and wearing round eyeglasses, spinning cotton, etcetera, etcetera. Except my Gandhi, my saviour, was not wearing a loincloth but a donkey jacket because he never quite accepted the fact that the weather in England in April could never live up to his expectations as an Italian man.

What is it about the Italian men in my life that they had to, by their code, resemble a twentieth century figure of historical importance? When he walked through my door and Luigi had bellowed, 'Hey, Rocco, fratello mio!' or 'Hey, Rocco, my brother!', I looked at him and all I saw was Gandhi in a loincloth. Much the same as when I first met Luigi at the Sun Inn, Hurley, all I had seen was a very downtrodden Mussolini.

Every day for two weeks I asked Luigi whether he heard from his friend Rocco and whether he was still coming to join our venture. 'Otherwise, I better start advertising for another chef'. Why he was delayed, what his intentions were, what he was playing at because I was by the beginning of week two on the verge of a nervous meltdown; every wasted day was nibbling away at what little money I had left in the bank since the other three staff members that I managed to recruit still wanted to be paid, including Luigi, who was getting paid a fortune to do little other than allay my fears that a chef called Rocco actually existed. 'He's a genius, he's worth waiting for'! was his usual, offhanded answer accompanied by a dismissive wave of his hand.

It was during the second week of that torturous wait that I realised that although Luigi was at that time my only friend, who knew almost everything about my life, had been present throughout the little collapses that I occasionally had that customarily involved a bottle or two of wine; had listened meticulously to me ranting on about my father, my upbringing, about everything, and even though I thought that I knew almost everything about *his* life – his ex-wives, his bankruptcies, his namedropping – I did not trust him one bit. I did not believe his assurances that Rocco was due tomorrow or the reasons why he hadn't arrived yesterday or the day before that. He disappointed me. The realisation that I didn't trust him had disappointed me. It had been like an awakening, a revival of my senses all of a sudden when I realised that my friend Luigi was treating me no differently from those guests he pretended to know when they'd appeared at the door of the Sun Inn.

Luigi was a fraud, and I had gone into partnership – not in a financial sense, the risk was all mine, but in an emotional sense – with an Italian charlatan who couldn't stop himself from lying to me. I hadn't fully believed his stories about Pavarotti and Lady Di either, but that hadn't mattered compared with the deceit of an absent chef whilst I stood in a refurbished restaurant that was ready to trade but couldn't. I was supposed to open for the Easter weekend, 2019, to take advantage of a town full of day-trippers when we would undoubtedly have been packed to the rafters which would have put some money back into my bank account. Easter had come and gone, the bank account was exhausted, and so were my nerves.

How long is forever? Forever is a fortnight.

The four of us had occupied the time, filled the void of the delay, by doing little jobs that did not really need doing and cleaning things that hadn't had the opportunity to get dirty. I was resolved to not pay them for sitting on their phones whilst drinking my coffee. Actually, everything that I had inherited from the previous tenant had cleaned up quite nicely.

'Everything cleans', my stepmother had taught me many years ago as we both scrubbed the carpet in my father's study which the dog had almost ruined because it turned out that it didn't like tuna which I had given him the night before as an extra special treat.

And everything works again, machinery and such, if you throw enough money at it. The ovens had required some attention, which had cost me almost a thousand pounds to bring them back from the brink. The extractor fan almost as much. The fryer had had to be condemned and a new one brought in. But tables, chairs, plates, cutlery, etcetera, all cleaned up quite nicely. Walls were freshened up with a lick of paint and decorated with Googled images of old-fashioned fishing villages and fisherwomen sewing their men's nets. The gas meter, by the way, was only re-installed after a barrage of emails and letters from me, and one from the agent to prove to the gas board that I was in no way associated with the previous tenant. The toilets were acceptable, but the floor in the *Ladies* was so rickety that any *Lady* with high heels on their feet would never get out again, but I figured day-trippers would not be wearing high heels, so I left it unattended until another time. It had never occurred to me to worry about the roof, to wonder whether the place was actually watertight, and you already know what happened to the poor guy from Chicago as he was about to place a plump prawn into his mouth. Some things, like roofs, just aren't worth worrying about. Roofs should be reliable, fit for purpose, just like friends should.

I employed a young man, Sean, to work in the kitchens. He was on a gap year from university, but not a gap year wherein he intended to see the world – fall in love, have his heart broken, by either a person or a place – but to earn money. I assured him of full-time hours. I employed him to assist the (non-existent) chef with whatever he needed assistance with; plating up, cooking perhaps, but really his job was to wash pots and clean the kitchen because *apparently* the singing chef was so accomplished, so at the top of his profession, that he shouldn't have to clean his kitchen himself. I liked him. I liked the fact that he was articulate and could hold a conversation; I liked the fact that he considered Luigi a lunatic. Most of all, I liked the fact that he hadn't cared about hours and money nearly as much as his parents obviously had and only wanted to finish early every shift because there was always somewhere better to be. He had been on an hourly rate, and I was always happy to let him.

I also employed a middle-aged woman called Linda, whose husband was extremely ill, but she'd been unable to ascertain any benefits for him at all and so who needed to work. And what a worker she was. That woman never stopped working even though she was English. She cleaned and cleaned until everything had sparkled. She even painted the walls and hung the pictures. A terrible waitress, but one hell of a worker. I liked her too, maybe even more, because the conversations I had with her were about hard, tough things that concerned death.

The plan had been to have two in the kitchen and two out front with me filling in the gaps between the two positions and, if the occasion arose, working the door because I was always good at it. Luigi had objected, insisting that Rocco should be given the wherewithal to choose his own kitchen staff because he was a great chef and that's what great chefs do, surround themselves with people they know they can trust to do the job.

"Yes, maybe so, but we need to start slowly."

"You will sort out front of house, Rocco will sort out his own kitchen!" Luigi had demanded.

"Let's just get open first, then after a couple of weeks, if we're busy …"

"You can have whatever front of house staff you want; you can have old woman slamming plates down who looks like Betty fucking Turpin, if you want (Luigi had been in England for so long that he had been able to grasp English cultural icons ahead of Italian ones) but Rocco, he needs his own staff."

"He's got his own staff, he's got Sean."

"But Rocco wants Frederico!"

"Who the hell is Frederico?" I gasped. Another one, I shouldn't have wondered.

"He is Dame Joan Sutherland's 'Gilda' to Pavarotti's 'Duke of Mantua'!"

"What the hell are you talking about, Luigi?"

"Rigoletto by Verdi"

"Who *is* Frederico?"

"I've never met him, but Rocco speaks highly of him, and he will only come if Frederico can come too. So you pay Frederico wage, capire?"

"Capire." And sigh. But looking back, I would rather have paid Betty Turpin.

"He's on the train!" said Luigi, looking up from his phone on day fifteen after the supposed, and pre-advertised, opening day. They had been the most beautiful, tender words that anyone had ever said to me. They sounded like a song or a poem spoken out aloud by the author themself. It had been the greatest thing I had ever heard, and my relief must have shown on my face because Luigi brought himself close to me. "He's been in Thailand!" he chortled.

"I don't want to know that!" I replied.

"Dirty, dirty, bastardo!" he laughed out aloud, thinking of his friend in a way that seemed to belie his statement.

Whether or not Rocco looked like Gandhi, even if he had two heads, I'd never been so pleased to discover that someone actually existed in my life. The myth, the man, had been made real when he stepped into my restaurant in his thick overcoat, thin and frail, and shivering like a scolded dog. Luigi introduced me to him formally when Rocco looked me up and down in an attempt to estimate the quality of the man whom he was going to work for and by the look on his face, he didn't much care for what he saw. Neither did I. He looked old, delicate, decrepit, past his best. His face was unshaven and drawn as though he spent too much time over a hot stove and the heat had cooked it, dried it out. In the moment of that handshake, I considered the poor Thai girl or man, or whatever, who'd had to 'entertain' him on his regular visits when he needed his release from God knows what. I hoped that it was the same person every time to mitigate the psychological damage that his visits must have inflicted on that country. More than anything, he looked weak, barely able to stand up, let alone run around a busy kitchen, and suddenly the insistence that Frederico would join him made sense. Frederico was going to do all the work, because that man in front of me barely had the strength to shake my hand. Perhaps it was the long flight that had laid him low? Maybe once Luigi had gotten him to his place, fed him and put him in a hot bath, he would come back looking like Gordon Ramsey in his prime? But that had been wishful thinking on my part.

But first impressions can be and usually are deceptive. Rocco turned out to be a sweet, gracious old man with many more social skills than his friend, Luigi. I grew very quickly to like him. He seemed to me to be a kind man, and that was important.

After letting go of my hand, he shuffled across the restaurant and craned his neck to see over the pass and into his kitchen. Again, he didn't seem any more impressed with the facilities as he had been with their benefactor. It's true that the ovens did look old, they were old, but he can't have known by looking at them that it'd cost me a small fortune to get them to work again, and Linda had done her best to get most of the old grease off. Then he wandered into the kitchen past the pass and had started to open cupboards and fryer lids with the same look of disdain on his face as though he was the health inspector. Then he found a laminate copy of the menu on the worktop and picked it up.

Luigi and I had prepared a fairly basic menu in the first instance, five starters, ten main courses – twelve, if you count haddock, cod, and a mixture of the two as three separate dishes – on the understanding that Rocco would have carte blanche to change things once he settled in. He turned the menu over to read the back of it, but it was blank. Instinctively, I knew he was looking for the Italian dishes, pizza, pasta, and seemed to despair that there weren't any. So I began to worry that Italian dishes, pizza, pasta, was all he could cook after all, and would he struggle with the particularities of Yorkshire puddings or even know what a cottage pie ought to look like?

As any good health inspector would, or any tradesman who knew that he was needed and would not be sent away, he sucked in his breath and clenched his teeth before saying in English, "Six-hundred-pound notes per week, Ce?" I must have looked shocked because he glared at Luigi as though he been brought in on false pretences, as though he had been conned.

"Ce, Rocco," Luigi exemplified with his hands as though his friend was worth every penny.

"Frederico, four-hundred!" Rocco followed up.

By then I nearly fainted. "That's a thousand-pounds per week between two employees," I gasped. "We're not even open yet; we don't even know if this place is going to work!"

"And I no like tax!" Rocco added for good measure, just a pinch of irony in the remark to season his truth, an exemplary chef. "I pay tax on just half of it, the rest …" and he made the internationally *filthy lucre* gesture with his fingers.

I sat down and rubbed my face with my hands vigorously, and in that private moment of despair, Luigi had silently urged his friend to start singing. I pulled my hands away from my face just in time to see the tail end of Luigi's prompt and the bemused look on Rocco's face because he hadn't had a clue what his friend had wanted him to do. But then the message was received, and he had started to sing – opera: Nessun Dorma by Puccini. And actually, it turned out that Rocco, that strained, skinny little Italian, had a tremendous voice and he sang it very well. The noise had provoked Linda to emerge from the toilets where she was hiding on the pretext of cleaning them again because, and I quote, 'If that Luigi were a golfer, he never hit a hole in one'! Her facial expression just about summed up the surreal, unexpectedness of a skinny Italian who looked like Gandhi singing opera at the top level of his voice. Sean hadn't lifted his head from his phone screen, probably too embarrassed to. Luigi had joined in at the end, at the crescendo at the end, although he couldn't sing to save his life and he kind of ruined it.

All'alba, vincero! Vincero! Vi-ncer-oooooo. And relax.

"Bravo, Rocco," Luigi had said when it was over. Rocco accepted the acclaim like he was Maria Callas on the stage at La Scala taking a curtain call, and I half expected a bouquet of roses to be thrown through the door by one of the baristas next door. Linda shook her head as though she just had an epileptic episode and was emerging from an *aura* when she slipped into a trans-like state and at the other end of it, she wondered whether it had all been real or not before skulking back into the haven of the gent's toilet. Come to think of it, she spent so much time in there that Luigi hadn't so much as missed a hole in one than peppered the whole place with golf balls like the far end of a driving range. *You're going to have to have a word with the dirty get, Lewis!* But really, I think she just used that private space and the time alone to check in with her husband.

"This place will work, Lewis," Luigi had said as he passed me and patted me on the back, evidently incredibly pleased with himself. "Pay him what he wants!" And in that moment, I imagined my restaurant filled to capacity inside with a queue outside waiting for a table, all singing along to Puccini arias, accompanying the singing chef.

Vincero means *I will win*. And they did.

You may ask why I was so stupid, why was I so gullible, so blind to the obvious. And you'd be right to ask that. I was all of those things. But when a man is given what he's never had but has always craved, then perhaps the question must evaporate into the steam of a hot kitchen, a kitchen at full throttle to be captured by the extractor fan and sent into the ether of the nether after. Looking back, I had been all of those things which are attributed to me. I was a stupid man, another one. But why? I can answer that question without pausing and thinking too much about it. Because those four years at the Sun Inn at Hurley had, looking back, been the happiest years of my life. Years that will remain in the recesses of my mind forever. Years that will define me, who I am, who I will be ultimately, at the end. Because whilst I worked there – at first a novice but by the time I left quite frankly a superb waiter – I met people that will be with me until the end. Perhaps not physically but in the confines of my subconsciousness, where they are fated to wait until a gadfly comes into my head and stings my mind and forces them all out of retirement. I met Luigi, and I met you. You, who pulled me up off my knees precisely when I needed someone to do it. And it hadn't necessarily needed to be you, but it was you, so that is that.

I may have given the impression that Luigi is an idiot, a caricature. And he was, is, both of those things. But in the quieter moments, when he wasn't being those things, he was a genius. He told me things that he probably hadn't told anyone before, things that had awaited in his mind ready and rehearsed but had been waiting for the right person to hear them. He told me about his first wife – the mermaid – whom he adored but who'd left him and had taken off with his money so that he didn't have the wherewithal to pay his staff at his restaurant in Leeds. He told me that he did not sleep for two weeks, that every morning he threw up in his toilet bowl. He told me that on the occasion of Pavarotti's visit to his restaurant that he hadn't had any supplies and ingredients in his kitchen with which to honour his menu and that he sent the kitchen staff off to the co-op down the street to buy pasta, passata, onions, anything, and had given them his credit card that he hoped, prayed, still had a balance left on it. I realised that Pavarotti's visit, that great man's presence in his restaurant, who'd probably sung to his entourage before they were fed, had finally bankrupted him. Much like when Queen Elizabeth the First had decided to tour the country with an entourage of five hundred, stopping off at one nobleman's ancestral home after another, she had bankrupted them all, and she knew she would.

He told me that he had four children to two different women but because of the circumstances of those women leaving him, he did not have a relationship with any of them except perhaps his eldest daughter to the mermaid but only very tenuously. He texted her only when he summonsed the courage to do so, and sometimes she replied. He told me that when he arrived in West Yorkshire in 1986 that he been astounded by the

71

griminess of the place and had wondered how this little island in the north had dominated the world. Every woman had called him *love* so that he actually thought that they were in love with him because the translation is *amore* which is used quite differently in everyday Italian. He told me that the job at the Sun Inn at Hurley had been his salvation, his answer to them all. He told me that at the age of sixty-four that there was one big adventure left in him which he longed for.

So, why had I been so stupid?

Because these people, these sad and lonely people: the little fat Italian who looked like Mussolini on a bad day; the singing chef that looked like Gandhi, who needed to fly to Thailand twice a year to find a physical connection with another of the species; the old waitress who looked like Betty Turpin, who had to work five twelve-hour shifts just to keep a roof over her dying husband's head; the young kitchen hand who looked as though he didn't want to be there and had wished that he was in South America; the girl who picked me up off my knees, who was there because she was trying to escape something, *and I will find out what it is she's trying to escape from*; all of them, and all of the people at the Sun Inn, Hurley, Berkshire, and John Bull's Traditional British Fish and Chips, Windsor, who were not my family, became my surrogate family. And it did not matter to me that I was paying them to be my family. In that regard, I was no better than Rocco on his frequent visits to Thailand. Every man needs his release.

Surrogate: noun; a substitute, especially a person deputising for another in a specific role.

Now, doesn't that sound pathetic?

72

Chapter Six

John Bull's Traditional British Fish and Chips didn't quite work out as I thought it would. But you might have figured that out by now. You might have also guessed that Luigi was never able to get his Italian tongue around the word *haddock.* You might also surmise that the singing chef never sung because he was always too exhausted or in such a bad mood that to sing would have choked him. And you'd be right. Oh, we'd had our moments in the ten months that we'd been open. Joyous moments with gilded edges when everything had just worked, as though someone, somewhere, looking down on us had clicked his fingers. And when the singing chef sang, no-one ordered haddock, Linda (at long last) laughed and had no reason to skulk away into the gent's toilet due to how many *gents* were in the restaurant, so instead, she had to stay with me, the whole thing just worked.

When Rocco began to sing 'O Sole Mio' while grilling a pre-prepared cottage pie, Frederico was batch frying countless amounts of cod. Meanwhile, Sean stood ready with the chips, mushy peas, and the plates. The heat lights on the pass shone like the lights above the stage at Covent Garden. And Luigi had been on the top of his game. He'd called everyone *signor* or *senorita,* and they all loved it. And when Rocco leaned over the pass and sang '*Ma n'atua sole, Cchui bello, oje ne',* his audience sang *O sole mio* right back at him. And I wandered around the restaurant, conducting them all. And Linda laughed; happy at last because she'd forgotten all about her half-dead husband at home. Sean watched, too inexperienced to join in, and upon noticing him, I realised in that moment how Brazil, Peru, and even Machu Picchu, could never compare to this; could never provide him with the same thrill, and nothing ever would for the rest in his life. Even when Linda opened a bottle of prosecco wrongly (she loosened the cork but then had gotten distracted by her conversation with a woman from Wales, where she had her honeymoon) and the cork was left unattended for too long and shot out of the bottle and went hurtling across the restaurant. Everyone ducked while they sang, and the cork nearly took Frederico's face off, but all he did was laugh. We all did.

"I meant to do that!" Linda announced, slightly embarrassed.

When I realised there was enough cash in the till to pay their wages, and with two thirds more coming into the bank on the Wednesday next week (Saturday night was when everyone sang O Sole Mio), everything had worked out precisely how I intended back when I first stood in front of that shut down building on the concourse of Windsor Old Train Station, looking up at a sign that said *lease me.* Alice may have had her Mad Hatter's tea party, but I had my O Sole' Mio night.

However, these golden moments with gilded edges when the restaurant was full to capacity and everyone sang along with the singing chef were few and far between. Don't get me wrong, when it worked, it worked really well. But most of the time, we had to hold an inquest at the end of service to ascertain what had gone wrong. In these moments, when Rocco moaned about the lack of adequate equipment ('the basic tools with which I can do job!') and when Luigi would always conclude the inquest by insisting that what the restaurant needed was 'food! People fucking want food! Pizza, pasta!' despite there being two very excellent Italian restaurants further down the concourse that were always busy because their

74

reputations were established and which probably didn't employ a Mussolini or a Gandhi. Frederico, by the way, turned out to be something of an Italian heartthrob who didn't resemble any famous figure from the twentieth century, thus destroying my supposition. He certainly reminded me of someone, but I was never able to pinpoint precisely who.

Chefs are, by their code, petulant creatures who think they're God Almighty. Rocco, on a morning whilst he sipped his coffee, proved to be all of the things I previously said he was, kind and gracious, a *real* raconteur with a fascinating bunch of stories in his locker. But once he was in his kitchen, and when service was at full throttle, he turned into a proper diva, a prima-donna of the most insufferable kind. Little wonder he sung opera. I'm surprised he hadn't insisted that we all called him *maestro*. Although, thinking about it, he must have known that he didn't stand any chance of being called that by Linda, who'd turned out to be something of an ally to me, perhaps my only ally in the business. Linda had turned out to be incredibly important to me, despite her dodgy waitressing skills and her ignorance to the power of a pent-up bottle cork. Linda turned out to be one of the most perceptive, shrewd, interesting people I ever met. She really did have a story to tell but lacked the eagerness to tell it, unlike the Italians.

After she finished cleaning the restaurant from top to bottom after the night before, and after I finished cashing up the till; once my deliberations about precisely how much money I had in the bank, when the rent or the VAT was due, what was coming in from the card payments in three days' time, and whether it would be enough to cover the wages, we always sat down, the two of us, for a cup of tea – none of that coffee nonsense with us two – before service resumed. When I say before *service resumed,* what I mean is: before I unlocked the door. Before normal service resumed, Linda and I would sit at a table next to the bar and have a cup of tea. I would always make it, and she would always, without fail, say: 'Oh, that's a nice cup of tea, Lewis,' whilst we listened to the Italians arguing in the kitchen, always in their own language, although occasionally we would hear Luigi bellow *for fuck's sake, Rocco*! in English.

At first, I craned my neck around the toilet wall and said something along the lines of: *what on earth has happened now*? But after a while, I gave up asking because invariably nothing had happened at all. After a while, Linda and I became exempt from their squabbling, realising that it had nothing to do with us, so we would instead just sit and sip our tea.

"He wants to change the menu now," I said to her one morning.

"Who does?"

"Luigi."

"Into what?"

"Pizza, pasta!" I replied just as something smashed in the kitchen and Linda jumped out of her skin. They may have been trying to kill each other in that moment, but Linda and I no longer cared.

"Then what will he do with his waist coat?" she asked.

"What do you mean?"

"Well, the current menu is displayed on the front of his waist coat because his hands shake when he's carrying plates to a table. So what's he going to do if you change the menu, buy a new waist coat? He's probably had that thing since the mid-eighties!"

I laughed at her quip. "He wants me to buy a pizza oven. He says he knows a man in Middlesbrough that can supply one for six hundred pounds, but for that price, we'll have to do a bit of work to it."

"They're going to bankrupt you, Lewis, you do know that?"

I nodded. I knew they would. And her comment cemented my desolation.

"You're a good man, Lewis," she said to me, placing her hand on top of mine and knowing precisely what her fellowship meant to me. "You're too kind for your own good. Too loyal to stupid people who don't deserve it. Too kind to go into business. Too easily persuaded. Why did you do it, Lewis? Why did you plough all of your money into this place?"

Then, the sound of Luigi from the kitchen, "For fuck's sake, Rocco, stop fucking complaining!"

"Because I imagined that someone would come back to help me do it," I replied, completely ignoring the sounds from the kitchen.

"Who? Who did you want to come back?"

As she asked that question, she leaned across the table and placed a hand on the side of my face, realising that I was on the verge of crying.

"It doesn't matter since she didn't come back when I asked her to." I now recall that I did actually cry, much to my shame. "She pulled me up from off my knees. And then she left me. But now I am on my knees again with no-one to pull me up." Then, a sound from hell erupted in the kitchen, but I didn't care. The Italians may very well have killed each other, for all I cared.

During another conversation at our little table next to the toilets, Linda told me that her husband had emphysema from his days as a miner.

"In the North?" I asked, presuming too much.

"In South Africa," she replied.

Her husband had been a gold miner in South Africa. They'd lived there for twenty years. Linda told me as she remembered those years with fondness that the sun always set on every day of the year, at six o'clock, because of that country's weird position on the globe. And when her family returned to England in two-thousand-and-three, her two daughters found it hard to believe that in England, at the height of summer, the sun barely set at all because of its own peculiar position on the globe.

"And nowadays, he has to carry a bottle of oxygen around with him wherever he goes, so he no longer goes anywhere because he is embarrassed by his little bottle that keeps him alive!"

"Can't the government help you both?" I implored her.

"I'm only fifty-eight, Lewis. Whenever I've tried, they just say, go out to work. So I do. And you have given me work, Lewis, so that I can pay the mortgage and he doesn't have to worry about anything other than that little bottle that keeps him alive. And so that I can repay him for everything he has done for me and our daughters."

Rocco, you're gonna fucking kill me, man!

Then, in mid-March, 2020, something happened. Something quite unexpected but more remarkable for it. Enter, stage left, *the disease*. An invisible antagonist that for me was like the presence of an angel on my shoulder who whispered *you're saved* in my ear. The day before, I stuffed six hundred pounds worth of notes into Rocco's white envelope, five hundred into Luigi's, and four hundred into Frederico's. But in order to stuff three hundred pounds into Linda's little white envelope, I had to go to the cash-machine outside the bank. Sean was long gone by this point off to find his own adventure, so perhaps he actually did fall down a rabbit hole because I hadn't seen him since Halloween the previous year. In my heart, I knew that it was the last time I would have to perform this peculiar ritual.

Not because of the disease that had floated over from China and had ravaged Italy but because of the Inland Revenue. I always paid my employees first and my suppliers second, but there had never been any money left to pay the VAT after that, and they were about to foreclose.

VAT. Value added. I always wondered what it was for until my accountant had explained: *if you sell a sausage roll uncooked, then there is no value to it ... if you, personally, cook the sausage roll so that the customer can walk away and eat it immediately, then you have added value to the sausage roll, and the government wants twenty percent of the retail price of that sausage roll ... or else you'll go to prison, Lewis!*

I knew something strange was happening because the week before, Linda had come into the restaurant brandishing a letter that she'd received from the government. The letter instructed her to 'shield' because they knew her husband was *vulnerable,* so she must not conjoin with anyone but her spouse. I think that had been the first piece of written confirmation from *the government* that confirmed she had been right about her husband all along – *but you wouldn't listen* - and the letter was like an official recognition, as though she was going to be awarded an OBE. But even then I hadn't grasped the

79

magnitude of what was going on, such were my personal tribulations. Even though, on that same spring morning, Luigi had been on his phone to his elderly mother back in Italy and had walked the length and breadth of the restaurant six times, completely oblivious to the fact that I had been there with him, listening.

"Mamma, you cannot go to the piazza at dusk anymore!" he spoke into his phone, obviously exasperated and beginning to realise that your parents, in the end, become your children. "Because if you get it, then it will kill you, Mamma! And I couldn't bare for you not to be there. I don't want to be an orphan! I can't bare that I'm not there with you!"

And when he ended the call, he cried. And then he cried even more when Rocco rushed out of the kitchen and hugged him tight because he knew. And Frederico shook his head sadly as though there was too much trouble for him to comprehend. And then I wondered: *what on earth has happened now?*

As a history enthusiast, I've seen all of those documentaries on the Discovery Channel or PBS about the Second World War. I've seen the black and white, otherworldly images of people in England in the autumn of 1939 huddled around the wireless in their sitting rooms to listen to Neville Chamberlain say: *and consequently, this country is at war with Germany*, along with all the connotations that statement had involved, subsequently. Total war. And so I watched Boris in March of 2020 on television saying more or less the same thing, although the war was no longer with Germany, of course. It was to be waged against something else, something unexpected, something that no one could have ever predicted, not even that old sage, Luigi.

Boris had said to the nation: *I must give the British people a simple instruction. You must stay at home*! And then, on the following Monday, he locked the whole country down. What he actually said to me, however, as an angel or devil on my shoulder, was: *Don't worry about a thing, Lewis. From now on until this is over ... **I'm going to pay the Italians!*** If I was playing bingo at that moment, I would have shouted, "HOUSE!"

Thank God for the coronavirus (little bit of irony, ever the chef and so on and so on).

Chapter Seven

What I'd really like to do at this juncture is bang on, and on, and on, and on about the Inland Revenue. About the virtues of *value added*. How a frozen sausage roll, when it's still frozen, is one thing. But when it's cooked through and probed so that it could never kill anyone – which involves paying staff – so that a customer can eat it straight away, then it becomes something else entirely so that the government can claim twenty percent of its retail value. That's what I'd like to do at this impasse.

But because of the extraordinary circumstances, I can't. So, I'm going to bang on, and on, and on about my half-sister instead. She has to be the most corroding person I've ever known. Not in the sense that she possesses a razor-sharp, acid wit that could cut you in two and bring you down a peg or two but corroding as in she seems to have the ability to erode any feelings of goodwill a person may (at first) have for her. I should try to temper my observations about my half-sister with the disclaimer that this is, of course, only my experience of her and that other people may have formed quite a different opinion. But I don't think my judgement of what people are *really* like has been too far off the mark in the past, so I will continue on the basis that my assessment of Jane Sinclaire-Sharp is not too far from the truth. The very fact that she wanted to hyphenate her surname when she married Michael Sharp and insisted that her sons carried that name throughout their lives too, just so that she could keep her precious *pappa* with her forever, even though it always made her sound like a lawnmower, should tell you all you need to know.

And this is not a character assassination either because she has no character. She's dull. Her voice is of a lowly quality and always monotone. She hardly ever laughs; in fact, I don't think I've ever heard her laugh, so I have no idea what her laughter may sound like. And she doesn't seem to like other people laughing either. Whenever the bald-too-young husband dared to laugh, she always scolded him with her eyes, and he'd go quiet very quickly. In conclusion: she doesn't laugh, and whether or not she finds something amusing is academic because she seems incapable of giving anyone the satisfaction of knowing that they've amused her. Sometimes I find myself feeling sorry for her because everyone ought to be able to laugh out loud sometimes, and the more desperate and darker the circumstances, the better. You would presume, wouldn't you, that someone who was incapable of laughing, who never found anything funny, must have gone through a terrible ordeal that had stripped them of that gift, that human right? An ordeal so vile that that one faction of humanness has been taken away from them. But not my half-sister. She had a blessed, gilded childhood; she'd always done precisely what she wanted to do. She is completely well-adjusted and secure in the world and in the knowledge of who she is, where she is, and where she is going. So now I must return to my original proposal, that it always comes down to the matter of character, personality, or, in her case, the lack of one.

Bland is the word I use to describe my half-sister, and whenever I think about her, my mind's eye always sees her dressed in beige with a grumpy frown on her face as though someone's upset her. She is the type of woman who, if she ever frequented my restaurant (which never did), she would screw her face up at the offering on the menu then order a piece of fish to be boiled, no batter, with perhaps some potatoes; boiled, no sauce, and everyone sitting with her would roll their eyes in despair. She is that type of woman. And very judgmental, too. Her life is so settled and ordinary, comfortable, and flat that she can afford herself the luxury of judging everybody else's life. A fisherman on a flat sea doesn't have to worry about drowning. She is so secure in the love she receives without having to earn it, that she has no empathy or sympathy for anyone who sometimes finds themselves struggling, either financially or emotionally.

If she ever follows her pappa's footsteps and becomes a psychoanalyst, she will simply tell her client to *pull yourself together. Worse things happen at sea, you know.* Then she'd charge them five hundred pounds for the advice. No, she would have charged them five hundred pounds first and then told them to pull themselves together, and the client would have left her consulting room none the wiser. I'll give my father his dues; at least his skill of being able to peer into his client's soul and diagnosing a loose wire (or something) had actually helped them. It must have done, or else he wouldn't have been so famous and renowned in the field of *dodgy wires.*

We all expected her to follow in my father's footsteps when she obtained a PhD in Philosophy from Bristol University. The photos of her graduation are still plastered all over my father's study, though I've always suspected that the real reason she studied there for six years was because she didn't want to get a proper job. Or perhaps she merely wanted to honour her promise to the old man that she would not turn out to be like me, and once she made good on that promise, she would then live off his money and find herself an equally dull man to worship her without having to work too hard to earn his devotion, with the resolve of never having to work a proper nine-to-five job.

A PhD meant that she was almost as intelligent as the old goat, and since this is Jane we're talking about here, I doubt he would have disagreed with that appraisal. I've never asked her much about her degree because I was never particularly interested, but I think her thesis was along the lines of humankind's inherent need for God. Not necessarily a Christian God but any old god or goddess, even Zeus or Mother Earth if needs be. That all living creatures have an inborn need to feel secure and nourished and belong to something greater than the confines of their individual, physical selves. Like a child needs a parent or a dog needs a master, or at least another dog. Her argument was that the necessity of God – the idea, the dream of God – was the same as a child clinging to its mother's leg when it was afraid, but the thread of her narrative had concentrated on a pet dog's need of its owner to feed it and to give it water and to make the dog believe that it belonged to them and to nobody else.

She is quite clever, actually. But she sorely lacks the imagination with which to profit from her intelligence. I, on the other hand, am not a particularly intelligent man, but I sadly possess an imagination that forces me to run away with it. My imagination is like a siren on a rock in the middle of the Mediterranean Sea singing her songs, and I am Odysseus, fated to turn my boat full way towards her to find out where the sound is coming from (see what I mean?). I was the man who'd fallen hook, line, and sinker whenever she'd take hold of my hand and whisper in my ear: *Lewis, come away with me.*

She had her thesis published in a trade journal that focused on such things and even received a commendation from a professor – turned TV personality – so famous in his field as my father was in his. She received her doctorate and became a Doctor of Philosophy. Dr Jane Sinclaire-Sharp. However, I've always thought that it makes her sound like a better specification of the same lawnmower.

I can only imagine the type of conversations she had with my father when she was home for the weekends. Earth-shatteringly good conversations they must have been. Important conversations of such a profound nature that the adrenaline pumping through their bodies must have made them feel like a jack-in-a-box. And all the while, my stepmother was standing in the kitchen cooking her famous beef Wellington, smiling proudly but with the resolve to keep out of their way. Then imagine the front door slamming closed as I dared to come back into the house, and they would roll their eyes at one another, and my father would despondently mutter, *here he is*. Thank God for the dog, that's all that I can say.

To give my stepmother her eternal dues, she'd always known what the two of them were thinking whenever I came back into the house, and she always overcompensated for them by greeting me almost as excitedly as the dog and saying something like: *here's my boy, home!* But it was only kindness and never completely genuine. And I always thought, *It should not be you who's saying that*. To my eternal shame.

A clever woman. Not my stepmother, God rest her soul, but my sister. Good for her. Good for her that she studied and studied and somehow found a way to connect to my father because I never could. What was I going to talk to him about? Luigi or the singing chef? The water from the roof that dripped onto the forehead of a man from

Chicago? It would have fallen on deaf ears, and quite rightly for the most part.

Fiona, the nurse, had a brother. When I knew her, he lived in Plymouth (where they were born). As her partner, I imagine that he never had the wherewithal, or the imagination, or the need to go anywhere else. And whenever we visited him and her parents in Devon, she always called to inform him that she was passing the Wicker Man on the M5 (you either know or you don't, but you can imagine what it is) and that she wouldn't be long now. It obviously had been a *thing* between them, probably from when they were children. The reverse of that journey had meant they were finally leaving the place where they were born, and they were so excited about it and about the proposition of the world beyond the border. Or perhaps it assured her that she was going home, and she felt the necessity to inform him of that, regardless of whatever else her life had unexpectedly thrown at her in the meantime. I always envied her the Wicker Man.

It gives me no satisfaction whatsoever to tell you that my half-sister and I have never experienced that kind of connection. *We two* had no such thing as the 'Wicker Man'. Except, perhaps, and very tenuously, New Year's Eve 1994 when I was twelve years old and she was eight. Our father did have a personality, by the way. He was not outrageously the life and soul of the party, nor was he one of life's natural performers, but he was always a good host, and it seemed that the people who were in his 'circle' absolutely adored him. But then, he'd always been one thing to his family and a completely different thing to everybody else. They'd appreciated his cleverness because he was a very clever man, and any event that he

87

and my stepmother hosted was always furnished with the finest wines and the most delicious food.

We always knew, my half-sister and I, when an event was coming up because my stepmother barely left the kitchen for three days and nights, and my father would always return from London with boxes of new world wines, unfamiliar gins, whiskeys, and an array of liqueurs in strange-looking bottles. Such events always gave me a little bit of a thrill. Their parties are one of the few joyous memories that I have brought with me from my childhood. I suppose it's because they were out of the ordinary. They were occasions that had been anything but routine, when excitement and anticipation would dominate the atmosphere in the house, and I would eavesdrop on their private conversations at night-time to find out precisely who'd been invited. And it was always big names; names like *Clifford and Maise, if he can get away from Parliament in time, you know how it is with him; Marjory's coming over from Maidenhead* (Marjory was a writer of historical novels usually centred on Henry the Eighth's court, and always brought a different woman with her every time, but they always had noticeably short hair). *And Peter's going to finally come because he's performing at The Old Vic. A Man for All Seasons, so try and keep him away from Marge because you know how prickly she gets when people ask her about the Tudors without paying her, but he won't be staying over because he has friends in Windsor that he wants to see the new year in with.* It had always been that kind of conversation and those types of names. And the anticipation built.

We two children were always given instructions in the afternoon of a party. We were told to keep out of the way, stay in our rooms, and try our best to go to sleep or *read a book or something*. We were always fed about six pm when my stepmother would watch us eat and urge us to go quicker, and when we finished, we were whisked away to our rooms quicker than our dishes and placemats made it to the dishwasher. We could never sleep because we always had indigestion. We were given instructions like: 'If you need to go to the toilet, then make sure no-one is upstairs first', in case the politician or the actor or the writer would emerge from the bathroom to find a Dickens-type waif standing in front of them, peering upwards and pleading, '*Please, sir, what's going on down there*'?

I don't know if my father and stepmother were ever aware of the fact that neither of us ever went to sleep. No such book existed that could compete with the excitement and exhilaration of sitting on the landing upstairs listening to adults getting drunker and drunker downstairs, and every hour that encroached upon midnight turned ever so slightly more menacing when particularly important people's personalities had begun to show true particularity. That's what alcohol does: it reveals the truth. It strips back the necessities of politeness when empathy and sympathy and tact get thrown out of the window. But it doesn't matter because, in the cold light of day with a banging head and a compulsion to vomit, sobriety reveals the real truth: that they were all as bad as each other. So, it doesn't really matter who said what to who because it had merely been the *drink* talking. And the truth gathers up its empty bottles and leaves thinking, *I'll try harder next time*. And everyone else goes about their business, still thinking that they're friends.

When the actor wanted to pee, he announced it as if he were standing on stage at the Old Vic. 'My darling, as much as I like to hear about what you did in Naples, and with whom, I'm afraid that my bladder is thirty years older than I am, and I need to take my leave!' And everyone laughed. But what he actually did was give us a *heads up* that he was coming upstairs, as though he fired a starting pistol which gave us the nod to get back into bed. He pissed for what seemed to be, from my twelve-year-old brain's perspective, twenty minutes solid. The house bathroom was next to my bedroom, and as I listened to the sound of his flow hitting the water, I wondered if he was ever going to stop; if that great man was going to be found dead on our toilet because every last drop of moisture had been ejected from his body. I thought that his next role should be a donkey because a donkey always pisses once a day for twenty minutes.

When I heard the toilet finally flush and the lock on the bathroom door click, I pretended that I was asleep. But unlike him, I wasn't a good actor, so when he curiously opened the door to my bedroom and peered inside, I was wide awake. And with all the gusto, dash, and euphoria of a performance, he gasped when he saw me, as though he was Bilbo Baggins looking upon the ring of power again, just when he began to doubt that it had ever existed. And then he projected, in that magnificent, villainous English accent, that was like he swallowed up the whole of Shakespeare's complete works: 'My God, A-lee-chay lives!' before withdrawing, stage left to the acclaim and applause of his audience resounding in his ears.

The thing about having an eight-year-old daughter is that, regardless of how much you had to drink the night before, you still have to be up before her. To my stepmother's eternal credit, she always insisted that we four should always eat breakfast together whenever the occasion arose that we were all in the house at the same time. And New Year's Day 1995, was no different from

90

any other day when that might have happened in her mind. It looked as if an atomic bomb had exploded in the kitchen. I'd never seen so much glass, though enough space was left on the kitchen table for us to sit and eat our eggs. My stepmother insisted that my father should join us for breakfast because she was sure that a soft-boiled egg would cure whatever ailed him. Plus, it was New Year's Day. We ate in silence at first because any noise at all was like a fingernail being drawn across a blackboard to my father's sensitive ears. But when my half-sister couldn't open her own egg, my stepmother ascended quickly and manoeuvred herself into a position to do it for her. In the temporary commotion of my stepmother opening my half-sister's soft-boiled egg for her, I asked, "Who is Aleechay?"

"What?" my father grumbled, looking at my stepmother but seemingly asking me the question.

"Peter came into my room, and said …"

"Peter is a fool, Lewis. Peter was drunk. When you grow up you will learn not to listen to drunk men!"

The ticking sound of the clock on the wall had never been louder. The sound of cutlery being scraped across the surface of a white plate had never, and can never be, louder. I had never seen my father's face set with so much fury and aggravation before.

"Let me do it for you," my stepmother said to my half-sister whilst looking at my father. "Have you got enough toast, sweetheart?" Something was going on between her and my father.

"Was Aleechay my mother?" I asked him as I slipped a solid piece of egg-white with just a speckle of yellow yolk into my mouth.

To this day, I cannot listen to the sound of a clock ticking without bringing the memory of that breakfast to

91

the forefront of my mind; without remembering just how furious my father became after the asking of a question.

"Be quiet, Lewis, and eat your egg!" he stirred, glaring not at me but at the white expanse of his own plate.

When my stepmother threw her own cutlery onto her plate, the force and resulting sound of it made my half-sister jump. "Why should he?" she bellowed so loudly that my half-sister started to cry.

"I don't know what you want me to do," my father said to her.

"Tell him, Martin!" I had never seen a woman so provoked by something in my life, and I have seen a lot of provoked women during the course of my adulthood. But something had arisen in my stepmother; something that had been so ferocious that it almost made my father teary too. "Tell him who," she did exclamation marks with her fingers, "A-lee-chay is! And let me listen because I would quite like to know too!"

My father placed his cutlery into the centre of his plate very gently, even though we could all see that he still had an egg left unopened. "She was a stupid woman who liked melodramas. She liked soap operas, American soap operas, Dallas or Dynasty, and such nonsense."

"And that's it, is it?" my stepmother snarled at him. "That's all you've got for the boy?"

"Shut up, woman. You're still drunk from last night."

His comment then made my stepmother sob too (was there no end to this man's talents?).

"I'm not drunk, Martin. I'm exhausted," she sobbed.

Finally, my father had heard enough, and he rose from the table with such sudden and unexpected force that his chair was sent hurtling to the far side of the kitchen.

"What do you expect me to do now?" he blasted at my stepmother.

Then she stood up too, but her chair wasn't sent hurtling. "Tell him the truth!" she yelled at him. "And let me listen too, because I'm tired of it all, Martin. I'm tired of trying to fight for you when I don't even know the nature of my opponent!"

"WHAT DO YOU WANT ME TO SAY?" he retorted angrily and desperately. "DO YOU WANT ME TO TELL HIM THAT SHE BROKE MY HEART?" then he started to cry too, and I wondered whether he was still drunk because alcohol can have the effect of making people cry as much as it has the effect of making them tell the truth. Then he settled down a little bit and stopped shouting and seemed to be talking to himself more than to us. "That every day I'm left to wonder where she went? Why she went? Why did she need to leave me? Just leave me there on my own WITH *HIM!*" he then stormed out of the kitchen.

And my stepmother sobbed so openly that she really didn't care whether the children were watching or not. In that moment, as the sound of the clock ticking came back into my head because everyone had stopped shouting, I had never loved my mother more. But, nevertheless, I took hold of my half-sister's hand because she'd never been so frightened (since she never heard her parents have a row before). But I had, since I was four years older.

So, that particular party, and that New Year's Day morning, is perhaps the closest thing that I can compare to the Wicker Man. Very tenuous, I know. But at least it's a memory that both of us can share, even though we're fated to look back on it with differing degrees of fondness.

I can recall thinking, as my stepmother hollered and my father strode out of the kitchen: *Jesus, I wish I hadn't said anything.*

~ End of Part One ~

Chapter Eight

So, as a consequence, I cannot listen to a ticking clock while in a quiet room, nor the sound of cutlery tapping upon a porcelain plate, without thinking back to that New Year's Day morning. And whenever I'm forced to think about it, I always carry a little bit of shame in my mind. Not because it had inconvenienced my father and sent him into a rage – which had merely been an added benefit to him giving me what I wanted – but because that New Year's Day breakfast had destroyed my stepmother. I can't imagine my father ever telling her anything that she didn't already know, but the truth, like a memory, is only made real when spoken aloud, whether slurred with drunkenness or not. The spoken truth turned her from a cheerful, happy-go-lucky mother hen into a leopardess, whose only function in life was to protect her young from harm.

The feeling in the house for a good six months after those soft-boiled eggs had been like the weather in Siberia (I imagine): ice cold with no fine weather to look forward to; hard, frozen ground underfoot; heavy going. My half-sister had been eight years old, so she still possessed the ability to worry only about herself; about being taxied to her ballet lessons, whether her bed had been made, what she was going to be given for dinner, what time her *Pappa* was due home and whether he'd bring her something from Hamley's, etcetera. He invariably did because my father tried to make good by overcompensating his affection for his daughter to the woman who'd been resolved to give him the cold shoulder. It is when I first noticed her sitting on his knee after dinner in the quiet moments before her bedtime, and she'd pulled on his nose and he made the

95

sound of a steam-train whistle. And when I first began to hate her because the trick seemed to work. The atmosphere thawed just a little every time she pulled on his nose. The ground underfoot became a little easier, and my mother had been forced to slink back into whatever hole she managed to climb out of. A clever man, my father; an even cleverer girl, my half-sister.

What my father had been resolved to do in those six months after the soft-boiled eggs was to appeal to the leopardess's instinct to protect her young from harm. My stepmother had known full well that she was always subordinate to my mother, a consolation, a substitute, never to be compared for the fear of failure. And suddenly it had been confirmed like a post office stamp on a paid bill. But she hadn't left him. Why? Because she wanted to protect her children. Not necessarily her natural daughter alone but me too. She could have easily walked out of that house on January the first, 1995 and taken her daughter with her and then sued that duplicitous bastard for every penny he possessed. She could have lived comfortably with her daughter in a house that backed onto the river. But she didn't leave him because she couldn't legally take *me* with her, and she nursed me the best part of a year before she fell pregnant with my half-sister. I was her son in her eyes, and she had been resolved not to leave me on my own with my father, and if she had, then she would never have known what would become of me and what would become of me was important to her. I loved that woman whether she was a substitute or not. Sometimes the substitute comes onto the pitch and scores the winning goal (I thank you). She was kind and good, a great cook and one of life's natural protectors. She was an exemplary mother; faultless. She just wasn't mine.

Even though, at the end of a primary school day, when I was eight years of age and when we children had been chaperoned by the teacher into the playground so that we could all be picked up by our parents and taken away, no one had come for me. I stood there wondering if anyone was ever going to claim me. When all of the other children had been whisked away to safety, I was left on my own atop a grassy knoll at the side of the playground, which granted me a better view of the road at the bottom of the school path. I never took my eyes off that road. My young teacher – though to my eight-year-old eyes, she was ancient and responsible – had been watching from the assembly room. When she finally came outside, she asked me: 'Who is supposed to be picking you up, Lewis? Your father or your mother?' And I answered: 'My mother'.

At that point, she appeared at the end of the pathway and was running towards me as quickly as she could while also pushing a buggy that had a four-year-old strapped into it, who must have thought she was on the Big Dipper at Blackpool Pleasure Beach; and when she reached me, she hugged me tightly while apologising for her lateness. She smiled at my teacher apologetically and gratefully. My teacher simply smiled back, sympathetically, because she must have known how hard it was to juggle all four of her balls to keep them all from dropping to the ground. I'd never been so happy and relieved to see another human being in all my life. But even then, she was not my mother.

Not my mother when I'd been picked for my house's football team at secondary school at the age of twelve. I *hated* football in all its forms, but my P.E teachers picked me for the team regardless. They probably suspected that all I needed was just a little nudge in the right direction. She hadn't been my mother when she'd been only one of five parents who'd braved the cold and the rain and watched from the touchline. Or when the ball hit me and fell at my feet, and everyone else on the pitch had stood stock-still when the world seemed to stop turning and when everyone was waiting to see what I did with it, she screamed: 'Kick it, Lewis!' and the other set of parents looked at her enquiringly, and she simply smiled proudly at them, as if to say: 'That's my boy out there!'

Even then.

Not my mother when I'd been thirty-two, and I'd come to the house at Henley for a cup of tea, and the steam from the tea masked my penitence as I informed my father that Fiona and I were parting; that I wasn't going to marry her despite his advice. He growled something. I can't remember what, and then he buried his face into his newspaper. Not my mother when she followed me to the front door, kissed me on the cheek, and whispered into my ear: 'It's either there, or it isn't, Lewis.'

'What is or it isn't?' I asked her, desperately longing to know what she meant.

'You'll know what I mean when it *is*,' she replied before closing the front door on me. But I smiled, which wasn't at all usual on so many other occasions when I stood on the doorstep of my father's house because I think, or rather suspected, that I knew precisely what she meant.

Even then, she was not my mother. But assuredly I say this – as sure as God made little green apples (one of her many adages) – she'd always been assured of the fact that I was *her* son.

She is about to slip out of the narrative now. But before she goes, I want to pay her an accolade: that although in my head and in my heart she was not my mother, nor could she ever play that role because my father was always in the way in her *head* and in *her* heart, I *was*. She'd been an angel sent from Heaven when a four-year-old boy – and a thirty-two-year-old man – precisely needed one. She was the right person at the right time. I adored her because we shared so many secrets together, secrets that my father and my half-sister will never know, nor would they be able to comprehend them if they did.

She died on the 19th May, 2016, six months before my thirty-third birthday, which was in September. My father found her on the kitchen floor after returning from his chess club meeting. She'd had a blood clot in her leg for months, but it had burst in her heart, thus killing her instantly. That's what the paramedics told my father, anyway. But I've always imagined that her final moments had been torture in its purest form: in the proper sense of the word. Her heart had burst because of my father, and by extension, because of me. But I'd been resolved not to bear the burden alone; that the lion's share of it must be my father's. My half-sister, by the way, is absolved of any responsibility, and bears no burden at all for her mother's death. My father had informed us both that she'd been preparing her famous beef Wellington when she died because he found a fillet of beef on the floor next to her – she must have been holding it when she collapsed – and there had been a rolled-out piece of puff pastry abandoned on the work surface covered in flour. What a lovely way to go: by giving them all what they want.

My father paid for an obituary to be published in The Times. And it was the correct thing to do because there were important people out there who would need to know – people who neither he nor my half-sister had the time or the inclination to contact. *Martin Sinclaire's wife is dead, oh I'm so sorry for that,* etcetera. *You know who Martin is, he's the man who cured me and who brought me to you.* The obituary in The Times had described my angel as being the loyal wife of *Martin Sinclaire, the beloved mother of Dr Jane Sinclaire-Sharp, devoted grandmother to her grandsons, Arthur and Martin ... stepmother to Lewis from Martin Sinclaire's first marriage.* Even then he had to make the distinction even though he paid for the obituary by the word, and the word **step** had cost him an extra one-hundred-pounds. *She died peacefully at home on the morning of the 19th May, 2016. Her funeral will be held* and so on and so on. But as I read it, I knew that she hadn't died peacefully at all. Nobody ever does. She died screaming: *what the hell did she have that I haven't got? Why was I never enough for you, Martin?*

The spoken word, preferably slurred with drunkenness, always reveals the truth. The written word, however, can sometimes suppress it; because it's always written in the cold, sober light of the morning. And then there are obituaries, which are always written in the third person narrative, which in turn puts a different slant on the tone.

The actor, Peter, had obviously been contacted directly – *he* didn't need to read about the news of her passing in *The Times* – because he'd been given the task of delivering her eulogy at the funeral. A funeral, by the way, that had been gammed to the rafters. Standing room only with people outside too, straining their ears to listen to what he had to say about her. And, in that cut-glass, note-perfect, English villain way that he had of delivering his lines, he said some lovely things about her. Some very poignant things that had stirred my father and had made him wonder about the character of the woman of whom the actor was speaking about; that had made him stop and think again and wonder what he could have won in different circumstances. But ever the actor, Peter had delivered an Oscar-winning performance. The congregation hung onto every one of his words. But I knew the tone of his voice, the glint in his eye, had concealed the truth. Ever the actor. So, he delivered a beautiful eulogy that summed my stepmother up to a tee and made us all mourn our loss, but every sentence that he uttered was punctuated with the word: *however.* I heard it. And so did my father.

I'm glad that she died when she did. Don't get me wrong, I thank God every day that she lived, because if she hadn't, then I don't know what would have become of me. But if she lived for any longer than her sixty-one years, then nothing that happened after her death would have been possible. She would have blocked it. The truth would have remained a drunken mess on a sitting room rug. And I would never have known.

You want to know what happened, don't you? Well, that is if you're still listening to me. If you are still listening, then you've got to agree, better than Dallas, this is.

She died six months before my thirty-third birthday, and when I think about it, the grief of no longer having her there, on my side, was what had put me on my knees in the wine cellar of the Sun Inn, Hurley, when I sobbed into my hands as quietly as I could to prevent the management from hearing me. It hadn't been my father's phone call, after all, that had triggered my response to the person who *had* heard me sobbing and who'd cared enough to pull me up off my knees. I didn't holler: *how dare he talk about her to me?* because I'd been thinking about my mother, but because I'd been thinking about my stepmother, in that moment. Grief can do that. It can creep up on you like a stealthy old fox, and before you know what's happened, you're like the remains of the chicken, with feathers and bones strewn everywhere.

'Have you heard from your mother?' What I should have hollered in that moment in that wine cellar was: *your wife's body is barely cold, you are a grievous, egotistical old man, and I hate you*. But what would he have done if I told him that I *had* heard from her? (I hadn't, by the way). What if I told him then what I know now? What would he have felt on the other end of that connection that I wouldn't see because it was only a phone conversation? Desolation, terror, or relief? The relief that comes from having received an absolution? Would he have been renewed? A better version of himself? Would he have felt like the contestant being given a second go at winning the star prize? Would he have flown to New York the following day, business class, once he begged me for her address? He would certainly have been free to do so as a widower and rich enough to fly business class, obviously.

I should have answered: *yes, she's still alive and living life to the fullest in New York City, and I fly out there at least one weekend every month, and we go to the zoo in Central Park and eat hot-dogs, and we laugh about you*. If only I'd known then what I know now.

I want to talk about Linda. I know, I know, I'm going off on another one of my tangents, but bear with me because I think she deserves a bigger part than the one she's got so far. Peter would have understood what I mean because as one of the world's great actors on the screen for the money and on the stage for the kudos, he would

102

have known that sometimes a bit-part player can appear and change the entire piece for the better; make the whole thing make sense with just one, significant line of dialogue. And you're probably thinking that I want to talk about Linda due to that domineering *mother-issue* thing that I may seem to have, but you'd be wrong because that particular prickling had been cured by my stepmother with the camomile lotion that was her kindness and empathy and her basic goodness. I want to talk about Linda because she was perhaps the most remarkable woman I've ever met; certainly, in the top three anyway.

Linda Finch was, on the one hand, very ordinary, and on the other, quite extraordinary. She was a hefty woman who'd no longer cared about her weight because food – eating whatever she fancied – was one of the few comforts that was left in her life. Her hair was of a weird blackish-grey hue like an Old English Sheepdog; her face always seemed to be flushed. If you'd passed her in the street, you would not have considered her at all; she would be just another human walking in the opposite direction. If she served you in a supermarket and even if she exchanged pleasantries about the awful weather, you would have forgotten all about her the moment you stepped out through the automatic doors into the rain and the cold. She was that type of woman. A woman you encounter every day. An everyday kind of person. And because (I presume) she hadn't gone to university to study Chaucer or Newton or Freud, the kind of person my father would have considered one of the 'stupid people'.

Luigi's assertion that she looked like Betty Turpin – that barmaid from that northern soap opera that if someone had forced my father to watch an episode or two, if he hadn't passed out through shame, he may have learnt something – was wrong because she looked nothing like her. But I appreciated his point. Luigi, in his chauvinistic, 1970s mindset, had thought that a waitress should always be young and beautiful, a woman on the cusp of greater things. A waitress, in his view, should always be young and beautiful and poorly paid so that she worked even harder to earn her tips. Linda had liked Luigi for reasons I cannot explain. He gave her a thrill and his behaviour and his over-the-top Italianises had regularly made her laugh out loud, although it may have been his incompetence as a waiter at the age of sixty-four that had amused her. I liked the way they'd argued with one another. In my mind, and in hers, it had been bantering between work colleagues, and that can only ever be a good thing from an employer's perspective.

Linda had always known precisely why Luigi didn't like her. Because she could do things in that restaurant that he never could despite his lifetime of training. But she always had the good grace not to think that a waiter, especially an Italian waiter, should be young and handsome and wearing tight trousers on the cusp of something greater: not wearing the remnants of yesterday's service on his waistcoat on the cusp of keeling over. Some waiting staff are beautiful and on the cusp of greatness – they toil at the edge of a life still to be lived – but some toil at the other side of a life well-lived with the aim of reclaiming past glories. And some toil in order to keep a roof over their dying husband's head. And that's all they toil for; turn up every morning for. But if, from time to time, they are distracted and actually allow themselves to enjoy it, all the better, from an employer's point of view.

It was in the December of 2019 that I first noticed the phenomenon that was Linda Finch, a full seven months since I first hired her, more for her cleaning skills than her waitressing skills because she had none. But when everything had been scrubbed and cleaned, at the point when everything was ready to go, I had no choice but to justify her minimum wage per hour by putting her to work as a waitress, even though she'd never waited on a table in her life unlike Luigi, who'd served Pavarotti and Prince Charles and the Sheiks and so many people in between.

It was the part of December, the early part, that was just beginning to whip up the excitement of Christmas without it actually being Christmas and containing none of the disappointment and comedown that the *actual* Christmas must inevitably bring. The lights in Windsor that year were exceptional. The council had seemed to pull out all the stops to make the town look like a Christmas wonderland in order to entice the tourists from London and the locals to spend, spend, spend, with good, seasonal cheer. They must have known what was going to happen. They must have known that December was everyone's last hurrah. They must have known that it was destined to be the last Christmas, so they'd given everyone the chance to make extra money by putting up more twinkling lights than they usually had. Blow the budget.

Yet, nothing in that December seemed to be any different from any that had come before. The town was full of tourists and locals shopping frenziedly. The baristas next door and further down the concourse had never been busier. The boutiques and the market stalls that sold hand-carved chess sets and tapestries depicting cats were booming. The restaurants were full except for ours. But there was less Chinese and Japanese than I expected, and *they'd* kept me afloat since May. So, my restaurant had bucked the trend by being quiet. Then again, it was always going to because *John Bull's Traditional British Fish and Chips* was not staffed by people who were young and on the cusp of something wonderful. It was staffed with people who were past their best at the end of something wonderful. By people who were trying to make sense of whatever essence that their lives had left them with. Including the leaseholder. So, it had been doomed from the offset because every business is, must be, a reflection of its creator's intentions and ambition, and it must grow from that seed. If in the businessperson's mind, they wanted nothing else but money, then the chances are that their business will succeed. But I wanted something else, so the venture had been doomed from the get-go, and fate had kicked me up the backside, saying *don't be so stupid, this isn't how you'll achieve what you want to achieve.*

And now I'm digressing from a digression.

It was a Friday at the end of the second week in December, and I spent the early part of the afternoon checking out the competition – although in their proven locations they were no such thing – to establish how busy they were, longing for them to be deserted as I was. But they weren't, obviously, deserted; they were all packed, and the tapas place even had a little queue going on, God damn them. It was obvious that the beautifully rich, the bourgeois of Windsor, didn't care much for traditional British fare because it was too colloquial for them, too northern, too grounded, and too familiar. It was the food of their youth, but they had grown up and had become sophisticated, had educated themselves to appreciate the more exotic tastes of the world because they'd seen the world and wanted the food that they ate to prick their consciousness and remind them of other times. And beneath the heat lamps, they could forget for an hour or

106

two about the rain and the cold and the ceaseless greyness of England in December. They could pretend that they were in Italy again or Vietnam, Spain, China, or wherever. My trade had come from the people from those places wanting to do the same thing but in reverse. But they'd stopped coming for some reason. I assumed that it was because of the ceaseless greyness of England, but it was something else entirely. In December 2019, no one on this side of the world knew about it yet, or if they'd seen it on the news, didn't really care. It wasn't yet a *thing.*

When I returned to *John Bull's,* I had been pleasantly surprised to see three tables occupied but wondered why Luigi was not attending to them or why Rocco was leaning over the pass with his head in his hands, looking very bored because all he was paid to do was cook. I would have been beside myself with joy if each of those three tables had had six Chinese or Japanese or Americans sitting at them, but such was my luck that three separate people were sitting on their own on three tables that had been set for six. Luigi's face had gripped an outraged countenance, and when I asked him what the matter was, he snarled: 'they only want fucking cups of tea!' Rocco had beckoned me over to the pass and when I reached him, he said: 'where are my orders, boss?' To which I replied: 'they only want a cup of tea!' 'Sad bustards,' Luigi added because he'd followed me to the pass. Then, more through devilment than an experienced eye for business, he walked to a table, pulled his little pad out of his waistcoat pocket, licked the tip of his pen, and asked his customer: "what would you like to eat, signor?"

"Just the tea, thank you," his customer replied ever so slightly embarrassed.

Luigi then moved to the second table. "What would you like to eat, signoria?"

107

"I'm happy with me tea, thanks."

By the time Luigi reached the third table, he been taken over by that temper that had ever held him back from being something absolutely wonderful, both professionally and personally. "Signor, what would you like to order from the menu?"

"Do you do teacakes?"

"For fuck's sake!" Luigi bellowed, his temper finally spilling over so that everything was saturated by it, as though it was Noah's flood and my customers had had to lift their feet off the ground in case they'd gotten their shoes wet.

When the door went again, both my and Luigi's hopes had risen to the occasion. *Go get 'em, tiger*, I thought as Luigi dashed towards the door.

"Just myself, I'm afraid," the old man said to him. *'For fucks sake'* Luigi had uttered beneath his breath but at least he hadn't said it out aloud. "Is Linda working today?" the old man asked as he removed his overcoat and hung it on the peg behind the door.

"She starts at five!" Luigi snarled, by then completely exasperated – completely overwhelmed.

The old man checked his watch which told him that he had forty minutes to wait unless she was early. It must have been worth the wait because he sat down at the table that Luigi had offered him.

"Do you want the menu, signor?"

"No need. I've already eaten."

"To drink, signor? A pot of fucking tea?"

"I've already had three pots of tea," the customer chortled, more amused at himself than the circumstances which he had found himself in. "What time is it?"

Luigi took his phone out of his trouser pocket to check the time. "Its 4:20, signor," ever the professional even though his customer was most definitely not Pavarotti.

"Well, it's perhaps a little bit early, but what the hell," the old man responded, suddenly quite excited. "What cocktails do you do?"

"One moment, signor, I will ask the owner."

"We don't do cocktails," I replied, utterly terrified. "Tell him we can do him a *sex on the beach*."

"You want me to tell him that?"

"It's the only one I know."

"'Sex on the beach'? He's about ninety fucking two. The last time *he* had sex on the beach, the Germans were probably bombing it!"

His comment made me laugh, and Rocco too, who'd been leaning over the pass behind me. For just a fleeting moment all three of us were laughing together and not at one another. "I love you, Luigi!" I sighed.

"For fuck's sake!" Luigi replied, half a smile on his face as he went back to his new table and told the old man that he was going to prepare him something special. What he then prepared him turned out to be luminous green, but Luigi had presented it to his customer proudly nonetheless: "Signor, your cocktail."

"What's in it?" the old man asked, bemusedly considering the glass of nonsense that had been placed in front of him.

"Everything!" Luigi replied. "What won't kill will cure, capsica?" And then he stepped away, leaving his customer to consider the concoction that had been placed in front of him, probably lamenting not having just ordered a pot of tea like all of the others because his 'cocktail' had shone so brightly that the air traffic bound for Heathrow had been distracted by it. Maybe not, but the other three people who were sipping tea at their tables

109

set for six had certainly noticed it and were watching what he intended to do with it, drink it or clean the redundant cutlery with it. *Drink me*, the cocktail said to the old man, because it had been so full of nonsense that it had gained the identity of a human voice in the impasse.

Then, ten minutes before she was due to start, Linda had stepped through the door, and all four individuals had stiffened their backs in anticipation. I watched from the pass; had smiled gratefully and nodded my greeting to her, and she grinned mischievously – that ironic smirk of hers – as she passed them all whilst removing her overcoat preparatory to starting work. I watched what happened; what affect her arrival had on those four sad, lonely people. She greeted the old man with the cocktail by his name, then made a comment about the bizarre concoction in front of him – something about mouthwash – then moved through the tables with the grace of a gazelle, all the while speaking to the individuals who'd been sitting at them, asking about doctors' appointments or if their friend had eaten their breakfast today. This was even before she had been allowed to remove her overcoat; whilst she walked amongst them on her way to the staff area that was in reality the dark corridor that led to the pot wash. It was astonishing. It was a sight to behold. I had never seen any of the people who were sitting in my restaurant on that cold December evening, but obviously Linda had; had served them all in the quieter hours when I wasn't there. And she talked to them, engaged with them, listened to them. Not necessarily all at the same time, but whenever they'd plucked up the courage to drag themselves in out of the cold and the rain. And they'd found a warm welcome, so they'd returned time and again. They'd discovered *empathy* in the form of an

110

overweight, greying waitress who to them was the most beautiful girl in the world.

What a woman. What an exemplary human being she was. One of the best people I've ever known. And even though she buried one of her daughters at the age of twenty-four, and the other one had moved back to Africa the following month because she struggled to cope with the grief of losing her sister, leaving her mother to tend to their dying patriarch by herself, she'd still had enough life left in her soul to enquire whether a friend had eaten her breakfast or what the doctor had said, to people she barely knew.

By the February of the following year, even the sad and the lonely people had not frequented my restaurant. They'd dared not, in case … well, in case. And the beautiful bourgeois of Windsor had not frequented the top-notch restaurants further down the concourse either. Nor the top-end coffee joint next door because people had realised that an authentic Italian coffee wasn't worth paying the price of, well … it just wasn't worth it. And I'm certain that a tumbleweed had rolled down the concourse of Windsor Old Train Station.

"I'm sorry, Lewis," she said to me as we sipped our tea. What she had been sorry about was the trouble that her letter from the government had seemed to cause me. "I can't stay here. I mustn't take *it* home. Because if he gets *it,* he will die. Do you understand?"

"Do you hate me?" I asked.

"Why would you think that?"

"For fucks sake, Rocco, give it a rest!"

"Do you hate me for making you work with Luigi?"

My comment made her laugh, so I was thankful for that at least.

111

"He's a good man. I like him, actually. And he thinks the world of you, Lewis, so that'll do for me."

"He gets paid to."

"No, it's more than that. He told me that he thinks of you as his brother, and I genuinely believe that he does. He cares about what happens to you, and so do I, and that's why I like him. He's a terrible waiter, but he's a good man." She wiped her brow. "It's so hot in here, Lewis. No wonder you haven't got any money with that heater on full!"

But the heater hadn't been on. I couldn't afford the electricity.

"Rocco, I don't fuck care anymore! Why don't you just piss off back to Thailand and your ladybird!"

She laughed as she brought her overcoat over her shoulders from behind her chair. "He's worried about his mother, you do know that, Lewis?"

"Why? What's the matter with her?"

"She's eighty-eight, Lewis. Things are really bad in Italy right now. He's worried that she will go outside so he rings her every day to make sure that she hasn't."

"Does he? How do you know?"

She couldn't seem to get her breath because something had caught in her throat, and she was unable to stop coughing. When she finally settled down, she said, "because he told me yesterday whilst we were having a cup of tea."

Once her overcoat had covered her whole body, she walked towards the door. Before stepping out into the cold and the rain, before she was overcome by the greyness of a February morning in England, she turned and bellowed towards the pass: "Arrivederci, Luigi, Rocco," in her cut-glass common south-eastern English accent.

112

"Goodbye, sweetheart," Luigi called back in the most genuine way that I ever heard anyone say goodbye. "Take care of each other, love."

"I'm so cold, Lewis," she said as she stepped out into the vast, grey expanse of the world. Before leaving entirely, she turned around and looking back at me sitting at *our* table, she said simply, "Thank you."

I never saw her again. But she has left this impression on me: that she was a woman who'd buried her youngest daughter, had lost her eldest daughter to the other side of the world, was nursing her husband to his inevitable early death because of the work he had done in South Africa that had been his solution to provide for his family, had worked sixty hours a week just to pay the rent and the bills and whatever else they'd owed to who-knows-who because the government had refused to help them.

Yet, she turned up ten minutes early for every shift; had befriended an array of unrelated people at one time or another on the quieter shifts when neither I nor Luigi had been present, so that in those cold, dank days of December 2019, some of them had found themselves in the same place for the same reason. And she greeted them as though she was seeing her daughter again; had enquired about this or that as though they'd been her best friends and she was privy to the intricate details of their story when in reality, I had known that all she knew about them was that they were sad and lonely because their lives had been touched by *life* and it had stung them just like her life had stung her. And when they'd frequented *John Bull's Traditional British Fish and Chips,* they'd encountered a person who had been kind to them when that's all they'd needed. And she listened to all their stories and had been interested in all of them. Even though she was probably

113

exhausted and waited and waited for the pause in the conversation that would allow her the time to disappear into the toilets on the pretence of cleaning them but in reality, she wanted the time to ring her husband to ascertain whether he was still alive.

What a woman she was. What a genius. And whenever I think about her, I am ashamed of myself because she faced the consequences of her life in a way that I have never been able to. Linda had not been a drinker of wine because where would that have gotten her, with all that she had going on, her responsibilities and such? She faced life full-on and had dealt with whatever it had thrown at her with none of the anxiety and inhibitions that I had when we sat at table eleven next to the toilets before service began and drank our cup of teas.

"What happened to your mother, Lewis?"

"I don't know. I hope she's dead."

"Why?"

"Because everything will be easier if she is."

"No, it won't, love."

I hope you've noticed that I've been talking about Linda Finch in the past tense. Because she died just a week after leaving her position when she clutched her letter from the government that had instructed her that she needed to isolate with her husband as though it was a letter from Buckingham Palace informing her that she was going to be awarded an OBE. As a responsible employer, my accountant and business adviser had 'advised' that I should keep a written record of my observations regarding my staff in case they ever tried to sue me for constructive dismissal. The aforementioned narrative is my *observation* of Linda. That, and the knowledge that everything that affects a human being's mind must come

114

from its childhood and almost never from its adulthood. Because an adult possesses the capacity in its mind to comprehend everything that this intricate, delicate, fleeting, complex thing that we call *life* can and will throw at it. But a child cannot; it must not. It should not.

I actually mourn Linda Finch. I think about her a lot. My greatest regret, my true lament, is that I never got the chance to introduce her to my half-sister – because my half-sister had never brought her little family to my stupid restaurant – because if she had observed Linda, as I had, then she would have known that her *thesis* was correct after all.

Linda's sudden decline and death had shocked the three of us that were left behind to try and prop up the crumbling structure that was *John Bull's Traditional British Fish and Chips*. Frederico had gotten himself out of England and back to Italy several weeks before when it became apparent that if he hadn't left when he did, then he would not be permitted to fly out maybe just a day or two later since his native country was on the verge of closing its borders.

Luigi had wanted to get onto that last flight to Italy too. He hadn't said as much, but I know him well enough. He was increasingly animated with agitation in those two weeks that straddled February and March 2020 but had been perversely quiet and thoughtful at the same time, which wasn't like him at all. This was not the same kind of tension that an irate customer or a wrong order had customarily caused him. This was different. As a professional waiter, particularly one who owns the business's reputation, whenever I arrived at a table with the wrong dish, or whenever a group had turned up for their reservation but whoever had taken the phone call hadn't written it in the book (Luigi was prone to that because he always struggled to understand their surnames) it was a nightmare. The customer would inevitably flare up in rage because of the inconvenience, not to say unprofessionalism, of someone's honest mistake. As one of the world's great maître-d's, Luigi had had to grovel and apologise to countless customers over the years because someone had made an honest mistake, and his customer had wanted to make a song and dance about it and make everyone else in the establishment aware that something disastrous had happened that really shouldn't have. And so had I on too many occasions. But what a waiter, a maître-d, actually wants to say to the customer is 'calm down, sir, madam, it is *not* the end of the world!'

Now that I think about it, I believe that's what I actually said to the woman from Chicago who'd made such a hullabaloo because we'd dared to have a leaking roof and a steady flow of rainwater had dripped onto her husband's prawn, that a group of Japanese women had physically reacted to her screaming and had probably mumbled to each other in their own tongue, *has a bomb gone off?* I said that to her: *it's not the end of the world*, immediately before I informed her that worse things than water dripping onto her husband's head will happen to them both during the course of their lives. And now I know that I was right. Even though I have no idea who she was, what her husband was called, whether they were rich or poor, etcetera … I *do* know that something worse than water dripping onto her husband's head from a leaking roof *had* happened to them.

That flight that Frederico had taken probably wasn't the last flight to Italy, but that's what it felt like. This was different, and that was the kind of drama that

116

was injected into a conversation about an aeroplane ticket, as though we were all living our lives as though it was a dodgy disaster movie. Better than the Towering Inferno but not as good as The Poseidon Adventure … not yet anyway. A flight which Luigi had wanted to get on, too. Linda had been right, he *had* been worrying about his mother back in Italy because if *she had got it*, whatever 'it' was, then it would have killed her. But he hadn't tried to book a ticket for that flight. And I pretend to myself that he hadn't because he hadn't wanted to leave me behind on my own amidst a crumbling building and a dying dream that had been my answer and *his* final hurrah.

Boris had helpfully informed the *British People* not to frequent pubs or restaurants or any public space where they would be exposed to something else of the same species that may be carrying 'it', but he needn't have bothered. Trade had died a death long before his decree but thank you for the advice, though. Windsor Old Train Station was deserted – not of every species because the pigeons (and probably the rats) were still there – of humans. So was the Castle precinct that just two months before had been so overcrowded with tourists and shoppers that I thought that all my dreams had come at once. And Windsor High Street, where the chain stores are, was empty too. When I stepped out of my restaurant for a cigarette, I hadn't seen another living thing, even though it was mid-March and the weather had been lovely. Where had they all gone? Boris had been elected in the early part of December the previous year by a landslide, but surely no-one actually listened to what he had to say? So, it must have been something else. It must have been everyone else's aspiration to stay alive that had kept them away because Rocco (it turned out) was an exceptional chef and a remarkably good interpreter of

117

Betty's Hot Pot. He was, as promised, a genius. So, it wasn't his cooking that had put them off. It must have been something else, something different.

On 23rd March 2020, Boris gave his *I must give the British People* speech live on television and so on and so on. As an owner of a restaurant business, I was given my notice to close my doors and shut up shop even though that particular boat had already sailed but thank you all the same. Trade had been non-existent for weeks already. Come to think about it, trade had been non-existent ever since we opened. But this was different because now trade was absent for everybody unless you happened to run a grocery store or even better, a toilet roll store. In March 2020, there were four things you couldn't get hold of for love or money: toilet roll, tinned tomatoes, rice, and – yes, you've guessed it, pasta, in any shape or form – because these four commodities seemed to be the staples of a human life. *If you've got tomatoes and pasta then you've got a meal, if you've eaten a meal then you need to shit* and so on and so on.

I've always thought that it was a ridiculous few weeks back then when the world seemed to explode and what was exposed in the debris had been toilet roll and the remnants of what the toilet roll … well, I won't dwell on what was on the toilet roll because luckily for you I don't feel inclined to go off on one of my tangents right now. *You must stay at home,* Boris had told everybody, and they did, and then some. There was some good news, however: he was going to let us all out for twenty minutes per day for exercise. Thank God the weather had turned out nice in England in March, that's all I can say. And we were all permitted to go to the supermarket once a day – one person per household – to buy essentials. But he never actually specified what *essentials* had meant. *Essentials* to me hadn't meant tinned tomatoes or toilet roll, not even pasta. I always went to the shop for wine. Even on one occasion, Limoncello! I always seemed to find myself behind a customer – an *essential shopper*, the nominated person to leave their particular household – with a tenner on a scratch card that they barely dared hand to the supermarket operative in case they'd snarled back at them: *seriously, you expect me to put my life at risk **for this**?*

You get my point? And the point: *it's not the end of the world, sir, madam!* When in actual fact, that's precisely what it felt like.

That last afternoon in *John Bull's Traditional British Fish and Chips* will live long in my memory, but in the years that will follow it, whenever a gadfly should dare to enter into my mind to sting me into remembering it, the recollection of it – the uncomplicated thought of it; the sheer human innocence if it; of a dream that was in the final throes of its existence, that had been a dream for all of us – will never cause me any consternation at all. Because that final afternoon had been beautiful; beatific and almost a religious experience. In its own way, it had been a wake, a lament, not for the lost opportunity, but for dear old Linda, who'd died.

Luigi had emerged from the drinks room with six bottles of the finest Pecorino. To this day, I'm still not sure whether he intended to try to steal them since I headed him off at the pass before he had the chance to whisk them away. "What a good idea," I said, incredibly pleased with myself because I obviously thwarted his plan, his original idea. He then had no choice but to open a bottle or two and the three of us had sat at table eleven next to the toilets, and we'd drunk fine Italian wine.

"Ce, Prego," Luigi said as he poured.

"Good health. Ognuno per se!" When Rocco had chortled, I asked what it meant.

"Every man for himself!" Luigi obliged.

Three bottles in and Luigi had been in a more subdued, reflective frame of mind. "To Linda. God bless you, sweetheart," he proclaimed, holding his glass aloft for the two of us to join him in his drunken toast.

"To Linda," we said. But I knew Luigi had been thinking about someone else and so had Rocco. And so had I.

"To Mamma!" Luigi slurred, holding his glass aloft for us to connect with but thinking more about Linda than his actual *mamma* in that moment.

"To Mamma," we obliged.

"You miss her, Luigi?" I asked. "You're worried about her?" I was very drunk by then, but it hadn't mattered because so were the other two, and it's always a relief to know that everyone in the room is just as drunk as you are, isn't it?

"She is my world."

"More important than Pavarotti?"

Luigi held his empty glass aloft again, preparatory to another toast. "To Pavarotti! God bless you too, you fat bastardo!"

"To Pavarotti," we all screamed, spilling our wine in the process of clinking our glasses.

Rocco, it turned out, was much more impressive when drunk than whilst sober. When he was sober, he was a pathetic, petulant spoilt brat of a man. But give him a glass of Pecorino, and suddenly he was the life and soul of the party. "He bankrupted you, Luigi, that man!" he stammered whilst sipping his wine as though he was Dean Martin. But he'd only had one glass. "That tenor from Modena bankrupted you, Luigi! Banka-rupia! You should never have trusted anyone from the north, Luigi!"

"Oh, but what a voice!" Luigi had by then been very, very drunk as he leaned in to speak confidentially to Rocco, his friend. "You know, he made me call him *maestro*. We all had to call him *maestro* all evening whilst we'd all been running around like lunatics just to please him, just to rustle up something for him to eat! But he was a great man. The greatest man I've ever met."

I heard what he said. "Even greater than Prince Charles, Luigi?"

"Gesu Cristo, what an idiot he was! Nessun confronto (no comparison). At least Pavarotti knew who he was, what a gift he been given."

"I preferred him in the seventies when he thought that he was Frank Sinatra!" Rocco slurred.

"Who?" Luigi demanded, angered by the interruption.

"Pavarotti!" Rocco snarled back.

"Why?" Incredulous.

"Because he sung better songs, that's all, songs that meant something to all of us."

"Like what?"

Rocco then began to sing something, quietly at first. *"Mamma, son tanto Perche retorno de te* (or: Mamma, your son returns to you). He sung it as well as Pavarotti ever could. A singing chef indeed, even though he was quite drunk.

"Why did Pavarotti bankrupt you, Luigi?" I asked. "Didn't he pay his bill?"

"Of course, he fucking did! It *was* Pavarotti, a man with more class in his little fingernail than a full-grown man can possess in his entire body!" Luigi responded angrily. Then he became more introspective as he peered into his wine glass. "By then I was already standing on the edge of the abyss. That night when he brought his entourage to my restaurant in Leeds and insisted that I close my restaurant to everybody else, they drank me out of house and home. The bill had come to one and a half grand. Imagine that! Imagine how much food and drink they'd had for the bill to come to that much. It was like all my Christmases had come at once, and I had a chance of paying the staff the following Wednesday. But he paid by card, not cash. And it took three days for the bank to clear the funds, and fifteen-hundred pounds was just enough to clear the overdraft, so on the Wednesday, the bank foreclosed on me. And I didn't have the cash to pay the wages, so my staff turned on me too like it was all my fault!"

"What did you do?"

Rocco had stopped singing all of a sudden. "He declared himself *in bancarotta*! And I never got my money!" he sneered.

"And Maria left me on the Friday of that week," Luigi lamented. "And took my daughter with her. Because I was bankrupt, a failed man in her eyes, and she no longer had a good enough reason to stay with me, but they were all I had left."

"The mermaid?" I asked.

"The mermaid," he replied, quietly.

"Then what did you do?" This *was* better than Dallas.

"I went home," Luigi replied whilst remembering and finally being able to laugh about it.

"*Mamma …*" Rocco began to sing again with the full force of his voice. They were both very, very drunk by this point.

"*Son tanto perche retorono de te!*" Your son has returned to you, a little bit less for wear. 'Because my life has stung me, so now I've come back to you!'

"*Mamma …!*" Luigi had risen from his chair to join his friend Rocco in the middle of the dining room floor where they'd embraced one another and danced as they sang their little song that I never heard before. Rocco's voice was so good. As good as Pavarotti's.

Maybe not, but it had been a beautiful sight for my eyes to see, and I laughed as I drank my Pecorino. It had seemed to be a fitting farewell, so I had been glad of it.

"Luigi, get up!" Luigi bellowed whilst his friend Rocco had continued singing their little song, but he was thinking about something else that the lyrics to the song had stirred in him, that the song had stung him with. "Luigi, it's time to get up!" They'd been dancing with one another as though they'd both been exiled to a foreign land and had found themselves, inadvertently, dancing towards the edge of the world. "Luigi, we need your sheets for the table!"

Luigi then pulled himself free from the dance and had come back to table eleven from where I was watching them. "Lewis, I'm so sorry," he exclaimed, "I didn't think about you!"

"It's fine, honestly!" I replied. In actual fact, it was all fine by me.

"What are you sorry for now?" Rocco demanded, wondering why he had to stop singing and dancing to the tune he was singing along to. Because he had known that his friend had a great many things to be sorry about already.

"Because he has never had a fucking mother!" Luigi snapped back at his hapless friend.

"What is he, then? An alien or something?"

Luigi, we need your sheets for the table is what Luigi's mother used to say to get him out of bed on a morning. I loved that even though Luigi had considered it an insensitive thing to say. I could have told them that my stepmother used to rouse myself and my half-sister out of bed on a school morning by shouting up the stairs: 'Lewis, Jane, I'm going to count to three. And woe betide you both if I have to get to three!' But I didn't tell them that. Because even then, she was not my mother.

Chapter Nine

My half-sister called me on my mobile phone precisely four times in the eighteen or so years that I possessed a mobile phone. That was one more time than my father did, so that was something at least. I won't dilute the narrative with descriptions of the first three since it would add nothing, and I no longer feel the need to go off on one of my 'tangents' because things are about to get interesting, and I haven't got the time. In any case, I can't remember the reasons she called me on my mobile those three times because they'd been ordinary things that she wanted to talk to me about, family events that she had no choice but to invite me to, 'I hope Fiona isn't on shift then because Father would like to have her there too', that sort of thing. But the fourth! The fourth time she called me on my mobile is when I realised that the world really had exploded.

Luigi, Rocco, and I were standing on the concourse of Windsor Old Train Station. The lights were out, the gas was off, and we'd left our wine glasses unwashed on table eleven as a memento to the failed opportunity to give an answer to everybody because it turned out that none of us had the answer to anything. I'd been struggling to find the key to lock the front door. Windsor Old Train Station was deserted, Windsor itself was a ghost-town. Not a soul around, not even in a car. There was no noise; from people, traffic, aeroplanes – even though Windsor was directly beneath the flightpath to Heathrow airport – nothing. The beautiful bourgeois had all vanished in a puff of smoke. We three drunken lords had noticed the strangeness of it as soon as we'd stumbled out of the building. It was as though the apocalypse had occurred whilst we'd been drinking Pecorino and the Italians had been singing *Mamma*. The Four Horsemen had obviously ridden up Windsor High Street and cut down anyone stupid enough not be hunkered down in their own houses. *Ognuno per se*. At least they'd all possessed a chess set, so that was a consolation.

"Gesu Cristo, I've forgotten my wine!" Luigi exclaimed, flaying his arms around like a gasping fish out of water before slapping his forehead with the flat of his hand like a failed mariner about to sink his own boat because of his incompetency as a mariner; when he finally let me in on his little plot to pilfer the pecorino.

"What wine?" I asked him, mischievously. But I didn't really care because he was worth more to me than half a dozen bottles of wine. In any event, there was no one left to sell it to.

"Oh, forget it, Lewis!" he replied whilst exhaling his disappointment and inhaling the exasperation, not to mention the inconvenience, of having to go to the supermarket to buy his own. If he bought some tinned tomatoes and some pasta at the same time, the *essential worker* on the checkout would be none the wiser.

"And Boris is going to pay me, Ce?" Rocco asked me because someone was obviously going to have to.

"Ce, Rocco. Boris is going to pay you now. But only eighty-percent of what I paid you."

He grumbled something in Italian that I hadn't understood and hadn't wanted to. "Better than nothing," he snorted. "And Frederico too, Ce?"

"Frederico left, Rocco. He got on the last flight out of here!"

"So, Boris no pay Frederico, no?"

"No! Frederico missed the boat!"

Rocco buttoned his donkey jacket up to the nape of his neck even though the weather in the March of England had been quite something. Obviously not to an Italian who'd had a penchant for Thailand. "I've never liked this Boris!" he sneered before turning away to begin the journey home. "Never trust a man who never looks at himself in the mirror!"

Even though Rocco had turned out to be a fabulous singer, and even though I never quite achieved a queue up the street to hear him sing, and even though he turned out to be an utter pain in the arse, I felt sorry for him when he walked away. After all, who could not feel sorry for someone who looked just like Gandhi? "What will he do now?" I asked Luigi as we stood together and watched the old man walk up the concourse of Old Windsor Train Station into the light.

Luigi sighed. "He will stay with me. We will form our own Italian bubble. And we'll no doubt watch old Italian movies, bad movies. And Rocco will laugh because they will remind him of his boyhood even though he has got nothing to laugh about. Until he can find a flight to Thailand, and then I'll be on my own!"

"To his ladyboy friend?" I interjected.

"To his son," Luigi replied immediately. "His son lives there."

I wanted to take Luigi by the scuff of his waistcoat and scream: *you've never told me that! I've been imagining all kinds of things!* But I didn't. Longing for a flight to his son had made total sense to me, but the thought of it had made me sad. "Let me know when he gets a ticket to Thailand!" I replied.

"Why?"

"Because then I'll tell Boris to stop paying him!"

When I finally managed to lock the door, I turned and looked at Luigi, and there must have been a desperate look in my eyes because he asked me, "What will you do?"

I had no idea. "Every man for himself, Luigi!"

Straight away he replied, excitedly, "Come and stay with us, Lewis. The three amigos, Ce?"

"For fuck's sake, Luigi, I want to go home!" Rocco hollered from the top end of the concourse whilst he was silhouetted by the bright sunlight with the shadow of Windsor Castle behind him.

I would rather have my eyes gouged out, I thought. But thank you for asking, Luigi. "I guess I'll have to form my own 'bubble'. I'll be all right."

Luigi held out his arms preparatory to embracing me. But I wasn't allowed to walk into his embrace when that's all I wanted to do. Because Boris had instructed us not to do anything like that. Contact between humans was forbidden, even though contact is our natural disposition. "I love you, man!" Luigi said, returning his arms to his side. "You are my brother!" And it was enough for me in that moment. His comment had actually given me some solace, some hope, at a time when hope was in sparse supply just like a toilet roll. Hope, in the March of 2020, was the *dried eggs* of its time. *Hope* was the 'dig for victory'! I have never been gladder of it.

As I watched the two Italians saunter down the hill towards the river, towards their home, I never felt so lonely in my life. I felt as though I oughtn't to have been there. I felt as though I oughtn't to have existed in the first place, since everyone I have known have seemed predestined to leave me. That I was a mistake, a consequence of something that I would never be able to control. As I watched the two Italians walk away, it had felt as though the world was ending.

Until, until … my phone vibrated in my pocket.

Five missed calls. I hadn't heard it, ironically. The name displayed on my screen was *The Toy* because that's how I saved my half-sister's number. Even then, I recoiled into the doorway of my redundant restaurant because I had been quite drunk and was afraid to answer the call in the event that I sounded drunk to one of the greatest 'thinkers' of our age. But I did answer.

"Hello!"

"Lewis?" Desperately.

"This is he." Casually, trying my hardest not to sound drunk.

"Oh, thank God! I've been calling you all afternoon, where are you?"

"I'm in Windsor, I've just closed down my restaurant …!"

"I can't get home, Lewis!" I may have been trying my darndest to sound sober but my half-sister had sounded as though she had been crying all afternoon. Her words were punctuated by her snivels, and her gasps were the consequences of her soberness. "I can't get a flight back. They've closed the borders!"

"Where are you?"

"I'm at the villa in Italy!"

Of course, you are! "And Michael and the boys?"

"They're here too. For fuck's sake, Lewis, where do you think they are?" Beside herself with panic, I never heard her swear before.

"Well, what do you want me to do, Jane?" Casually trying not to sound drunk.

"I can't get home!" she sobbed.

"To whom?"

129

"To my Pappa!" She paused to sob a little bit more but I could tell that she was doing her best not let me hear. "There's someone from Macmillan who goes to the house twice a week, but …"

"Why didn't you tell me you were going away, and I would have kept an eye on him?"

A pause. "What good would you have been?"

"What good can I be now?"

Another pause. "You're the only hope I have! You're the only one left!"

It turned out that drunkenness and desolation are the same thing after all. Because if drunkenness forces a person to speak the truth, then so too does desolation. And the truth is for the most part unwelcome, whether made real through too much wine or being forced to say it through desperation, it is almost always an unwelcome visitor. "He's your father, Lewis! As much as he is mine."

"What do you want me to do, Jane?" Casually.

When what I really wanted to say, to scream, to my half-sister was this: *finally, you've realised it! Finally, I have too. And Luigi, and everyone else has realised it. We've all realised it at the same time. And it is like an awakening, a new dawn. It is like the sunshine, this realisation, this desolation, this drunken truth. It is like being born all over again. And everyone else, locked away in their houses, whether backing onto the most famous river in the world or not, knows it too. They can sense it too. They can sense that something is happening. An awakening. Their own awakening. Whatever an awakening means to those others hunkered down in their houses, it is happening to them too. And it's happening to that old cow in Chicago also. It's happening to all of us at the same time.* But most of all I wanted to say to her*: I* *have a part to play in all of this after all, and my part in it is to speak a universal truth, which is:* what are they without us, what are we without them? *And it only took a fucking virus floating in the air for us all to realise it! That's how easy it was, after all.*

But I hadn't said either of those things; I don't even think that I said them to myself word for word. Because a thought doesn't need eloquent prose to accompany it. It just is what it is. A simple thought – dancing through the mind like Margot Fonteyn – is always strong enough to carry the sentiment so that the sentiment endures because that was the whole point of it. A thought always speaks the truth.

What I actually said to my half-sister – what my reaction had been – was something along the lines of feigned surprise and alarm that a Macmillan nurse was involved already in our father's care. Because I knew what a Macmillan nurse represented. They represent the *End* of a life. They are the agents sent by God – or the government – to see a person safely away because both of those entities care how it's done. And it must always be done correctly when possible. They are a gentle stroke on the back of an ancient hand-made blue because the veins have evolved to the surface, so that another type of nurse can take a sample of blood easily. They are the gentle touch of a hand on a forehead that brushes a wisp of hair away from the eyes so that they can still see clearly what needs to be seen in their final moments. They are the gentle pat on the back that seems to say *well done, for a life well-lived,* but they don't care whether that life has been well-lived or not, or whether the pat on the back was even deserved. Because every living thing, at the end of its life, deserves the same treatment. They exist to see us off. The code of their profession is to make the *end* as easy

131

as possible, just like the code of an engineer for British Rail is to ensure that an old diesel train doesn't squeak too loudly as it pulls into the station where it must terminate.

"Why didn't you tell me? I cannot know unless you tell me." The irony in this whole conversation, of course, is that my stepmother had died in such a way that she hadn't afforded herself the luxury of having someone stroke the back of her hand or to tell her *well done, for a life well-lived,* as the agent had brushed a wisp of hair away from her eyes. Nor had Linda, who'd died gasping for oxygen, I'm sure, thinking not of herself but of her poor husband who was about to be left on his own, and then what was he going to do? But at least my stepmother's funeral had been gammed to the rafters, unlike poor Linda's.

"What difference does it make now that you know, Lewis?" she asked exasperatedly. "And in any case, having a Macmillan nurse doesn't necessarily mean that he's going to die tomorrow or the day after or next week or the week after. A Macmillan nurse is offered to anyone with a terminal diagnosis, but we've only had one for the past month or so, just to help me out a little bit, if that's agreeable to you?"

I hadn't cared for her passive-aggressive tone but then I rarely had. "Of course, it is, whatever's best. What are you doing in Italy?" My tone was accusatory, questioning her motives for abandoning her *pappa* when he needed her most. It seemed a strange time to visit the villa at Porto Sant'Elpidio.

"He almost insisted we came out here," she replied. "He received word that Enzo had passed away and he was fretting about the place without him there to keep an eye on things."

"Who's Enzo?"

She sighed exasperatedly again. It seemed that whatever I said was enough to enflame her annoyance with me. "The caretaker, Lewis, Enzo Ballerini, the guy who's been in your life since your birth!"

"Oh, Enzo. I thought he was called Ennio. I'm sorry to hear that." But really, I couldn't have cared less, except that news of his death had confounded the gloom of a sunny March afternoon in Windsor: everyone was dying all of a sudden. I was pleased that Luigi had already sauntered away before Jane had rung me because I would have had to tell him what she told me about poor old Enzo, and it would have made him even more concerned about his elderly mother back home.

"But really, I think Pappa had seen how exhausted I was beginning to feel, so he insisted that we all take a break away." Her tone had turned melancholic, I noticed. But it was a phone conversation and I couldn't see her face so she may have just been picking a strawberry out of a strawberry Daiquiri for all I knew and was momentarily distracted. "For one last time!"

"One last time where, at the villa?" I probed, suddenly interested.

"Yes, that's what he said. Isn't it a strange thing to say?"

"Is he selling it?"

"If he is, then he hasn't discussed it with me," Jane replied snappily.

"Nor me." I was more sardonic in tone with my remark.

"Well, I know that he hasn't discussed any such thing with you, Lewis!" In other words: *of course, he hasn't*.

"Why would he want to sell it? He doesn't need the money and, well, I don't want to sound insensitive, but

133

you'd think that he has things on his mind other than worrying about his olive grove or the lawn now that Ennio's dead!"

"Enzo!"

… "Now that Enzo's dead."

"I think that maybe he was just confused or was lamenting the fact that he personally will never visit the villa again," Jane had concluded, but I knew the old goat better than she ever gave me credit for, and I knew that he was cleverer than that, whether he was dying or not.

"Is that why you rang me, to tell me that the caretaker is dead?" I was sitting on a green, metal bench in front of the Henry the Eighth Gate at Windsor Castle adjacent to the old train station. I was the only person around as though Henry the Eighth was in one of his bad moods and anyone caught wandering the streets was in clear danger of having their heads lobbed off. *Off with their heads for being* **out**! I never quite perfected the art of walking and talking on a mobile phone at the same time, so I had to sit down. The bench was of the top order. The Aston Martin of benches. My legs had moulded themselves into the seat part so that it had felt as though my feet had been lifted off the ground. And the Pecorino was beginning to take its toll, so I had been extremely glad of the bench's flawless design. A statue of Queen Victoria loomed large in front of me, and I was pleased that she was looking in a different direction, down the high street towards the barracks. She was another one who'd lob your head off at the slightest exasperation. She always seemed to be miserable. Her sculptors had always depicted her as a miserable old bag, even though she ruled a quarter of the world, so had had a lot to be grateful for. It was as though her face had seemed to say, *I don't want it, I didn't ask for it, and now that I have it, I don't know what to do*

134

with it. All I want is my husband back with me. When I looked to my left, the Royal Ensign was flying proudly atop the Round Tower, indicating that our current queen was in residence. Luckily for me, she does not seem the type to want to *lob off* your head just because you've found yourself outside sitting on a bench talking to your half-sister in Italy when being outside really wasn't an acceptable thing anymore. But talking out aloud in the open air, seemingly to yourself, was, so all was well.

"I rang you because I can't get home, Lewis!" Jane snapped at me. "I'm worried about him. He isn't answering the house phone."

"Have you tried the Macmillan woman?"

"It's a man, and I haven't got his number."

"What about the old woman next door?"

"Elsa, she goes in every day to check on him, but she's not answering either. Michael, have you washed your hands? I don't believe you. Go inside and do it now and remember to sing happy birthday to yourself twice!"

I had been momentarily confused by her aside until I remembered that her bald-too-young husband was called Michael and I had just been given a snippet of how she talked to him. I imagined poor Michael skulking back into the house with his head hung low with his sons laughing at him. "Is it his birthday?" I asked her, bemusedly.

"No, why?"

"Then why does he have to sing happy birthday to himself twice?"

"Are you drunk again, Lewis?" Snarly now.

"I was," I replied. "But now I'm strangely sober all of a sudden."

"If you could just stop drinking for a little while and emerge from your pathetic bubble of regret and failure that you live your life in and take notice of what's happening in the real world, then you'd see that something *is* indeed happening, and people are dying!"

I sighed and hadn't cared that she heard me sighing. "When are you coming back?"

"I don't know. There are no flights to the UK next week anyway, so I don't know."

"Do you want me to call in on him?"

"Well, what do you think?"

I sighed again. And it was true that I certainly felt sober all of a sudden and was pleased that I hadn't had to pay for the Pecorino because it had failed to do its job. "I'll call around in the morning."

"Are you kidding me, Lewis?"

"I can't go now!"

"Why not?"

I looked around. "Because there are no taxis or buses! I've no way of getting to Henley from here."

It was her turn to sigh despondently, and she hadn't cared that I heard her either. "I don't care how you get there, Lewis, just get there as quickly as you can! And take some things with you because you're moving in with him!"

Now who was kidding who? "What?"

"You're going to have to form a father-son bubble, and you're going to have to keep him safe!"

"He's got Elsa!" I protested.

"She isn't allowed to go around anymore, she's from a separate household!"

"Yes, but it's only next door, it's not like she has to catch a flight!"

"He's your father, Lewis!"

But he hates me, I thought to myself. *He won't want me there.*

136

"Just sort yourself out, Lewis!" Jane had been nearing her conclusion and her tone had finally turned customarily demanding. "Keep him safe, protect him from this. I'm trusting you to do the right thing. Because if anything happens to him while I'm stranded in Italy, then I will never forgive you and our relationship will be over!"

I'll smother him with his pillow then! I thought. What a wicked thing to have thought. What a nasty gadfly that one had been that had flown into my mind through one ear and out of the other. The worst type.

As soon as I finished my call with Jane, I rang Luigi straight away. I was still sitting on the most comfortable bench in the world. I still hadn't seen another human being. I imagined the queen looking out of her window saying, 'Philip, come and have a look at this idiot. Doesn't he know that there's a virus floating around?' Maybe if she had actually known what I was doing there in front of her castle, she would have felt sympathy for my dilemma and driven me to Henley herself in the Range Rover? 'Won't be long, Philip. This man's chickens have come home to roost!' A gracious queen indeed.

"Ce, Prego." That's how Luigi always answers his phone.

"I need a lift!"

"Where to, for God's sake?"

"Henley Upon Thames."

"What for, the fucking regatta?"

I paused. For reasons I cannot explain, I was reluctant to tell him the reason. Probably because I'd told him too much already; too many things that he hadn't needed to know, and if I told him, then it would look like I was back peddling from the truth. Eventually, I had no

137

option but to tell him why I needed a lift. "I'm going to have to move in with my father for a couple of weeks."

The sound of laughter that was emitted from the speaker on my handset was like 'The Laughing Policeman' since Luigi had recognised my dilemma straight away. I heard Rocco in the background asking what was so funny. Luigi had told him to shut up and mind his business.

"I can't, I've had a drink."

"Yes, but are you *really* drunk, Luigi?" I probed, desperately.

"I was with you just fifteen minutes ago, what do you think?"

Fifteen minutes before, he'd been incredibly drunk, and so had Rocco. They'd both been so drunk that they'd held each other's hand as they'd skipped part way down the hill, which had made me laugh to myself because they knew that I was watching them. Even then, I was tempted to coerce him into driving me to Henley with assurances that there wouldn't be another vehicle on the roads. But Luigi had been perfectly correct to deny my request in the first place. "Get someone else to do it," he concluded. "Ciao, ciao, ciao," in rapid succession is how Luigi always ends his calls.

The only other person who would have been able to give me a lift to Henley was Fiona, and believe me, I'd been tempted to ring her just for that reason. Until, as I brought her name and number to the screen of my phone from my contacts list, I realised that I hadn't seen or spoken to her in such a long time that to do so then, with that request and for that reason, would be proof positive that when I left her, she'd gotten off the hook. And I hadn't wanted her to believe that there was any other reason that I contacted her again, other than my request

138

for a lift to Henley, because I undoubtedly knew she would read other things into it. Better to leave her alone.

So, I walked from Windsor to Henley-Upon-Thames. Fourteen miles in all. I called in at my flat in Maidenhead to collect some things so at least I had a little time to recover. I took a slight detour once at Maidenhead, which took me past Fiona's complex, and if she had seen me walking by from her window and rushed out to discover what I was doing and where I was going, and I told her, and she insisted on taking me the rest of the way in her car, then that would have been a different set of circumstances altogether. But she hadn't seen me, or if she had, had backed away from the window.

But thank God the weather had turned out fine in March in England, 2020. Thank God it hadn't been snowing or raining or blowing a gale, which would have been more normal. Nothing seemed to be normal anymore, and in actual fact, it was unseasonably warm: too warm for such a long walk. As I walked through Maidenhead towards the roundabout that would take me towards the Henley Road, the only other human being that I encountered was an elderly gentleman walking towards me. Now, under normal circumstances this wouldn't have registered, but nothing was normal anymore, and Boris had told us all to keep a two-meter distance (unless you belonged to the same household or were in a 'bubble' with someone in a separate household). I'd never seen this old guy before, nor him me, but we found ourselves on a direct trajectory towards one another. Breaking the two-meter rule seemed to be inevitable, and there was an awkwardness in both our approaches as we started to wobble because neither of us knew what to do. The old guy smiled at me as he approached, but I knew the only thing on his mind was: *have you got it*? *Because if you* *have, then you'd better not give **it** to me! I've only come out for my daily exercise.* And vice-versa, but my daily exercise had been a darn site harder than his.

The old gentleman, perhaps the gentlest man I ever met, simply smiled at me before crossing the road, and we both breathed the amplest sigh of relief. It was over, this torment. Ten meters or so on the other side of the road, and he crossed back again to get back onto the correct trajectory that would take him to where he intended to get to before another human being had gotten in his way. I recall thinking: *what the hell is going on?*

It was dusk on an unseasonably warm March evening by the time I arrived at my final destination, where my journey finally terminated. And I'd been exhausted, a spent force, a relic of what I had once been before the journey had begun. I gasped for air, and I had to take a deep breath before stepping over the threshold of the *big house* at Henley. A deep breath before the plunge. On that occasion, there had been no one there to greet me. No, *I haven't got any money, Lewis*; not even: *Ah, Fiona, how are you?* Nothing. There was nothing. There was no stepmother gleaming with joy because her *boy* was home. Nothing. There was no welcome there for me. I felt an overbearing sense that everything that I'd ever known was over. There was no noise or at least, no noise from people anyway. All I could hear were the birds in the trees who'd reclaimed their dominion over the world; over everything, because the humans were hunkered down inside their houses because Boris had told them to. They were glad of a world where the humans were confined to their houses. But at least the humans had their chess sets, so that was something of a consolation – something for them to do in the meantime.

All I heard once I crossed the threshold into the *big house* at Henley was the sound of a clock ticking. And yes, that's right, it *had* prompted me to think about my stepmother and about that New Year's Day breakfast in the nineties that had turned her into a leopardess. And it made me feel sad and ashamed to think about it again. But at least it forced me out of my exhaustion. The sound of the grandmother clock ticking away in the front room as though nothing had happened was like an adrenaline boost administered to the fleshy part of my upper arm to give me the energy, the currency with which to approach what was going to come next in this quite extraordinary adventure.

Chapter Ten

It's strange how one of the closest people to you can seem like a stranger. I was standing on the black and white tiled floor in the hallway of my father's house, but I felt like a stranger, an interloper, no better than a burglar. I hadn't moved an inch since stepping across the threshold since the environment once I'd been inside the house hadn't seemed very much different from the surreal environment outside. The only thing that had changed was the sound of a clock ticking instead of the sound of birdsong once I'd closed the front door behind me and had shut that bizarre world out. I was holding an overnight bag that was precisely that: it contained a change of clothes and underwear and socks that, without being laundered, would only do me one night because that's the length of time I'd intended to stay. Just enough time to have made the effort that my half-sister had demanded of me for her to be satisfied that I'd done precisely what I'd assured her I would. The old goat would not want me there any more than I wanted to be there and that overriding sense of being a nuisance, an unwanted distraction, was why he was like a stranger to me, and vice-versa.

In that moment in that hallway, I thought again about my dog, Andrew. I know, a stupid name for a dog, but not as stupid as Jesus, which is what I'd wanted to call it for no other reason than to give myself the opportunity of standing in the street or the park to shout *Jesus, where are you? Jesus, come back! Jesus, it's time for tea!* And to present all onlookers, passers-by, the opportunity to think: *Jesus, what an idiot!* But really, I'd suggested that name for the dog just to give my father the opportunity to roll his eyes at me again. Because when you're eighteen and you have a sense that that's what someone wants to do to you, you feel an impulse to facilitate it in any way you can. You feel a desire to prove them right. Mainly, I'd thought about my dog again because I'd remembered a time when there had been a welcome for me in that hallway. A sloppy, waggy, over-the-top welcome when his claws would always slip on the black and white tiles, and I'd had to steady him and slow him down. Daft thing.

Frankly, I couldn't quite believe that I'd been standing there in that hallway clutching an overnight bag. I'd been aghast that my half-sister could even consider me a suitable substitute for her or my stepmother, even for Elsa, the old woman who lived next door. My natural inclination had been to turn around and tiptoe the hell out of there, closing the front door quietly behind me so that the old goat would never have known that I was ever there. All I'd wanted was to be in my little flat above the opticians on the Bath Road at Maidenhead, eating junk food and watching TV. I hadn't realised it until I'd found myself standing in the hallway of my father's house, but I was overdue a dose of solitude. I'd wanted, maybe even needed, to be on my own for a little while; and not worry about whether my customer's order was correct or if the Italians were going to get along. I no longer needed to worry about the VAT or the gas bill or whether the card payments would hit my bank account in time for wage day; whether the other restaurants further down the concourse of Windsor Old Station were busy when I was quiet, as though they all knew the secret of being able to drum up trade that I was never privy to because it turned out that I was a terrible businessman. The pandemic had come along at precisely the right time when I'd needed something to happen and had rendered such concerns and

143

pressures defunct, abstract and not worth worrying about in the bigger scheme of things. The entire world may have been locked down, but I had been set free. Free to care only about myself.

Because things had gone quite seriously bad at *John Bull's Traditional British Fish and Chips.* It turned out that my great, immaculate masterplan was, with the realisation of it, a terrible idea. Luigi had been right, but then he invariably is. There is a gap in the market for traditional British cuisine because no one wants it. Not even when it's done well by a chef who cared about what went across the pass, who occasionally sang Verdi or Puccini. Not even when it's done with a twist, sprinkled with a little bit of Italian magic. Don't get me wrong, I'm aware that on the coast – Devon or Cornwall, Yorkshire, anywhere there's a sea breeze and the shrill of gulls – people may very well want fish and chips, etcetera, but in Windsor Old Station, it had just seemed wrong, out of place, a little bit peculiar and to the beautiful bourgeois, an unwelcome addition to their little paradise of correctness and devoutness to the finer aspects of a human life.

I'd been standing on the edge of the abyss, probably in the exact same spot where Luigi had been standing. Pavarotti and his entourage had come along and pushed him over and I'd expected something similar to happen to me. I was prepared for it and, towards the end, longed for it. The stress had become unbearable. The kind of pressure that, when it's placed on top of someone, crushes them repeatedly until they become dust, and when caught in the wind, scattered asunder. It had been a mounting pressure that was like a wrecking ball, swinging in and pounding and pounding until it got its way and I collapsed. Or not. I almost had, but as the pressure and the stress had pounded me, I had longed for something to happen, had prayed for something, someone, to spring me from my solitary confinement. I had been on my knees again, but this time there was no one there to pull me up. There is no equivalent of a Macmillan nurse for someone who is about to topple into the abyss.

The A5-sized brown envelopes from HM had begun to arrive so frequently that towards the end, the postman had been almost hesitant in his delivery of them, close to tears on some mornings, whether through pity or joy, I cannot know. My accountant and business advisor, but never a friend, had informed me: 'Lewis, unfortunately, your main creditor is Her Majesty the Queen, and she wants her money'. Or what: *Off with his head.* Luckily for me, our current queen never seemed that type to demand my head on a silver platter to be served with onions and British lamb. 'Or she'll drive you into bankruptcy. She'll close you down'. Well, that was better than the alternative, at least.

It was strange how he'd evoked that little ninety-odd-year-old woman, who was like the world's grandmother, who had never seemed to change, who had been ever-present, certainly in my life and probably in yours too, as the entity that was hunting me down. I was on the run, but surely, I could outrun a ninety-odd-year-old woman?

You get my point? The point was that I hadn't really cared whether Her Majesty had gotten her money because I'd known that I could outrun her because she'd be too preoccupied trying to hold onto her hat. And I hadn't really cared about the gas board either, because they were grey men in grey suits who'd been paid more in a year than I could earn in a lifetime as a career waiter. All that had mattered to me was paying the Italians, and Sean

145

whilst he was with me, and Linda because she'd needed to keep the roof over her dying husband's head. That's all I'd cared about. And that's where all of the money went with nothing left over to pay those other entities. Or me.

Frederico, by the way, that essence of Italianises, that gorgeous man who was the very essence of Italy, who'd rendered Luigi and Rocco as mere imitations and a disgrace to their order, had only worked for me because Rocco had found himself working for me. Because Rocco was his mentor, his teacher. Rocco had been to him everything. Rocco had been like his father, and he'd followed him wherever he'd gone: London, Naples, Hong Kong, Leeds, Middlesbrough, Brighton ... but never to Thailand, thank God. I'd never really had a conversation with Frederico because it had occurred to me early on that his loyalty did not lie with me, the man who'd paid his wage, but to Rocco. That hadn't mattered. I won't dwell too much on Frederico because he is too damn handsome to worry about. Except he adores Rocco, almost worshipfully so. Linda had told me that he had three daughters back in Italy who lived with his mother, but she didn't know what had happened to the woman who'd borne him three daughters because she hadn't liked to ask, sensing that there was a story to tell there; but that's where his wages had been sent, nevertheless. And I'd been glad to pay him. It had been my privilege. When he'd gotten onto that last flight out of here, my accountant and business advisor had advised me that I owed him eight-hundred-pound sterling in holiday pay. That had felt like a gentle nudge over the edge into the abyss. That had been my Pavarotti moment.

When I'd Googled *the easiest way to* ... Well, I won't say what I'd Googled. I can't. And for the purpose of the narrative, I mustn't. It would be a distraction. But I will tell you that I prayed, how I'd prayed, and to whom. I'd prayed by sitting at table eleven next to the toilets. Not by placing my hands together and looking to the ceiling – which had been, by then, fully repaired and was, at the last, waterproof. The prawns were safe! – but by sipping my tea and whilst I looked into my teacup, I'd beseeched whomever I had been evoking in my mind's eye, whomsoever is narrating the story of my life, and I said to them *come on, you can do this. Now is the time. Give me a way out. Do something. If you're really there, then do something that will help me. You've got this. You've **got** me. So do something and give a man a chance. Or else, it has all been for nothing* ... But it was not God to whom I'd beseeched, it was my mother. It was to the third person to whom I had prayed. My half-sister was right, as she invariably is.

Yet, by beseeching my mother in quiet contemplation, had I assumed that she was already dead? Does she exist existentially because I exist? Was she in the ether, as God is in the ether: omnipresent? But I have never been in the least bit religious because neither had my father, as one of the world's foremost psychoanalysts, been a religious man. He was cleverer than that. I had no connection to God. God had not involved Himself in the details of my life, so I'd never involved myself in the intricacies of His. There's only so much devotion that a man can give, and all of mine was spent on my mother. The mere thought of her: her jet-black hair tied tightly behind her neck; her blood-orange lips; the silk scarf around her neck. That sense of belonging to her, and no one else, least of all God. And that she belonged to me also. The sense that she was narrating the story of my life so must know what happens in the end? The third person. Just as God is the third person in a religious person's life.

147

Yet, it is not such a peculiar thing that I prayed to her to help me then. Because we all do it, don't we? We all beseech those who have gone before us. We all evoke the image of them in our mind's eye. We all pray in our own way and not necessarily to God. We always have, we always will. How many times has a human being said to themselves: *oh, he would have loved this if he were here now,* or, *what would she do if she were still here? How would she play this because that's how I'll play it?* And we've done that for as long as human beings have existed. Because we are all just the consequence of whatever has gone before us. We may, in adulthood, find a resolve not to be like the people who are responsible for us, but it is always futile to think like that because, in the end, we are. That is the ripple effect of history.

History isn't Henry the Eighth, Elizabeth the First, Victoria, Elizabeth the Second. History is you, it's me. I suppose that's why people spend good money on websites that search a person's family tree. I suppose that's why Stonehenge was built all those thousands of years ago; why the fields of southern England are dotted with mounds that contain human remains, long, long before the concept of God even came into being. Not the God in a bad Charlton Heston movie, but the God in your imagination, the authentic version. The pyramids, the Colosseum, Angkor Wat, Uluru, and so on and so on … they've got nothing whatsoever to do with God. They exist in reverence to the people – our forebears – that have gone before us. That's what I think, anyway. It is the reason why I prayed to the woman who'd given birth to me all those years ago whilst I'd been sitting at table eleven gaping into my empty teacup. We are, all of us, a consequence of something. And the circumstances matter because all of us are the consequence. We are the ripple effect of history; we are the water breaking against the earthen bank, whether you like it or not. We are the youths leaping over a raging bull, and the lucky ones get to walk away. When the memory of that ordeal turns into myth, then perhaps we can begin to live. And yes, all that we can do – those of us who are left behind, abandoned, is play with whatever hand has been dealt to us: ace of spades, king of clubs, queen of hearts.

Hark at me, the philosopher. But when I prayed for her to do something that would help me, I could not have known that she would, that she could. I could not have known that she would do something so extreme, so over-the-top, as to conjure up a virus that would lay the entire world low; lock them all up in their houses with their chess sets. And all for me? I'd thought: 'my God, you're good, lady, whoever you are'! I actually thought that she was God because that's precisely the kind of thing that He would do, and if you believe the narrative, He has on many occasions. Yet now I know that all she wanted to do was put her side of the story from wherever she was.

I hadn't turned around and tiptoed the hell out of that house, as you might have guessed. And I hadn't because of an overriding sense that my narrator, the author of my story, had deemed it necessary for me to be there. So, I'd stayed. But I stood stock still, taking not even the slightest step from the spot where I'd been standing, as though I was a March hare caught in someone's headlights, stunned into the submission of standing still. I was like a pawn on a chessboard waiting for the player to make her move, hoping to put the king in check. Whilst I'd been standing stock still, I'd wondered whether my mother had ever been in this house. Had she been with my father when he'd purchased it in the

149

eighties? Had it been their home together along with the villa at Porto Sant'Elpidio? Had I been born in this house or at the villa in Italy? Probably in the Royal Berkshire Hospital, but the fact that I didn't know had caused me more discomfort than I'd been prepared for. I'd actually been born in the maternity wing of the San Giovanni Addolorata Hospital in Rome, and it turns out that I'm a Roman, but more of that later. The point is that I didn't know anything about my creation; where I'd been born, whether or not my mother had actually lived in the house that I'd been raised in, nothing. I'd taken it for granted that I'd been born some place because contrary to Rocco's barbed comment that I may be an *alien or something*, I am a human being, and human beings have to be delivered into the world from a woman, regardless of where it is. A human life is the consequence of something else. I'd wondered whether I'd been created through love or lust, because the two things are quite different. One is tender, the other is violent, and little details like that make a big difference. Little details like that can explain everything.

Had my mother nudged my father into buying that house because she'd adored the black and white floor tiles in the hallway since they'd reminded her of a warped chessboard where the king and the queen could play out their little game? Had she, in the eighties, adored the ornate cornice work in the dining room so she'd whispered in my father's ear, 'buy it, Martin. Buy it for me'. So, he had, just because she'd whispered the instruction in his ear? I hadn't known anything about the circumstances of my creation because I'd never asked. Being a quiet, introverted child has its many benefits, but it also has its pitfalls. The benefits of being a quiet child is that everything can be taken for granted; the pitfalls are that as an adult, nothing can be anymore.

My earliest memory, as you know, is of my natural mother kissing me on the forehead with her blood orange lips and whispering in my ear, *How long is forever? Sometimes it is just a moment. Happy birthday, Lewis*, preparatory to leaving me there on my own in that oversized deckchair. Other than that, my earliest memories are all formulated around that house, so maybe she had once lived in it with me after all? Then, step forward my stepmother, who I recall picking me up from off my knees and walking me around the dining room, gently rocking me to stop me from hollering (my father had been trying to work in the room next door, probably) so who knows?

I know, I know, that I have aforementioned that my stepmother is about to slip out of the narrative, but sometimes things aren't as straightforward as they seem, are they? Because my second earliest memory is of her gently rocking me back and forth in her vain attempt to shut me up. Now I know that she doesn't slip out of the narrative at all. That she is omnipresent and has a big part to play at the end, for which I am eternally grateful to her. None of this would have mattered, of course, if my father hadn't deemed it necessary to separate me from my stepmother and my half-sister by his overuse of his four-letter words: *step* and *half*.

The player made her move; she'd moved her fingertip from the top of my head and had committed herself to her strategy. I'd stepped forwards and had been committed to finding out where, precisely, my father was because I could not hear any noises within that house that sounded as though life existed within it anymore. Contrast that sound of silence – apart from the grandmother clock ticking competing with the sound of the house phone ringing – with all the hullaballoo and the commotion of human life that had once prevailed in that house, and you may get a sense of the sudden concern that had overwhelmed me. Suddenly, it had not all been about me anymore.

He hadn't been in the living room at the front of the house because that's where I'd looked first. The house phone, however, had been ringing off the hook and I'd known instinctively that it was my half-sister trying desperately to connect with him from the villa. To no avail because I'd let it ring and ring until finally, she'd given up trying and the ringing stopped. *Poor Michael,* I thought, because at the other end of the line on the other side of the continent, she'd been so frustrated by that lack of connection with her pappa that she probably thumped that poor, bald-too-young man squarely on the jaw before sending him away to wash his hands again. I hope that he didn't sing *Happy Birthday* to himself whilst looking in the mirror but something along the lines of, I don't know, maybe something along the lines of *Ding Dong, the Witch is Dead, Which old Witch, the Wicked Witch*? Both of those songs, by the way, can be used when administering CPR on someone who's heart has had enough. The tempo is exactly right with both of those songs. The tempo: *one, two, three, four*, whilst you're pumping down on a person's chest in an attempt to reactivate its heart, is the perfect rhythm for a human heart to reconsider its options; for it to pause and think to itself: hang on a minute, there's a little bit more that I'd quite like to see, thank you very much. Ding Dong!

He hadn't been in the dining room either because that's the room that I ventured into next. Nothing, except a huge mahogany table that was set for – get this – thirteen people. A pristine room that was ready to go and always had been. Thirteen people at a dinner party is only unlucky if the host only has twelve chops, as Peter the actor had once proclaimed, channelling Groucho Marx in his exuberant, over-the-top way that only actors possess. And everyone had laughed.

There had been no point in my going into the kitchen because my father had always avoided that room as though it had contained a psychoanalyst's chaise lounge, so what would have been the point? That room was the domain of my stepmother and always had been. It's where she died when her heart had finally had enough. No, the drama in that house on that weird day was all contained upstairs. Surely a man as arrogant as my father would have more shame than to die in the kitchen. The kitchen is where God dies, no one else. No, the drama in that house was in the bedroom and always had been, as it is in any house. Because a bedroom is a very private space where people connect with one another privately, and the truth needs none of the idiosyncrasies of drunkenness. It's a room that within, the truth abounds. The bedroom is a room in everyone's house where the truth bounds about like a March Hare; inconvenient, disruptive and a nuisance.

And it was in the master bedroom of the *big house* at Henley where I found him. When the house phone had started to ring again.

Chapter Eleven

I'm sorry about this but, suddenly, I feel the need to go off on one of my tangents again, so I'm going to talk to you about young Sean. Remember him? The young university student who'd had to spend his summer working at John Bull's Traditional British Fish and Chips because his parents could not afford to send him trekking in the mountains of Peru? I imagine that that's precisely what they'd been inclined to do for him, but that the consequences of their collaborative life together had prevented them from doing what would have been the correct thing to do for an adored son who was finally taking a break from his studies. I imagine that they'd wished that they could send him off on his adventure, hoping that *life* would find him, or that he would find it, and he would return to them a man with a story to tell them. But they couldn't, because they hadn't had the disposable money to present to him that he would undoubtedly need if they were going to enjoy his adventure as much as he did. They could have just put a sign around his neck that said, *Please look after this Englishman*, and someone in Peru may have found him and precisely done that, but what would that have taught him? He would have still taken everything for granted upon his return; he would not have learnt that nothing can be taken for granted. In other words, their boy would have been returned to them, undelivered, and not the man that they were longing to meet.

So, as a consequence of – in his words – their poverty, he had to get a job. And he'd gotten himself a job as a kitchen hand to the greatest chef in the world, and one who'd sang like Pavarotti to boot, although I doubt whether he'd know who Pavarotti is. And the only reason I want to talk about young Sean is because during that summer of 2019, he'd learnt that *life* doesn't exclusively live on top of a mountain in Peru. In actual fact, it doesn't dwell there at all. Machu Picchu, after all, is a dead old town with not much going on. Human life does not, it must not, gravitate towards a wilderness, almost by definition; it must exist where human beings do. And during that summer, he'd found himself working a truly dreadful job in a truly dreadful restaurant. My overriding hope for him is that when we returned him to his mamma in the September a little bit less for the wear, he'd told her: 'That was the greatest adventure I ever could have wished for. Better than Machu Picchu'. If we hadn't returned to her the man that she so longed to meet, then at least he'd have been returned to her with the resolve not to be like me. Just like my half-sister had once had the same determination not to be like me.

During that summer, he'd been regularly bawled at by the chef because he hadn't washed his pots quickly enough or had chopped the onions quickly enough, or he had taken his eye off the fryer, and the chips had come out overdone, but whatever they'd been accompanying had been cooked to perfection by Rocco and Frederico, so they had to do even though they'd ruined the whole dish and probably the chef's reputation. 'Mamma Mia, give me the strength!' Rocco was forced to snarl, slapping the flat of his hand to his forehead in exasperation because that is what great chefs are supposed to do, and in any case, it wasn't his fault that he'd been presented with a naïve, inexperienced boy as a kitchen hand.

During service – and believe me, we'd had many shifts, the five of us, when that restaurant had been rammed – Rocco's job was to cook, to stand guard over his hobs and his ovens; to keep watch over a dozen pans at once containing a dozen different elements to half a dozen dishes. Frederico's job was to assist him in any way he could and to relieve him of the burden when a piece of fish was fried to perfection, or a steak was exactly right, or when a pie had turned just the right colour of golden brown when Rocco opened the oven door to check on it: then to take it all away from him and plate up, place the completed dish under the heat lamps on the pass and then press the bell for service.

My job, and Luigi's and Linda's, was to react quickly to that bell and serve our customers. Luigi had always reacted as though he was the Italian component of the Olympic one hundred meters sprint race. Linda less so and had always taken her time to give herself the opportunity to smile and acknowledge those customers who were unfortunate enough to have been seated close to the pass. Me, halfway between the other two, sprinting but trying to make it look as though everything was under control because I owned the lease and was the manager, and if I stayed calm, then so would my customers. We three would seat the customer, make them feel welcome whilst we took their order, get them a drink in the meantime, create an ambiance, etcetera. Rocco and Frederico's job had been to cook their order and poor Sean's job had been to do everything else and more in between. And sometimes it worked well, other times less well, but regularly service had been such a disaster that an enquiry was needed at the end of the shift.

All too frequently, I arrived at that pass to collect an order preparatory to serving it to my table and had dared to look into the kitchen only to see young Sean on the verge of crying, such was the stress that he'd been under. Too often, I'd witnessed the angry countenance on

156

the chef's face, the frustration on Frederico's. Too often, I had seen the sad look in Luigi's eyes as he sped past me because everything was going wrong. Too often, Linda had to calm us all down with her kind words and her nominal empathy that seemed to me to be inexhaustible. Too often, I had felt guilt and shame for bringing these people down to the circumstances of my reality, like I was Hades luring them all into my underworld. Because every business is a true facsimile of its creator's intentions, and my intention was never solely about making money.

And yet when that business worked, it worked very, very well, and an enquiry into the service had not been necessary, so we'd all just gone home. I have aforementioned that Saturday night when the 'Singing Chef' had sung. That halcyon night when everything had actually been *the* true facsimile of what I'd intended from the start. When I'd looked across the pass and seen young Sean sandwiched between Rocco and Frederico, who had their arms around his shoulders as they'd all rocked from side to side, and even though Sean hadn't known the words to O Sole Mio, he tried to join in anyway, completely embarrassed but loving every second. Whenever I think about that night, that gilded moment, I tag it *The O Sole Mio* night. But for one O Sole Mio moment, there were a hundred *fire alarm* moments.

The *fire alarm* incident occurred, unluckily for me, on the same evening when that couple from Chicago had decided to eat at John Bull's Traditional British Fish and Chips. Of all the array of fine eateries in Windsor, they had selected my establishment as the venue for their final meal in England before flying out from Heathrow the following morning, back to the good old US of A where no such nonsense exists. They had wanted, the wife told me at the enquiry, to sample traditional British fayre before leaving the UK, as their last memory in this country because they'd heard so many negative things about it that they thought 'it can't be as bad as people say'. But it is, it most certainly was.

Everything had been going so well. That night had been on course to be another one of those halcyon nights, when the singing chef was on the verge of breaking into song. Almost there. Luigi had been in the kind of mood where he'd shaken my hand and had whispered: *I love you like you are my brother.* Linda had been at her halcyon best, spreading light over everyone she served. And looking back, I wish that she'd been responsible for that couple from Chicago instead of that group from Japan. Luigi had been attending to the elderly couple from Chicago, so maybe that's why it all started to go so wrong. But not yet. Not yet.

The food, the traditional British fayre, that night had been cooked to perfection. Everyone had been happy with what they had been served. Even the king prawns seemed happy to have been cooked until they'd turned pink; even they seemed to have a smile on their faces. They had been perfection personified. And then the extractor fan broke down and suddenly the kitchen had filled with fumes and smoke which almost choked Gandhi – sorry, Rocco – rendering him tuneless, helpless, and furious. LEWIS!! Came the call. DING DONG, DING DONG. When I arrived at the pass, Luigi had been there to greet me. *What on Earth is going on now?* I thought to myself. Rocco had been choking, Frederico had been trying to soothe him, slapping him on the back, and so on; Sean was standing at the fryer looking on, helpless because he was too young to care.

"We have no fucking extraction!" Luigi proclaimed as quietly as he could because we had an open kitchen so that if he'd been inclined to bellow his statement, then everyone in the dining room would have heard him, including Linda. "And Rocco can't fucking breathe!"

"Just smack it!" I whispered.

"Smack it?" Luigi enquired, puzzled. "Smack what, the chef?"

"Just smack the fucking extractor fan, Luigi!" I replied as quietly as my voice would allow me to be but quite urgently. "It's probably only a short circuit! It'll come back on."

"Your chef is fucking choking, Lewis! Look at the state of him, he can barely stand up!"

But then, he never could anyway. He'd always been too weak to stand upright on his own legs and feet. Frederico, as I recall, had been trying his darndest juts to keep his mentor, his father, on his feet, whilst he'd been gasping for breath. Then, I clocked Sean, who'd been standing in front of the fryer, who'd looked a little bit this and a little bit that. When he came towards the pass so that he could hear clearly what my instruction was, I said to him, "Sean, just give it a whack."

"Give what a whack?" he asked.

"The fucking chef!" Luigi added, unhelpfully.

"The extractor fan!" I interceded. "Just give it a whack, and it'll come back on!"

But it hadn't come back on and Frederico had looked at me as though to say, *What do you expect me to do now?* Was this how it ended, with the singing chef laying on the kitchen floor because the fumes of his kitchen had overwhelmed him? Verdi, Puccini et all a distant memory? Luckily for the singing chef, just in time, the fumes from the kitchen moved out of the kitchen and spread themselves out across the pass and into the dining space so that my customers choked too, to accompany the singing chef, but this was the opposite of O Sole Mio. The fumes from the kitchen had suddenly overwhelmed us all.

And they triggered the fire alarm. Ding Dong. The fire alarm panel had been secured to the little bit of wall that was adjacent to the pass before the building opened up to form the dining space. I ran as quickly as the British representative in the Olympic hundred-meter sprint race and put in the code and had silenced the fire alarm temporarily. My customers looked at me gratefully as they'd scraped their cutlery over the white expanse of their plates because even though they'd been choking at the fumes and were gasping for air, at least they could finish their meal in peace. But then the fire alarm went off again. The fire alarm had short-circuited in the excitement.

"Every fucker out!" Luigi hollered whilst he'd urged my diners to get up and run for their lives. Every man for himself, etcetera.

"What the hell are you doing?" I asked as I'd dragged him back towards me.

"The fire alarm!"

"But it's only going off because the extractor fan has packed in not because there's an actual fire! In any case, no one has paid yet!" What a desperate man I must have been.

"Your chef is nearly fucking dead!" Luigi retorted angrily.

"The chef was almost dead when he arrived!" I replied snappily. "Everybody sit down and finish your meals!" And they had, bless them all.

"What on earth is going on now?" Linda asked once she'd arrived at the pass, aware that something *was* going on.

"Open the front door, Linda, and do a man a favour," I instructed her, and she'd duly obliged. "Sean, open the back door!" And my instruction to both of them had alleviated the immediate concern of the kitchen fumes. The fire alarm, however, was not so easily placated.

It went off again, to the shock and dismay of my clients, but when I put in the code and pressed the 'silence' button, nothing happened. My customers began to get very jittery and were beginning to wonder whether they should have listened to the little Italian waiter instead of the English manager. The only way to silence the fire alarm was by standing at the panel with my finger pressed firmly on the 'silence' button; the moment I removed my finger: Ding Dong. So, I had to stand there for what had seemed like an eternity with my finger pressing the silence button, all the while smiling gormlessly at the poor foursome on table one who were sitting right in front of me and from where they had a full view of the kitchen. Some customers had been reluctant to sit on table one because it was too close to the action, others had been delighted to sit there because the actual workings of a busy kitchen had fascinated them; they'd obviously seen too many Gordon Ramsey documentaries. The foursome that had been sitting on that fabled table on that fateful night had only done so because there had been nowhere else to seat them, and they'd been hungry, that's all. They must have wondered why the manager was standing next to them with his finger pressed on the fire alarm, smiling helplessly at them. When they looked into the kitchen, they must have wondered why the chef was on his all fours crawling towards the back door, with his commis chef accompanying him and urging him to stand upright. "He'll be fine," I assured them.

161

From my position at the fire alarm panel, I'd been able to reach across to the top of the pass and press the bell. Luigi, as though the sound of that bell was to him a starter pistol and always had been, had arrived promptly, long before Linda did. The first thing he'd seen was the chef crawling towards the open back door towards fresh air. "Look at him! Look at the state of him. You've killed your chef, Lewis!"

I laughed to alleviate the tension that my waiter's remark had caused the foursome on table one. "He's a character, this one," I said to them. Then I whispered in his ear, "Luigi, when I take my finger off this button, the fire alarm is going to go off again, and frankly, if I don't lower my arm soon, it's going to drop off!"

"What do you want me to do?" he asked, bemusedly.

I recall that I'd taken hold of his hand and had directed it towards the fire alarm panel, prompted him to extend his index finger, then had manoeuvred it next to mine. I removed my finger and replaced it with his and we managed to get away with a very lacklustre ding, no dong, and no one was any the wiser. When Linda finally arrived at the pass, she'd asked me what on earth was going on, and I told her precisely what had been going on. I recall that for the first time, I'd snapped at her, and she'd looked shocked. "Have you called an electrician?" she added, unhelpfully.

"I've been standing here for fifteen minutes with my finger on the *silence* button, how the hell can I call an electrician?" Snappily.

"Well, I don't wish to add to your trouble, Lewis, but the couple on table nine are asking when they'll be getting their meals."

"You just go back to your table and tell them that they'll get their meals when we've resuscitated the chef!" I snarled.

"Lewis, you need to calm down!" she replied, walking away.

I know what you're thinking: that the couple from Chicago had been sitting on table nine. If only things had been that simple. They'd been sitting on table six close to the door. A perfectly nice, elderly couple from Slough had been sitting on table nine, and quite rightly, they'd asked Linda how much longer they would have to wait for their food since they only ordered fish and chips, not a very well-done sirloin steak. Luckily for them, they hadn't been able to see into the kitchen, but more fortuitous was the fact that Linda had seated them and not Luigi; otherwise, they would have likely died of heart failure instead of hunger.

What then followed was akin to a joint English-Italian Olympic relay race in order to keep the fire alarm 'silenced'. The four of us had taken our turns, the fourth person being young Sean, who found the whole thing hilarious. During my 'free' time away from the fire alarm, I'd called the electrician, but he hadn't picked up because *his* business had been all about the money and he'd made way too much of it already to care about me. On my fifth visit to the fire alarm panel, I'd given up caring what the foursome on table one had thought we were all doing there. But they must have known that something was amiss. Not necessarily because the staff had intermittently stood in front of them with their finger on the 'silence' button, but when they looked into the kitchen and had seen the chef shinnying up the side of the fridge to get himself back onto his feet, with his sidekick, Frederico, egging him on as though he was the coach to the last marathon runner to enter the stadium. I may be remembering this next bit wrongly, but I'm sure that that foursome had applauded once the chef had gotten back onto his feet. And to think that when I'd first shown Luigi around my empty premises all those months before we had actually agreed that having an open kitchen would be an asset, especially since I'd procured for myself a 'singing' chef.

"Get him to sing something, Frederico!" I said, across the pass, craning my neck so that I could see into the kitchen.

"He can barely breathe, and you want him to sing?!" came the reply.

"What did he say?" I heard one woman on table one say to her husband, confusedly.

"The manager wants the chef to start singing!" her hapless husband replied. And my shame was complete, because on a second look, my chef could barely stand up. Nevertheless, a little bit of Verdi or Puccini would have gone down quite nicely by that point, and the chef would have proven himself worth every penny.

Somehow – probably when I'd broken the formula in order to ring the electrician again – our relay had gone astray, so each of us had found ourselves, somehow, relieving the other at some point. Whenever I relieved Linda, for instance, she always smiled at me kindly and patted me on the shoulder as though to say *there, there*, or maybe to get my wind up; whenever I relieved Luigi, he had snarled something along the lines of *is this what I've been reduced to*, but not necessarily as politely as that. And Sean, whenever I'd relieved him, he was crying, not through stress, but with joy. Whenever they relieved me, I'd always said, 'Let me try that electrician again'. And on and on we went, the four of us. It was whilst Linda had been standing at the fire alarm that I'd heard that woman from Chicago scream. A sound from Hell that had made the Japanese leap out of their skin, and Luigi to drop the tray of drinks that he'd been carrying towards table eight. Crash, bang, wallop. Once I'd reached the couple from Chicago, the wife had been out of her seat, strangely mopping her husband's forehead. The first thing that I noticed was the pink prawn on the tip of his fork, poised halfway between freedom and his gaping mouth. I hadn't seen the steady stream of water dripping onto his head from the ceiling until his wife had screamed the instruction to look up. "Oh dear!" I spoke.

"What kind of place is this?" the Chicago woman screeched making sure that everyone else in the restaurant could hear her. And they did.

"We seem to have sprung a leak!" I lamented lamely, examining the ceiling. But what I'd been thinking was *get me Linda*! And to that end I'd summonsed Luigi to my side. *Leave the glass, and just get here, will you*!

"This is our last meal, and I wanted it to be extra special!" the silly old bag sobbed dramatically as she wiped her husband's forehead again. Why hadn't he just moved his head? Anyway.

"Not your last meal ever, madam," I replied. "Just your last meal in the UK! You will both eat again I can assure you! Can I ask you both to move to another table if that's alright?" But there wasn't another table spare to move them to. I'd needed Linda.

"Where's Linda?"

"She's at the fucking fire alarm!" Luigi snarled. "What's the matter?" And I'd told him what the matter was. "I'll deal with it," he suggested because he hadn't wanted to go back to the fire alarm. "I've dealt with worse!"

To my eternal shame, I'd by then had enough and had let him. At first, it had been all *signoria* this and *signoria* that, but for the first time in his life, his Italian patter hadn't worked because he'd been talking to her breasts and not to her face, and the old woman from Chicago had slapped him across the face, such was her fury and frustration and her determination not to be patronised by a little Italian waiter who looked like Mussolini because she'd probably already met his type before. To her eternal credit. And all the while the prawn remained suspended in the twilight zone between being one thing or another.

"Linda!" I barked quietly.

"I can't," she replied because she was standing with her finger on the 'silence' button.

"Sean, take Linda off!" I said to that young man, but in any case, he was already on his way to do his shift! It had been his turn anyway.

Ding Dong.

"What on earth is happening now?" Linda enquired once she'd gotten to the sphere around table six, that by then had been like the exclusion zone to a nuclear explosion.

"The roof's leaking now!" I sighed.

"They only want a free fucking meal!" Luigi interceded, unhelpfully, and so loudly that the woman from Chicago had heard what he said.

"NO! We only want to eat our meal without drowning!" she retorted furiously. She'd then proceeded into a full-blown row with the Italian waiter, who was, she proclaimed loudly, the most incompetent, chauvinistic man she'd ever had the misfortune to encounter. "And I'd thank you to speak directly to my face when addressing me and not to my breasts because they will not answer you, you creepy little man!"

"Incompetent? Me? I've closed my restaurant for Pavarotti! I've served Prince Charles!"

"Luigi!" I urged him with an unspoken instruction to shut up.

"Well, she's getting on my bloody nerves now!" Just when he began to calm down, he turned around and preparatory to walking away from her once and for all – because he'd known that he'd finally met his match – he snarled: "I hope you're sailing back to the States tomorrow and that your fucking ship sinks, signoria, then your husband will know what it's really like to get fucking wet!"

"Get me the MANAGER!" she blasted, finally losing her mind.

Luigi pointed at me. "He *is* the fucking manager!" he told her.

"Well, I've never, ever, in my life …" she was so shocked that she could barely speak to me. Her husband, by the way, hadn't moved, nor had the prawn on the end of his fork. Now, I may be remembering this wrongly, but I'm almost certain that the prawn had moved its head to look at me then the woman from Chicago, intermittently, depending on who was speaking, because it had wanted to know who would prevail. But by then, I'd had enough, not just of her, but of the Italians, the fire alarm, the leaking roof, the extractor fan, my absent mother, the father who would have preferred me not to exist, my abhorrent half-sister who'd been too damn up herself to ever bring her little family to my restaurant when that's all I'd wanted her to do; the woman who'd left me there on my own … everything.

167

"Lewis, you just need to breathe!" Linda urged me once she'd realised that I'd had enough. "Breathe, Lewis. Not through your nostrils, breathe through your mouth. Deep breaths, that's right."

But it didn't work. There's only so much that a deep breath can achieve. "Worse things will happen to you and your husband during the course of your lives than water dripping onto your husband's fucking head!" I snapped. She was so appalled by my lack of customer service skills that she almost passed out, but at least she'd gone quiet at last. "It doesn't, fucking, matter. Nothing, fucking, matters!"

Now, imagine the whole restaurant watching us. Imagine their shock. They had all stopped eating; there was no noise from their cutlery scraping over white, porcelain plates. Then imagine, at that impasse, the sound of the chef singing '*Your tiny hand is frozen, come and warm it next to mine*' by Puccini, across the pass, because he'd known that he should and that maybe it would help.

"Too fucking late, Rocco!" I bellowed, storming out the front door.

I've been told that subsequent to my exit, Sean had been laughing so much that he'd taken his finger off the 'silence' button. Ding Dong. And that Luigi evacuated the building, but in the pause of the hullabaloo of an evacuation, the old man from Chicago had finally eaten his prawn.

That night had been the moment when I realised that nothing actually matters at all. That's not correct: some things do matter. But not fire alarms, extractor fans, dripping water and un-eaten prawns. Sean had probably considered it the greatest night of his life. He had probably gone home that evening and proclaimed to his mother, 'That was better than Machu Picchu'. I believe that he'd

168

been – probably still is – studying medicine. But even if, in the years ahead of him, he discovers the cure for cancer and therefore all of human life's concerns, he will, I'm sure, still look back on that night in John Bull's Traditional British Fish and Chips when the extractor fan broke down, and the fire alarm had short-circuited, and water from the roof had dripped onto the forehead of an old man from Chicago and will always consider it the greatest night of his life. I hope so, anyway, otherwise what was the point of it?

Nothing ever has to make sense, is what my father had written on the first page, the publisher's page, the legal bit where nothing matters, of the copy of *Alice in Wonderland* that I'd discovered when I'd been foraging in my father's study when the only sound had been the grandmother clock ticking in the room next door. It was the same copy that I'd sneaked out of there all those years ago when I'd needed something to present to my A-level English Literature tutor when I'd been eighteen, but I hadn't noticed the dedication, written in his own hand, until then. Even if I had, it would not have made sense. Then, it had made perfect sense. My father? Oh, him!

He'd been sitting on the edge of his bed when I found him, trying to pull his trousers over his legs. He'd given me a fright when I walked into the master bedroom because he had looked old and very frail all of a sudden, a mere shadow of what he once was which had been strong, dogged and abundantly alive. Then, sitting on the edge of his bed, he had looked as though he was about to disintegrate altogether at any moment. Just dissipate into the ether in a puff of smoke. He barely had the strength to keep himself upright much less to pull his baggy trousers over his skinny, frail legs that seemed to be just as thin at

169

the top as they were at the ankle. He looked like the last survivor of a Second World War prison camp. And the reason that I got a shock when I'd stepped into the room was because he hadn't looked like that the last time I had seen him. I cursed my half-sister secretly, not because she had inconvenienced me with her instruction to move in with him, but for having the selfish courage to whisk her little family away to Italy and leave him behind because she must have surely doubted whether she would ever see her pappa again if he looked anything like that when she'd left. If she had pulled on his nose at their parting, he would not have had the strength in his body or the preparedness in his mind to make anything like the sound of a steam train whistle.

Chapter Twelve

What had shocked me most about my father that day when I discovered him in his bedroom was that he had actually looked pleased to see me. Well, relatively speaking. He hadn't rolled his eyes or sneered his usual put-down about not having any money. There had been the outline of a smile on his mouth and a look of relief on his face since he had been floundering on the edge of his bed with his baggy trousers halfway up his legs and when he heard someone shuffling around downstairs, he had been anxious that it was the old woman from next door come to check on him, so he had been relieved to find out that it was only me.

He had actually said that to me: "Oh, it's only you," as he sighed out and hung his head. There had been no formal greeting between father and son, nor was I expecting there to be. If there had been, then it would have been forced and false and whatever else my father was, he was not that, and neither am I. We had both stuck rigidly to our well-rehearsed roles, but it had been a little more cordial than usual, that's all. However, if I hadn't turned up when I had, then I'm sure that he would have died then and there on the edge of his bed with his trousers halfway down his legs. My half-sister had been perfectly correct to have been worried enough to assign me to the task of rescuing him because he had been too weak to do anything for himself.

"What are you trying to do?" I asked him. They were the first words I said to him since being back in his house. What I should have done was shout loudly: 'I'm back!' with a good measure of mischief because I was suddenly in control and calling the shots, as though the

171

last survivor's camp guard had turned up again, doggedly refusing to relinquish his command. *And before you croak it, you old goat, I want to know what you did with my mother?*

"I can't get my trousers on," he replied, so ashamed of himself, so bemused by what his illness was doing to him all of a sudden, that he started to weep into his hands. I had never seen him cry before, not even in the immediacy of my stepmother's passing. I had never seen anyone so vulnerable before, so exposed by their situation that they had no choice but to reveal their helplessness to their archenemy: hands in the air in abject surrender. Some enemy I turned out to be since I knelt in front of him and helped him.

"One leg at a time, Dad," I said, gently manoeuvring his legs into his baggy trousers one at a time, then placing his slippers on each foot to finish the job properly. He didn't say anything to me whilst I was helping him, but when he placed his hand on the top of my head as though he was blessing me, it was a genuinely tender moment. The tenderest moment we had ever shared, him and I, that had suddenly made me want to start crying in reply to him. And I wondered whether all of this archenemy stuff – the *oh woe is me* outlook on life – was just me, just the way my mind was wired and had nothing whatsoever to do with him because the frail, vulnerable old man sitting above me on the edge of his bed did not seem capable of propagating any such atmosphere of bad feeling. I had always suspected that all it would have taken was just one glimpse of tenderness from him to bring me in from the cold, and I was right, that was all it took, that one blessing as his ancient hand rested on the top of my head. And all the bad feelings had just dissipated into the ether.

The telephone began to ring again. My father had a phone next to his bed too and could have easily reached it from his perch; whether or not his trousers had been halfway down his legs wouldn't have mattered to the person on the other end of the line. "That'll be your half-sister," he bemoaned. "She is worried about me."

"You could have answered it when it was ringing earlier," I replied, confusedly. "But you didn't."

"Neither did you when you were downstairs!" A hint of mischief had spread out across his face. "She probably thinks that I've died already. Let her think that for a little bit longer. It serves her right for abandoning me."

"She told me that you insisted that they all go to the villa!"

"I probably did," he sighed. "But only for three or four days, not the self-imposed emigration that it's turning into."

"She can't get a flight home. Believe me, she's trying to."

"I know," he conceded. "And she's right, I did encourage her to go to Sant'Elpidio because she adores that villa … she finds peace there and gives herself the time to think about things. Time that we all need. I wanted her to go to the villa one last time."

"Why are you selling it, because Ennio died?" I enquired.

"Who is Ennio?"

I had to think hard about what the old caretaker was actually called. "Because Enzo's dead?"

"Ah, poor old Enzo. He has been with me at the villa since the day I bought it off his mother. All those years." He'd been in a sad, reflective frame of mind all of a sudden, any hint of his mischief had gone. "He was a fine gardener but a great man. He will be missed, but I suppose it is no longer my problem to worry about, is it?"

The old goat had indicated that he wanted to lay down on top of the bed, so I helped him up with his legs. "Jane has asked me to move in for a while, just until she can get back. Is that alright?" Because I still hadn't been certain that it would be.

He closed his eyes, so I moved quietly towards the door. "I haven't got any money left, Lewis," he replied. He hadn't opened his eyes, but the mischievous smile had returned to his face indicating that I was, after all, welcome to stay. "However, I would imagine that you have made so much money in that fabulous restaurant of yours in Windsor Wonderland that you no longer need it?"

He did not see my wry smile on my face. His comment had been tongue-in-cheek, I knew, and it had been one of the funniest things I think I have ever heard him say. He was not known for his irony. "You'd think, wouldn't you?" I replied.

"Not really. I do know what TripAdvisor is, Lewis. What on earth did you do to that couple from Chicago?"

I finally laughed out aloud. "Don't ask," I sniggered. Just as I was about to close the bedroom door so that my shuffling about downstairs wouldn't disturb him, he opened his eyes and was looking directly at me.

"Selling it? The villa? Lewis, I have no intentions of selling it."

Incidentally, since my father has mentioned it, during the ten months that John Bull's Traditional British Fish and Chips was functionable, we managed to acquire two-hundred-and-seventy-two reviews on TripAdvisor. Twenty-three five-star reviews, three four-star reviews

174

(strangely), one-hundred-and eighty-three-star reviews because we were nothing if not mediocre, eight (yes, eight) two-star reviews because we were not mediocre enough for some people, and fifty-eight one-star reviews, which had always seemed cruel and had affected every one of us whenever they had popped up on our *page*. The woman from Chicago's review had gone on and on and on to such an extent that she'd rendered it unreadable. Talk about going off on a tangent. She seemed to have had it in for Luigi in particular, whereas I'd gotten away with being merely incompetent. But not one mention of that poor prawn in the entire piece, when *it* had been the real victim of those circumstances on that horrible night, and not her husband.

The majority of the five-star reviews had popped up in the days that had followed the O Sole Mio night when the singing chef had finally sung. Those lovely people had written such things as *one of the best nights out we've had* or *the greatest experience we've ever had in a restaurant.* So near, but yet, so far; the story of my life. Come to think about it, all of the four-star reviews had referred to that O Sole Mio night too, but the authors of those reviews had lamented the fact that the chef had not sung in English, as though they'd been expecting him to sing 'just one Cornetto' or something. The highest position we'd managed to get to on that fabled website was two-hundred-and-eight out of two-hundred-and-thirty restaurants in Windsor. God only knows what those other twenty-two must be like because it doesn't bear thinking about.

But the real surprise about my father's evocation of TripAdvisor was that he'd even been bothered to read them at all. Thinking back, I reckon he couldn't wait to log on. What must he have thought? 'Better than Dallas, this', is what he'd probably thought. Certainly, more entertaining than his chess club, anyway.

You might have guessed by now that I spent more than one night in the *big house* at Henley. I actually spent the entire summer there because it turned out that there was life in the old goat yet. Because it had turned out that my half-sister hadn't been able to get a flight back to the UK or whenever she had – I imagined her tip-tapping on the keyboard and just at the moment when she'd secured four tickets from Fiumicino to Gatwick, either Arthur or Martin or Michael, or maybe all three of them had started coughing – she had been thwarted every time she had tried to press the *secure flights* button. I could imagine her frustration, the sense that she was stranded on the wrong side of the continent whilst her pappa was knocking on death's door; the stress of not knowing if she would ever see him again. I imagined her pacing the stone floor in the villa with her phone glued to her ear as she tried desperately to connect. She had rung the house phone every day, sometimes several times, to check in and make sure I was keeping my side of the bargain of keeping her pappa alive, at least until she had managed to fly back. Sometimes I hadn't answered her call. Other times the content of the phone call had gone along the lines of 'he's fine, he's sleeping now', because he invariably had been. On some occasions when he had not been sleeping, he'd indicated that he had not wanted to speak to her because nothing had changed in the three hours since her last call: 'Tell her I'm still here!' and so on.

During one such phone conversation, once I'd told her that her pappa was sleeping again, she had announced that she had found a flight from Ciampino to Manchester that could get her back by the Thursday of that particular

176

week, but it would mean that she would have to leave Michael and the boys behind in Italy. "Well, that's all right, they'll be fine," I assured her. "Michael is a secondary school teacher, he knows how to manage teenage boys," when what I was really thinking was that poor Michael would probably be glad of the break since there are only so many times a man can sing happy birthday to himself without going insane.

Jane declared her unease at leaving them behind, not because she was doubtful that her hapless husband would be able to manage – cook and keep house – but because the two of them had never so much as spent a night apart since the day they had gotten married. *That poor man,* I thought to myself during the course of that phone conversation. *That poor, bald-too-young man.* Then she suddenly announced that she'd decided not to take that flight because she was worried that once she had arrived safely back in the UK in Manchester, she may never be able to get a flight back out again; back to the villa and her sons, her bald-too-young husband whom, it was then obvious, she undoubtedly adores. And vice-versa probably. Which had come as something of a shock to me because I'd always assumed that all of the affection, empathy, devoutness that she was able to contain in her mind had been solely there to facilitate her worship of our father. Not so, it seemed.

So, after I put the receiver down after that particular phone conversation whilst my father was asleep on the top of his bed upstairs – he always refused to actually get beneath the bedding – I found myself wondering whether her and her husband's relationship with one another was yet another example of my mind coming up with its own, cynical, *woe is them,* conclusion. It suddenly dawned on me that the people closest to me had formed relationships

177

with one another that had nothing to do with me because I had spent my life, as Jane had once put it, in my private bubble of regret and self-pity, so I assumed that everyone close to me must have had the same kind of hang-ups that I did. Not so, it seemed. My half-sister, it turned out, was more worried about her little family than she had been about her dying father. The bald-too-young husband that I'd always felt sorry for because I assumed – wrongly – that he had been browbeaten and crestfallen was, it turned out, the love of her life and she hadn't wanted to leave him. It had come as a revelation to me and suddenly she had shot up in my estimation of her.

As a consequence of my half-sister's revelation that she actually loves her husband, I imagined the two of them wandering around the land that encases the villa at Porto Sant'Elpidio hand in hand through the olive grove, through the orchard, all the way down to the boundary fence where the row of Cyprus trees are, overlooking the town and the turquoise Adriatic Sea beyond. As a result of my half-sister's revelation when she'd refused to come back because she would not leave her beloved husband behind, I imagined the two of them like a pair of rampant rabbits. Even a man as accomplished as my father wouldn't have been able to analyse that particular image in my mind. And all the while, I was stranded on the wrong side of the continent looking after my father who had customarily been in a bad mood, particularly when his coffee had not been to the specification. As for the food I cooked for him every day, nothing had ever been good enough and he had been forced to wonder whether I had actually ever been in a restaurant much less owned one.

178

"You are a restaurateur, Lewis, yet you can't cook. Have you not learned anything from your chef?" I had learned a great deal from my chef, but not how to cook, unfortunately. *Any more of that and I'll summons my chef to this house, and then you might learn a thing or two, you old goat,* I thought to myself.

What a delicious prospect that would have been: my father sitting on the sofa wearing his baggy trousers, tray perched on his delicate legs, cutlery in his hands as he patiently waited for his meal. Luigi fussing around him and telling him all about Pavarotti and Prince Charles, the sheiks, the mermaid, et all; Rocco singing Verdi or Puccini in the kitchen. Even my stepmother could never do that. And all the while my father would be just sitting there waiting for his meal with a look of incomprehension and befuddlement on his face just like that poor prawn had had. Or not, who knows, he may have even enjoyed himself? He may have even learned a thing or two.

And after they'd gone, he would ask me: 'When are they coming back again? They were a tonic!' At the very least, his assumption that *the world is full of stupid people* would have been validated. Thinking back now, it would have been worth breaking the law and bringing two people from a different household into our household just so that I could have witnessed that bemused look on my father's face. He would have encountered Luigi; he would have been almost dead when he met him but brimming with life when he left him. 'Never the twain shall meet', I concluded whenever I'd been tempted to do it.

Anyway, he had always eaten, begrudgingly, whatever I cooked for him because he had the sense to know that once he stopped eating, then it was curtains for him! He sat around on his sofas a lot, reading copiously, filling his mind with whatever he could because his mind,

179

unlike his body, was at full throttle and full steam ahead. We barely ever put the television on because he had not wanted to be reminded that the world is full of stupid people and that the people in charge were the stupidest of all. We barely mentioned the virus because the virus had not mattered to him; the virus had not inconvenienced him at all other than the fact that it rendered his beloved daughter useless; other than the fact that he had to spend his last few months in the company of his son, who was the person he had been expecting to spend them with the least of all. Curiouser and curiouser.

After he finished his meal – well, he'd eaten as much as was necessary to keep him alive anyhow – he had always needed to lay down on top of the bed. I always stood behind him as he shinnied up the stairs in case he toppled backwards, and there I would be, a safe pair of hands to prop him back up again as though I was the goalkeeper in the England (or Italian) football team. *Steady now, one step at a time, Dad.* Every time that happened, neither of us had the wherewithal to know that if he had toppled backwards, then there would have been nothing that I could have done to prevent him from falling to his death, and he would have taken me down with him because none of his family had ever studied basic physics. If he had fallen backwards, then there would have been nothing that I could have done about it because the pull of gravity would have been too strong, and besides, what would gravity have cared that he was too weak to stand upright? That was biology's problem.

My father had always been preoccupied with the mind, and so had – by extension – his daughter, and me too if you count my A-Level failure in English Literature. He had always deemed the mind to be just as important as the law of gravity or the theory of relativity because, according to him, only the human mind can comprehend either of those things. 'The human mind can comprehend everything that there is to know, it is that powerful', I once heard him say to my half-sister during one of their conversations that I had rudely interrupted when I had dared to come back into the family home. 'But it does not possess the capacity with which to withstand the consequences!'

During the course of that conversation, whilst I'd been standing in the hallway with the dog fussing around my legs, I'd looked up and seen my stepmother who was standing in the doorway of the kitchen with her finger against her pursed lips as though to say *stay quiet for a moment, Lewis, and do a woman a favour.* So, we both heard him say: 'Galileo can tell you how the Earth rotates around the sun; Newton can tell you how the processes of gravity can pull an apple to the ground; Einstein can explain the concept of time, but none of them can tell you *why* it matters. Because that is our job, Jane. Because only a human mind can comprehend such things. A chimpanzee can't, can it? An elephant can't, can it? But a human mind can. And most of them select not to bother to try. Some people think too much. Others don't think nearly enough, because they dare not in case they will discover something that they would rather not see or know about. So, if you're looking for God, then go and find Him in the human mind because he exists no-where else.'

Most of the time during those three summer months of 2020, I had been incredibly bored. Frankly, there had not been much going on in that big house. My father, suddenly my only company, had been asleep more than he was awake, and I'd had to tiptoe around trying not to make a sound that would awaken him. My father turned out to be *not* the life and soul of the party. My father, that colossus of a man who had dominated my life for better or worse, turned out to be a waif, upon a second look. A skinny little man who did not possess the strength to climb up the stairs unaccompanied. He had been a man on the edge, not just of his queen-sized bed but on the edge of his life also with all of the connotations that had involved. With all of the complications that had involved too.

I found myself alone in that big house at Henley because the company had not been fit for purpose. I had found myself missing Luigi (yes, that's right) and Rocco; I even found myself missing my half-sister because her daily telephone calls had not quite cut the mustard. After all, there's only so many times a man can utter the words *he's sleeping* without going totally insane. After four weeks, once the novelty had worn off, I had found myself sitting on the sofa staring at the 1980s Bakelite telephone (in cream) and longing for it to ring.

Chapter Thirteen

Chess is what saved my soul in that summer of 2020. Chess, yes, that's right. Of all the things that could have cured my relationship with my father, it turned out that the solution all along had been chess. Come to think about it, the solution was never going to have been bike riding, was it? Even though every other family combination in the entirety of the country was riding their bicycles. Everyone, suddenly, had rediscovered the pure, unadulterated joy of riding a bicycle. They were everywhere all of a sudden. Everyone had suddenly appreciated the glory of being outside. Thank God the weather had turned out fine, that's all that I can say for all their sakes, or else what would they have had to do: play chess or some such nonsense. But the weather *had* turned out fine, for all their sakes, and everyone had rediscovered the simpler things in their lives. Fathers and mothers had finally discovered their children as though they had been Henry Morton Stanley standing on the shore of Lake Tanganyika, saying such nonsense as 'Dr Livingston, I presume?' You get my point?

And the point is that everyone had discovered something in that summer of 2020, and it had not necessarily needed to have been Dr Livingston himself. People, suddenly, had discovered that the world will keep on rotating around the sun whether or not they had stepped onto a London Underground train. Galileo had been right about that particular, indisputable fact all along. The Tube had almost ground to a halt in that spring/summer of 2020. Imagine that. The London Tube had ground to a halt, so they had all had to find something else to do. Maybe that is all I need to say on that particular subject.

But it was certainly true that during those summer months of 2020 that my half-sister had discovered or had rediscovered her love for her bald-too-young husband. Because she finally realised that he and her two sons were the future, whereas her *pappa* was the past. And there's never any sense in dwelling in the past, is there? She *had* walked with him hand in hand through the olive grove and the orchard towards the Cyprus trees, and I don't much care for what she has to say on this matter because I know that I am right. Maybe that is why my father had insisted that they all go to the villa in Italy in the first place. A very clever man, my father.

"Ciao, preggo."

One time whilst I had been bored, I rang my friend Luigi on his mobile phone.

"How are you?" I asked.

"This guy is doing my nuts in, Lewis!" Desperately.

"Who is?" Mischievously.

"Rocco!"

"Why?"

"Because he won't stop fucking singing, that's why!"

"Really? That's more than he ever did for me."

"Jesu Cristo, this flat is too small for the both of us!" Shouting. "I'm gonna have to fucking kill him, or I will go insane, Lewis. Every day he scours the internet for a flight to Thailand, and when he can't find one, it's all my fault. Like I created this virus. I say to him, Rocco, ride a fucking bike or something because there's nothing that I can do to help you. We are all in the same fucking boat!"

"So he sings?"

A pause.

"Jesu Cristo, his singing. To think that I used to like it. You once said to me that he reminded you of Gandhi. Well, now I wish he were Gandhi because some fucker would have shot him long before now."

"Other than that, how are you bearing up?"

"I'm not doing so bad. Although yesterday I had to get out of the flat, so I went to that Tesco Express, you know the one, beside the coach park? Because I am allowed out once a day to buy essentials. Anyway, to cut a long story short, I was run over by some old guy on a bike!"

"On a bike?"

"Some old twat was riding his bike that he evidentially hadn't ridden since 1985, and he ploughed right into me."

"Were you hurt?"

"No, but he was, the daft …."

"What were you going for?"

"Mushrooms."

"Well, maybe they can be classed as essential, Luigi."

"Rocco was cooking something or other."

"Was it good?"

"Not worth the effort!"

"As long as you enjoyed your meal?"

"*Si, Rocco, sto arrivando cazzo!*" Or 'yes, Rocco, I'm fucking coming!' Angrily.

"What's happening now?" I dared myself to ask.

"He's decided that now he wants a bath, and he can't find the shampoo. I'll have to go, Lewis. I'll call you tomorrow. He can't find the shampoo even though he's as bald as a, how you say, coot?"

"Well, that's precisely how we would say it and thank God that's how you say it too."

"Ciao, arrivederci. And don't ever forget, Lewis, that I love you like you are my brother."

That phone conversation with Luigi had been a highlight of sorts but most of the time I spent in the big house during that summer had been uneventful and very boring. My father had slept for eighty percent of the time, the other twenty was probably spent playing chess and trying to eat whatever I had conjured up in the kitchen by way of a hot meal. The Macmillan nurse was a middling sort of chap called Lee; he had dropped his visits to once a week and even then, he hadn't really done much other than check on my father's medication and whether or not I was familiar with what he had been prescribed to take and when. His weekly visit had not really benefited my father at all, he'd always considered it a nuisance and a distraction but at least he'd been polite to him. Lee would always enquire about his pain level on a scale of one to ten, ten being unbearable. My father would always reply with 'somewhere lower midtable'.

"Like my team, Reading," Lee replied the first time my father had made the comment.

"Quite," my father replied off-handedly, refusing to be drawn into a conversation about football.

I would always listen to their conversation from the hallway. "Are you eating, Mr Sinclaire?" Lee would always ask him.

"I'm willing to eat but my son can't cook," he would invariably reply. And it always gave me a thrill to hear him use the words, *my son*, because before then, I can't recall having ever heard him say it. Lee was always so wrapped up in his PPE that often my father had struggled to hear what he was saying, so I would always have my own private chat with Lee in the hallway, socially distanced, of course.

"There's no need for him to be in pain, Lewis," he would tell me. "Make sure he knows that."

I don't know why but I had always followed him to the front door, socially distanced, of course, to see him off. Lee would always remove his face mask as soon as he'd gotten into his car, and as soon as the wheels were moving, he would light up a cigarette because I could see the smoke coming out of his window. I would stay on the doorstep until his car disappeared. I can't explain why, but it had become something of a ritual and besides, it had been a change of scenery. I would stand there taking in the fresh air and wondering what weird alternative universe I had slipped into that had embroiled me in my father's illness and assigned to me the task of being his physician.

Then, one time close to the end, Lee left a syringe filled with a clear liquid on the sideboard in the living room whilst my father had been sleeping upstairs. "You'll know what to do when the time comes," he said to me calmly as he'd gone down the steps towards his car. "You've got my number, Lewis, if you should need me." And on that occasion, I cried on the doorstep and hadn't seen whether Lee had lit up a cigarette or not. I don't mind admitting that his parting gambit had made me incredibly sad because it had indicated that the end was not far away, and I hadn't wanted to lose him just yet because I had just begun to beat him at chess. But more of that later.

I suppose, like everyone else at that time, the highlight of my day had always been to get out of the house for my daily dose of exercise. I never ventured far because I could never leave the old goat for too long, normally a gentle stroll on the flat to the most famous river in the world, where I would sit and watch the swans who would intermittently float by and look up to the bank and wonder where the hell everyone has gone? Sounds exciting, doesn't it, but for a good couple of months, that was about as exciting as my life got. Then I'd stroll back again towards the street where I had found myself living unexpectedly. I would inevitably find myself on a direct trajectory towards some other thing of the same species, and we would do what I have labelled *the sidewalk samba*, but it was nothing more than a shuffle of the feet, a swaying of the shoulders, the odd sidestep but most of all an embarrassed and alarmed expression to accompany the movement of the body. I had never personally crossed the road to get out of someone's way because I had always left that to my adversary, but I had on many occasions stopped walking and taken a step back into a driveway until someone had sped past me, smiling, and nodding their graceful appreciation. *My pleasure.* The most curious thing about that whole samba sidewalk thing was that invariably people had looked at me as if to question my motive for *being outside*, as though I should have been wearing a sign around my neck that said *I'm out for my daily exercise*, without the sense to realise that they had been *outside* as well; otherwise, they wouldn't have seen me, would they? At that time, everyone had known their own reason for being outside but not everybody else's, so a good sprinkling of suspicion was essential in order to perform the *sidewalk samba* properly.

I had gone to the supermarket maybe three or four times a week, but those trips out had never been a highlight at all. They had been a drudge; a walk into Hell. The only thing that had differentiated the whole

188

experience of going to buy *essentials* at the store in the town centre was that there is no requirement to queue in order to get into Hell (as far as I am aware) and a temperature is positively encouraged. I could not drive and still can't. I have never needed to learn how to do it, so I have never bothered, that's all. But it had meant that I could only buy what I could carry home, which was not a lot. Enough supplies for two nights' meals at a time, that's all that I could manage on each trip into Hell. I could have stretched it to three nights had I not bought the wine, but every man needs his release, don't they?

So, chess is what had saved my sanity. For the twenty percent of the time that my father had been awake, he had insisted that we play because chess had kept his mind alert when it could have so easily have been burdened by the trouble that had existed further down in his body. Chess, for the most part, had kept his pain level safely mid-table. He had not liked us to have the television on because I suppose a man who knows that he is dying does not want to watch other people who don't know that they're dying, screaming, and shouting their assurances of *life* that would have just sounded absurd to him.

So, we sat there, the two of us, every afternoon into the early evening, playing chess in almost silence, apart from the grandmother clock ticking away in the corner of the room. But at first, I had not been particularly good at it. I learned in the weeks that had followed that first game how to play better, but even then, I was not up to his level or the level of the other combatants in his chess club when he had been well enough to go. At first, I had yet again been a disappointment to him. The first couple of times that he had gotten my king in check after four or five moves, it had been a thrill, but twenty times later, and the

189

thrill had begun to wear thin. My father, it seemed to me, had needed – had longed for – a worthy opponent. Then, at the end of May, I was resolved that he would have one.

Thinking back to those three months now, I realise that I had been incredibly lonely in that house. I had rambled about the place all day long with nothing much else to do but investigate its nooks and secret places, particularly in my father's study-come-library at the back of the house that neither my half-sister nor I had been permitted to venture into when we had been children and very rarely my stepmother either, come to think of it. That dark room filled with books and secrets had been my father's personal province that he ruled over since the day he'd moved into that house, like a sub-Saharan tyrant. 'Get out!' he would shout whenever I ventured anywhere near the entrance to his squat at the back of the house when I had been young, and I always backed away teary-eyed into the safe enclave that was my stepmother's kitchen where the air had always been warm and dry and fragrant and welcoming. That smallish room at the back of the house had always intrigued me; I had often wondered what he did in there alone, but then I suppose that every man needs his escape, his release from the real world. Especially a man as renowned as my father; one of the world's great thinkers.

So, I suppose it was because he had needed peace and personal space within which to think about things, and there had been nothing secret and intriguing in there at all apart from the gathering of his thoughts within the conclave of his mind. I had, of course, dared to venture in there when I had been younger, and he had been at his work in London. There was a Tube strike as I recall so I had known that he would be late home, so I'd gone in there to find a suitable book to read for my A-level assignment that had been due the following morning, and I found that copy of *Alice in Wonderland* by Lewis Carrol. But as soon as I had grabbed that book, I backed out of that room as though the tyrant was still in residence bellowing his instruction to *get out* or that he'd merely been on the toilet because tyrants need the toilet more than us ordinary people. Tyrants go through toilet roll like there's no tomorrow. Tyrants live on the edge; tyrants all have a sense that their whole performance could be called out as being unauthentic at any time, and the game would be up. Tyrants rule in the knowledge that sooner or later their secrets will be found out and then what the hell are they going to do?

When my father slept in the daytime, he had slept very soundly which always reassured me that he hadn't been in too much pain and had been nestled safely somewhere mid-table after all and that he hadn't been just putting on a brave face for the Macmillan nurse. As a consequence of his deep sleep, induced by weakness and by being ground down by the consequences of the way his life had panned out, I had been safe to prowl and snoop around the entire ground floor, including his study-come-library. Quietly, of course, because I had always been aware that my sole function in that house had been to cause him as little or no disturbance or inconvenience at all. But just to be there on the end of the line whenever my half-sister deemed it necessary to call. To help him off the bed and down the stairs whenever he had woken up; to prepare for him a disastrous meal that Rocco would have put straight into the kitchen bin whilst slapping his forehead with the flat of his hand and saying: *Mamma Mia, give me the strength!* My job had been just to be there, and I was, but whilst I had been there, I had been incredibly bored and lonely, so I'd rummaged through everything. Quietly, of course, so as not to disturb him.

So, for two of those three summer months, I had been like Henry Morton Stanley exploring the centre of Africa, and I had discovered all sorts of things that I had not known to have existed. For example, a black and white photograph of that great Irish-English actor, Sir Peter O'Shea standing with his arms around my father, both of them dressed for dinner and obviously Peter had said something hilarious – as he invariably did – because it had caused my father the disturbance of being amused: positioned on the flat bit of the grand piano that had always been in the bay window of the living room, always un-played. The flat case of that grand piano in the bay window was full of photographs of the great and the good, the hoity-toity, when suddenly it dawned on me that all of those people (yes, including a prime minister, but I will not tell you which one it was) had at one time or another been *cured* by my father's expertise. The flat bit on that grand piano was his CV, but I had not noticed it before, for example.

But then, but then, when I summonsed the courage to venture into my father's study-come-library whilst he had been asleep on the top of the bed upstairs, I discovered something quite extraordinary and quite revealing. Not only had I discovered that battered, first-edition copy of *Alice in Wonderland* by Lewis Carrol again; not even the dedication on the first page, the boring page before the story begins, but a polaroid photograph that he had hidden bang in the middle. Ding Dong! It had fallen out when I opened the pages of that book. I picked it up off the floor and had looked at it. It was a photograph of a woman, a beautiful woman with hair as black as jet. Even though it was a polaroid photograph – you know, the type that before the iPhone you'd had to shake that little white square in the air in order to develop the image that it contained; a little white square of photograph paper that had instantly been ejected from the camera at the moment the image was captured when everyone stood around and waited for the image to come to the fore so that they could all see what they looked like (that's the one) – her lips had been the colour of a blood orange.

I cry a lot. I always have. I blame the wine. I had cried on the doorstep of that house at Henley when the Macmillan nurse had left me that syringe that waited on the top of the sideboard and whenever I walked past it, it seemed to say to me *use me, Lewis. Do it.* I had cried and cried my eyes out when my stepmother died; I had cried when I had found out that Linda had died; I even cried when I left Fiona the nurse, even though that had been all my own doing. And I am not ashamed to say that I cried in that study-come-library when I finally found out what my mother looked like. Suddenly, there she was, nestled precariously in the palm of my shaking hand. And she looked a lot like me.

Dr Livingston, I presume?

I feel thankful that I am here to meet you, Mr Stanley.

The queen can go wherever she wants to. Unlike a knight that is constrained by the rule of four squares up and two across; the rook on his vertical trajectory; the bishop on his diagonal trajectory; and the pathetic little pawns that can barely move in any direction. As for the king, all the other pieces have to do is protect him from being cornered so that he can still make his move. I had always known how to play chess, but I'd never been able to play well, unlike my father. And during that summer

193

whenever we two had played, I had always seemed to lose my queen early on in the game. Once the queen is lost, the game is up.

"Check-mate!" my father said one time close to the end. "For goodness' sake, Lewis, please try and give me a game! Please try to understand the basic law that you must try not to lose your queen!"

"I didn't see it coming," I replied, frustratedly, falling back into my sofa that had been adjacent to his and almost kicking over the gameboard.

"Evidently!"

The thrill of winning was still evident on his face, in the glint in his eye. And because he had been a dying man, the thrill of being vanquished had still been evident on my face. And the glint in my eye had never been so shimmering because I had kept that polaroid of my mother in my pocket ever since I discovered it. "One of these days, I *will* beat you, you old goat!" I said, standing up and stretching my back because it had ached through all of the hunching that is just as much a part of a chess game as the chequered board itself.

"Maybe when I'm dead, Lewis," he replied whilst resetting the board. "Now, what delight are you preparing us for dinner tonight?"

I ventured towards the door preparatory to going into the kitchen and preparing for us both our evening meal, and in that pause, I thought about that photograph of Sir Peter the actor and my father in their dinner attire – that had probably been taken after one of his premiers in the West End – and replied: "Fish fingers and chips, Dad, because I'm good at cooking that!"

"I don't even know what that means, Lewis," he replied whilst still resetting the board.

194

What I ought to have done in that moment of defeat was take my polaroid out of my pocket and wave it in the air saying: 'Look what I have found. Check-mate, you old goat!' But I hadn't. And I hadn't because I had promised my half-sister that I would keep him alive until she managed to get home. In any case, I was determined that the syringe filled with a clear liquid would kill him and not his heart. If I had shown him that polaroid, his heart would have packed in, and what would have been the justice of that?

"What does it come with, this gastronomical delight?" he followed up with as I had been walking out of the room.

"Mushy peas or garden peas, signor?" I replied.

In actual fact, he quite enjoyed his meal. He had been a little unsure and confused about the whole concept of a fish finger to begin with, but once he had gotten into his stride, he had eaten them heartily. I will not go as far as to say that my father had discovered a whole new taste sensation that he had wanted to repeat over and over, but he almost cleared his plate, nonetheless. I sat opposite him on the adjacent sofa and watched his every mouthful and had been heartily relieved that he had at last eaten something that was not soup and bread. Chips had always been an anathema to him, but he had even eaten most of those too. He had selected to miss the delights of mushy peas, not even garden peas, but I had found an in-date tub of potato salad in the refrigerator, so I had served that as an accompaniment, which he had enjoyed most of all because it had been soft and easy to eat.

Between us, as we ate, was the reset chessboard, and in that moment, it seemed to me that the occasions when people sat around that magnificent dining table set for thirteen, or even at the kitchen table, to eat their meal, were long gone. Those occasions were suddenly a relic of a distant past. My father's and my stepmother's dinner parties – even their New Year's Eve parties – had been legendary; an occasion that was relished by all who had been invited, when the sound that had filled the house had been of laughter, jeering and the mumbling of exceptionally intellectual conversation. All just a distant, otherworldly memory to him as he sat night after night eating his meal from his lap in the living room. A meal that had invariably been overcooked or undercooked, too lacklustre when I couldn't be bothered or too extreme whenever I had tried to experiment and prepare him something special. Maybe it hadn't been my cooking that had been the problem. Maybe it had been his lament for the good times when Peter was at his exuberant best. Curiously, the reason why the dining table had been perpetually set for thirteen (I later found out) is that his own father, my grandfather, the British Rail engineer, whom he had never talked about, had been the youngest of thirteen children. Now, isn't that curious?

One evening when he asked me what culinary delight, I had prepared for his evening meal, sarcastically and crankily, of course, because I would not have had it any other way, I'd told him: "Nothing. I have not prepared you anything, Dad." He looked surprised. Not disappointed necessarily, just surprised by my reply, semi-appalled by my insolence.

"Shall we just play again, then, Lewis?" he asked me. The reason why I had not prepared him anything to eat was because I had arranged for Rocco to prepare him something to eat instead. I had made the phone call to Luigi the previous day and requested that Rocco should prepare for my father a meal that I was sure would please

196

his delicate and sophisticated palate. I had wanted to make him happy to eat again, that's all.

The two Italians arrived precisely when they were told to. A knock on the front door that had sent my father into waves of shock since he assumed, incorrectly of course, that it was Lee the nurse. Thinking back, I wish that I hadn't arranged any such nonsense in the first place because the look on his drawn, worn-out face had been one of unbridled horror and panic. He had been so ill by that point that any thoughts of dinner parties for thirteen people, or New Year's Eve parties when people had filled every crevice of the house except for mine and my half-sister's bedrooms, had just been abhorrent to him and he wondered how he had ever had the energy to entertain such nonsense in the first place, all those dim and distant years ago.

Knock knock: "Who's there?"

"Who the fuck do you think? It's Luigi!"

"Luigi who?" Bear with me, it'll be worth it.

"Luigi the Squeegee, the fucking window cleaner!" he replied snappily.

"You can't come in, there's a pandemic on!" I whispered through the jar in the front door. "Leave it on the step."

"Oh, for fuck's sake, Lewis," I heard him sigh. Then much louder, so that the entire street must have heard him: "Just get back in the car, Rocco, he won't let us in! What was that?"

"What did he say?" I had asked Luigi because I had heard Rocco mumble something beyond the confines of the front door.

"Rocco says you owe him fifty-five pounds!" Luigi replied through the jar in the front door.

"Tell him that Boris will pay him," I laughed in reply. Luigi laughed too on the other side of the front door. Then, when I had been sure that I heard the sound of two car doors slamming shut, I finally opened the front door fully. I waved at them both, my two Italians. Luigi, from the far side of the car had extended his arm to wave back at me; Rocco, on the nearside, had leaned out of his open window and had made the *filthy lucre* gesture with his hand. It felt good to see them both again, even if it had been just their hands in various gestures of affection.

What they had left for me on the front doorstep was a plethora of food wrapped in silver foil. I gathered them all in, one by one, and walked back towards the kitchen as though I was ten years old again and had just won the jackpot on Crackerjack, minus the cabbage, thank God. Once in the kitchen, I unwrapped the silver foil and what had been revealed to me was a perfectly cooked – perfection personified – beef Wellington, and when I unwrapped the other silver-foiled parcels, there had been all the trimmings. I have aforementioned that I cry quite a lot, and I cried again then too in that kitchen on that evening. Not the over-the-top kind of crying that people do at funerals because, just because, who the hell cares; but a more delicate type of crying when moisture fills one's eyes because one is looking at one thing but thinking about something else. It had been that kind of crying; that kind of moisture. And since we are talking about moisture, oh, my God, that fillet of beef. When I cut into it to make two portions the juices had just oozed.

But my father couldn't eat it. He did try a mouthful, then another, but not much more than that before he placed his plate on the coffee table whilst announcing that the beef Wellington was not as good as his wife used to make, and frankly I had found it hard to disagree with him when that is all I had wanted to do because that beef Wellington was destined to cost me a further fifty-five pounds. Because Boris was not going to pay for the cost of the fillet of beef, after all.

But he did not say, in the exact words, *what my wife used to make*. He had said, precisely: 'Not as good as your mother used to make'. And then upon realising what he said, he had looked as though he was a man about to be run over by a steam train with its whistle full on and full steam ahead. Startled all of a sudden; a little bit this and a little bit that. He looked as though he had been a man who had inadvertently said the wrong thing. But, unbeknown to him, he had precisely said the right thing at precisely the right moment. What a clever man my father was.

But that beef Wellington had been every bit as good as the ones my stepmother used to make, if not considerably better, and my father had known it. The reason he had not eaten very much of it was because he had been so weak and ill by then that his body could not face it; his eating days were nearly over. I feel foolish now for having arranged that meal for him in the first place; I feel ashamed that I had not recognised the deterioration in him that had seemed to happen very quickly, maybe within a week or so. But when you're hunkered down with a dying man, you don't notice such things straight away; the human eye is not that sophisticated. In the same way the human eye would not notice the decomposition of a corpse if it were constantly looking at it.

So, after I cleared away our dinner plates into the kitchen, we had simply played chess again and something remarkable happened. I kept hold of my queen for the majority of the game. My father had tried his darndest to capture her, but I managed to manoeuvre her out of harm's way whenever it had been my turn to move. I had been playing very defensively but what else could I do when I was playing a grand master? You guessed it: my queen placed his king in check, and I only had my rook, two pawns and a knight left on the board too. He could barely believe that such a thing was possible and the look on his face proved it; he had been astonished and bewildered in equal measure as he hunched further over the board to examine his options. Then, when I looked at the board again after my initial burst of excitement, I realised what he had already fathomed out, that it had actually been check mate. The game was up for this tyrant.

"It cannot be," he sighed whilst rubbing his face to free it from the shock.

"It is, look," I insisted. "You can't move that way because of that pawn, that way because of the knight and my rook has all the bases covered!"

He leaned back in his sofa but had stopped short of giving up the game. "Do you know what I fancy, Lewis?" he said, determinedly.

"What do you fancy, Dad?"

"A glass of lemonade," he announced. "Proper lemonade made with lemons."

"We haven't got any."

"They sell it in supermarkets nowadays, I believe."

"Do you want me to go to the shop?"

"If you don't mind."

I had done as he told me for once in my life. Before leaving the house, I instructed him not to meddle with the board until I returned, and he assured me that he would not. But, of course, he did.

Chapter Fourteen

That night had been a lovely, warm mid-May evening and even though it was nine-thirty PM, the sky was as light as it was at midday. The approaching sunset was going to be spectacular it was clear. The walk into town had done me some good. It cleared away the debris in my mind even though I had found myself wondering what else besides a bottle of lemonade that I could buy in order for my journey to the supermarket to be classed as 'essential' to the cashier. I settled on buying some bread and a bottle of milk even though we hadn't needed either, because those two items are essential to everybody, surely?

The late evening birdsong soothed my mind and with the absence of traffic noise, I even heard an owl hoot, or twitter, or whatever the hell owls do. There was still no air traffic noise either and I imagined my half-sister still sitting at her computer tip-tapping on the keyboard searching for flights, going out of her mind when she hadn't been able to find one, and Rocco too, probably. *Good luck to them both,* I thought to myself as I turned onto the high street. There had been no other human beings around, so the sidewalk samba had not been necessary. I even crossed the high street without stopping to check for oncoming cars or busses, such was the ease with which I had adapted to the new circumstances. Come to think of it, it had been astonishing how most people had adapted to the new circumstances of their reality with relative conformity. We had been given a simple instruction and most people had done as they had been told. Except, I had been out for the third time that day; once to the supermarket earlier and once for my afternoon saunter to the river, so I felt a little guilty for having been

201

out on the streets again. But who would know? In any case, I was running an errand for a dying man who fancied a lemonade, so no-one with any compassion and empathy would have minded, surely?

But it felt so good to be out of that house again, even if I had been breaking the rules. The evening had turned out to be a disappointment so the walk along Henley high street had been welcome, it had salvaged something from a discouraging day. Even though I had finally gained the upper hand in a game of chess, my father had not been able to eat one of the finest meals that had ever been placed in front of him, either in a posh restaurant or on his lap, and it had been an indication that he was falling further towards his death. I suppose it had come as a disappointment and a shock to have finally realised what my half-sister and probably her husband too had known all along: that his death was imminent and inevitable, and there was nothing that I, or Lee, or anybody could do to prevent his illness from completely overwhelming him. The sound of the birdsong had been a welcome accessory to my walk.

Suddenly my mobile phone vibrated in my trouser pocket (I had long since adopted the practise of keeping it on silent) and when I brought it out and looked at the screen, it had been my father calling me on it for that third time. Seeing the word *Henley* displayed on the phone screen whilst I had been meandering along its high street seemed absurd and a little abstract. As I have aforementioned, that third time my father had called me on my mobile phone had not caused me any disturbance or panic at all, just inconvenience. The inconvenience of having been disturbed; my solitude had been disrupted by a very needy housemate.

"Are you alright?" I asked him, suddenly beginning to wonder whether he was, actually, alright.

"Of course, I am, Lewis," he replied, brusquely, as though why wouldn't he be.

"What's the matter? Why are you ringing? You never ring my mobile."

"Scrap the lemonade, Lewis," he insisted. "And get me a bottle of Italian Limoncello instead. I would like to taste it again. Preferably one that has been pressed and bottled on the Amalfi Coast."

"I'm on Henley high street, Dad, not the Amalfi Coast!"

"Well, just get the best bottle that they have. Money is no object, Lewis."

Nor has it ever been, you old goat, I thought to myself. "Ok, Dad. But if they don't have one, do you want the lemonade after all?"

"For goodness' sake, Lewis, of course they will have one." And then he hung up.

Do you see what I mean? Compared to the first two times my father had called me on my mobile phone it had been like nothing, just an urge to communicate with me with a remarkably simple instruction. The semblance of a normal conversation; just natural interaction between a father and his son as though nothing had ever happened. It had been a quite surreal phone call, not because of the normality of it, but because it had been yet another symptom of his aching and ailing body but of his vibrant mind too.

I struggled to reassure myself that a bottle of Italian Limoncello would be deemed any more *essential* than a bottle of lemonade, perhaps less so to the cashier who would have the unenviable task of checking me out. At least I hadn't been going to the supermarket to cash in a lottery scratch card with a pound winnings on it as some people had because I had found myself at one time or another lining up behind them. As long as I bought milk and bread at the same time, all would be fine, and I could slink the hell out of there undetected.

Whilst I had been walking and talking on my mobile phone to my father as I walked along Henley high street, I had not noticed that the birds had stopped singing. The birds had flown for cover all of a sudden, aware that there had been a storm brewing in the skies long before I had been aware. The sky had turned very dark and suddenly nine-forty-five pm in May was everything that it always ought to have been. Then it started to rain, and I had become aware of my inadequate clothing for the weather in England in May, that may be one thing one minute, but quickly becomes something opposite the next, come what may. It had not been the drizzle and damp that one gets in November or December in England or the damp mist and fog you get in February or March or the showers between the sunshine in April, but the sudden, unexpected downpour of biblical proportions that you tend to get only in May or June in England after what had otherwise been a perfectly lovely day so you hadn't bothered to put on an overcoat.

And I had gotten soaked to my skin. Every part of my body seemed to have been wet and quite unexpectedly. I will try not to sound as melodramatic as suggesting that a storm cloud had burst over the top of my head but that was how it felt. No, we were all in the same boat; me and the other eight people who were standing in line outside the supermarket entrance at the top of the high street. I will not mention the name of the supermarket, but it was the posh one that you don't find in the east end of

Glasgow or on the Britwell estate, Slough, and it was limiting the number of customers that it could admit through its entrance so that by the time I joined the back of the line, they had been operating on a one in one out basis. I had almost given up since I'd known that the store closed at ten pm but when a very polite young man came out to inform me that I would be permitted to enter but anyone else behind me would be turned away, I settled down on the inevitability of having to ask for a bottle of Italian Limoncello, preferably one that had been pressed and bottled on the Amalfi Coast, because I would not have the time to look for one by myself once I'd gotten inside. With that thought, I had hunched my shoulders in a bizarre attempt to keep out of the rain and had bellowed my cheeks preparatory to breathing out the longest melancholic sigh that I ever had.

Then I saw her standing there, fourth in the queue: Fiona the nurse. Of all the people, what had she been doing in Henley? I thought about calling out her name because right then, on that night, it had felt good to see a familiar person, but I hadn't because I hadn't been sure of the rules regarding calling out for someone's attention whilst standing in a line at a supermarket. So, I sent her a text message instead, which when her phone had vibrated in her pocket, she pulled it out and looked at it before turning around as per the message's instruction. She waved tentatively whilst trying to smile, then she had broken from the line to join me at the back, thus losing her space forever because even though compassion and empathy had still existed in the world, not that much that would let her back in.

"What are you doing in Henley?" I asked.

"I work in Reading, Lewis, the M4 is closed so this is the only way home, and I needed some stuff, so I pulled in."

She looked exhausted; haggard, pale, and stressed. She looked much older than her thirty-three years. She had still been dressed in her nurse's uniform; she had abided by the rules and stood two meters away from me, but I wanted to pull her closer and give her a hug that may have reassured her that she was standing in the pouring rain with a friend. But rules are rules, so I hadn't done that.

"How are you holding up?" I asked her because it looked as though she could barely stand up much less hold up.

"Things are really bad, Lewis," she replied whilst rubbing her face with her hands. And since her hands had already been at the level of her face, she started to sob into them. "I'm so tired," she sobbed. "I am so sad right now."

I did not know how to react to her sobbing. Ordinarily, I would have given her a hug because one of the most important things that my stepmother ever taught me was that a hug given genuinely can cure almost anything. But rules are rules, and in any case, common sense had to prevail over sympathy and Fiona was a nurse who had just finished a shift on a Covid ward at the Royal Berkshire Hospital, Reading, and I was a redundant man living in a bubble with his dying father, so you get my point. But really, what had been the point of my hesitancy? What difference would it have made if I had taken Covid back into the big house and to my father? Better that he died from that, surely, then from the encroaching pain that had put an end to his eating days already. But not his chess playing days, or his mind and his voice. It seemed to me that Covid had killed quicker than cancer does, and I still wanted answers, so that is why I had been hesitant to give Fiona a hug so that is why I hadn't.

"How is your father?" Fiona asked me once she had calmed herself down and upon realising that I was not going to give her a hug when that is precisely what she had needed me to do.

"He's bearing up. He doesn't eat a lot now, so I'm a bit worried."

"It's not going to be long now, you do know that don't you, Lewis?" she replied. It had seemed to me to be one of the most insensitive things that anybody had ever said to me, but on second thought, Fiona was a nurse who had just finished a shift on a Covid ward and quite frankly, she could not have cared less. But I was wrong, she had cared. Because when someone is living in a bubble with someone who is dying, then there is absolutely no point in anyone else giving you platitudes and false hope. Fiona had cared enough not to have said anything that would have filled me with any sense that there was any hope left in the world.

"How's your family, Fi?" I responded in kind, lacking the wherewithal to say anything else.

"My brother died!"

"What?"

She seemed to be on the edge of crying again; what I mean to say is, it had been an exceedingly difficult thing for her to say out loud, but she had been waiting for the moment when she could tell someone and I had happened to be there, that's all.

"I'm so sorry to hear that, Fi!" And actually, I had been, because I had known how much he meant to her, how close their sibling relationship had been that I had hitherto envied because my own relationship with my half-sibling had been hung on a very tenuous New Year's Eve.

"You know that he had bad lungs, Lewis," Fiona replied. I nodded but actually I hadn't known that at all. She had probably once explained her brother's condition to me whilst driving down to her home in Devon and maybe whilst passing the Wicker Man, but I obviously hadn't taken any notice because at the time I had been so wrapped up in my own problems, my own trouble, that anybody else's had just sounded like nonsense. "Well, he got *it*, and he died. My parents held his funeral two weeks ago, but I couldn't go because, well, just because of the circumstances." And then she wept so openly and so loudly that I wished that she had stayed in line and had not been bothered to look at her phone, or that even when she did, would not have cared that she had read a message from me. But she had read that message. Her phone had vibrated so she had taken it out of her trouser pocket and read it and had turned around to encounter me again. God help her.

"I can't believe it, Fi," I responded again, even though I could have easily believed anything that anyone had selected to tell me. Someone could have told me that the moon was made of cream cheese, and right then in the pouring rain whilst I was standing in line awaiting permission to enter Waitrose (shit, I was determined not to say), I would have believed them because at the ending of the world, anyone will believe almost anything. At the ending of the world anything is possible. "All I want to do is hug you, but I can't, Fi."

"No, you bloody well can't!" she replied, firmly. "You've got to think about your father." Suddenly, her tears had given way to her laughter. Those two human reactions are never too far apart in any case. "And there's a sentence that I never thought that I would say," she said.

"It's been a strange year so far, hasn't it?" I mumbled melancholically in response.

Fiona started to cry again but tried to keep her sorrow a secret from the other people in the queue. She had not been thinking about my father but about her brother; I'd known her well enough to have known that. Have you ever tried to grieve in public, in secret? It is the most difficult thing that a human being can attempt. Much harder than climbing Everest; more draining than running a marathon through the Sarah Dessert; more straining than standing at a fire alarm for twenty minutes with your index figure pressed on the 'silence' button. But grieving in public, in secrecy, is precisely what Fiona attempted to do. She had been prepared to attempt the impossible, and it hadn't worked out for her because the other people who had been standing in that queue all turned around to see what all the fuss was about, and I wished that I had been somewhere else. To my eternal shame.

Rule (noun): one set of explicit regulations governing the conduct or procedure within a particular area of activity: *those who did* break the rules *would be dealt with swiftly,* for example. But rules be damned. Rules are meant to be broken. And I did break them. I had broken the rules in the pouring rain, because I felt an overwhelming urge to hug that poor woman, so that is precisely what I did, against the rules. And Fiona hugged me back so tightly that I thought that my eyes were going to pop out of my head. She had clung onto me so tightly that it was as though I were the mast of a sinking ship. And she sobbed openly at last. At last, her grief had been set free on my shoulder; I was already soaked to the skin so what difference would a few tears make?

But I was glad that I had my back to the queue because I recall that I'd winced. Not through pain – Fiona is slight of frame and strength – but with embarrassment. The embarrassment that comes from being the one who is being hugged, like a puny nephew at a party on New Year's Eve, whilst their parents looked on adoringly. I had winced because of my shame: shame because I had known that I could never be the man whom she had so longed to meet. I winced through guilt: guilty of not loving her, because *it* is either there or it is not, and it had not been, even then, nor had it even been there in the first place. I had winced because I had realised that at one time or another, *it* had been there. Not with Fiona, but with someone else, but at the time I hadn't had the wherewithal to realise it.

'You'll know what I mean when it is, Lewis', my stepmother had told me. But I had not, because I had been so wrapped up in my own troubles that anything else had just seemed like nonsense. As Fiona hugged me – because she needed to, and I had been willing for her to do it – in the pouring rain as we awaited permission to enter the supermarket – I finally realised what my stepmother had been talking about all those dim and distant years ago on the doorstep of the big house at Henley, when the welcome had been less than welcoming. *It's either there or it isn't, Lewis, and you'll know what I mean when it is.* In the pouring rain, I realised that I already had known what my stepmother had meant, but also that I had been so enveloped by my own misfortune that had dominated my life thus far, that I missed my opportunity to realise what my stepmother had once meant to say to me. That is why I *winced* – my eyes bulging out of their sockets, happy to have my back to the waiting queue for the supermarket – because whilst Fiona the nurse had been thinking about me and about how happy she was that she was hugging me, I had been thinking about … *you*.

Something then happened that I still can't quite explain. The manager had come out onto the street – obviously, the manager because he was wearing an exceedingly good-looking, crisp suit that had fitted him so well that he could have almost been an Italian – and he made a beeline for Fiona and me at the end of the queue. Maybe he was the Covid police, who had been alerted to the fact that we had broken the rules by *hugging*? But no, he was just a supermarket manager who had been alerted to the fact that an NHS nurse was standing at the back of his queue, sobbing.

"Please, come with me, madam," he said to her, extending his arm and almost bowing his head. "You do not have to queue. Is this your partner?" Referring to me.

"No," I replied quickly.

"Yes," she replied, even quicker.

"Please, come with me. It is our pleasure," the manager said. Now that is how to manage when I realised that I had never quite got the hang of it after all.

"I can't come with you," I whispered to Fiona as she followed that young man's instruction to go with him. I had been a little bit embarrassed and a little bit overwhelmed.

"You hugged me, Lewis, so now you are in my *bubble*, or else we've broken the law," Fiona chortled. "And besides, you'll get in quicker."

And besides, she had hold of my arm so pulled me along with her towards the entrance, all the while remembering to stay two meters behind the manager, who was proud to have led the way. The other people who were standing in that queue in the pouring rain had given us a round of applause as we stepped past them. We had both of us been very embarrassed by the whole experience, but such was the difference in our characters that Fiona had lowered her head as she passed them whereas I had almost given them the royal wave. I had been half-tempted halfway along the line to stop and shake the hand of a middling sort of man and ask him, *What do you do? How nice.* Curious.

Once through the doors, the staff had been alerted to the fact that there was an NHS nurse about to enter their supermarket, so they all gathered next to the entrance, and they too had given us a resounding round of applause as soon as we entered, and some of the other customers who had already been in there, too. Fiona smiled at them all graciously; I had started to cry, because as aforementioned, I cry quite easily. Because I felt like a fraud. I had been in that supermarket under false pretences. I knew that, and so did Fiona.

She picked up her basket whilst smiling graciously to acknowledge those other people's admiration of what she did for a living. I, myself, had not needed a basket so I just stood next to her, because if I had gone my own way around the supermarket without Fiona, then the fraud would have been revealed.

"Stop crying, Lewis, for goodness' sake!" she snarled at me, suddenly embarrassed by my lack of control. "What's got into you?"

"I don't know what's happening, Fi, but it is the most beautiful thing I have ever experienced," I replied. And it truly had been. There had been no fraud in my emotion.

"Well get your shit together, Lewis, because we haven't got long, they close in ten minutes," Fiona responded as she had stridden along the fresh aisle, and I

212

had struggled to keep up with her. Then she stopped in front of the fresh meat. "That felt good!" she sighed.

"What did?"

"Finally having the opportunity to tell you to get your shit together."

I had known precisely what she meant. Someone should have said it long before then. "What do you need?" I asked.

"Something quick, something easy, a ready meal or something because I have to be back at work at six am," she replied.

Are you out of your tiny mind? I thought to myself, incredulously. *Is that even legal?* Then again, what is the point of the law at the ending of the world?

"And milk," she added, heading off towards the dairy cabinet. "You know what I'm like for my coffee on a morning."

"Three cups before you leave the house," I chuckled, and Fiona had been glad that I had remembered that fact about her.

"What about you, what do you need?" she followed up with.

"A bottle of Limoncello," I replied quite nonchalantly, realising how ridiculous it sounded.

My reply stopped Fiona in her tracks, and she looked at me doubtfully. "You have queued in the pouring rain just to buy a bottle of Limoncello? Are you actually an alcoholic, Lewis? Please tell me that you are."

"If I was then I would buy something stronger, wouldn't I?" I replied. "Why?"

"Because if you are actually an alcoholic, then it would actually make me happy."

"Why?" Incredulously.

"It would explain a lot."

And she would have dodged a bullet, which is what she had meant to say. But I wasn't, I am not, an alcoholic. "My father has a fancy for a glass of authentic Limoncello. But they'll keep it behind the counter, so if it's all the same to you, I'll bide my time until we get there."

Fiona sighed again whilst she picked out a litre bottle of semi. "Of course, he does. And what the great Martin Sinclaire wants, someone will fetch it, and he does not really care who. Fucking Italy again. That fucking villa again! Why doesn't he just sell it, be rid of it once and for all because it seems to me that it has caused him – and you – nothing but grief!"

"I know."

"Anyway, why is it you? Where's his beloved Jane?"

"Stranded at the villa."

"For God's sake!" she gasped as I followed her into the bakery section. She picked up a Parisian stick. "What is it with you people? Why do you all live in the past? What is done is done, just like this French stick ..." she waved it in front of my nose, almost taking my head off with it, so I I'd had to duck. "It is *done*. It is what it is. It is what it was meant to be all along." She sighed again, disparagingly. "You people," she concluded. "If any of you did my job, then you would realise that there is no 'past'. All there is, is the hope that there may be a future."

She then backtracked on herself because she had forgotten that she needed butter because what use is a French stick without it? I followed her.

"My sister goes there because she knows it's there and she likes the sun, that's all. I haven't been there since I was seventeen."

"I know, you've already told me that." She prefers salted butter.

"And I think he *is* selling it."

"He really should. It has done none of you any favours, that place."

I stopped in my tracks. "But for me, the past is not done," I whimpered, pathetically.

Fiona brought herself close to me again, sensing that I needed to be hugged. "I know that too, Lewis," she said to me, unsalted. "But I don't think that there's anything you can do about it now, after all these years. Or is there?"

"I've been playing a lot of chess with my father. It seems to take his mind off things. Before I came out, I had his king in check. I think it might even be checkmate," I said, randomly and quite excitedly.

"Good for you," Fiona replied offhanded because there had been too much trouble on her mind to not care. She had forgotten the one thing that she had gone in for, a ready meal, so she had stridden swiftly back towards the fresh aisle, and I had to trot to keep up with her again, like a child whose mother had told him not to wander off or else. "With your queen, I shouldn't wonder?"

"Yes, actually." I had failed to recognise her barbed point.

"And so he fancies a glass of Limoncello all of a sudden?"

"Yes, and I fancied the walk."

"In the pouring rain?"

"It was quite nice when I came out."

This was a side to Fiona's character that I had never encountered before: a flippant, sarcastic tone to her voice that seemed to ridicule me and my family in a way that I

215

had never experienced from anybody before then. Luigi had occasionally made the odd mocking comment about my father and my *mother issues,* but he was such a ridiculous man who'd had no right to say anything after the ridiculous life he had led so they just bounced straight off me. But Fiona's condemning pitch had been perturbing because up until then, the only side to her character that I had been familiar with was her caring, empathetic, encouraging side. She had been perfectly correct, of course, but I hadn't known that she had it in her to express it so damningly, that's all. Right then, I felt like a nuisance, a parasite on a leopardess's back and her instinct had been to brush me off with her tail and then get on with her life.

When she had gotten everything that she needed, we joined the back of the queue for the checkout. The supermarket was limiting the number of customers who were allowed in at any one time to ten, and the other nine had been standing in line for the till. Nine, since Fiona and me had counted as one as far as that polite, courteous manager had been concerned. I was standing by her side, feeling a little uncomfortable and wishing that I hadn't messaged her whilst we had been waiting in the pouring rain for admittance. But I had – it had seemed the correct thing to do – so there we were, the two of us, at the end of the line.

And we waited and waited for the chance to move a step forward onto the next yellow hazard strip that the store had stuck onto the floor tiles as an instruction for what two meters actually was. "I bet someone's cashing in a handful of scratch cards," I sighed, whilst craning my neck to see what the holdup was all about. "As if they're *essential.*"

"And a bottle of Limoncello *is*?" she replied, mocking me and my father again.

"Yes, on this occasion, it is." I had been proud of my retort and when Fiona chuckled, she seemed to have concurred.

"Who was she, Lewis?" Fiona asked at that impasse.

I was taken aback by her sudden, unexpected question. "Who was who?"

Straight away, she countered: "Who was the woman you left me for? And where is she now? What went wrong? As if I need to ask."

The woman standing in front of us heard what Fiona had said and she turned her head slightly to see the faces of the combatants that had suddenly made her long wait for the checkout seem a little less like purgatory. This was better than Dallas.

"I don't think this is the time or the place, Fi," I replied.

"Why not? You can't come to the flat, can you, and we can't meet for coffee somewhere, so this place is as good as we're going to get. And since I may never see you again, I would quite like to know what that woman had that I didn't, if it's all the same to you?"

"What makes you think that there was anybody?"

"Because it ended too quickly. I had done all of the hard work ... I had ingratiated myself to your father and your sister ..."

"Half-sister!"

"Oh, for God's sake, Lewis!" she gasped. "We'd had a perfectly nice life together. We had a lovely flat, we both worked, I'd cooked and cleaned for you and ironed your clothes. I had mothered you, which is what your father had told me that I should do ..." The woman in front had been so engrossed in our conversation that she had temporarily forgotten her manners and had belched. "… so why was I never enough? One minute we were planning our trip to Devon, the next, you were gone. Nothing could end that quickly unless there had been someone else involved. So, who was she? And what did she do that I didn't?"

"She pulled me up off my knees when that's all I'd needed anyone to do," I replied.

"For God's sake, Lewis," Fiona whimpered, angrily. "You were always on your knees!"

"Because I didn't need a mother, Fi! I already had one … my stepmother …!"

"She never liked me, that woman, I'd always felt it."

"Because she *knew*." I had been just as frustrated as Fiona had been. We had indeed been combatants as we stepped forward to the next yellow hazard strip; one step closer to the checkout. "Because I had told her all about …"

"All about who? What was her name?"

"What does it matter now? She has gone. She left me, like everyone else has!" I had been very aggravated by that point: like father like son.

"And whose fault is that?" Snappily.

The manager, either because Fiona had been wearing her nurse's uniform or because he had been made aware that we were having some sort of altercation in his queue – he could control a pandemic within his supermarket with his yellow hazard strips but not the circumstances of a couple of human lives – approached Fiona tentatively. "Madam, you do not have to queue," he said to her, tenderly, as he gestured for her to follow him once again towards the checkout. What a manager. We stepped out of the line when the woman who was standing in front of us had looked at that manager and her expression seemed to say: *are you kidding me? Now I'll never know what the hell happened. Who the hell was she?* I believe, in terms of the drama, it is called a cliff-hanger.

"Sixteen pounds forty," the checkout operative told Fiona.

For a bottle of milk, a ready meal, a French stick and a pack of butter, I thought to myself, disbelievingly. *At least Dick Turpin wore a mask!*

"And a bottle of Limoncello, if you have one," Fiona replied.

"Certainly have, madam," the checkout operative said, turning around to face the array of spirits that were behind her.

"Preferably from Amalfi," I whispered in Fiona's ear.

"It doesn't really matter does it, Lewis?" Fiona said to me, exasperatedly.

Beep. "£29.80 madam. Thank you. Your receipt, but before you go, I just want to say, 'thank you'."

Those other customers – apart from the woman who had been standing in front of us – and the staff had seen us off with another round of applause. Fiona smiled at them all, but I had felt like a schoolboy who was being escorted off the premises by his furious and disappointed mother after he had been caught shoplifting. Once we exited through the automatic doors, another two had been permitted to enter and they entered as though they had been the contestants on a gameshow that would permit them to have whatever they could get their hands on in the short time that they had. Good luck to them.

"I'd better let you have this," Fiona mumbled, pulling the bottle of Limoncello out of her carrier bag. "Goodbye, Lewis."

I didn't find the correct words to say to her, so I said nothing at all; I had simply taken the bottle of Limoncello from her. But I had known how she felt right then at that moment of parting. I had known precisely how it feels to say goodbye to someone who is the love of your life whilst wondering 'what did I do wrong?' I had known, at that moment, how she felt to see someone walk away from you who was very much alive whilst feeling grief as though that person had died.

Fiona turned right towards the carpark; I walked straight ahead back down the high street. "I owe you for the Limoncello!" I called back to her.

"It is my treat, Lewis," she shouted back without turning around. "Tell your father that I am thinking about him."

"I will, Fi."

"Fraud!"

When I turned around to see who had shouted that word to me, I saw an incredibly angry man who had been standing in front of me whilst I had waited in line for admittance before I had messaged Fiona in what then seemed to me to have been another lifetime, another dimension. As I walked back along the high street towards the big house, I found it difficult to argue against his sentiment.

"I'm absolutely soaked to the skin," I announced once I had shuffled through the front door and whilst

220

removing my jacket that had been ill-prepared for a torrential summer downpour. My father then emerged from the side door to his study-come-library: a little, frail old man with an angry countenance on his face. "What an ordeal I have had," I said whilst shaking my head like a dog that'd just leapt out of the bath.

"There's a book missing from my bookshelves, Lewis," my father said to me, sternly. There was life in that old tyrant yet, it seemed.

"Is there? What book, I wonder?" Nonchalantly.

"You know which book. *Alice in Wonderland* by Lewis Carroll, and I would quite like to see it again."

I had deflected his derision and disappointment by going into the living room because it seemed to me that that was the only option I had. The chessboard was the first thing that I saw. "You've changed the board!" I gasped, angrily.

"No, I haven't," my father responded, coming into the living room from the hallway.

"Yes, you have. Before I left, I had your king in check by my queen, but now that I look again, that isn't the case anymore. You have moved that pawn!"

My father came closer to examine the board for himself. "I most certainly haven't," he pronounced defensively. "Perhaps you are remembering how things were quite wrongly, Lewis?" He then smiled mischievously as he collapsed back into his sofa because his expedition into his study had taken the wind out of him. "You've got to be a man to play in my league, Lewis," he sneered at me. "Are you that man?"

Chapter Fifteen

I recall that I said to him in reply, "You mean, you've got to be a *cheat* to play in your league?" And I had been silently pleased with myself.

"Nonsense, how dare you?" my father sneered in response to my accusation, but if he'd had a moustache, he would have been twirling the edges of it right then like the villain that he was, Dick Dastardly, etcetera. However, the glint in his eye was a pleasure for me to behold. Was that why he had enjoyed his chess club so much during the course of his twilight years, every Tuesday night: to have been able to cheat openly, at last, knowing that his opponent lacked the wherewithal to reveal the fraud? Had the fraud been the aspect of his game that had given him the greatest thrill: his ability to cheat openly more than his skill at actually being able to play by the rules?

"My move, I believe," he chortled, whilst pulling himself forward from his slouched position on the sofa and moving his king out of check. "Now what are you going to do?"

I had to think carefully about my response because my opponent tended to cheat whenever I turned my back. "I'm going to pour you a glass of this very, very expensive bottle of authentic Italian Limoncello ..." I pretended to look at the label closely as though I needed eyeglasses ... "pressed and bottled, so it says, on the Amalfi Coast." I then made the international *filthy lucre* gesture with my fingers. "You owe me fifty-five pounds, by the way." Because if I said twelve-pounds-sixty, he wouldn't have drunk it.

I examined the board, his move out of check. "That pawn was not on that square when I left!" I snarled, exasperated and frustratedly. Never more so.

"I did not touch that board!" my father leered, defensively. "All the time you were out of this house, I have been in my study!"

He winced through pain, as I recall. Too much pain for any human body to have to endure. And even though he had never appreciated the whole 'football' analogy, I had known that he had been rapidly climbing the league, regardless. However, I had not cared so much about his discomfort as my response to it as I meandered towards the grand piano in the bay window, and when I picked up a photograph of my stepmother – an image of pure beauty smiling at me as though she were saying to me: *finish it, Lewis, find out* who *she was, because I would quite like to know too* – only to move it away from that copy of *Alice in Wonderland* by Lewis Carrol, that I had hitherto concealed beneath that photograph of that fabulous woman. "Looking for this, I shouldn't wonder?" I pronounced, proudly.

My father cringed through pain once again. Once it had worn off, temporarily, and he recovered, he asked me, "Why on Earth did you hide it under that?"

"Because I knew it would be the last place you would look for it."

Then, I gave the book back to him whilst I studied the board once again, determined not to lose *this* game, out of all the other games that I had lost, hitherto. And he grabbed it out my hands as though it had contained the secret to solving pain, any kind of pain. "What a strange creature you are, Lewis," he sighed, reproachingly. "But then, you always have been too quiet for my liking, too eager to think about things that were, or are, or may never have been."

"What are you thinking?"

He had been clasping that tattered copy of *Alice in Wonderland* close to his chest. "I think that it's time you poured me out a glass of that Limoncello," he replied. "Whilst I consider what I am going to do after you have made your move."

I poured him out a large measure because whilst I read the label, I noticed that it had only been fifteen percent by volume, and he had needed to get drunk, that's all; because I had known that the truth, in drink, will always without. I had been studying the board whilst my father downed his drink whilst flicking hopelessly through that battered, tattered copy of *Alice in Wonderland* by Lewis Carrol, first edition. Then, I made my move. Just that same pawn that he had moved, back onto the square where it had been when I had left the house, but his king had been safe, for the time being, because he had moved his king in the other direction.

He studied the board again whilst handing me his empty glass for a refill, which I had been only too happy to do. "You know how angry I get when someone has been in my study," he grumbled. "When you were a child, you had barely dared to peer through the door. But I suppose the game has changed now, hasn't it, and while I have been confined to my bed on the next floor, you have felt emboldened to go in there, pilfering my books."

"Borrowing your book. I do believe that I've just given it back to you. Libraries and studies in most family homes are accessible to everyone who is a member of that family, but not this one. In this family home, the library-come-study is out of bounds to everyone but the keeper of his secrets!"

"Don't be absurd, Lewis," my father snarled as he downed his second glass of Limoncello.

"And it's not the first time that I have borrowed that book, either. I 'pilfered' it when I'd been at college, too."

"*Alice in Wonderland*?" he mused. "Why?" Then he gasped in pain again and held his abdomen with his free hand.

As I refilled his glass, I told him why, about the A-level assignment that had required me to read something, but I had not had the drive or the determination to read something too weighty or complicated. "But I did not notice the dedication on the first page when I was seventeen."

"But this time you have?" He leant so far over the board that he was almost standing up. A look of awkward fury had cast itself on his face. "You can't see it, can you, Lewis?"

"See what?"

"You've beaten me. You have finally got me."

"You mean the book ... the dedication? I don't know what you mean."

"It's check-mate! I can't move," he sighed as he collapsed back into his sofa. "I think I need another glass of that Limoncello, which, although it is palatable, it was most definitely *not* pressed and bottled on the Amalfi Coast. Nevertheless, it's all we've got, and we are where we are, aren't we?"

I had not read the board correctly; I had not realised that my move with that pawn had put him in checkmate, and when I studied the board again, I still hadn't. I had gone through every possible move that he could have made; his king to that square, or that square, until it dawned on me that actually he was right: he could not move anywhere. I had him tied up; done and dusted; a

225

busted flush. And I have never been so pleased with myself in my life. The only thing that had been missing from that moment of elation had been the feeling, because of my incompetence as a chess player, of having been able to have said to him: checkmate, Father … again.

"What were you looking for when you were flicking through that book?" I said instead, and it had felt just as satisfying.

My father brought himself forward; a move that seemed to have caused him a tremendous amount of pain again. "Where is it, Lewis?" he demanded. He had glanced through that book one more time, paying particular attention to the first page. "I must have been out of my mind when I wrote that," he gasped, half in horror and half in shame.

"Wrote what? When?" I pleaded with him, but really, I had known precisely what he had been referring to and his comment confirmed to me, once and for all, that he had actually written that dedication in his own hand, however many years ago. I had begun to wonder whether the handwritten dedication on the first page had been there when he'd bought the book in the first place; had been the reason that he bought it. He had confirmed, in that instant, that my mother had actually once existed, and that the photograph of a woman that I'd had concealed safely in my back pocket was *her* after all.

"I must have been very naive to have written something like that," he continued, suddenly enraptured by the book that he held in his frail, old hands because the game of chess had very quickly lost its ability to enthral him. "I must have been very much in love with that woman to have oversimplified the contents of a human brain. When I'd written that, I had been making a specific observation to her, but it reads back as a generalisation, which it cannot be." He seemed aggravated and beside himself with worry all of a sudden, which is precisely not how I had not wanted him to be. Things were bad enough as they were and the pain was showing in his face; in his eyes; in the way that he'd looked at me, like a dog on a scorched street. "Nothing ever has to make sense", he gasped. "What on earth was I thinking? *Everything* has to make sense; otherwise, what it is the point of a human life?"

"Some people think too much, Dad," I replied, jittery all of a sudden because it had seemed to me that the shock of looking at that book again might actually kill him, and not the cancer that was galloping all over his body like Dick Turpin on Black Bess, demanding more than was necessary, *your memories or your life*. "The human brain has the capacity to understand everything, but not the wherewithal to withstand the consequences."

My comment seemed to settle him. He remembered the occasion when he had first said it. My reply had brought his daughter and his wife back into his mind, I was quite sure of that. It had brought back to him a time when none of this nonsense had mattered, when the house had been filled with life. He settled down. I hadn't had to slap him out of his delirium; a restlessness and confusion that seemed to cloak him because he had either had too much to drink or his mind had been sent hurling into the nether after because he'd just lost a game of chess. Anyway, he settled down.

But the pain had been evident on his face. He was, by that point, Manchester United or Barcelona or AC Roma, and I began to wonder whether this was the right time to call Lee the nurse. *Not yet*, I thought to myself. Not yet. *Let's just see how this thing goes.*

Then he said something to me that to anyone else would have been a lovely thing to hear, but to me, it had just sounded like nonsense. "I love you, Lewis," he mumbled. "It's important to me that you know that before I go."

Nonsense. "You're not going anywhere just yet, you old goat," I replied. "You're just drunk, that's all it is."

"What did you call me?" my father demanded, semi-furiously.

"An old goat. I've been calling you that my whole life because to me, that is precisely what you are!" And I hadn't cared because the game really had changed.

My father chuckled to himself; well, as much as he had been able to chuckle in the circumstances since the ability to chuckle had shot him up the league. "I used to call my father, your grandfather, the *oily rag*," he chuckled.

"Why?"

"Because every time he returned to the house, he had seemed to me to be covered in oil and grease, and whenever I looked at him, I had been determined *not* to end up like him. I'm sorry for that now, because all my father had ever intended was to give me the best crack at life that I could have possibly gotten off anyone. Which is more than can be said of me. He was a better man than me." He had been feeling sorry for himself. He had been in that drunken state when the truth is the shot and melancholy is the mixer.

"But nothing is that simple, is it, Dad?" I replied, and I had meant it. "There is always much more to a person's life than the circumstances of their arrival, isn't there?"

My comment had seemed to stir something within his ailing body; a glint in his eye that had seemed to say *I've still got my mind*. Because my reply had reminded him of who he was; it reminded him of much weightier conversations that he had had with my half-sister and countless others during the course of his glittering career. I poured him out another glass of Limoncello and he appreciated my gesture.

"I think that it is because we have no say in the circumstances of our arrival that the people who created us become the dominant figures in our lives, Lewis," he said in reply to me. "And therefore, our adult lives – our adult minds – are subjugated by the way we interact with them. What do you think?"

I feigned cautious thought; I do believe that I'd actually cupped my chin between my forefinger and my thumb. "Lots of fabulous people have made a success of their lives despite the circumstances of their arrival."

"Of course, they have," he snarled back at me. "I have, for instance. But you are not getting my point!"

"Which is?"

"That the people who created us, brought us into the world, must – almost by a definition – be omnipresent in our lives. And the smarter ones, like me, can suppress the urge to acknowledge it and get on with their lives … but the less smart …"

"The *stupid people*?"

"… the less smart allow it to dominate their lives! They get hung up on the whys and wherefores of everything. *Why am I here? Why can't I love someone? Why am I cruel? Why do I let someone else do cruel things to me?* Etcetera, etcetera."

"Then surely, I disprove your thesis?"

"Why so, Lewis?"

229

"Because I have never known my mother, I don't know her name, what she looked like, or looks like, or why she abandoned me. I have never had a particularly close relationship with you, not like Jane has had, and yet I have made a real success of my life despite not being particularly smart." Yes, I had been speaking paradoxically, and it had amused my father.

"If that's the case, then you can give me my money back before I die," he sniggered. Then he repeated an earlier jibe: "I *can* read TripAdvisor, Lewis. I suspect that the woman from Chicago can disprove your own, absurd thesis in turn, and we could go on like this for the rest of the evening."

"You mean talking bullshit?"

"Not getting anywhere. Going around in circles. Not getting to the point."

This was it; this was the point when my father had decided that he would like to have a conversation about my mother. This was the moment that I had been waiting for. This had been the purpose of the Limoncello; why I had been prepared to queue for it in the pouring rain when I could have just run home instead and told him that the store didn't stock it. My father had been nearing the end of his life; that much was obvious by the pain he'd been in which by that point had him in a restless state: one minute leaning forwards and the next slouched on his side on the sofa. He hadn't known where to put himself. If he had been a dog, he would have been paddling the length and breadth of the house and I wouldn't have dared to go near him in case he bit me. But my father's mind was still intact. He had been as coherent and sharp as he had ever been, perhaps even more so because of his circumstances. My father had known that he was running out of time. He hadn't had much more time left to say very much at all, so he had been resolved to say only the things that were important. Not necessarily for me, but for himself. And I had known precisely how Bilbo Baggins felt upon discovering that dull, little ring. Curiouser.

I had not said a word as I handed that little, dull photograph back into my father's care. He had been hesitant to accept it at first, probably because he'd known that the conversation could only go in one direction after he had. I imagine that he had felt like Bilbo Baggins too for a second or two: longing to see it and hold it again when he thought that he'd lost it, but slightly afraid of what would happen to him once he did. Once he had accepted it into his trembling hands and looked at the image of that woman who was impressed upon it, the effect on his body had been just as potent as a shot of morphine, and he bolted forwards in a sudden move. He had been temporarily recovered enough not to have felt the pain. It was as though he'd been looking at the Turin Shroud and had been cured. And to continue the religious analogy, he had been just as charged with emotion as a Buddhist monk would be at the moment of his enlightenment, when everything had suddenly made sense and all of the hard work, the sacrifice, had been worthwhile.

But I had not said a word to him during his moment of enlightenment, his deliverance, because despite my longing to know everything that there was to know about that woman, the moment belonged to him. I could tell by the pained expression on his face that it was no longer the tumours that had been causing him the discomfort but those damnable gadflies stinging his mind at that moment. It was his memories that had suddenly caused him to be uncomfortable, his regrets. Funnily enough, I felt sympathy for him and an overwhelming urge to try to comfort him. I had not quite reached the stage where I'd felt the need to go over to the sideboard and pick up the syringe that Lee had left for me, but you get my point.

"Alice!" he whimpered, whilst looking at the photograph longingly, almost bringing it to his lips so that I thought that he was going to kiss it. "My Alice!"

That moment had been precisely the right moment for me to finally say something because despite his private recollections, despite his memories having been stung back into life by those god-damn gadflies, it was like *hello, I'm here*! "I'm sorry, what did you say?" I said, quite bemusedly. I had been very confused.

"That's your mother's name, Lewis," my father replied, just as confused all of a sudden. "You know it is. Don't you remember that New Year's Day in …."

"Al-ee-che!" I barked back, breaking his momentum. "That was the name that Peter had said to me! Not Alice. Fucking Alice? Who the fuck is Alice?"

"Al-ee-che is the Italian pronunciation of the name Alice!" he replied gently. Ever so gently.

"But Peter the actor was Irish, so how do you work that out?" I was, by that point, quite angry.

And so had he by that point. "Because Peter had been there with me in Italy in 1980-God-knows-when. And he heard how her name was pronounced, that's why. And that was how he had always referred to her … *Aleeche*. Ever the actor, the centre of attention."

I recall that I had grabbed hold of that tattered, battered copy of *Alice in Wonderland* by Lewis Carrol again. It had been sitting on the sofa next to my father. I had brandished it in front of my father's face as though I had been Chairman Moi brandishing his Little Red Book.

"So, what the fuck is this all about, eh? 'Nothing ever has to make sense'!"

My father calmed down sufficiently to have been able to reply. "I had taught her how to speak English by teaching her that book," he said softly. Very softly.

"So, she wasn't English? *Isn't* English because I'm not even sure of the 'tense' that I should use right now, because I don't know whether she's still alive or dead!"

"She was, is … I don't know either … an Italian."

"Hang on a minute, stop talking!" I gasped. "So, I am half Italian?"

"You know you are."

"How do I know I am?" I barked.

"Surely, I've told you that much already?" he whimpered.

The anger had been slowly bubbling up in my stomach. You know that feeling when you know that you have to speak because there's something important that you have got to say, but all you really want to do is scream! "You have never mentioned that woman's name to me at all!" I snarled, furiously. Actually, I could have struck him across his face at that point, and if I had been wearing a glove then that is precisely what I would have done. Unfortunately, this was last year and not the eighteenth century, so I hadn't been wearing a glove. "I tell a lie. You once did. You rang my mobile on my birthday whilst I was at work, and you asked me whether I'd heard from her. But that was the only time apart from that New Year's Day breakfast that you have said anything about her to me."

"Surely not," my father sighed, but his sigh had not belied the truth.

"So, that's her, is it?" I asked after a pause to regain my equanimity, referring to the polaroid photograph that he held in his trembling hand.

"Yes."

"I need a drink."

My father handed me his empty glass. "So do I. Throw the rest of that rubbish out, if there's any left in the bottle. I may as well be drinking lemon squash. There's a bottle of Irish whiskey in the bottom draw of my desk that Peter gave to me on New Year's Eve 1994. It must be well aged by now. He told me that I would know the right time to open it. I think it's time to taste it, don't you?"

Curious. "Give me the key then," I demanded, holding out the flat of my hand.

"It isn't locked. It has never been locked. I don't even think that there is a key, Lewis." I sighed before turning around and walking out of the room. "And in the same draw you will find a leather-bound scrapbook that I bought in Amalfi in 1980 ... oh, I can't remember the year, but you will know it when you see it."

Even though I had been given permission by the tyrant himself, I still walked into his library- come-study as though I suspected that the tyrant might be in there waiting for me, sitting behind his desk stroking his cat and uttering an absurdity like *ah, Lewis, I've been expecting you,* with a movie-villain glint in his eye. I looked at the bookshelves. Freud, Thorndike, et all, of course; dozens of books about Italy; *The Thorn Birds*; medical journals about the human mind, galore; lots and lots of other books too: a gap where *Alice in Wonderland* ought to have been. I had never been behind his desk, which was positioned in front of the window. I had never seen his desk chair before and it turned out that it was a remarkably simple thing that hadn't looked comfortable at all. Maybe that had been the point of it: the seating equivalent of a horse-hair shirt? Because by that point, it had been evident to me that his library-come-study had been his room filled with memories and remorse. It had been where he had stored away the notion, the endless possibilities, the dream, and the design, of his alternative life.

I pulled the bottom draw of the desk open tentatively. Wait, rewind a moment or two. I had actually rummaged through the papers that had been strewn across the surface of the desk first when I had come across his *last will and testament,* but it had not interested me in the least. His portrait had been glowering down at me from above the mantelpiece, and it seemed to say *don't you dare. Not yet!* Knowing what I know now, I should have read it, but anyway, I hadn't, so that is that.

As promised, the bottom draw of his old captain's desk had not been locked. There, sure enough, was a bottle of Irish whiskey. Underneath it, as promised, was a leather-bound A4 sized scrapbook. Class always shows, and I had been assured of its Amalfi provenance by the leather straps that were wound around it and tied in a loose knot to keep it closed. Once I loosened that knot and opened the book, it had become apparent straight away that this was, indeed, a memento of his alternative life. The first page contained a photograph – a really good, black-and-white photograph that must have been taken by a professional – of my younger father and my younger mother embracing one another. One or the other must have said something hilarious because they were both laughing. Not a posed smile that people normally offer a camera, but both of them were almost on the edge of delirium with amusement. Someone had obviously said something gut-wrenchingly funny. In black-and-white, it had been obvious to me that my mother had been an Italian. There is no other way that I can describe her: the most beautiful Italian siren that you've ever seen in your life.

I recall that I had cried at that moment. As aforementioned, I cry quite a lot.

Chapter Sixteen

"Have you ever really loved a woman, Lewis?" is what my father asked me once I'd delivered a large measure of Irish whiskey into one of his hands, and the scrapbook into the other. "A woman who was not your mother?"

His question had seemed to me at the time to have been precisely the right thing to have said in the circumstances. But when I settled on the sofa adjacent to his and sipped my own glass of Irish whiskey, it had quickly become apparent that he had not been speaking hypothetically: he required a genuine answer. He had been waiting for my answer. He had been eager to know and looked at me with that expression on his face that I had recognised from all of those other chess games wherein I had been roundly defeated. I recall that I had gulped back my whiskey and so had he and then I refreshed both of our glasses and whilst reaching over to his side, I said, "Yes," casually, because it had been obvious to him that I had, so there would be no point in denying it.

"Who was she? It was not Fiona, I imagine?" he countered with.

"No, it wasn't her."

"Then who was she?"

"I saw Fiona again, by the way, in the supermarket." I thought that I'd made a move that had moved me out of check. "She sends her regards and wanted me to let you know that she's thinking about you."

My comment seemed to make him happy. "She often asked your half-sister what she was doing wrong, why she wasn't enough for you, why you'd always seemed to have been thinking off message," he scoffed.

237

"And your half-sister always assumed that it was because of your mother. That you had *mother* issues to contend with before you could possibly love another woman. I don't blame her for falling for that old chestnut because that was her training. That kind of reasoning had made her name, after all. But I'd always suspected that it wasn't as straightforward as that. I'd always suspected that there had been someone else, and so had your stepmother, because she had seen the look in your eyes so many times before in mine. So, I ask again, who was she, Lewis?"

Gulp, top-up, gulp. "Top up, you old goat?" I asked, but it had been a hypothetical question because I had already topped up his glass without waiting for his answer.

"Go easy with that," he objected without really objecting. "It won't have been cheap, if I know Peter." Gulp. "Who was she?" he repeated. He was not going to be put off finding out, I knew.

"She was the person who pulled me up off my knees," I replied.

My father sighed. "Of course, she was. Why am I not surprised? What, if I need to ask, were you doing on your knees in the first place? Too much wine the night before, I shouldn't wonder."

I corrected him immediately. "My stepmother died, and I hadn't given myself time to grieve. I hadn't thought that I needed to grieve for her or whether I was even supposed to. And then you had rung me on my mobile to ask whether I'd heard from my actual mother, which seemed to be an absurd question to ask me, because, of course, I hadn't. Then, all of a sudden, everything had just gotten too much for me to bear so I had collapsed onto my knees."

"So you were actually on your knees, and she'd had to pull you up? You're not speaking metaphorically, then?"

"Actually on my knees."

"Because I had rung your mobile?" He had been incredulous. Incredulity, where I was concerned, had always come easily to him.

"Because of everything. Because my stepmother had died, because you'd asked me about my mother, because I wasn't in love with Fiona but knew that everyone else was. Everything."

He held out his empty glass for a refill; I duly obliged. "So, she pulled you up from off your knees, you'd looked into her eyes and that was that … you fell in love with this mystery woman?"

"There was more to it than that."

"What's her name?"

"Cristiana." Gulp

"Really?" Gulp.

"She's Italian, alright?"

"Of course, she is," he chortled. "Like you." Then he had not been able to suppress his high-spiritedness any longer and laughed out loud, much to my annoyance. Calming down, he added: "I'm sorry, I shouldn't laugh." Then he laughed again. "I can understand that with your stepmother dying, and me enquiring about your *actual* mother, and poor Fiona thinking that if she didn't mother you, then you'd be off, why you would find yourself on your knees." He had been trying very hard to suppress his joy by this point. "Talk about mother issues: you had them coming at you from all angles, didn't you?" You know that sensation when you have to purse your lips and breathe through your nose just to try to stop yourself from doubling over with laughter? Well, that was my father by

239

that point. "You'd been *mothered* to the point of no return!" With that final assertion, he actually doubled over with laughter. No mean feat for a man at death's door.

"You're analysing me!" I objected.

"I am not, how dare you? You can't afford me!" he retorted, sniffling.

"You are. You're analysing me!"

"Don't be absurd, Lewis," calming down.

"I hope you weren't like this with your patients?"

"Of course, I wasn't." Whimpering, his laughter petering out. "Would I be the man I am today if I'd been like this with my actual, paying clients?"

"So that's the difference, is it, money?"

"Circumstances are the difference," he retorted, breathing deeply in an attempt to calm himself down. "Do you know how your Uncle Peter and I first met?" I shook my head bemusedly. "I had been very junior in that practise, so they'd passed it to me, but Peter the budding actor had sought counselling because ..." He had then broken off because he'd had to suppress a laugh again, "... because when he'd been a child, he had witnessed his mother being head-butted by a goat!" Then, as though all of the pain had been ejected from his body, he collapsed back into his sofa, laughing so hard that I had been worried that he was going to die laughing. Calming down yet again, he whimpered, "I'd had to leave the room to consult with my superior colleagues, then we'd assured him that it was allegorical for his desire to perform since most children would have found it hilarious. And we charged him a thousand pounds for the service. Bearing in mind that this was in 1981 and the price of a house was only eighteen thousand. What an idiot. The world is full of stupid people. But I felt sorry for him. No, I had felt guilty at the cost, so I offered to buy him dinner. A little place in Soho where we'd hit off, him and me, and from where we have never looked back. I recall that I had the duck-a-la-orange, and he had the scampi in a basket. This was, after all, 1981."

This was a side to my father that I had never encountered before. I recall that I checked the label on that bottle of Irish whiskey to ascertain the percentage by volume because it seemed to me that it was a miraculous spirit that seemed to alter a man's personality. It seemed to have been more magic potion than alcoholic spirit. Limoncello be damned!

"Cristiana was a waitress at the Sun Inn, Hurley. She started after I had so I was given the task of buddying up with her to show her the ropes. I liked her straight away. She hadn't been able to speak English so well … in fact, that's why she was in the country in the first place, to learn English. If she had been English, then she wouldn't have worked a job as a waitress, she would have been running the restaurant, if you know what I mean?" My father had been sipping his whiskey at last and listening attentively as though I was reading him a story whilst kneeling next to his bed. "She was, is, intelligent, empathetic, astoundingly beautiful, and she didn't suffer fools in any language, but that establishment was full of them. Particularly Luigi, whom she considered an utterly incompetent clown."

"Who is Luigi?" my father interrupted.

"*Luigi*! My Luigi, my friend, I've told you about him."

"Ah, the guy on that TripAdvisor review?"

"That's him."

"Well, his reputation as a waiter has gone international, Lewis, because he's as well known in Chicago as he is in Italy."

"Yes, but he's always been very good to me, Dad," I replied. I hadn't known who I was really defending, that little Mussolini doppelganger or myself. "But he was, is, a terrible waiter," I had to conclude. I didn't mention Pavarotti or the whole Prince Charles, Lady Di thing because it would have just sounded ridiculous. It would have been no defence of that man at all.

"This Cristiana had got the measure of him from the moment she'd met him, then?"

"She can't suffer fools as easily as I can."

"I like her already," he scoffed. "I presume that once she'd grasped the English language, she bolted the hell out of there?"

"After we'd had an affair that to me had lasted an eternity but in reality, it had only lasted a matter of weeks."

Gulp. "If she's as intelligent as you make her out to be, then she wouldn't have had a love affair with you unless she loved you, would she? And yet, where is she now? Why didn't you marry her? And please don't blame Fiona because people leave one another all the time if the circumstances demand it. If I know you, Lewis, you won't do anything that you don't want to do. If you try to disagree with me, I'll bring into the conversation the subject of your A-levels."

I recall that I'd drank a little too much Irish whiskey by that point and had started to cry. "She probably looked at me and had seen the biggest fool of them all." I put my feet up onto my sofa and wept a little.

My father leant forwards on his. "I think that she'd known that she couldn't build her life around a man who can't stand still. Because you can't, Lewis. You are perpetually rotating on the spot so that you are forever missing the view that's directly in front of you. One minute it's there, the next, it's gone."

I had taken exception to his statement and brought myself forwards on my sofa, my feet firmly on the ground again. "You *are* analysing me! What am I? One last client before you die?"

Gulp. "You are my son, Lewis," he barked. "And there isn't a psychoanalyst in the world who would dare analyse his own son. Because if you are not necessarily a true facsimile of me, then you are most definitely a consequence of who I am, how I have lived. Who in the hell would want to analyse themselves? Not even Freud would dare. There isn't enough money in the world."

We had both of us snivelled for a little while. "Where is she now, this Cristiana? Because pardon me for prying, but I'd begun this conversation by asking you if you've ever really loved a woman who was not your mother, then all of a sudden, we're talking about someone whom I've never heard mentioned before. Which is fine, since I asked the question, it was your prerogative to answer it. And you did. What was meant to have been the opening gambit of my explanation to you about your actual mother has turned into something else. Which is fine by me. A man has to have his eyes fixed firmly on the road, but a little detour every now and again has never done a man any harm."

"She left me. I'd opened her cage, and away she flew."

My father laughed again. "I think you're drunk, Lewis."

"So are you," I replied bitterly.

243

My father picked up that polaroid photograph of my mother and studied it as though it were a paper about to be submitted to the Lancet magazine. "Who is this?" he asked me, showing me the face side of the photograph.

"It's my mother," I sobbed.

He looked at it again. "Yes, it is. I can't deny it. But at the time this photograph was taken, she wasn't, she was *my* Cristiana! And you are just like her. Not only in looks – every time I look at you all I can see is her – but in your ways too, behaviour, mannerisms, traits, whatever you want to call them. Because she could never stand still for long enough to see the road ahead either. She was always rotating on the spot, thinking of other things that were not directly in front of her." Gulp. "So, I like this Cristiana woman, whoever she is. I will never meet her now, obviously, but if you ever do again, then please tell her that I thought the world of her, because I know precisely how she felt!" Gulp, again. "We shouldn't play chess, you and I, Lewis. We should play fucking dominoes!"

Chapter Seventeen

Ding Dong, the phone rang. My father rolled his eyes because he'd known who was on the other end of the line. But I panicked just like I panicked when I had been sitting on that bench in front of Windsor Castle when I'd had too much to drink. "That'll be your sister," my father sighed.

"My half-sister, you mean?" Clever.

"Whichever!" he barked across the aperture between our respective sofas. "Answer it, Lewis. Put the poor girl out of her misery."

"What will I tell her?"

"Tell her that her *pappa* is pissed!"

"I can't tell her that," I protested vehemently. "You know how much she worries about you!"

My father sighed resignedly. "Give me the phone, Lewis, I'll answer it myself." And he did, *"Hello, Martin Sinclaire speaking. Ah, Jane, my darling girl, how are you all bearing up over there? Me? I'm absolutely fine, Jane. Do I? Well, I don't know how because I haven't touched a drop. Yes, I've had my meal. Oh, something with potatoes, I don't really know what it was, but I ate it, nonetheless. Lewis? Yes, he's here somewhere, you know what he's like for wandering. Looking after me? Well, he's doing his best in the circumstances."* With that remark my father winked at me, and I shook my head in frustration. *"I think he's drunk again, Jane. He found a bottle of Irish whiskey in my desk draw, and he's guzzled the lot! I know, a disgrace indeed. I couldn't agree more. I wish that you were here, darling."* Wink. *"No, I'm absolutely fine, you won't get a flight anyway. No, I won't go anywhere, I promise, I'm not going to die anytime soon."* But then he looked sad all of a sudden, sober.

"Anyway, what have you all been doing? Oh, it's lovely there. I wish I was there to see it too. Yes, one day I will be there again. How are Michael and the boys? I bet they are. Because we all need time to discover ourselves, Jane, don't we? You know that more than anybody. Just enjoy yourselves, darling, whilst you all have the chance to. I'm doing just fine precisely where I am. Lewis ... oh, Lewis ... will be fine in the morning. I suppose that I'll be doing our breakfast. I know, you've hit the nail bang on the head. He is a disgrace." Wink with the added measure of an affectionate smile. *"You go then, darling, and see what they're up to. I'll see you all very soon. Much love to Michael and the boys, Jane. Choo-choo!"*

"I know that I won't see her or my grandsons again," my father lamented whilst sitting on his sofa clutching his side because there is only so much that alcohol can do. "But I couldn't tell her that. Or was I wrong to give her false hope? Was I wrong to have released her from the burden of worrying about me? Is the truth always necessary? Is the truth always what we long to hear?"

My father had been beside himself, looking on to see what happens next. He had been in so much pain that he had flopped onto his side, filling the entire surface of his sofa.

"What do you need?" I asked, beginning to panic again. I had been worried that he'd drunk too much, and the alcohol had begun to interfere or react against his prescribed medication. I had cursed myself for not having thought about the consequences before that point. Then he seemed to have recovered a little as though the pain came in waves, and one had washed over him, and in between them, he could breathe and talk and recover a little in time for the next one. All he could do was wonder how bad the next one was going to be, and it seemed that with each wave of pain that washed over him, he'd disappeared just that bit more, as though the wave was corrosive and each time a layer of him was washed away. I asked him if he wanted me to phone Lee the nurse.

"No, please don't," my father pleaded. "He'll only ask me that ridiculous football team comparison about the league."

"I don't think it's a bad analogy, to be fair to him. It gives him a scale to work with as opposed to having to work it out for himself just by looking at you. I think it's quite clever, actually."

"But how can I know where I am in the league when I don't know how bad the pain is going to get? I may think that I'm at the top of the league but as far as this cancer is concerned, I have barely kicked a ball. I can't know how bad the pain is now compared to what it will be."

I thought about the syringe that I had hidden in the draw of the sideboard. Was this the time to administer that particular medication? Perhaps it wasn't the pain that it was intended for but the fear in the old goat's mind? Lee should have told me if that was the purpose of it: to gauge his state of mind rather than his level of pain, and I would have. But all of a sudden, he was sitting upright again, and he was talking comprehensibly; his eyes hadn't looked startled. He hadn't looked frightened, even though, thinking back, he must have been.

He then proceeded to explain that it hadn't been the pain that had been the worse part but the sadness, the loss of opportunity. "Not knowing how life will affect my grandsons," he added. "What kind of men they will become." As he talked, he rubbed his mouth and I had noticed that his hands were trembling so much that they were barely any use at all. "Knowing that I shall never see my daughter again."

"You may, yet." I lied because by then I'd decided that the truth was an unwelcome guest in that house. "Things *have* to start getting better soon and then the flights will resume, that's all she's waiting for."

"I won't," he replied resolutely, pursing his lips and glaring at me with his wide eyes. That's when I realised that Fiona had been right: the end wasn't far off. "That's the saddest thing about this whole situation really. I had known that I would never see her again when I'd seen her off that morning, but I'd had to put on a brave face. Have you ever said goodbye to someone with the innocence of an affectionate parting whilst knowing that you will never see that person again?"

"Yes," I answered straight away. "I know how you must have felt."

My father then took hold of his leather-bound scrapbook, untied the loose knot and opened it. He had seen that black and white photograph on the first page again and gasped with astonishment, or sadness, or regret. Hard to know. Maybe he gasped at the sheer brilliance of the photographer because it is a very good photograph. I recall that I had instinctively stepped across the aperture between our respective sofas to sit next to him on his. He had not asked me to and seemed a little perturbed by my impertinence at first before resigning himself to the inevitability of it. When there are two people in a room, then a scrapbook or a photograph album cannot, it must not, be viewed alone.

"What was so funny?" I asked, looking at that photograph again.

"Oh, I can't remember, Lewis. Peter was one of life's natural wits so it may have been anything."

"Peter took the photograph. Peter was there?"

"Peter was everywhere!"

When he turned the page, the next photograph had obviously been taken on the same day because my mother was wearing the same dress. In this one, she was standing on her own with her hand propping up an olive tree, obviously striking a pose for the camera because she had been told to for comic effect. My father gasped in astonishment again. Not sadness or regret, I was sure, but pure astonishment at the sheer, natural Italian beauty of that woman. I think that I gasped too, not through the astonishment of her beauty but the incredulity of my father letting her leave him in the first place. Don't get me wrong, my stepmother was a beautiful woman too, but her beauty was not in her appearance but in her goodness, in her soul, the way she had been able to just naturally take care of all of us at the same time. I was sure that the woman in that photograph would be incapable of matching the feats that my stepmother had managed to achieve, but even so: why would any man let a woman like her leave him? What on earth had gone on out there?

The next page contained a colour photograph of the villa itself, which it seems to me is the true protagonist in this story. Just like Southfork in Dallas was the reason that they'd all fallen out in the first place. No, the villa had been the backdrop, the scenery on the stage at Covent Garden or La Scala or wherever, which is a much better comparison than that tired, old American soap opera theme and one that my father would have appreciated more, I'm sure. I'd only caught a glimpse of the fourth photograph because my father closed the scrapbook very quickly, but I have lately discovered that it is a photograph, in full colour, of my mother holding a three-year-old me in her arms. Perhaps on the very day she abandoned me, but more of that later.

"What good are my memories?" he snarled whilst slamming that scrapbook of his closed. "Memories can't take the pain away. Memories are not a solution to anything, and they never will be. Memories equal regret, and what good can ever come from that?"

I had taken exception to his proclamation. I felt aggrieved that he had closed that scrapbook prematurely. "Consequences equal memories," I snivelled. "Memories equal answers … resolution. For me at least."

Once my father mellowed, or perhaps once another wave of pain had washed over him to claim yet another layer, he looked at me in a way that I had never known before. Longingly, with not a hint of the despondency that I had hitherto been accustomed to. In that moment, I realised that my father did love me after all. His trembling hand brushed the side of my face. He barely had the strength to lift his arm, so I had appreciated the gesture all the more. "You are my saving grace, Lewis," he whispered. "You are the silver lining. You are the consequence of this cancer that's eating me up from the inside. You are the antidote to the pain, to this whole pandemic even. Because without either my cancer or this pandemic, you wouldn't be sitting next to me. Consequences, what a fabulous word. I wish that I'd taught your mother the definition of that word instead of the words *curious* and *nonsense*. If you want an explanation, a resolution, then are you sitting comfortably, Lewis, because here it comes …!"

Gulp.

Chapter Eighteen

If there was ever a nagging doubt in my mind that I was my father's son, then it was allayed when he'd gone off on a tangent even wider than any of mine. I had actually done as he suggested; I made myself comfortable on my sofa, brought a cushion over my knees and perched my half-filled whiskey glass on top of it, and waited for him to tell me everything. My body had been pumped with adrenaline all of a sudden, which had the effect of making me tremble, which I knew was not the effect of the whiskey. My stomach seemed to be filled with boiling water. I had to breathe deeply since the anticipation of discovering who my mother was and why she abandoned me all those years ago had almost overwhelmed me. If my father's agony had come in waves of pain, then mine had come in waves of expectation, and only he had the cure, the syringe that would allay me.

But he had begun by giving me an in-depth exploration and explanation of his long-standing friendship with Peter O'Shea, the actor. It seemed to me to have been a very strange place to start. I appreciate that every story should start at the beginning – except for mine, of course – but my father had seemed to have gone right back to the Big Bang. It hadn't made any sense. I had already known that his friendship with Peter the actor had been a close one, almost brotherly to the extent that as children, my half-sister and I had called him *uncle*, so why he felt the need to explain it and evaluate it had simply seemed a little bit bizarre. Perhaps it was the effects of his medication mixed with a strong Irish liquor that had sent him on a tangent. Or maybe it was because of his penchant for regression therapy that had prompted him to begin before the beginning; that same technique that had discovered that our Uncle Peter's anxiety had been triggered as a child when he witnessed his mother being head-butted by a goat.

Anyhow, my father had lamented his ability to make friends easily. Acquaintances, apparently, he'd had many of those. But friends, real friends, were what he had always struggled to find, or when he'd thought that he had, he hadn't possessed the skills to make the friendship endure. But during that dinner in Soho in 1981, my father and an anxious Irish actor called Peter had just hit it off, and unlike the scampi in a basket, that particular friendship *had* endured to stand the test of time. When he then broke off from his sequence to ask me whether I had ever encountered a friendship such as that myself, I thought about Luigi immediately and answered that I had. Thankfully, he hadn't asked me who with, so I hadn't had to explain. It would have sounded ridiculous to his sensibilities since my relationship with Luigi *is* ridiculous and really oughtn't to work. So I had understood why Peter was so important to him. I listened obligingly because I had appreciated what *real*, brotherly friendship means to an only child such as my father. Me too, almost. I hadn't been an only child. I had been a *half*-child.

But then it all made sense. My father had merely been setting the scene. What a marvellous raconteur he turned out to be. Almost Ustinovian in range and depth. If he had ever appeared on the Parkinson chat-show, then he would undoubtedly have been invited back on.

"Later that year (1981), Peter and I decided to take a trip abroad. I had never been abroad before. Poor Peter had been struggling to make a name for himself on the English stage. He'd had some bit parts here and there, but hardly King Lear or Hamlet, and he'd been feeling very sorry for himself. His anxiety was off the scale. But I had just obtained a big promotion within my Harley Street Clinic, and in addition, I had inherited my parents' estate following their deaths, so I had been feeling quite cock-a-hoop, if you know what I mean?" He chortled, almost choking on his memories.

"And you went to Italy?"

"Yes, funnily enough, we did," my father snorted. "How ever did you guess? Peter had needed to get away from London to lick his wounds and regroup, but I needed to find adventure. And what an adventure I found. I can't really remember why we'd found ourselves in a little town on the Adriatic Sea called Sant'Elpidio a Mare, but we had." He strained his mind to the extent of its ability when I had thought that another wave of pain was about to wash over him at precisely the wrong time, but it turned out that it was only those damnable gadflies. "Yes, I can ..." he announced happily. "I recall that Manchester United or Liverpool were playing one of the big Italian teams in a football game so the only flight I could get for us both was to Perugia." He laughed again. His memories were bringing him joy and I had been glad to see it. "When we'd got off the plane and had got through check-in, we hopped on a bus that we'd thought would take us into Perugia itself."

"But it didn't, I'm guessing?" I remarked. "It took you to the coast?"

"Yes, that's all it was, Lewis. The wrong bus," talk about the ripple effects of history, "that terminated in Porto Sant'Elpidio. But the sight of the sea was quite something, much better than the hills of Perugia, so we decided to stick around for a while to see what that little town had to offer. It turned out that what it had to offer

253

was even more spectacular than the shimmering sea." At that point, he would have touched Michael Parkinson's knee. It's worth mentioning at this point that the name *Perugia* had resonated with me much more than the name of that little town where my father's villa was located. Much more.

"Peter and I had wandered around the place for most of the afternoon looking for a place to stay when suddenly we had found ourselves on the edge of the town. Finding oneself on the edge of that particular town is a very easy thing to do because it isn't a big place. A little bit down a very narrow lane lined with Cyprus trees, we stumbled across the opening to an incredibly decrepit bed and breakfast called *Mamma Gloria*. Gloria, by the way, is the Italian translation of *glory*, and that is precisely what we found there. I don't think that I need to elaborate on the fact that Mamma Gloria was your grandmother, Lewis, do I? Because we haven't got the time."

Gulp. "So, my maternal grandmother was called Gloria who owned the B&B?" Astonished.

"Of course, she was, it's all perfectly straightforward, Lewis, if you keep up. This isn't *Alice in Wonderland*. Everything will make sense, but if you drink much more of that whiskey, then in the morning, you won't remember any of it, and I'm sorry to have to inform you that I won't be around for much longer to explain it again, nor will I have the inclination to. So pull yourself together and buckle up for the ride, son.

"Mamma Gloria was the epitome of what you would expect from an Italian proprietor. She was hefty, straightforward, spoke with her hands ... she was a stereotype. As for her cooking, oh my God, her cooking. Most of all, she had been grateful that a young

254

Englishman and a young Irishman had somehow found their way onto her land, because we had been her first paying guests of the season, so she had pulled out all of the stops. You see, there aren't that many people who visit Sant'Elpidio. He just hasn't got the pull of say, Saint Peter or Saint Francis."

He then opened his leather-bound scrapbook again and flicked through the pages until he found what he was looking for, then turned it around to show me a very small, barely coloured photograph of a middle-aged woman who was smiling through her embarrassment of having to endure the agony of having her photograph taken. "That's her," my father chuckled. "That's your grandmother, Lewis. Do you see what I mean?"

I had seen what he meant. She did look like the epitome of an Italian mother. The sight of her had been enough to make me weep openly, which had nothing whatsoever to do with the effects of the Irish whiskey, I promise.

"The very first time that I saw your mother was when Peter had nudged my arm to break me off from my breakfast and said, 'Would you look at her'. So I did, and I have never stopped looking at her since. Now, I don't believe in love at first sight, do you? When you'd first met this Cristiana, did you fall in love with her in that instant, no. I've had many conversations about this over the years with one client or another, and I don't believe that *it* exists. Even though from time to time I have had to conclude that *it* does, just to get them out of the room, but *it* doesn't. Something does, at that first meeting, but it most definitely cannot be called love. *It* is something else. Perhaps, rather than *it* being called love, *it* is fate, or destiny, or some such nonsense. *It* is serendipity. Now there's a word that defies a definition if you want one."

255

Serendipity (noun): having your breakfast plate cleared away by the most beautiful woman in the world.

There you go, for added measure.

"There is always a trigger to *it*," my father continued. "For you, it was when this Cristiana woman pulled you up from off your knees because I had rung you on your mobile phone, I have no doubt about it. Am I wrong?" He wasn't. "For me, it was when, unexpectedly, your grandmother died on day five of our stay."

"She died?" Incredulously.

"Quite suddenly and quite unexpectedly. Her heart gave out, apparently, according to the paramedics but I am in no doubt whatsoever that she'd decided to die once she had encountered me and your Uncle Peter because she had known that one or the other would take good care of her children."

"Children?" Gasping and gulping.

"Her daughter, whom she'd described in the preceding four days prior to her death as *flighty ... thinks too much, can't stand still, doesn't want to be here,* probably to put us both off the scent... and her son, whom she had described as *my simple boy.*"

"Don't you dare, Dad!" I gasped, rasping for breath, because I'd known what was coming. So I had pre-empted the inevitable. "Ennio was my uncle?" Beside myself.

"Ennio?" my father retorted snappily. "Who the hell is Ennio? Enzo was your uncle, yes. And surely, I don't have to show you a photograph of him? Surely you remember him, Lewis?"

It had been too much for me to understand all at once. As I recall, I had sped out of the room. "Well, you did ask," my father called out to me as I made my escape.

I had found myself in the kitchen because I would not have dared to go into his study-come-library again without permission. Strangely, I had made us both a cup of tea because when a man knows that he's had too much alcohol, that's all he needs. My father had summonsed the energy to follow me into that fated room. When reality strikes, it strikes, and I had to help him sit down on a chair next to the table and he almost flopped over it through weakness and fatigue because the stroll from the living room to the kitchen had taken its toll on him. Yes, that's right, we had both found ourselves drinking tea at the kitchen table in the big house at Henley.

Happily, we had given ourselves a pause, an impasse of sorts, whilst we had sipped our tea. That moment had been the opposite to that moment in 1995 when my stepmother had been turned into a leopardess. That is to say, it had been calm and quiet with not a hint of menace in the air. My father broke the pause by asking, "Do you know who Victor Kiam is, Lewis?" randomly.

"My fucking grandfather, I shouldn't wonder," I replied groggily.

Laughing, my father replied, "No, as far as I know, Victor Kiam is not your grandfather. He was an American entrepreneur who used to appear on TV commercials in the eighties. He was a spokesman for shaving products, as I recall. His catchphrase was 'I liked the product so much that I bought the company'."

"What about Victor Kiam?"

"Well, that was me, back then. I had liked that villa so much, it had given me something, but I cannot explain what it was."

"My mother?"

"Probably. Anyway, I had liked it so much that I bought it!"

"Just like that?"

"No, of course not *just like that*. Nothing is ever just like that. But when your grandmother died, it was to me whom your mother came to for solace, not Peter. Because she'd probably sensed that I would make everything alright, and I did, I could, for a while."

I thought about the entire scene for a moment or two. "Are you sure it wasn't Peter?" I asked him. "Because I don't look like you." Curious.

"Peter was gay, Lewis!" my father replied, snappily, frustratedly, because I had broken the thread of his commentary. "Peter was in love with me! And since, at the time, no-one else was, I had milked that goat for all its worth. Being gay in Ireland in the seventies and eighties was not necessarily the right thing to be, and not in London then either to a lesser extent. Peter's anxieties hadn't come from his experience as a child when he'd witnessed his mother being head-butted by a goat … they had all arisen from his sudden realisation that he was different, that he was about to disappoint everybody, not least his mother. Clever, aren't I?"

I recall that I hung my head. I really wished that I hadn't asked. I wish that I had just discovered that scrapbook in the bottom draw of his desk whilst clearing out the house after he had died and come up with my own conclusion. "Peter was even cleverer. When he'd seen what was happening, he told me that I could never hope to contain that woman. As Gloria had warned me, she was just too flighty, like a horse that refrains from taking the bit because it knows that once it has taken it in its mouth, it will never run free again. But for a while I did contain her. For a while we had been happy together. For a year at least, we had been happy together. My gilded year. I had secured the lease on her family villa with the money that I had inherited from my father, and as far as she had been concerned, her beloved brother, Ennio, had been saved." He snapped his head. "Ennio! Who the hell is Ennio? You've got me at it now, Lewis. ENZO! Her beloved brother, Enzo, was safe, not damn Ennio, whoever he is! I don't care what the hell happened to Ennio, whoever he is!"

All those names were swirling around in my head like a tempest containing all the information that I had ever required. My grandmother, Gloria, my Uncle Enzo, my mother, Alice or A-lee-che. I had seen what they looked like in old photographs that had been concealed in the bottom draw of my father's desk for as long as I had lived in that house; never locked, it had never needed to be. I had been given what I had been longing for all my life, yet those faces and names had left me cold.

After the initial shock of discovering them, I felt nothing towards them after that, which had disappointed me. It seemed that for me the thrill was all in the chase and not in the reveal, but maybe that was because they were all dead. My grandmother and my uncle, certainly, but I had still been a little unsure about the fate of my mother at that point, but I had been sitting at my stepmother's table in her kitchen, so she was as good as dead whether or not she actually was. Maybe I had merely been stunned, like a pigeon after a long flight from the continent suddenly flying into a window: bang, there it was to thwart it and bring an abrupt and painful end to its journey. The more I think about it, the more convinced I am that's what it was, shock because latterly I have taken to thinking about them all quite a lot with a degree of fondness and familiarity.

My father had sufficient energy left in his ailing body to continue. I hadn't goaded him for any more information, but he had been eager and anxious to say some more. It had been as though he had needed to get the rest off his mind before he died, so I listened attentively. It was by then very late in the evening; the game of chess was a distant memory to join with all the others. The rain, I recall, had not ceased and was battering the French doors that led out onto the garden. A portent hint of what was to come out of my father's memory bank next.

He sipped at his tea. The tea had seemed to pacify the pain. I could not recall ever having seen him drink a cup of tea before then. It was all of that strong Italian coffee nonsense for him. The tea had seemed to have done him some good. He should have drunk more tea if you ask me, then none of this may never have needed to happen.

"Peter left Sant'Elpidio in the August," he mused. "He said he had an audition to attend in London, quite a big part in a Hollywood movie about some Roman emperor or other. I hadn't believed him at first. I thought that it was just an excuse to get out of there since he had already affirmed that the one part that he did not want to play was gooseberry between myself and your mother. But anyway, he must have been telling the truth because he'd gotten the part and the movie was quite successful, and he was on his way to becoming the star that he was to become. Good for him.

"But I was glad when he'd gone because I wasn't due back in London until the end of the October, so your mother and I had spent two months alone at the villa in the sunshine. Two months during which we had got to

260

know one another very well. Two months during which she had enraptured me … given me everything that I had ever desired. She taught me how to be somebody else, somebody that I had never thought that I could be." He leant back in his kitchen chair and sighed so deeply that I'd actually leant forward in mine to ascertain whether he was ever going to breathe in again. But he did. "Those two months were the most perfect, uncomplicated time of my life. Halcyon days of never-ending joy and promises. There I was in Italy at a villa that I now owned in love with the most beautiful woman that I had ever seen. A woman whose gratitude to me knew no bounds, because I had saved her ancestral home and had kept a roof over their heads." Sigh. "Oh, the trees, the sea, the sky. It was as though I was seeing the whole world in its glory for the first time. Does that make sense?" I nodded. I had known precisely what he meant. "It's important for me to tell you, Lewis, that for quite some time your mother and I had been happy."

"So, what happened? What went wrong?"

"I learned that everything that glitters is not gold!" he replied, mordantly. "That's not good enough. That was a terrible metaphor, and I've always deplored uttering such nonsense. What I mean to say is, life … real life … isn't a bed of roses!" He then actually thumped his thigh with his fist using what little energy and strength that his body had left in it, such was the extent of his frustration at being unable to find the correct words to describe the emotion that had been waiting in his mind for its chance to shine for who knows how long?

"It doesn't matter. I know what you mean. Go on."

"When I told your mother that I would have to return to London by the third week of that October, and even though I had assured her that I would return at

Christmas, she demanded that I take her with me. Since I had already begun to surmise what would become of me if I did not return to London at all, it had seemed to have been the perfect solution. But I knew what was waiting for me once I'd returned to London. I knew the calibre of the people who were waiting for me to return. The path had been laid down at my feet before I had gone to Italy, a straight path to success. Do you understand?" I nodded.

"Your mother couldn't speak very good English, but I was sure that I wanted her with me at one function or another once we'd arrived in London. I had wanted to introduce her to the world beyond Sant'Elpidio. I had wanted to teach her that life does exist elsewhere, and she was longing for *life* to happen to her, I knew. She would be a tentative, conscientious pupil. She had suddenly become that important to me. Suddenly, I could not comprehend any aspect of my life without her. I was on the threshold of something big, something remarkable, once I returned, but all of a sudden, I'd known that I couldn't do any of it unless she was by my side. Does that make sense?" I nodded again. "So I bought that book." Then he became restless. "Where is it? I can't see it," searching the tabletop with his hands as though he was blind all of a sudden.

"It's in the other room, Dad. It's safe." Reassuringly.

He calmed down. "I bought that book in a little shop close to the port whilst I ought to have been buying fish for our supper. Partly because it had her name in the title, but mainly because it was short and manageable, unlike Thorndike or Tolstoy or Austen, Dickens, Shakespeare!" He thought deeply and at length. "What would have been the point of teaching her Shakespeare? How could she have learned English words from him?"

262

A little bit deeper than the Thorn Birds, but anyway… "But it doesn't make any sense, Dad."

"It has her name in the title!" he snarled, firmly. "So that was a start."

He became fidgety again, concerned that he had found himself in the wrong room, my stepmother's room, where there were no books. Or there were books, recipe books, but nothing by Thorndike or Freud or Sinclair or Carrol or McCullough. But really the kitchen chair had been too uncomfortable for his skeletal body to bear, so I'd helped him out of that room and steered him towards the living room where the two books that were important to him were waiting on the sofa where he'd left them. The soft, cushioned fabric had welcomed him back once he collapsed into his sofa. The sofa welcomed him back and had moulded itself around his emaciated body, and he found a measure of comfort. I had resumed my perched position on my own sofa as though we had been about to reset the chessboard. It would be a chess game wherein *checkmate* was no longer an option. He picked up his scrapbook and opened it on a page that contained just a simple photograph of my mother that he studied assiduously as though he was doing his homework and had to memorise the verse.

"Did she learn English easily?" I asked him.

"Very. They say that it's a very difficult language to learn, but she had learned it quickly because she had read that book that I'd given her over and over, so that by the beginning of the October, I felt confident that she would represent me very well once we had returned to London."

"And did she?"

"Your mother is a very intelligent woman, Lewis."

"Is?"

"Was … I don't know. All I know is that together we'd knocked their socks off. Now, there's a metaphor that I'm happy to release from my mouth. Together, we wowed them all. Me and her. Her and me. I'd had someone by my side, that is to say, associated with me, whom they'd all agreed was a genius."

"They? Who were they?"

"My new employers. The partners in the practise that I had joined and their wives! All of them."

"Did she ever step foot inside this house? Did you and she buy this house together?" Longingly.

Looking around my father answered, "No, I bought this house with your stepmother when she was pregnant with your sister. Your mother never stepped foot inside this house."

"Half-sister, you mean?"

"Shut up, Lewis. We haven't got the time!"

Then, he'd gone off on one of his tangents again, which infuriated me. "What is love, Lewis? What do you think? I think that it has got nothing whatsoever to do with sex. Love is most definitely not a physical reaction to something else of the same species. It is much deeper than that. I think, whilst considering sex, we have to strip ourselves right back to the animal that we are. Consider a lioness. She will make her scent known to all but will only breed with the strongest of her species, the king of the pride. In the full and safe knowledge that her offspring will be the best that she can produce. But is that love? No. It is survival. Her genes will survive. She and the lion will live forever. And once her cubs are born, then her only instinct is to ensure that they survive, and even if their father should threaten them, she will protect them with

264

every instinct that she has left to the last tooth. But is that love? No. It is something else.

"So I have to conclude this, Lewis, by saying that love is a particularly human trait. And better people than me, more accomplished people than me, have tried to get to a definition of love for thousands of years without success. Love is particularly human just as eating eucalyptus is particularly koala. Love is what has made me my fortune! Love is what has kept a roof over our heads. Or at least trying to understand what love is, has. Love is 'I can't do this unless you're standing by my side'. Love is 'I can't live unless you are alive to watch me', because what would be the point? Love is 'I do not want to be alive unless you are'. Otherwise, what would be the point?

"I don't really know what *love* is, truth be told. I have made my fortune by telling people, stupid people, what they have longed to hear. The truth is, I don't have the answers. I made my fortune by pretending that I did. In that, I am a fraud, and I suspect, hope, that you've found me out at last, Lewis!" Check, you old goat, because I had found him out for the fraud that he was. "But none of that matters now, does it? Nothing really matters at the end of a man's life, does it? In the end, it all comes down to the manner within which a man is prepared to die. When he either remains the fraud or he comes clean. That's all that matters in the end." He turned the scrapbook around so that I could look upon the vision of my mother in black and white. "Let me introduce you to your mother, Lewis." She was beautiful, in every sense of the word. She was everything that I could have hoped that she would be at the end of all things. "The greatest person that I've ever met. Beautiful, undoubtedly;

265

intelligent, absolutely; Italian, God yes; a lover, my God; complicated, I've never encountered anyone like her …"

"So, what went wrong?"

"You did!" Beside himself with the sadness that transpires from some truths. "She fell pregnant with you. And you changed everything. When she told me that she was pregnant, we had been beside ourselves with joy. When you were born, we had been besides ourselves with joy. In the year or so after you were born, your mother had seemed to change as she struggled to reconcile herself to the fact that she'd had you to take care of apart from herself and your Uncle Enzo. And she just couldn't do it."

I had been confused. "So, she had post-natal depression or something?"

It was obvious that my father was reluctant to say much more on the subject, but he had no choice but to continue with his thread. "No, she didn't have anything like that. That's what I'd thought too, but no. She just didn't like you. She didn't want you."

"Thanks very much," I whimpered, rubbing my eyes. The dream that was my mother was quickly turning sour. But was he telling the truth, or was his statement his last attempt at hurting me before his decaying body finally gave in?

"But I did!" he announced proudly and firmly. "I liked you, I wanted you." It was affirmation that he wasn't lying after all. "So I did everything for you. I fed you, changed your nappy, bathed you, tried to make you smile because you seldom smiled or giggled. Your Uncle Enzo could make you giggle though, but then he could make anyone giggle, that man."

"I can't remember that," ashamed of myself all of a sudden.

"No, you won't. Because whatever I did was never enough. You always wanted her. You would always be looking for her. It used to break my heart when you used to reach out your arms to be picked up by her, but she never picked you up."

The one memory of my mother that I had retained in my mind for all of my life seemed to contradict everything that my father told me about her. Because it was a sweet memory. You know the one: blood orange lips, hair as black as jet tied in a ponytail, the sensation that I belonged to her and her to me, etcetera. So, is a memory a true facsimile of what actually happened? All I know is that after that parting, I never saw her again. So I absolve myself of any responsibility. It was not my fault that she had to leave. It was not my fault that she hadn't liked me or wanted me. It was not my fault that in the years that followed my father had grown to resent me as though it all *was* my fault. But it was not. I know that now.

As my father told me what had actually happened on that day when she'd had to leave me, abandon me, when the truth was coupled with that one memory that I already had, the whole scene had been clear in my mind. I could just see it all happening, and it *was* better than Dallas. I wish that as my father told me what happened, she had been standing in front of me, because never mind a goat, I would have fucking head-butted her! Bang! Take that, you rotten bitch. Payback time for Lewis!

Chapter Nineteen

I recall that I wept openly at last as my father had told me precisely what had happened on that day at the villa at Sant'Elpidio when my mother had no option but to leave. She'd either left or my father would have called the Carabinieri. The choice had been hers: go away and start a new life somewhere else or go to prison. Because it turned out that my mother had tried to kill me. My father had walked into my room and saw my mother holding a pillow over my face. He had not been lying to me when he'd told me that my mother hadn't wanted me, hadn't liked me. If anything, he was being kind with his choice of words, because she'd wanted to murder me! But what if she had succeeded? What then? What a waste of a life. Or not, because maybe my life has not been so important after all. Perhaps it would have been better for everyone involved if she had succeeded? I don't know. And neither did he, which is why our relationship had been so complicated, confused, delicate. My mother, it turned out, was a psychopath. My father had been a psychoanalyst. Me, I was caught somewhere between the two of them.

"She had a vision of her life that did not involve me or you," he sighed. "I had come along to finance it, and you had come along to ruin it. She was almost there. She had me fooled. But you, you were something else entirely. She couldn't fool you." Another wave of pain seemed to wash over him just as I'd thought that he was about to join me on my sofa to put his arm around me and comfort me. It had not been as bad as the last time, so he had recovered quicker. "For as long as I live, I will never forget that moonlit night when I happened to walk past the doorway to your room, and I'd seen her trying to smother my son with his pillow!"

Too much information. Too much of anything is never a good thing. Too much love, too much hatred, too much Irish whiskey, too much analysis. "What did you do?" I asked pensively.

"I rushed in and wrestled her to the ground. She had been beside herself with despair. She hadn't really wanted to do it." It was as though another wave had washed over him again, except this wave had been a different kind of pain, a different kind of torment. "She had been so sad that she screamed out a sound that I would never care to hear again from anybody. It was the sound of Hell. She'd been that sorry." My father then flopped forwards on his sofa, almost knocking over the chessboard with his limp head. "I can't really explain what happened next without it sounding absurd. Seeing as we were both on the floor, and since I'd known that I would never see her again, we had made love. What is love, Lewis? Assuredly I tell you that it is *not* sex. We had sex on your bedroom floor whilst you had been screaming for your mother. If she were here now, then she'd probably tell you that I'd raped her! Assuredly I tell you now that I did not. The following morning, I told her to pack a bag because she was leaving. To her credit, she left without an argument."

How long is forever? It is, well, forever. But *forever* is what you make of it. Because *forever* doesn't care.

"I do not intend to say anything else," my father lamented. "Enough is enough for one night. I would like to go to bed now."

Normally, I would have escorted him up the stairs by standing behind him as he ascended the staircase in case he toppled backwards and there I would be to catch

269

him as he fell. But not on that night. It had been obvious that he didn't have the energy or wherewithal to even stand up, so I had lifted his delicate body in my arms and carried him up the staircase to his bedroom. Thankfully, the staircase had been wide enough for me not to have caught his head on the banister. Quality always counts. I had almost thrown him onto his bed because by that point, my arms had been throbbing as though I had been Geoff Capes throwing a hammer in the Olympics, and they needed to be rid of their burden. I then helped him remove his shirt, but he couldn't help me remove his trousers, so I had done that by myself. I hadn't cared so much about his underpants or his socks, strangely. All I can recall is that I'd put him to bed. His head rested upon his pillow and for a few seconds at least he had found comfort. "I need to be quiet now," he said to me. "I need to be still. I need to be at peace."

It had been the first time that I had heard someone say *I need to be quiet now.* And I have not heard anyone say that sentence since. *I should shut up; I have said too much,* yes, of course. But not that, in the way that he said it to me. I know now that what he'd meant was that he had needed to be at peace. Because if he was at peace, and therefore still and quiet, then the next wave of pain could not cause him anything like the torment that those others had. If he remained still and quiet, then perhaps the pain would not notice him at all. And yet I still could not let him rest in peace. "A genius. You said that your colleagues and their wives considered her a genius. Why?"

"Go downstairs, Lewis." He already had his eyes closed. "Look at my scrapbook. Find out for yourself. I can't help you anymore."

What is a word? People say words without thinking about what they're saying or why, but to the listener, the recipient of those words, they are critical. My father had uttered that one word that may be my mother's salvation, her redemption: genius. According to his associates and their wives, that is what my mother was. Genius: noun, plural: *an exceptional natural capacity of intellect, especially shown in creative and original work in art, music, etc.* She may have been a psychopath but if she was a genius at the same time, then there was hope for her after all. I had wanted to know what my father had meant so I followed his instruction and went downstairs to look at the scrapbook again. I sat alone with only a table lamp for illumination because I had turned out all of the other lights so that my father could sleep. That's when I had seen that photograph of my mother holding me in her arms. The curious thing about looking at it – which I had for quite some time – was not seeing the face of my mother, I had by then become quite unsensitised to her, but seeing my own face as a baby. You know that sensation when you look at an old photograph which you are in, and knowing what happened next, you home in on yourself, don't you? Just to see what you looked like back then.

More curious was wondering whether this photograph was taken in the days immediately before she tried to kill me. If it was then, maybe her genius was in her acting skills, which would have been better than Peter's if that was the case. I hadn't been sure. I had been the right age from the way I'd been sitting upright in her arms beneath an olive tree, but who knows? No, my mother's genius had been in her creativity. She had been an artist, a very accomplished artist. The second half of that scrapbook is filled with her sketches of people, landscapes, seascapes but mostly people. I had known that

271

they had been her sketches because each one of them had been signed by someone called *Alice Ballerini*. Suddenly I had discovered my maternal surname: *Ballerini*, which means someone who likes to dance. If I decided to hyphenate my name by deed poll, it would have been Lewis Ballerini-Sinclaire, which would not have sounded like a lawnmower at all. Even more curious was the discovery that my maternal line was called the *Ballerini*s, the people who danced. The people who had built and owned that villa for countless generations were called the *Ballerini*s. I was a Ballerina. Well, you know what I mean.

One of the sketches seemed very familiar to me. It was a preliminary sketch of my father sitting in the open air in profile, looking at something or other that had caught his attention in the distance. It was familiar to me because I had seen that pose before.

I rose from my sofa and had dared to venture into my father's study-come-library again because that was where I'd seen it. I turned on the big light, and sure enough, there it was: a portrait of my father in oil, hanging on the chimney wall above the mantelpiece. I had, of course, always known that it was there. I recall that when I had taken that book off his bookshelf when I had been an A-level student, as I withdrew from that room, I'd flicked that portrait the finger.

My father was depicted in oil paints, sitting in the open air with his villa – the Ballerini Villa – in the background to give a perspective to the fact that he dominated it all. He is looking out to the sea; there is just enough of the sea in the corner that forms a direct trajectory to his eyes. I think that my mother depicted him looking out to sea because he was not an Italian and she knew that his story was elsewhere even if his heart wasn't.

272

It is a masterpiece. I still have it now, hanging on my wall. So well executed in hues of blue, brown, and orange with subtle hints of green. The likeness is unmistakably Martin Sinclaire in his prime in all his pomposity. My mother had captured his pretentiousness perfectly.

It was as though I had discovered a Michelangelo or a DaVinci or a Goyette or more pertinently a previously undiscovered Klimt. When I discovered that my mother was a genius and when I had forgiven her everything. She had been absolved of her sins whilst I gazed upon a portrait of my father that hung in his study-come-library at the big house at Henley. Almost. The one thing that I cannot forgive her for is the fact that she must have thought that I would stop her. That because she had given birth to me, she would not be permitted to become the great artist that she had known she could be, as though the two things were mutually exclusive. I cannot forgive her that because if she had permitted herself to get to know me, she would have found in me a kindred spirit. If my mother had ever eaten fish and chips, or cottage pie, or a roast beef dinner at John Bull's Traditional British Fish and Chips, then she would have discovered that I am just like her. That's why I can't truly forgive her; because she never gave herself the chance to get to know me. She never knew what she could have been, could have had, could have won.

Right then, I had gone back into the living room and picked up the house phone.

"Ciao Prego, what's up?" Luigi asked.

"How are you?"

"In cima al mondo, Lewis." Delightedly.

"What does that mean?"

"On top of the world, Lewis."

273

"Really? Why?"

"Because Rocco has found a flight to Thailand at last, and he's booked his ticket!"

"That's good for him," I replied, and I had been genuinely pleased for him. "Finally, he can go to his son. And you're on top of the world why?"

"No more fucking singing, Lewis. Finally, a bit of peace and quiet."

"But you'll be on your own once he's gone."

A pause whilst Luigi thought again. "No more singing. No more fucking opera. But I'll still have you, Lewis, my brother. You're not far away."

"You'll always have me, Luigi," I responded to allay his sudden jitteriness. "When does he fly out?"

"Next Tuesday, thank God!"

"In the meantime, I need you both to do me a favour."

"Another one?" Even though I had always paid them both for services rendered.

"Another one, Luigi."

I slept in the armchair in my father's bedroom because I had been certain that he would not survive the night. The armchair was positioned next to the window where in better times my father had liked to sit and watch the world go by on the street below whilst he'd done his crossword in *The Times* and whilst, no doubt, my stepmother had prepared for him something wonderful to eat for his lunch or breakfast in her kitchen downstairs. I hadn't slept very well. In fact, I had slept with one eye on him. His trick of keeping quiet and still seemed to work because he slept very soundly. So soundly that on two or three occasions I thought that he was dead and tried to ascertain the facts by taking hold of his hand that laid on top of his bedsheets and clenched it vigorously, but every time I did, his hand was withdrawn and was accompanied by a desperately sad sigh, or maybe it was a whimper, which confirmed to me that he was not dead after all. There was life in the old goat yet.

I think that I'd fallen into a sound sleep around five am in the morning, just as the sunlight of a new day was breaking. I think that I dreamt very vividly, *mother,* of course. Because my father had introduced me to her at last, which is why I had been convinced that he would not survive the night. In my dreams, she was holding me in her arms again. She kissed me again with those blood orange lips but I had been wriggling and resisting, told her: *Let me go, let me live.* Let him die peacefully in his sleep. But now I know that no-one dies peacefully in their sleep. Now I know that there is no easy way out of the mess that is *life* for anyone. There is no escalator like those at an airport that has a sign in illuminated letters with the instruction: *Uscita* or *Exit.* Yet, that is not necessarily true. The truth is not the sole responsibility of drunkenness; it is also the product of death. The truth will out at the end of things, I can assure you. You can either go peacefully or in agony. The choice is yours.

I don't think that my father had expected to survive the night either, so when he opened his eyes, he had been so spooked by the thought of a new day that he wished that he hadn't. Maybe it had been my snoring that had brought him back from the brink of death. He had awoken me from a deep slumber by deliberately knocking over the water glass on his bedside table. To my credit, I responded instantaneously by leaping out of my chair and picking up the glass, then asked him if he was alright as I placed it

275

back onto the tabletop whilst I had been crouching on my knees by his bedside.

"What's for breakfast, Lewis?" he asked me mischievously.

I had still been half-asleep as I replied, "Well, I don't fancy soft-boiled eggs, do you?"

"Not at all. They are a skill that I suspect you, dear son, do not possess."

"We have bread for toast. I think we have some sausages, but I can't recall why … cereal, porridge!"

"A cup of tea will do just fine."

"Porridge will do you a lot of good, Dad."

"I'll just take the tea, Lewis, but thank you."

So tea it was. And carrying a tray of crockery up that staircase had proven to be a lot more problematic than carrying a human being up it was. Everything on that tray had vibrated so much that it seemed to me that they were about to topple off it, so I had to take it one step at a time. Perhaps my hands had been shaking. Too much Irish whiskey the night before. That whole endurance test had not been aided by the fact that my mobile phone had been vibrating in my trouser pocket the whole of the way up.

The sensation of release when I placed that tea-tray onto my father's bedside table must have been obvious because my father chortled. Never had a pot of tea with slices (wedges) of lemon on a saucer and milk in a jug been delivered to my father with so much performance and hullaballoo, incompetence. It had been good to hear him chuckle, though. "Shall I be mother?" I asked whilst taking hold of the teapot.

He chuckled again. "Someone has to be," he replied. But I had been so exhausted, or hungover – it was hard to tell – that his quip simply washed over me, so I had just poured his tea, then flung a lump of lemon into it because all I had wanted to do was check my phone to see who had been ringing me. Not who I'd hoped, but anyway: guess who? That's right.

"Ciao, preggo," I said once he picked up.

"Fuck off, Lewis, that's my line," he snarled back.

"Are you alright?" I asked him.

"I am, are you?"

"Not really."

"I rang you to let you know that Rocco has agreed to do it."

I had been standing on the landing outside my father's bedroom. "He's agreed to do what?"

"What you asked me to ask him to do last night!"

Damn you, Peter, and your Irish whiskey. "Which was what, exactly?" Vaguely remembering something; some such nonsense that I must have said but had forgotten about.

"But he wants paying."

"Paying to do what, exactly?"

"What you have asked him to do. For fuck's sake, Lewis, do you want him to do it or not?" Exasperatedly.

"Yes, of course I do." *But if it's another beef Wellington, even a roast beef dinner, then I wouldn't bother, if I were him.*

"Then what time do you want us?"

I had to think. I almost collapsed through the exhaustion of having to think. "Lee is coming at two, so perhaps teatime, Luigi, if that's alright?" Still no idea.

"Who the fuck is Lee?"

"Lee is my father's nurse."

God-damn you, Peter, and your Irish whiskey. God-damn you Peter, for knowing everything.

277

Peter the actor, by the way, died just a year after my stepmother. Thinking about it now, I have no doubt that his death must have hit my father hard, so much harder than my Uncle Ennio – sorry, Enzo's - death did. At the time, I had been so absorbed in my own trauma that his death had not resonated with me at all. Knowing what I know now, and having had the opportunity to Google him, I wish that it had resonated with me because the part he has played in mine and my father's lives was Oscarworthy. His death had been recorded in *The Times*, not in the oblique *marriages, deaths and births* section, but as a full two-page obituary, written by someone who had known him well. Who knows who? *Peter O'Shea has died. The Irish actor will be best remembered for his portrayal of Nero in the 1982 movie* Burn *when he starred with Peter Ustinov as Seneca. But more memorable are his performances as Casanova* (ironically) *in the movie of the same name in 1991, and as Seb Shalp, the megalomaniac Bond villain who wanted to destroy the world in the 1996 Bond movie* ... who cares? *In two-thousand-and-two, he was awarded an honorary Oscar for his services to film and theatre. He is survived by* ... I hadn't read that far.

But I wish that my mother had painted him also because then his portrait would have hung on the wall directly adjacent to my father's. There isn't so much as a rough sketch of him in my scrapbook, only a black and white polaroid photograph.

Lee the nurse did not come that day, or ever again, as a matter of fact. He rang the house phone at lunchtime to inform me that he had been in contact with a family member of one of his patients that had tested positive for Covid and that he'd had to self-isolate for two weeks. He asked about my father's condition, and I'd told him about the increasing rapidity of his waves of pain, and that he'd stopped eating. I'd become worried when he went silent on the other end of the line before assuring me that my father would be assigned to another nurse straight away, but it was unlikely that she'd visit today, probably tomorrow. "Don't forget, Lewis, he does not have to endure the pain. Remember what I told you to do."

"OK, I will discuss it with the new nurse tomorrow," I said.

Surprisingly, my father seemed disappointed when I told him that Lee would not be coming for at least two weeks and the reason for it. He had still been laying in his bed; in fact, he hadn't got out of bed all morning. I had stuck my head into his room numerous times; sometimes, he had been laying facing the window with his eyes wide open, frightened, or astonished; the other times, he had been asleep. *Asleep* is misrepresentative of what he was when he had not been either frightened or astonished: semi-comatose, unconscious is perhaps a more accurate description. I had been more contented on those occasions when I'd looked in and had seen him 'asleep' because it meant that he was between those waves of pain. I resumed my seated position on the landing outside his bedroom with my back resting on the railings of the staircase where my half-sister and I used to sit during those New Year's Eve parties. Thinking back, I suppose that I was sitting guard over him.

"Pity," he said. "I would like to have known how his team is doing … whereabouts in the league they are now."

"The season ended some weeks ago, Dad. I think they ended the season somewhere near the bottom, but they weren't relegated."

279

"Lucky them."

"I thought you weren't interested in football?" Things always take a while to sink in with me; I frequently miss someone's point, their true meaning, until it's too late. Thankfully, on that occasion, it had only taken me a couple of minutes to get his point. "Oh, what about you? How are you doing in the league?" I asked.

"I won the league days ago, Lewis," he whispered. A wave washed over him again and he almost rolled to the far side of the bed, my stepmother's side. His legs had risen from the mattress pulling the bedsheets away from their foundations. He ended up in a contortion of Houdini proportions. "Now I think I'm about to win the world cup," he gasped with what little breath that his lungs had left in them.

Which is when I'd known that my father would not survive another night. This was it. This was the moment I had been dreading from that very first moment when I'd been standing in the hallway of the big house contemplating turning around and getting the hell out of there. How much easier would it have been if I'd been sitting in my flat at Maidenhead watching junk TV, or waiting on tables at my restaurant, then to receive a call from my half-sister informing me that my father had died? She wouldn't have troubled me with the grizzly details of his death, just that he'd passed away, that's all. But this, this was a burden, a responsibility that should never have been mine to bear alone. God-damn you, Coronavirus, for grounding those flights! I thought about ringing her to tell her what was happening. Why should she be strolling along the coast arm-in-arm with her bald-too-young-husband and their little brats following close by whilst I had to deal with the grizzly circumstances of our father's death? It wasn't fair!

280

Anger is a symptom of panic. But in a panicked situation, anger subsides very quickly to leave only pragmatism. Anger never gets anyone anywhere. If I had rung her to tell her that her *Pappa* was going to die today, what could she have done? Nothing; she would have panicked and felt helpless, hopeless, and that would not have been fair either. I was not helpless. I had suddenly found myself very necessary, tolerated because I was necessary. That's not fair on my father. I had been there, that's all, and he needed me to be. Besides, in those past weeks, we'd had some great games of chess. If I had rung my half-sister and told her what I'd known, she would have rung back every five minutes, and I didn't have the time to placate her. I had a job to do.

One of them was to carry my father to the toilet in his en-suite bathroom because cancer can destroy your vital organs, but it can't, must not, destroy your dignity. He thought that he'd been about to soil himself, but after what had seemed to me to be an entire epoch, he did not *pass* anything. How could he have? He had not eaten anything for days. Thankfully, I hadn't had to carry him back to his bed because he insisted that he walked there by himself. One final walk, unaided, to his death bed. He sensed that once he had gotten back into his bed, he would never get out of it again. He had known that his time had come, and so had I.

Ding-Dong, the front doorbell rang. *Who the hell is this?* I thought as I'd sat my father down on the edge of his death bed. "Who is it, Lewis?" my father enquired because he hadn't had the wherewithal to entertain guests anymore.

"It's probably the woman from next door," I assured him. "I'll get rid of her."

Ding Dong. "I'm coming!" I snarled, scuttling down the stairs. Guess who? That's right.

"Ciao. I know I'm not allowed to come in, Lewis, but you need to plug this in," Luigi said, handing me an electric plug on the end of a very long electric cable. I still had no idea precisely what it was that I'd asked him and Rocco to do for me, but when Luigi tells you to do something, you do it. Ever the master, ever the mentor, ever the *buddy*. So I plugged it in without wondering why, then I went back upstairs because I had left my father tottering on the edge of his bed. He had been precisely where I left him, thank God.

"Who was it?" he asked me. Now, I could have told him the truth. I could have told him that it was my over-the-top Italian *brother* who was a doppelganger for Mussolini with his friend and sidekick, Rocco, who was the dead ringer of Gandhi. If I had said that, then it would have proven his theory that *the world is full of stupid people* and maybe then he would have died peaceably. Who was it? *Not who you were expecting it to be.*

"They had the wrong house. It was someone delivering a parcel," I assured him.

Then something happened that neither of us had been expecting. From out of nowhere, all of a sudden, to take us both by surprise, came the opening movement of O Sole Mio by Giovanni Capurro. That swirling piece of music that other people thought was the accompaniment to an ice cream advert or *It's now or never* by Elvis Presley. It truly was now or never. Who was at the door? Who had been ringing the bell? You know that feeling after drinking too much whiskey the night before so you can't quite remember what actually happened? I think that I'd actually arranged for the singing chef to sing for my father, and I had never felt such a fool in my life as when

I'd been sitting on the edge of his bed next to him, and we'd both heard that opening flurry of musical notes emanating from the street below. My chickens really had come home to roost.

And yet. And yet...

... I sped towards the French windows to look down upon a scene that I had absolutely not been expecting to see. There were Luigi and Rocco standing in the street. Some sort of speaker was situated on the roof of Luigi's car, which is where the noise, the disturbance, was coming from. There was Gandhi, sorry Rocco, standing in the street with a microphone in his hand, donkey jacket, et all. There was Luigi, giving me the *thumbs up* as if to say, 'we're here, just like you asked.' There had been my father on the edge of his death bed, wondering what the hell was going on. As for the neighbours, they had all come out of their houses and were standing in their front gardens, wondering what the hell was going on too. What was going on was simply beautiful, sublime. What had been going on, it turned out, is the greatest moment of my life. And until my dying day, I will never forget it. Nor will his neighbours, hopefully. What had been going on was a musical memory, a reminder that whatever else happens to you, it can't take away the memories, it can't take away the hope.

My father had wanted to see, so I opened the French windows wide, turned the armchair to face the balconet, and helped him to get there. Just in time for our tenor's high C in the middle of the aria when the neighbours all applauded and cheered his performance. Rocco was a mixture of a 1950s crooner type of singer by the way he held the microphone and an operatic maestro by the way he sang. What a performance he put on for my father and his neighbours; what a star he was. Pavarotti, eat your

283

heart out. He was Pavarotti, Caruso, Domingo all rolled into a donkey jacket, singing their hearts out at Caracalla or Carnegie Hall or the Royal Albert Hall when in actual fact, that stupid, skinny little man was performing on the street below my father's bedroom window. It was the best rendition of O Sole Mio that I've ever heard, and my father loved every second of it, every note, every high C. The neighbours, of course, hadn't had a clue what it was all about, but at least it had given them a reason to come out into the open air. They couldn't venture any further than their front gardens, but they'd been able to acknowledge one another at last, nod and smile, recognising that they were all privy to a quite extraordinary moment. Even Luigi seemed proud to be associated with that guy Rocco. *Exalted, adjective: in a state of extreme happiness; rapturously excited.* Because that is what it was: an exalted moment for everyone involved.

It ended, as all exalted moments should, with a standing ovation. Well, it would have done if everyone hadn't already been standing, and my father had no longer been able to; otherwise, he would have too. Cries of *Bravo* resounded from across the street. Rocco took a bow, and well he should. Luigi had given me yet another thumbs up, so proud of his friend and their collaborative feat that he'd been almost bursting. Bravo, Rocco. Bravo, maestro.

"Is that where my money went, Lewis?" my father asked.

"Yes," I replied, strangely quite ashamed of myself all of a sudden.

"It was worth every penny," he assured me.

As I closed the French windows, I waved down to Luigi and Rocco. Luigi had been watching me intently whilst Rocco had his back to me because he'd been

284

absorbing himself in our neighbours' adoration. I remember that the room had gone very quiet once I had closed the windows. Then a wave of pain that was like a tsunami washed over my father taking with it what little of him was left. "You need to get back into your bed," I said to him, lifting him out of the armchair.

"I don't want to go to bed," he resisted. "I want to watch the news!" Panicked and astonished again.

Except the wave did not subside, it did not break, which meant that it was no longer a wave. The pain was now constant, a flood. My father could not bear it any longer, I knew. I had known precisely what to do in those circumstances. When I returned to the bedroom from downstairs, my father had been slouched over the armchair, no longer able to sit upright. He had still been conscious, though, so when I revealed the syringe, he asked me what it was. "It's for the pain, Dad, that's all." Without thinking too much about it, I administered that liquid into his arm, into his blood vein on his arm, with the skill that I hadn't known that I possessed. Fiona would have been proud of me right then, and so would Lee have been if he'd been there. God-damn you, Covid.

He had not bled, which assured me that I had administered it correctly. "I just want to say," I said, "thank you, Dad."

"For what?"

"It is because of you that I am living now."

"Was it a curse that I put on you, Lewis? Because *life* is a curse."

"No," I assured him. "I wouldn't miss it for the world."

So there we were the two of us, a dying man and his son. Just when I thought that he'd died, he came back to life, reanimated if you will, to take me by surprise. "The world is full of stupid people," he snivelled.

"Not now, Dad. Not again," I sobbed.

He placed his hand on my face. "I am the stupidest of them all because I let her go. Are you stupid, Lewis, like me?" They were his final words. He died. Or at least I thought that he'd died. The fact was that I hadn't been sure. There had been no nurse standing with me in that room to confirm that he had. I squeezed his hand to ascertain the facts, but that had been the limit of my expertise. Suddenly, Luigi appeared beside me. He really oughtn't to have been in the house in the circumstances. What did that matter, then? He had known precisely what to do. He placed his fingers against my father's throat then uttered those words which I will never forget, "He's fucked. I'm sorry, Lewis."

I lifted myself from off my knees then sobbed so openly and loudly that Luigi had no choice but to hug me. It was an act of pure kindness for which I will have a cause to remember that little, gruff Italian for the rest of my life.

We went downstairs after that, closing the bedroom door behind us. Ding Dong, the doorbell rang. It was Rocco, sticking his head through the front door and demanding his money. "Fuck off, Rocco, you Bastardo! Wait in the car!" Luigi affirmed, and Rocco withdrew from the front door whilst making the *filthy lucre* gesture with his fingers.

"How much does he want?" I asked my friend, going into the living room to find my father's wallet because I had been sure that he would have wanted his debts to be settled.

"Five hundred pounds," Luigi chortled.

"Five hundred pounds?" I protested. "For ten minutes worth of singing?"

286

"He doesn't come cheap," laughing and semi-appalled at his associate's behaviour.

Ding Dong, the phone rang. Guess who? That's right. "Your dad has died, Jane," I told her. I had been very empathetic, and my tone had been one of genuine sadness at having to deliver such news.

Silence. "You promised me, Lewis." Sobbing. Then, her yowls of *Michael! Michael! Michael!* And I imagined her collapsing onto her knees beside the telephone table in the hallway, or wherever the house phone was in that villa, because her grief and shock had got the better of her.

"I know. But there's only so much that a man can do." Sobbing with her and hoping that poor bald-too-young Michael had gotten to her quickly.

Chapter Twenty

The timing of my father's death, although dreadful for my half-sister half a world away, was perfect for Luigi. Because Luigi's sidekick, Rocco, had gotten the hell out of there to the other side of the world the following Tuesday, on an Emirates flight to Bangkok from Heathrow. To his son or his ladyboy – I don't know – but he hadn't cared about the baggage allowance, which was just as well because if he took that donkey jacket with him, it must have cost him an extra two-hundred pounds, which Boris most certainly would not have paid for. Arrivederci, Rocco, and thanks for everything. So, on the Wednesday morning, Luigi had come back to the big house with a rucksack so big that I'd wondered whether he intended to move in permanently. I know what you're thinking: that he'd spied an opportunity; that he was a menace; that he was a parasite on a pedigree, Disney-type dog's back. No, he was my friend.

   In the two or three days after my father passed away in that armchair, I had been struggling, to be honest. Wait a minute, just a cotton-picking minute: why do I have to be anything other than honest right now? Why do I have to feel ashamed of being on my knees again through grief? Why is there always shame attached to grief because there always is. If not shame, then regret. One or the other is always attached to a person's *grief.* I am not ashamed to say that I had found myself on my knees again because of my father's death; I had only just begun to like him. My regret is that I had only just begun to like him, understand him, in the six weeks that I spent with him in the big house at Henley because I'd had no choice in the matter. We had played chess night after night, when he had opened up and revealed himself in all his glory, like a Cob swan rising from the surface of the water and ruffling his feathers on the most famous river in the world. To my surprise, the glory was all his and not my mother's. Is a memory a true facsimile of what actually happened; is a photograph? They are not! The truth is the only true facsimile of what actually happened. But the truth, whether spoken through drunkenness or not, relies on the appointee to reveal it. My father had revealed it at the last – fuelled by a very strong Irish whiskey – and the truth had changed my mind completely, full way towards him. Up until that teatime when he died, I had loved my father truly for only six weeks. Yet, he had passed away when I was thirty-seven. So, for thirty-six and a bit years, my mother had held sway over me; had dominated my life, the way I lived my life, had been responsible for my trouble, had turned me to drink. She had ruined my relationship with a perfectly good woman; had ruined my relationship with my half-sister so that the only comparable reasoning to *The Wicker Man* was a very tenuous New Year's Eve party in 1994 when we had found ourselves sitting on the upstairs landing at the big house listening to the hullabaloo from the adults' downstairs, and we had both been terrified as though our house had been full of ghosts.

My mother had been responsible for everything because that bitch had tried to kill me, and then where would you be? You wouldn't have a story to begin with. How long is forever? It is precisely thirty-four years. In the days and nights that followed my father's death, I drank copious amounts of alcohol, sobbing whilst I scrutinised that scrapbook page by page, photograph by photograph, sketch by sketch, to try to fathom out what had actually happened. The truth is that I will never really know what happened at the Ballerini Villa at Sant 'Elpidio in 1984, and perhaps that's just as well. The Thursday of that week was the last time I have drank alcohol. With good reason, since I had been so drunk that I was sick on the black and white tiled floor in the hallway as I tried to make my way to the downstairs bathroom. Luigi had to clean it up after he had escorted me upstairs, taken off my clothes, and put me into my bed. Before I had gone unconscious, I recall that I had heard the house telephone ringing: *Ciao, Prego. Who am I? Who the fuck are you? His sister? He hasn't got a sister. Ring back tomorrow. Ciao.*

Tomorrow was the day of our father's funeral which was probably why I had gotten so drunk. You know, the stress of it all, the thought of it. What can I say about my father's funeral? It was perhaps the most bizarre day of my life, not to mention his. The limit on the number of people who could attend a funeral during the lockdown was set at thirty. You have to set this number against the fact that if my father had died during normal circumstances, there would be three thousand people who would have wanted to attend. My half-sister would have booked St Pauls if she had been able to, and she would have filled it. That great cathedral would have been rammed with his colleagues, his associates. The producers, writers, and directors of his television documentaries that he'd made for the BBC in the noughties. His editor and his publisher, whom he had made rich. His patients whom he had cured, a contingent of the congregation that would have included actors, writers, artists, politicians, and yes, even royalty. Minor royalty, mind you, but royalty, nevertheless. One of those would have given the eulogy in Peter's absence. I wonder what they would have said. The congregation in that great cathedral would have sung at least three hymns, one of which would undoubtedly have been *All My Hope on God is Founded*. Would the eulogist have mentioned my mother, I wonder? Or me, because the two are inextricably linked. What essence of Italy would my half-sister have instilled into the proceedings because there surely ought to have been some reference to his love of that country? An aria by Pavarotti as his coffin was carried out or in. It doesn't really matter since my father had a *lockdown* funeral at Slough crematorium.

The essence of Italy at his funeral was courtesy of Luigi. The government's guidelines for a lockdown funeral were severe: no singing of hymns, facemasks must be worn, everybody should maintain a two-meter distance from one another. Basically, get it over and done with as quickly as possible and then get the hell out of there, *run for your lives* because there's some other poor bugger who needs to be cremated next. The early summer of 2020 had been a boom time for funeral directors. It had been one out, one in, much like the queue for the supermarket. For those who were not able to attend because they were self-isolating, terrified, or stranded in Italy in the sunshine, remote streaming was to be made available. Needless to say, my half-sister and her brood had absolutely no intention of missing it, not for all the lemons on the Amalfi Coast. On the morning of my father's funeral, she had rung my mobile eight times to ascertain the correct link to use, the precise time to join the proceedings, what I had planned for his send off, etcetera. It was a very stressful morning, particularly when I realised that I did not possess a black tie, so Luigi had to cut his in half. So we'd worn half a tie each, which we could barely fasten around our necks. All we had managed to achieve was a black knot at the collar of our

291

shirts, but it hadn't mattered because it wouldn't show up on a live stream, would it?

The hearse arrived precisely on time. The funeral directors were all wearing masks. As Luigi and I had come out of the big house, I noticed that my father's neighbours had come out of their houses again to see him off. It was not another O Sole Mio moment, but their gesture had touched me, nevertheless. I think that Luigi had waved at them all, and bizarrely some of them had waved back. We had only needed one limousine to follow the hearse to Slough because at that stage, it had only been me and Luigi. One of the undertakers had leapt out of the hearse to sanitise the car-door handle preparatory to us getting in. That had confused Luigi no end.

"Who's giving the eulogy?" my friend asked me once we made ourselves comfortable inside the car.

"Marjory."

"Who the fuck is Marjory?"

"My father's friend. His lifelong friend, as a matter of fact. She knew him as well as anybody."

"What's she going to say about him?"

"I don't know, I've left it up to her. But I think it'll be good because Marjory is a writer." Having thought about it, I began to worry that she might compare my father to Henry the Eighth because although she was very accomplished in her field, her field was limited. Marjory was one of the world's foremost authorities on the Tudor period of English history, but that's all she was. Ask her to write something about life or love or loss, or pain or joy, sunshine, storms … and she would flounder like a fish out of water. In the car, I wondered whether Marjory had ever met my mother because I had not been sure that she could have. The dates just didn't seem to figure.

As it turned out, only thirteen other people attended my father's funeral. The crematorium had only been at half capacity, such were the circumstances. I counted them as Luigi and I followed my father's coffin into the little chapel that they have at Slough Crematorium that is attached to the furnace behind the red velvet curtains. Thirteen, unlucky for some; unlucky for him. But I had remembered Peter's quip that thirteen at a dinner party is only unlucky when the hostess only has twelve chops, and it gave me comfort. Marjory was there, of course, who looked every bit the septuagenarian that she was, but the woman who was with her could not have been much older than thirty, a pretty woman with long hair. Marjory scowled at me as we processed down the centre aisle behind my father's coffin. She would have preferred my half-sister and her sons but what she had gotten was me and Luigi. I vaguely recall that my stepmother's brother had been there with another woman, but I can't be certain because I had only met that man once when I was a child. He was a postman in Reading, so hadn't been made very welcome or had felt uncomfortable at the big house at Henley, where people only ever talked about important things.

As for the rest of them, I hadn't a clue. Probably his chess club. Except for the one face that I did recognise: Fiona. She smiled at me to reassure me that she was there for me and not because she'd had any affection whatsoever for my father. That's what a person needs at a time like that: help, support, succour, a benefactor. Now there's a good Latin word that essentially means a *kindly helper*. And she was, just by being there. T*wo-thirty* was the time that I'd told my half-sister to join the live stream. Lights, camera, action!

Most of the thirteen that made up the congregation observed the rules perfectly. They had all worn black face masks, had all stood two meters away from one another. The postman had stood two meters away from his daughter (I presume, but who knows?). Marjory had stood two meters away from her younger lover, a rule that I presumed the younger woman was more than happy to have had the opportunity to observe at last (although, who knows?). Fiona had been standing on her own anyway. The only ones who had been standing at close proximity to one another had been the members of his chess club because they make up their own rules anyhow.

The eulogy: what can I say? The presiding clergyman called Marjory up for her to play her part, but she fluffed her lines. Talk about a fish out of water. That, by the way, just about sums up her walk towards the pulpit because unbeknown to me at the time, she had been waiting for two new hips, but because of the current crisis, her operation had been cancelled. Marjory, the writer, had almost crawled towards the pulpit when I had looked over my shoulder to see her younger lover shaking her head in despair and disgust. "Look at the fucking state of her," Luigi whispered in my ear. "I hope she talks better than she walks."

"We are here to remember my friend, Dr Martin Sinclaire, OBE," she began. A strong start, I'll give her that. But from then her eulogy went downhill; it had been all bullet points on a page that she was reading from. Martin was born ... *no-one cares*; his father was an engineer for British Rail and his mother was ... *who gives a shit?* He obtained his PhD in philosophy from the University College London in 1979 ... *blar*. He met a woman whom he would later marry, called Sandy Monroe, in 1985, to whom he would have a daughter, Jane

… Wait a minute, just a cotton-picking minute, what did you just say? You seem to have skipped a year or two?

Luigi sensed my discomfort. "What's the matter?" he asked me.

If I had been sitting at the London Palladium, then I would have booed or hollered: Get Off! Instead, "She isn't describing my father at all," I replied, solemnly.

Luigi knew me well enough to know when I was riled. The countenance on my face, the way my shoulders vibrated through anger, was more or less the same reaction that I had when I had discovered his little plot to pilfer my Pecorino on our last day at John Bull's Traditional British Fish and Chips. "Don't you do anything to embarrass me, Lewis," he whispered in my ear.

"Get off, move aside," I instructed Marjory as I took up my position at the lectern, and Luigi had sighed resignedly. *Lights, camera, action.* Marjory had been relieved of her duties, and in actual fact, she had been very relieved to have the opportunity to sit down at last. "Where's the camera?" I asked the priest, or vicar, or presiding clergyman or whoever the hell he was.

"The camera?" he replied, a little bit confused.

"For the live stream!"

He had to think about my proposition for a little while before directing me towards a little red dot in the corner of the chapel beside the door. "I think that might be it," he told me before withdrawing because I think that I had moved so quickly that I had broken the two-meter rule. It was my turn. Something had risen in me, and to this day, I can't really describe what it was because ordinarily, I am a very reluctant public speaker. Frustration, more than likely. Frustration at having been air-brushed out of that family for most of my life. Anger

295

that my mother had been overlooked; Italy had been overlooked entirely. Maybe I had been premature in my ejection of Marjory, and she may have been building up to it, craftily constructing a tone of suspense as any great writer would, but I doubt it. Bullet points were what she had been about probably, due to the pain in her hips, so she hadn't really cared to put the effort in. Or she hadn't known what I knew?

I had spoken directly to the red light. "What Marjory has told you is perfectly true, I'll give her that. My father was a very clever man. He belied his mediocre upbringing to gain a doctorate in his field from one of the world's great universities. So what? Who cares?" A gasp from my audience which assured me that I had shocked them all. "But he wasn't as clever as the letters after his name might have you think. In one aspect of his life, he had been very stupid. The world is full of stupid people, and he was one of them, quite frankly.

"My father loved Italy. Italy, his little piece of Italy, was his lifelong obsession. Italy was his mistress, and everything he'd strived to achieve was only to please her. My father first went to Italy in 1981 with his lifelong friend and confidant, Peter O'Shea … that's right, the actor. Whilst lost, they stumbled across a dilapidated old villa called Villa Ballerini, the *house of the dancers*, where he met a woman who would change his life irrevocably … is that a word? I think it is. Anyway, the villa had been run by a woman called Gloria as a bed and breakfast, so they stayed a while amidst its crumbling charms. At breakfast on their first morning, my father met my mother. My father did not believe in love at first sight, but I do. I am certain that as my mother cleared away their breakfast plates, my father had fallen in love with her

296

there and then, and he did not stop loving her, thinking about her, for the rest of his life …"

I was certain that at that point I noticed that spiteful red-light flash faster and faster; I could imagine my half-sister's despair and fury on the other end of the link. I imagined her thumping her gormless bald-too-young husband as he tried to comfort and reassure her. But, as aforementioned, sometimes my imagination can overpower me, so who knows? Maybe she had been enthralled, as Marjory's lover and Fiona and another man that had caught my eye, seemed to be.

Marjory had left her bullet points on the lectern and since at that juncture I had needed to take a moment, I read what she had written. *The BBC,* yeah, whatever, *the bestselling books*, so what? *The OBE at the Palace* when that queen should have sliced his head off for being so stupid! Her conclusion had angered me though. *He died peacefully at home, and I think the saddest thing about his passing is that his beloved daughter, Jane, is not able to attend today due to the current crisis. I know that she is looking in via a live stream, so Jane, I just want to let you know that we are all thinking about you at this sad moment in your life. To conclude, I quote Gloriana herself, Elizabeth the First: 'I may not be a lion, but I am a lion's cub and I have a lion's heart!'* There it was. I knew it. I bloody well knew it! I almost choked through anger when I read that bit.

So, I ranted on. "For three whole years they had been happy together," I raged. "My father had bought the villa when that matriarch, Gloria, died suddenly. Screw Gloriana, this is all about Gloria!" I directed my remark directly towards Marjory. I had, by that point, been very angry. The congregation, all thirteen of them, had been very shocked. The red flashing light had almost exploded.

297

"And they had a son together. A son that they named Lewis after my mother's favourite author." Once more at poor Marjory, who had begun to realise that her aching hips were suddenly the least of her problems: "And here I am! Lewis Ballerini-Sinclaire!" Which roughly translates as *Lewis, the dancer, bot boy don't he drone on and on.* "Just like Henry the Eighth had a son too, but nobody ever writes about him either! It's all about the daughters!" Then, as I recall, to my eternal shame, I flicked Marjory the finger when she had almost fainted, and the presiding clergyman had gasped in shock. This was either the worst, or best, funeral he had ever presided over. As I stepped down from the lectern I had proclaimed loudly: "Al-eech-ay lives!" Gasps of shock all around, like the beginning of an operatic chorus.

As I put my mask back over my face, mainly to hide my shame, Luigi asked me, "Better?"

"Better now, thank you," I sighed, settling down at last. "But I suspect that I've been eulogising to the alarm censor, not the actual camera!"

"You are stupid, fucking idiot!" Luigi whispered, chuckling.

The committal was committed in shock. "Would you all please stand for the committal," the vicar said, slightly unnerved, slightly aghast, obviously out of his depth and sinking fast. Obviously, a novice because funerals can be all manner of emotions, as this one was. Everyone stood up. Marjory had to be helped up because she'd only just sat down, bless her hips. "To everything there is a season and a time to every purpose on Earth, a time to be born and a time to die. Here in his last act in sorrow but without fear in love and appreciation ..." he'd had to read his notes ... "we commit Martin Sinclaire to his natural end." He crossed himself, poor man. Poor,

298

disillusioned man … "to be accompanied by a song chosen by his son, a beautiful Italian love song. Please listen as we say goodbye."

When I sat down, I had been emboldened, empowered by my forthrightness; finally, the head of my family and I had taken back control. What happened next completely destroyed my credibility. Why can't I ever win? Probably because I had stupidly let Luigi pick the music that would accompany my father's coffin through those red, velvet curtains. He had assured me that it was a famous Italian song called 'Bella Ciao' that his Mamma used to sing as she prepared his favourite meal, pasta Fagioli. He had chosen it because the translation was *Goodbye Beautiful,* so he'd thought that the title was pertinent, knowing what he did. The title was, but the rest of it was completely inappropriate. I recall that I read in a newspaper, *not* The Times of London, about a funeral wherein the family had selected the love song from the movie 'The Bodyguard' to accompany the coffin's withdrawal beyond those red curtains. You know the one, the Whitney Huston classic. Because of a misunderstanding or miscommunication with their funeral director, what they actually got was the theme tune from the classic 1980s television comedy 'Minder', and you know that one too, sung by Dennis Waterman. Completely inappropriate for anyone's funeral, bar Dennis Waterman's own. I wonder if that family saw the funny side. Anyway, it was a bit like that, except the funeral director had precisely found the right song, just the wrong version. So my father's coffin had disappeared behind his red velvet curtains to a tune so jolly and uplifting that the congregation, not to mention the vicar, had gasped in disbelief all at the same time to make a sound that was like a fierce wind blowing the chapel doors

299

open. I could almost hear my half-sister's squeal all the way from Sant 'Elpidio.

"What the hell's this?" I mouthed to Luigi, myself in disbelief, spying over my shoulder and daring myself to look at the flashing red light.

Luigi leant towards me and whispered, "My Mamma used to sing it slower!"

It was too late to have done anything about it; the song seemed to go on and on, building in tempo as it did. I found myself tapping my foot to it, and I noticed that the vicar was moving his head from side to side to the tempo as though he was Zorba the Greek. Thank God that we'd all been wearing masks because I knew that beneath them, everyone was trying to stifle a laugh that would have been completely inappropriate as my father's coffin tracked its way towards the incinerator with the red velvet curtains slowly closing in front of it to spare us the shock of seeing what happened next.

The song ended approximately four hours after it had begun, or that's what it felt like. Once the red velvet curtains had been fully closed, the vicar removed his mask and I just knew that he'd been laughing behind it; I could tell by the way he had to get his breath back. "That was a very moving tribute," he said, gasping. Sarcastic bastard. "Thank you, Lewis," *for giving me the greatest moment of my career.* "And thank you all for coming," he said to the congregation. I just knew that they'd all been thinking *we wouldn't have missed it for the world*, as though they had just said a combined *Amen.* "Because of the current crisis, I would ask you all not to gather in front of the chapel …" (fat chance of that) "… but to be on your way as quickly as possible. May the grace of God be with you all." Then he had sped so quickly from that lectern into his little room adjacent to the chapel that it was as though he had needed the toilet urgently or to laugh out loud at last.

Luigi and I had been obliged to walk out of the chapel first then wait outside for the others to emerge too, one by one. They were like the animals stepping off the ark once the flood had subsided and Noah had told them that they could go now. Dry land at last after an eternity adrift on a boat with other animals that, in other circumstances, they would rather eat than accept their right to exist. They all looked exhausted.

Eight of them had simply walked past us and offered us a sympathetic smile. They were probably the members of his chess club who were no doubt thinking: 'No wonder he never mentioned that he had a son' or 'who the hell is the other one who looks like Mussolini?'

"Grazie, arrivederci," Luigi said to them, kindly, as they walked past him.

Marjory and her younger lover were next out, but she'd just limped by us without acknowledging us at all; her lover had had to help her down the steps one by one, one step at a time. "Gesu Cristo, imagine having to wake up to look at that!" Luigi lamented as we both watched her slow descent from the chapel, willing her to stumble and fall. "Who the fuck is she anyway?" I am almost certain that she flicked the finger back at me once she'd gotten into her waiting car.

The man I had noticed earlier who seemed to have appreciated my effort at some sort of appropriate eulogy for my father was next. He paused in front of me, maintaining a distance, of course. "Thank you for mentioning Peter, Lewis," he said to me. "I know how much your father meant to him and what he did for him."

"My pleasure," I replied, on the edge of crying.

Then he simply drifted away. "Who the fuck is Peter?" Luigi asked me, confusedly.

"It's a long story."

Fiona was the last out of the chapel. She paused in front of me too. She is beautiful. But she did not maintain her distance; she stepped forwards and hugged me tightly. "Good for you, Lewis," she said to me heartily. "Good for you."

"Thank you for coming," I replied haphazardly. "My father loved you, Fi!"

Withdrawing, she replied: "No, he didn't. He *loved* you, Lewis. You were always on his mind. All I was, was your chance to get over yourself."

"I'm sorry. Was it the worst funeral you've ever attended?" Then I immediately reproached myself because in that moment, I remembered that she hadn't been able to attend her brother's funeral in Devon. I had cringed by my choice of words, my turn of phrase.

"It was just about right," she laughed. "You do know that your half-sister is probably already on a flight back here to sort you out, don't you?"

"God help me."

"Bye, Lewis," she concluded.

"Is that the nurse?" Luigi whispered in my ear as we watched her leave.

Which is when I wept openly at last because it was over.

On the other side of the road, I noticed a woman loitering with intent. She had been looking at me intently, trying to catch my attention. A tall man had been standing with her at first, but once she had caught my attention, he backed away. I was in no doubt whatsoever that this woman and I were destined to meet one another. It was a

302

strange experience for me to be drawn to someone across a busy road so strongly that I had crossed it without being concerned about the flowing traffic. Cars sounded their horns as this madman crossed, and one of them had to slam their brakes on. Talk about the butterfly effect: if that man hadn't had the wherewithal to hit his brakes, then I would never have known what was to come next on this extraordinary day.

It was not my mother if that's what you're thinking. The woman, in her mid-thirties, was the spitting image of my father. I mean, his doppelganger; she had the same nose. "Is your name Lewis?" she asked me, tentatively, with a north-eastern American accent.

"Yes," I replied bemusedly.

She held the flat of her hand against her nose as though she thought that it was about to fall off. She wept as she said, "I think that I'm your sister!" in a very strong New-York American accent.

.

Chapter Twenty-One

"I'm sorry, what did you say?" I spoke after a pause, during which I contemplated what she had said. During a vacuum into which the whole of my life, and all of my grief, could have been poured into.

The woman finally removed the flat of her hand away from her nose. "My mother was Alice Ballerini, my father was called Martin Sinclaire, an Englishman."

"So were mine!" I gasped.

"Then I think that qualifies me as your sister, don't you? I read about his passing in the New York Times, and I said to Daniel I've gotta go there."

"Who the fuck is Daniel?" Luigi asked her, poking his head in between us.

"Luigi, please give me a moment," I scolded him. It was the first and last time that I have sent him away from me.

He skulked away down the street with his shoulders hung over his body like a scolded schoolboy. "Capisco, whatever," he snarled. "Gesu Cristo, at least fucking Dallas had a commercial break!"

"Daniel is my husband," the woman then said to me. "He is the love of my life. Daniel is the person who has got me through all of this." And suddenly, as if the woman had been Debbie McGee, Daniel had sprung up as though he was Paul Daniels. Oh well, you get my point.

"Hello, Lewis," he said to me, wanting to shake my hand but knowing that he wasn't allowed to. "Boy, are we happy to meet you, man." He had seemed happy to meet me, after all the years, after all of the drama and turmoil that I had instinctively known that they had been through. Daniel had, has, a full head of hair, that was so abundant he could have styled it in any way that he desired to, whatever the mood had taken.

"Look at your hair!" I whimpered, lacking the wherewithal to say anything else. It was all I could think of to say to him, and frankly, I had wanted to run my fingers through his thick, luscious hair.

"His hair?" the woman responded confusedly.

"It's a long story," I replied to her. I had not known what else to say to them. They were total strangers to me, and in my defence, I had just incinerated my father whilst a very dodgy Italian song had played in the background.

"Is that your partner, Lewis?" the woman asked me, referring to the Mussolini doppelganger stomping his way along the sidewalk, or pavement?

"You mean my business partner?" I said, disorderedly. "He never put a penny in!"

"No, I mean is that your *partner*?" she followed up with, determined to know one way or the other, having obviously witnessed us both emerging from the crematorium together.

I have aforementioned that sometimes it takes a moment or two for the penny to drop. Sometimes, when I have missed a person's point, it has been too late to correct them, but thankfully on that occasion, the penny had dropped by that woman's emphasis, in that strong New Yayk drool, on the word *partner*. "Oh God, no," I insisted. "He's my waiter!"

"Your waiter?" All three of us were getting more confused with each passing second.

"Yes, my waiter and my friend," I told her. What I had really wanted to say to her, to scream out aloud, was, *I don't know what you expect me to do right now!* Instead, in the awkward pause, as we watched Luigi stomp away to the end of the street in somewhat of a huff, we had then

305

looked at each other for a prolonged period of time. She had seen in me her mother and I had seen in her my father. The obligatory DNA test that the characters insist on having done in dodgy soap operas was not necessary. Her arrival and subsequent announcement that she was my sister was not in doubt. It was obvious to me that she was who she said she was. I had a sister. Not a half-sister or a second sister once removed, but a full, bona fide sister. And she had a brother all of a sudden. She is about five foot six – or whatever the American equivalent is – has long dark hair like her mother, green eyes, is slim in build like her mother, is incredibly stylish like her mother (she'd worn a silk scarf around her neck), and has a hooter like a hornbill like her father that had mesmerised me at that first meeting because I wondered that if I'd pulled on it would she make a noise like a steam train whistle?

She is an American woman. Her husband is tall and slim – athletically slim, not skinny – very handsome and has a beautiful head of golden-greyish hair that he wears swept back over his head and kept in place by a gallon of hair gel, or whatever the American equivalent is to a gallon. My sister is called Gloria. Yes, that's right. My mother named her after our grandmother.

"What do we do now?" I asked her, bewilderedly, slightly in shock. She'd had more time to prepare. She had been the sibling who had dropped the bombshell and it had exploded right on top of my head. "I need a drink," I concluded desperately.

"Most places still seem to be closed in this country," Daniel, my brother-in-law, lamented.

The off licenses aren't, I thought right then, imagining that we three could just sit on a park bench and drink strong liquor straight out of the bottle, passing it down the line in turn, whilst reminiscing and bewailing our misfortune. In the circumstances, that would not have been a bad thing to do, but instead I had suggested that we all go back to the big house at Henley. "I would like you to see where he lived," I said to her, and she agreed that she would like that.

The limousine driver looked at me disbelievingly when we all shinnied into the back of his car and made ourselves comfortable. My sister had looked embarrassed as though she ought not to be there, but as far as I was concerned, that was precisely how she ought to travel to our father's house. The driver shook his head, and I knew that he was thinking, *it's not a taxi, sir*. The car pulled away from the Slough Crematorium in stately fashion but unlike the journey there, the driver had pulled onto the M4 motorway to get us home as quickly as possible. We alighted in front of our father's house but this time, the neighbours had not come out of their houses to welcome me home, for which I had been thankful because a lot had happened in the three hours since I had embarked with my father on his final journey, and I had returned with company.

My sister adored that house. She looked at it in that quintessential American way of observing something by their standards. To her, the house was small, quaint, and archetypically English, like something out of a Jane Austin novel. I did not tell her that it was worth two-point-five million pounds sterling or that the night before, I had puked all over the black and white tiled floor in the hallway upon which she was now standing. "How lovely," she sighed. "What a lovely, welcoming house."

She was looking at it objectively, of course. She had no idea whatsoever of the trouble that had existed within those four walls, but also of the laughter and joy too sometimes. Every time I stepped foot into that hallway, I had thought firstly about my dog, Andrew, and secondly about my stepmother, who was always rushing out of her kitchen to greet me. I had always heard my father's voice in my mind saying, 'I haven't got any money, Lewis' … or 'here he is!' despondently. Because a house triggers a memory like nothing else can. A family home is the biggest, maddest gadfly of them all and stings the mind like a syringe the size of the Shard in London. A house is where *life* happens, whether it's an Edwardian terrace in Henley, a villa at Sant'Elpidio, Italy, or a second-floor apartment in Queens, New York City. A house is the stage upon which *real* drama happens. Drama that is not so mellow; comedy that is hilarious; melancholy as though it can only exist there; grief as though it were a chapel.

If I had been invited to step into that second-floor apartment at Little Neck, Queens, I imagine that I would have felt the same compulsion to be as condescending as my sister was when she stepped into our father's house. All I would see would be the rising damp, all I would hear would be the sirens and horns on the road below, all I would smell would be the garlic coming through the ceiling from the apartment below. Because walls cannot talk. A fact of physics that humankind has lamented for as long as human beings have dwelled in houses. If only they could.

I felt sorry for my sister because even though I had not known our mother for long, I *had* once known her. Had felt her embrace, the touch of her body against mine, and I have the photos to prove it. I have a memory of her, and even though the truth has come along to discredit it, it still exists in my mind even now. A memory is resilient, if nothing else, so I have forgiven her. She is redeemed. But my sister had never known our father. So, as she wandered into the living room and gasped with delight at the chandelier and the ornate cornice work around the ceiling, the picture rail from which hung paintings of Henley the town, river scenes, Italian seascapes, etcetera. When she'd evoked an image of Mr Darcey when her husband, Daniel, had followed her into the room, as though she were at Disney or wandering around Windsor Castle and looking at paintings of Henry the Eighth or Queen Victoria, I had been resolved to bring her back down to earth with a bump, because why should she be feeling so happy right then? That house was *not* Disney, or Windsor Castle, or quaint olde England, it was where *life* had performed on its stage.

Ding Dong the house phone rang. Yes, that's right.

"I've been trying to get you on your mobile, Lewis!" The lawnmower, that's right. And a very revved-up lawnmower to boot. More like a strimmer than a lawnmower right then.

"Oh, really," I replied, innocently. "I've had it turned off for obvious reasons."

"You had to do it, didn't you?" my half-sister snarled all the way from Italy. "You had to make it all about you!"

What I wanted to bellow down the house phone all the way back to Italy was that is precisely what I had not done. I had made it all about *him*, our father! I had precisely given the right eulogy at the precise funeral where it had been necessary. Even the song, Bella Ciao, was perfect, just the wrong version, that's all. I had known it in my heart that my father would have been proud of me for the first time in his life, even though he was dead. So, screw you, Dr Jane Sinclaire-Sharp. But I had not said that. Instead:

"I can't really talk right now, Jane, so I'll ring you later!"

"Why? What's happened now?"

"My sister has turned up," I replied.

"What?" Horror-struck, probably thinking more about the two-point-five-million-pound house than the fact that I had another sister.

"It turns out that I have a sister," I whispered into the receiver joyously. The most joyous, delicious news that I have ever delivered to anyone. "She's just coming out of the kitchen, so I have to go." The sound coming out of the receiver end of that house phone was like one of those chainsaws revving up to cut down an ancient Brazilian Nut Tree in the Amazonian rain forest. "Love you, Jane, but gotta go. Much love to Michael and the boys!" And I slammed the receiver down just in time for my sister and her husband to step back into the living room, as I imagined that my half-sister had been so frustrated and angry that she thumped that bald-too-young husband of hers square between the eyes to send him hurtling to the far side of whatever room their phone had been in.

"What a beautiful kitchen," Gloria said politely.

"You have no idea how beautiful it is," I replied, vaguely, thinking about my stepmother and her famous beef Wellington. Thinking about where and how she'd died. Anyway, thinking about her at that moment, not my father, not my mother, only her.

It was to the kitchen that we manoeuvred ourselves because as any gracious host would, I had offered them a drink. "Tea or coffee?"

"Oh, tea, I think," Gloria answered excitedly. "We're in England after all." As though the tea in England was different from the tea in New York or anywhere else. So I boiled the kettle, got the best teacups out of the cupboard, and made the tea in a pot.

"Shall I be mother?" I asked, looking at them both in turn (it never gets old, that one).

They had positioned themselves at the kitchen table, side by side, where Jane and I had sat all those otherworldly years ago. Gloria looked very mystified. "Excuse me?"

"Tea, Gloria, how do you take your tea?"

To her credit, she'd reprimanded herself for being so ignorant. "Oh, just a little bit of milk for both of us, thank you."

When I opened the fridge, there wasn't anything remotely like milk in there. There was barely anything in there; a bit of butter, but that's all. "I haven't got any milk," I said, ashamedly. "I don't drink … milk … and Father took his coffee black and strong and his tea with lemon."

"Lemon will do just fine," Daniel said.

"Are you lactose intolerant, Lewis?" Gloria asked me.

No, I'm a borderline alcoholic, all I drink is wine and when the occasion calls for it, Irish whiskey, I thought to myself as I'd scoured that kitchen for anything resembling a lemon. But there wasn't one. The fruit bowl had contained only a rotten banana. "I haven't got a lemon either!" I sighed resignedly as though to acknowledge what a terrible host I was. My stepmother would have been appalled at my ineptitude.

My sister sensed my shame. She was embarrassed. She stood up but with the good grace not to have sent her chair hurtling to the far side of the room. "We've imposed ourselves on you too soon, Lewis, and I'm sorry for that."

"It's fine," I assured her. "It's just that, right now, I'm a little bit this and a little bit that, if you know what I mean?"

311

"Of course, I do," she assured me, empathetically. "If it was the other way around and you walked up to me on 59th Street, then I would feel a little bit this and a little bit that, too."

"Fifty-nine what, exactly? I thought you lived in Queens?" A little fact that I had managed to ascertain during the ride back from the crematorium.

"My mom and I lived in Queens," she replied, slightly more embarrassed. "Daniel and I live in Manhattan now."

Daniel, it turned out, was an executive for a television streaming service (yes, that's the one), so I am glad that I hadn't told them that the house at Henley was worth two-point-five million pounds because he would have simply shrugged his shoulders as though to say *so what*? It would have been pocket change to him. Everything is relative.

"Black tea will do just fine," my sister concluded. So I poured them out a cup of tea from a teapot into China teacups, which they had gone gaga over. "English tea, in a teacup, in an English house," Gloria laughed to her husband.

If it weren't for the damn allotments, you'd probably be able to see Mr Darcey swimming in the nude in the second most famous river in the world, after the almighty Hudson! I thought to myself. Right then, I had hated them both.

The thing about arriving unannounced is that you can never really know what kind of welcome you are going to receive. I had, up until then, been a gracious host, if somewhat a little bit inept. But as Gloria and Daniel had clinked their China teacups together as though they were toasting their combined success; as though they had been taking tea with the queen herself, I had been resolved to bring my sister back down to earth with approximately the same level of *bump* that her announcement on the street in front of Slough Crematorium had caused me. To that end, I had broken their little moment by saying to my sister, "I want to introduce you to our father, Gloria!" Because this was not quaint olde England or Disneyland.

I led them both into my father's study-come-library. Even then, I had to pause in the doorway in case he was still sitting behind his desk. He wasn't, of course. Because he was dead, and I'd just cremated him. I took her by the hand and led her in – she had been absorbed by that room. *Oh, Dan, look at this* – and positioned her in front of his portrait that hung above the mantelpiece. A portrait of him as a young man. "Dr Martin Sinclaire OBE, the foremost psychoanalyst of the late twentieth century. Our father." My sister looked at that face on the wall above her, and it must have been like looking in a mirror. She had been transported by it. "Behind him, see, is the Villa Ballerini where our mother was born and raised. Our mother painted this picture."

What happened next was the intended effect of my devilment. Gloria crumpled into her husband's body and sobbed so openly and loudly that I had expected her to pass out because her body had become so limp, and he'd had to keep her upright with his arms. "This is what we wanted, Glo," my brother-in-law said to her, kissing her on the top of her head to reassure her that he was right. "This is why we came. To find out what happened." He pushed her away from him, towards me, so she'd had to stand on her own two feet. "I'm going out for a walk," he announced. "I'll leave you two to it. How do I get to the Thames from here, Lewis?"

313

"Turn left once you're out of the front door and follow your nose, you can't miss it," I told him. But don't expect to find Mr Darcey swimming in it, or Ratty, Badger, Mole and Mr Toad rowing along it, because life doesn't work out like that. All you'll see is a couple of swans and maybe a few ducks, and if you're lucky, no people.

During his absence, my sister and I had talked about things. About this and that at first, until one or the other of us had dared to mention that great, pompous, beautiful elephant in the study. "Oh boy, I could do with a drink!" Gloria exhaled once the conversation had turned onto the inevitable. *You really are my sister,* I thought to myself as I fetched her a glass of red wine from the kitchen. "Are you not having one, Lewis?"

"I don't drink very much," I replied. "Well, not after last night anyway."

It had been my pleasure and my honour to have told her all about her father, the kind of man he was. His passion for chess, what a good host he was when the occasion demanded it of him; what a quite extraordinary examiner of people's minds he was and of the glitterati that he had 'cured' during the course of his career. Gloria had been enthralled all over again. I had shown her his scrapbook when she had looked at black and white photographs of her mother, her father, her mother with her father, Peter the actor, the villa Ballerini, and me as a three-year-old child. We had looked at it together whilst we had been sitting at the kitchen table, and I had pointed out who was who because it hadn't meant anything to her.

Insisting that I turn back the page, Gloria exhaled, "Wait a minute, isn't that …?"

"Peter O'Shea, the actor, yes."

314

"He's like a megastar, Lewis. I've seen so many of his movies!" Starstruck.

"He was my father's best friend. He was like a brother to him. My half-sister and I used to call him 'Uncle' Peter." Take that, Daniel, because your streaming platform cannot compete with that, and your penthouse apartment (I supposed) and all the money in your bank account cannot buy that kind of kudos. I had never loved my 'Uncle' Peter as much as when my sister had been looking absorbedly at his black and white photograph. I think at that point I had rushed into the living room to fetch the photograph of him and my father dressed in their finest outfits that had always sat on top of the piano in the bay window, just to accentuate my point.

"There's so much that I don't know," Gloria sighed.

"You and me both," I chortled.

The fact was that we were strangers, my sister and me. Well, relative strangers, attached only by a desire to know the truth. To finally be able to understand why our parents had been so stupid all those years ago. She had wanted to know everything there was to know about her father and only I had the information that she had craved all of her adult life, whereas I had wanted to know the same amount of detail about my mother.

I had gone first since she had made the effort to cross the Atlantic during a pandemic. I had told her all about him, but I won't repeat it now since we haven't got the time and besides, it's already been said. I did tell her, however, that the important bit, the part about when our father had fallen in love with our mother, and what had happened between them at the Villa Ballerini, I had only found out myself barely a week before. And only then because of the extraordinary circumstances that had

315

forced me to 'isolate' with him in his house whilst my half-sister was stranded on the other side of the continent, so there had been nothing else for him to do but play chess and drink whiskey and tell the truth. It had been as though I was reading her a bedtime story, something like *Alice in Wonderland*, so absorbed in my words she had been.

Whilst her handsome husband had been walking along the Thames no doubt looking for Ratty or Mole, or maybe even Oliver Twist, or Henry the Eighth, I had introduced her to one of the most extraordinary English characters of the late twentieth century, who happened to be her father. Incidentally, I did not tell her about John Bull's Traditional British Fish and Chips, or of the dream that I had for that place; or that Rocco, my chef, had sung O Sole Mio to her father in the street, and the neighbours had loved every note, every high C. Or anything about Luigi, or Pavarotti, or Prince Charles or the Sheiks. Because it would not have made any sense whatsoever. It would have just sounded like nonsense.

In reply, an hour or so and a few more glasses of red wine later, Gloria told me all about my mother. I listened just as absorbedly as she had. Alice Ballerini had arrived in the US with enough money from my father to start a new life, a mind full of regret but also with a sense that her life was about to begin again in a new country filled with opportunities and gullible men. It seems that the only thing that was hampering her purpose and desire was that there was a new life growing in her womb, which she had not bargained on because she had not known about it when she left. So my sister had come as a bit of a shock to her, a reckoning, and her punishment. Which, reading between the lines, had formed the basis of their relationship because Gloria had not spoken about her with any degree of fondness at all. I hope that I had not spoken about my father with the same level of gloom, but I suppose that in parts, I probably had.

So, my mother had secured the lease on a second-floor apartment in Little Neck, Queens, New York, because she had needed somewhere to live but my father had not given her that much money to allow her to settle in Manhattan, which was where she must have preferred to be. The dream of New York is not Little Neck, Queens. The dream, the aspiration for anyone arriving at JFK, is to make it all the way to the top of a skyscraper, to be able to look down on the world. For someone as complicated and wound up as my mother was, not to mention talented, her dream must have been to mix her paints with the best of New York society. It turned out that in the end, she had, but at the beginning of her new life, she had struggled. Her greatest asset, more so than her talent, which has never got anyone anywhere, was the way she looked. She was a beautiful Italian woman and when she first arrived, no-one knew that she was pregnant with my sister. So, apparently, she had worked several menial jobs in restaurants to pay her rent. Italian restaurants, more than likely, and I imagine that the proprietors of those joints had been overwhelmed to have an authentic Italian siren serving their pizzas and pastas. I never really knew my mother, obviously, but I imagine that that particular part of her early life in New York had been like purgatory to her. She must have considered that time as her penance for having had to leave me for having tried to kill me. Every pizza or pasta dish that she served to a group of cackling wise guys must have felt like self-flagellation to purge her of her sins. It would have been a short period in purgatory for someone like her if it had not been for the

317

swelling in her belly. A fact of nature that it seems she never forgave her daughter for.

How easy it would have been for my sister to gloss over those early years of her upbringing to concentrate on the gilded years in Manhattan when our mother had secured a position with an auction house that specialised in fine art and when she had made that particular proprietor fall hook line and sink in love with her, daughter, et all. Probably because of the effectiveness of the red wine, Gloria did not gloss over anything. She needed to purge her mind as well, not of sins but anger, so she had given me the bleak version, the unabridged truth. And it had been bleak during those early years. Gloria told me that she had been taken into the care system when the woman in the neighbouring apartment had alerted the authorities that she was left home on her own while her mother was out with a suitor. She had been five years old when she had been placed in a children's home and I had imagined a scene out of Annie, and they'd all sang *it's a hard knock life*, but judging by Gloria's sad countenance, it had not been precisely like that at all. It had obviously been a horrible time for her.

Daniel is a multi-millionaire TV executive; they own a luxury apartment in Manhattan and a substantial residence in the Hamptons – a cliché, I know, but facts are facts – so it would have been so easy for my sister to have fraudulently claimed that her life had been blessed with good fortune and the love of a good mother, but she had not put that kind of spin on things at all. She had not glossed over the truth, to her credit. In fact, that whole conversation had almost been an exhalation of her wrath and sense of injustice in one, continuous, relentless, ferocious breath. 'Breathe, Gloria,' I wanted to say to her because, at one point, she had seemed poised to have a

318

heart attack. *It doesn't matter now.* Except, it did, it does, because we are all a ripple effect of history, a consequence of how our parents chose how to live their lives. My sister is most definitely not a fraud. She does not boast about their money, their houses, their success. If anything, she is the opposite of a fraud, whatever that is. Genuine, I suppose; a bona fide lovely woman who'd had a terrible start in life, that's all.

She had been returned to her mother when she was ten years of age since her mother had reformed herself to a certain degree. Returned to that apartment in Little Neck, Queens, but that had not mattered since all a child wants, longs for, needs is to be with their mother, and it doesn't matter where it is. In any case, I'm sure that it was better than the children's home or being passed around between one foster home to another, between people who hadn't really cared unless they were getting paid. Just like Marjory only ever entered into a conversation about the Tudors when she was being paid. I wish that I hadn't flicked Marjory the finger in the chapel, thus destroying any chance of a future meeting, because I would have liked my sister to meet her. Gloria would have destroyed that hipless historian with just one look. It had not been all plain sailing after that, however, since our mother had had one wisecracking wise guy after another. Men who to Gloria had only been a name beneath a hat. She had not dared herself to get to know any of them because it seems to me that they were in her life one day and gone the next. Men with names like Tony or Marco, Luca, and Mario, who had been only too pleased to have had a woman like our mother on their arm but who had considered my sister a nuisance, a trip hazard that had gotten in the way of what they really wanted.

"I think I got off lightly," I sighed once Gloria had calmed down. "I think I dodged a bullet."

"You really did, Lewis!" she replied ardently.

To say that my mother's life in New York had come as a great disappointment to me is an understatement. Gloria's description of our beautiful mother had left me reeling with disenchantment. Her hair seemed less dark than I remembered; her lips a little less orange; her smell a little less fragrant. Imagine a balloon being burst because it had been blown up just that little bit more than was necessary, and you will get an image of how I felt right then. She had let me down, my mother, at the last. Yet, who am I to judge her? I wasn't there because she had left me behind. Gloria's exposition of our mother's character had been opaque, to say the least, spoken in the first person, from her own experience of her. There was some hope, however …

"Oh, it wasn't all bad, Lewis," Gloria said. "I used to love it when she took me to Macy's, or Central Park, or the Bronx Zoo." My sister's eyes frosted over. "In Macy's, she used to spray me with every scent bottle on the counter until a cloud of a dozen different perfumes had shrouded me, and we'd laugh and run out. At Central Park, she used to nudge me mischievously when a man in lycra ran past us. At the zoo, she would pull me towards the Ape House and point at a gorilla and say, 'He's your father, Glo. So now you know'! And we would laugh." They had been very private memories that I had not been privy to but at least I still had my one. "And things had gotten better once we'd moved to Manhattan," Gloria continued. "She seemed to settle down. I had always known when she'd been steady and calm because she would paint. She was a very, very talented artist, our mother, Lewis." She had sensed my disenchantment. "My

320

apartment is full of her paintings. When you come over, you will see them for yourself."

"Am I invited, then?"

"You are my brother, Lewis," Gloria insisted. Maybe it was the wine talking, but hopefully not. "And now that I've found you, well, I'm sorry if this isn't what you want to hear, but I am never going to let you go!" It had been precisely what I wanted to hear. There had been an affiliation between Gloria and me from that very first meeting on the street in front of Slough Crematorium, and even though neither of us had known anything about the other, it was obvious from the way we both looked, me like her and her like him; from the way we had looked at one another, that we were siblings. A product of the same, dodgy stock. Two bewildered ripples of water breaking against the earthen bank, or against each other; against the curb, against the bookshelves of our father's study-come-library. Or, if it had been the other way around, and I had gone looking for her, against the Rockefeller Centre or the hot dog stand in Central Park, or Gino's Pizzeria and Gelato on the main street at Little Neck, Queens, because if I had known ten years ago what I know now that is probably where I would have gone in search of my mother. But I wouldn't have found her. Neither would I have discovered that I had a sister because ten years ago, she was living in Manhattan with her gorgeous television executive husband, whose hair really ought to be used in a shampoo advertisement.

"Was?" I probed.

"Was what?"

"You used the past tense to describe our mother's artistic streak." I paused afraid to ask. "Is she dead, then?"

Gloria paused too. She then gulped back every last drop of red wine in her glass before announcing, matter-of-factly, "She killed herself when I was twenty-five!" Her announcement had merely added another measure of drama and sorrow to add to everything else that had been said in that kitchen. "She hung herself in her apartment. I found her two days later. I was supposed to meet with her on the day she did it, but my girlfriends had organised a trip to Long Island, so I hadn't." Grief and regret: twins, like Romulus and Remus. Grief and regret: siblings, like Elizabeth the First and Mary Tudor, if you pardon me. Or like Lewis Sinclaire and Gloria Ortiz. I had never been so angry in my life. How dare they, the two of them, have left us two like this? How dare they! God damn you, Mother, and you too, Father, for letting us find out like this. The world is indeed full of stupid people, and you two take the biscuit.

Daniel arrived back at the house just in time to hear me ask his wife why she had not tried to seek us out before today. Gloria had been preparing to answer but her husband's appearance in the kitchen doorway had thwarted her. "Did you find the river?" she asked him, wiping her eyes.

"Stunning, Glo," he answered, enthusiastically. "It is everything you have ever imagined in your mind's eye. It is like a silver thread holding history together." Poetic. My brother-in-law, the poet. He sensed her unease though, so he stopped waxing lyrically. "I'm not interrupting, am I? I am, aren't I? You two haven't finished talking."

"Lewis has just asked me why I haven't tried to find him until today," Gloria said.

"She did, Lewis," Daniel added, rushing to her defence. "We came over on the tenth anniversary of her mother's death. We stayed in the Harte and Garter at

Windsor." Very posh and very expensive, since it was located directly opposite the Henry the Eighth gate at Windsor Castle. When Charles married Camilla that was where the world's media had stayed, and I recall that the balconies had been aglow with television lights, but anyway, I digress. "And we actually came to this house. Glo had some ludicrous idea that she could just knock on the front door and say to the old guy, 'Hi there, I'm your daughter!' I told her life isn't like Dynasty, Glo." *Dallas*, but who cares.

"But I did see our father, Lewis," Gloria added. "I saw him on the doorstep as he was kissing goodbye to your sister …"

"Half-sister!" I protested.

"Anyway, she pulled on his nose, and they'd laughed together, and I knew then that I could not impose myself on their lives. Everyone had moved on, so what would have been the point of ruining their lives with my selfish, stupid announcement about who I was? Suddenly, who I was did not seem to matter."

"But what about me? I had not moved on. Did you ever pause to think about me?"

"Of course, I did," she assured me, touching my face with her hand. "But you were nowhere to be seen. If he had been saying goodbye to you, Lewis, on that doorstep, then perhaps I would have had the courage to cross the street."

Moments, simple consequences. How might things have been different for me if my sister had crossed that street? "It's all water under the bridge now," I concluded.

"It is," Daniel affirmed. "And it needs to be." Ever the executive, he looked at us both, had taken hold of both of our hands, and neither of us had been in any doubt about who was in charge. "They are both dead now!

Gone. History. They don't care anymore, so why should you two? Live your lives and just be glad that as a consequence of their stupidity all those years ago, you now have a brother and you now have a sister," looking at us both in turn. To Gloria: "Your stupid mother was pregnant when she left your stupid father, but so what?" And to me: "And you have obviously spent your entire life feeling aggrieved because your mother left you. So what? Worse things than that happen to people all of the time!"

It's worth mentioning here that at the time of their visit, Daniel had been the executive producer on a documentary series about the refugee crisis in Syria. God-damn him. God-damn him for being so gorgeous, for having hair that my bald-too-young, quartered brother-in-law had not had since secondary school. God-damn him for being right. I could not wait to introduce him to my half-sister, because I had a feeling that they would get along fabulously.

And then we three had hugged; very American, and for me, very awkward, because I am very English. Then something dawned on me. If I had been drunk in that moment, that awakening, that smack across my face, would have sobered me up instantly. "Oh, shit, shit, shit," I exclaimed, panicking, pulling myself away from their embrace to the amusement and surprise of my houseguests.

"What's happened now?" Daniel asked suspiciously, curiously.

"I forgot about Luigi!" Imagining him strolling up and down in front of the crematorium at Slough, waiting for the limousine to come back for him, that was never going to come back for him because the driver had clocked off hours ago.

"Who's Luigi?" Daniel asked me.

Gloria glowed. "He's his waiter," she answered for me, and to this day I am still convinced that she thinks that we were lovers. "Go get him, Lewis," she urged me. "Bring him home."

Ding Dong, the house phone rang. *That's* right. I answered her call, but I did not have the time to spare.

I ran all the way down Henley high street, past the queue for Waitrose, across the bridge, and on and on until I picked up the Maidenhead Road which I assumed would be the road that my friend would come back on. If he decided to take a different route, then that was not my fault. I had seen him coming towards me at a place called Hurley, that's right, where the Sun Inn is and where I had first encountered him. He need have called Marjory for her lack of athleticism because he looked like one of those marathon runners at the end of the race, the ones who need to be helped over the finish line one misplaced step at a time, when the race marshals deliberately hold a ribbon that a fitter, faster athlete had broken through hours before; looking on admiringly but secretly thinking, 'Jesus Christ, won't you hurry up, we want to go home?' The ones who get the biggest cheer because God loves a trier. He looked exhausted because he'd had to walk all the way from Slough crematorium to Henley. The sight of him staggering along the sidewalk, pavement (oh, whatever) had made me laugh. Once Luigi had seen me running towards him, he had regained enough of his strength to become customarily angry.

"Bastardo!" he bellowed at me, staggering towards me. "You are fucking Bastardo, Lewis Sinclaire! You fucking left me behind! You are a fucking C …."

"See you next Tuesday, Lewis," is what my half-sister had said to me on the house phone. "Because I have finally found a flight back to the UK, and we land at Gatwick next Tuesday at three-PM, so make sure you're there because I have a few things that I would like to say to you. You broke your promise, Lewis. You let him die, and I don't think that I'll ever be able to forgive you. And that funeral, what in the name of God was that funeral all about? Once I'm back, now that things are getting back to normal … hang on a minute, Lewis … *oh, shut up, Michael, and go and wash your hands* ... I intend to have a proper memorial service for my pappa …" In St Paul's Cathedral, no doubt. But that doesn't matter right now because I have bigger fish to fry.

To spite his anger, I hugged him once I had reached him, and he seemed to calm down. My friend, my little Italian, Mussolini doppelganger with his dyed black hair, whom I had abandoned temporarily because I had thought that I'd had bigger fish to fry. But I had not. As I pushed him away from me once our embrace had ended, I asked him, "Why didn't you just go back to your flat?"

"Because my keys are in your fucking house, Lewis!" he answered, scarily enraged.

"It is not my house," I lamented.

"I don't fuck care anymore!" he replied, gasping for breath because he had already walked too far. "Whoever the fuck house it is, my keys are in there!"

"She was pregnant when she left, Luigi," I said to him, ardently, because there was not another living human being alive on the planet in that moment who would have known what I was talking about. I recall that I had been almost *bouncing* on the spot in my emphasis on the word *she.*

"Who was?" he asked, almost too angry to care. "Don't tell me, your fucking mother? Because that's all you care about, isn't it?"

"Cristiana was!" He gave himself a moment to consider what I had said. But I had been too excited to wait for his response: *the fucking waitress?* So, I had concluded the story for myself. "That's why she left me because she was pregnant! Look at me, Luigi, what kind of father would I have made for her child? Much better for her to have gotten the hell out of here and raise the child on her own."

A deep breath proceeded his reply: "The fucking waitress at the Sun Inn?" Astounded.

"She was pregnant when she left me."

"How do you know that?"

"Because I have seen the photos."

"What fucking photos?"

"On her social media. She went home to Italy, and she has a child who's about four years of age."

"So what? How do you know it's yours?"

"Because he has the same nose as my father!"

"Who does?"

"My son, Luigi, my son!" Beside myself through turmoil I announced, "I need to find a flight to Italy. I need to go to Italy now."

"Lewis, my brother, my friend," Luigi said to me, assuredly. "If you go to Italy, then you will have to quarantine for two weeks when you get back. And then what the fuck are we all going to do?"

"There is no-one left to worry about, Luigi, apart from me and you," I said emphatically. I had been determined to go, but my friend had been afraid of living in the UK without me. Because everyone has their own, private agenda. It has nothing whatsoever to do with the past, but it is all about the future for each one of us and argue against that fact of life if you dare! My brother-in-law had been right: it was time for me to live my life. "I don't intend to ever come back," I told my friend. Right then, my friend had been afraid of what would become of him once I had gone, if he had been left alone. "I need to book a flight to Italy!"

I had broken away from his embrace and was striding away from him towards the sunset that was the big house at Henley, because that is where the money, and my passport, and my clothes, had been.

"Why?" Luigi demanded, too exhausted to keep up with my pace.

I turned. "Because the world is full of stupid people, but I am not one of them," I said to him.

Luigi stopped walking and was standing stock-still. He had been thinking about his ex-wife, the mermaid, and the daughter that they'd had together; more pertinently, he had been thinking about his mamma. "Then I'm coming with you."

"Luigi, if you come too then *you* will have to quarantine when you get back!"

"I don't want to come back," Luigi said.

Epilogue (the Third Person)

Lewis found a flight from Gatwick to Perugia for himself and his friend Luigi the following Tuesday, the same day his half-sister, Jane, was due to fly back to the UK. The cost of their tickets was extortionate, but Lewis had somehow managed to pay for them both. The love of his life, Cristiana, lived with her father in a small town called Foligno, not far from Perugia, which is why they had flown there, and most definitely not because he had intended to visit the Villa Ballerini because that place had been the last thing on his mind. Luigi contributed towards the trip by paying for the taxi that took them from the airport to that small Umbrian town.

As Lewis packed his bags on the Monday afternoon before his flight, he assured his sister, Gloria, that it was perfectly fine for her and her husband to stay on in the big house at Henley for however long they wished, so they did. The time was a very purifying experience for Gloria since once her brother had gone, she felt as though the spirit of her father was with her at last because that had been his home. Every night she drank a very full-bodied Valpolicella, ate fine Italian cheeses that they procured from an excellent delicatessen on Henley high street and looked at that scrapbook from cover to cover. She looked at photos of her mother and her father; that great actor, Peter; her three-year-old brother; her Uncle Enzo; her grandmother and namesake; and not least that damn villa. She tried to make sense of it all. It did not occur to Lewis that on the Tuesday evening, his half-sister, Jane, and her family would arrive at the big house and demand to know 'who the hell are you?' Or perhaps it had.

"I'm Gloria, Lewis's sister, and you must be Jane?"

329

"I am Jane, yes, and *I* am Lewis's sister!" Jane retorted angrily, scouring the house for her half-brother. "Where is he? Lewis! Lewis! Lewis …?" she called out, but Lewis was not there.

"He's gone to Italy," Gloria told her happily because she knew why he'd had to go.

Cristiana lived with her father on a small farm on the outskirts of Foligno. Lewis already had the address because she texted it to him the day after she left in the hope that he would come to his senses and join her there. But he hadn't because he had been too wrapped up in his own bubble of trouble at the time, too contented to let a bottle of white wine diagnose his problems and cure them. Actually, at the time, it had not occurred to him that the reason she sent him that text message was because she had wanted him to join her. Lewis had always been slow on the uptake when it comes to another person's point or the proper intention of their words or messages.

The taxi ride from the airport had taken the pair of them through some truly exceptional countryside because Umbria is perhaps the most beautiful part of Italy. It is positioned in the centre, has no coastline, is not preoccupied with money like in the north, poverty like in the south, or hung up on history like Lazio or Campania in the middle: it is neither this nor that. So its hills just roll away one on top of the other until they disappear into the distance like a gentle wave on a calm sea. But Lewis had not looked at the scenery in the same way Luigi did. It was as though he was actually the Italian and therefore anesthetised to its beauty, and his friend was the first-time visitor, enraptured simply by the thought of it never mind the actual sight of it. Lewis had been too nervous to look at what was unfurling out of his car window. He had been worried that Cristiana might have moved in the four or so years since she left him, or since he had last heard from her. Then he remembered that she once told him all about that little farm in Umbria, about her domineering father who had struggled all of his life to eke out a living, so one of the reasons she had come to England in the first place was to send money home to him. So, he was reassured that she had probably not moved. A farm in Umbria is not something a man like her father can ever leave, so by extension, neither could she. That realisation only made him even more nervous.

"What if she doesn't want to see me?" Lewis said out of the blue, panicking all of a sudden.

His sudden outpouring of nervousness took his friend by surprise. "I'd be more worried about her father coming at you with a fucking shotgun if I were you, Lewis," Luigi sighed. "Look, if she turns you away, then you'll just have to come and live with me and Mamma in the house."

Oh, God! Lewis thought, ungratefully. *What a mistaka to maka*, or *what the hell am I doing here?*

The taxi driver stopped the car and mumbled something in Italian which Lewis had not understood. "What did he say?" he asked his friend.

"This is where the satnav has told him to stop, and he's not prepared to go any further," Luigi answered. "This is it, Lewis. This is your intended destination."

The car had stopped on the main road adjacent to a narrow farm lane lined on either side with Cyprus trees. Lewis gulped anxiously as he got out of the taxi, opened the boot and took out the small suitcase that contained all of the necessary things that he thought that he would need once he started his new life and then closed the boot. The taxi driver's inclination when he heard his car boot slamming closed was to speed off, on to his next destination with Luigi still inside. Luigi told him to stay precisely where he was and to not do anything impulsive, which was not like him at all.

"We'll wait here, Lewis," he said to his friend, who was standing at the entrance to the farm lane holding his suitcase. He looked like a schoolboy on his very first day at school, desperately clinging on to his satchel because the satchel was the only link he had to home.

Lewis set off walking down the narrow farm lane. Every now and again he turned around to be sure that Luigi was still there. "Go on, you'll be fine," Luigi assured him out of the taxi window. He did not have to walk far before he saw her. There she was tipping pellets into the donkeys' trough: the most beautiful Italian woman he had ever seen. Just as beautiful as he remembered she was. More beautiful. He stood stock-still. When she turned around and saw him standing there, she dropped her bucket and the pellets scattered around her feet. The donkeys thought that it was a feeding frenzy, so they almost toppled her over. She climbed over the fence and walked towards him along the lane because she had not been sure that her eyes were not deceiving her. So, they found themselves walking towards one another, slowly, a little bit this and a little bit that. Once she was sure that it was him, she ran towards him, and he ran towards her, and they took one another in their arms and spun and spun each other around until they were both dizzy.

"Guida fino al tuo prossimo rientro," Luigi instructed the taxi driver. Or drive on to your next drop off. The taxi driver sighed relievedly, and as the car pulled away, Luigi leant out of the window and hollered in that

332

Italian-Anglo way that that he had of speaking: "I love you like you are my fucking brother, Lewis!"

Once the taxi had sped off to its next drop off, Lewis had then gone off on one of his tangents again, and in the rush of blood to his head that comes from realising that you are right, and you always have been, he then proceeded to tell Cristiana pretty much word for word what she already knew. Poor woman. "Why are you telling me all of this, Lewis?" she asked him bemusedly.

"Because …" he paused, he hardly dared say the words again, "… because the world is full of stupid people, but it's important to me that you know that I am not one of them."

A young boy then ran up to them. He was approximately four years of age, certainly no older than that. He ran up to them whilst kicking a football. The football stopped rolling at Lewis's feet. Lewis was caught unawares because he had not expected to meet him so soon. He had barely finished telling the woman his story about himself. "Buttalo indietro, signor," the young boy said to him, almost insistently, longingly, waiting to see what he did with it.

"What did he say to me?" Lewis asked her.

Cristiana laughed along with her son. They laughed at his stupidity. "He wants you to kick the football, Lewis," she replied.

And the world stopped turning because it seemed to him that everyone was waiting, watching to see what he did with it. In that moment, he thought about his stepmother again. He had not thought about her in a long time. In his head, he heard his stepmother bellow from the side-lines: *just kick it, Lewis*! So he did, and he sliced it into the donkey field.

"Stupido Inglese!" the young boy hollered at him as he ran away from them to fetch his football.

His mother chuckled to herself.

"What did he say?" Lewis asked, bewildered, wondering what he did wrong.

"You stupid Englishman," Cristiana replied. "But don't stress too much about that, he's learnt it from his Nonno. It is what he says to him whenever he does something wrong."

"Stupid Englishman?" Lewis gasped, incredulously. "But he is not English."

Cristiana gasped too. "No, what is he then? L'Italiono, Ce?"

"Ce, the Italian," Lewis confirmed, gasping.

Lewis had made a memory with his son that his son had then carried with him for the entirety of his life. Lewis had done so by conjuring up an image of his stepmother in his mind. Because his stepmother had once said to him: *just kick it, Lewis*, so he had. But even in that moment, that memory, she *was* not his mother. Because **I am**! That's right, it's me speaking to you now, because I think that I should have a bigger part in this than the one I have been given. Because I have my own story to tell. My name is Alice Ballerini. I have never married any man who would take my name away from me. I am a Ballerini, a dancer! I always was. I always will be. But I was a terrible mother. It just wasn't my cup of tea, that's all. But I thank God that Martin was a terrific father. Because, in the end, he brought my son back to me over a game of chess …

"Come on, Lewis," Cristiana said to him, taking hold of his hand and leading him towards the big house at the end of that lane lined with Cyprus trees, towards the setting sun. "Let me introduce you to my father."

334

"Oh, God!" Lewis lamented as she took hold of his hand and gently pulled him towards the farmhouse.

A week later, his father's last will and testament was delivered from his solicitor in Henley, an old chess-playing associate who had crossed all the T's and dotted all the I's precisely how his client had wished. That old son-of-a-railway-engineer bestowed upon his daughter, Jane, the big house at Henley and the entire contents of his estate, which amounted to something in the region of six million pounds. He bequeathed to my son the villa at Porto Sant'Elpidio and one-hundred-and-sixty thousand pounds. A strange amount, but he had been determined to deduct the money he had already given him since he had originally intended to leave him two-hundred-thousand pounds. But Lewis was contented with what he received. It was enough. He wished his half-sister no ill fortune at all.

Incidentally, before I go, before I rest in peace at last, I just want to let you know what became of Luigi. Or, *Zio Luigi*, as my grandson came to call him *(Uncle Luigi)*. When the taxi driver had pulled away from the farm lane on the outskirts of Foligno, he had taken his second passenger to his own drop off point. His mamma lived in a house in a town called Ancona, fifty-two kilometres up the Adriatic Coast from Sant'Elpidio. The taxi fare had almost bankrupted him.

"Gesu Cristo, at least Betty Turpin wore a fucking mask," he snarled at the taxi driver when paying him (he'd meant Dick Turpin, but it didn't matter since the taxi driver still wouldn't have had a clue what he was talking about because he didn't speak English). That little sexagenarian, Mussolini doppelganger withdrew his

335

suitcase from the boot and then the taxi sped off leaving him standing in a cloud of dust. The screeching of car wheels brought his mamma to her front door. She had not been expecting him.

She was the very essence of what you expect an Italian *mamma* to look like. She wore a pinafore dress and an apron because she was perpetually cooking something or other. Luigi had been so happy to see her alive and well, but she had borne an angry countenance on her face as though he had interrupted her from something important. He walked towards her, clutching hold of his little suitcase, then stopped in front of her. His mamma gently placed her hand on the side of his face, her eyes mellowed at the sight of him.

"Look at you," she said to him, lovingly, longingly. Then she became customarily angry again and used the same hand to smack him across his head. "You break my heart every time I look at you!" she snarled. "Get in the house, the neighbours are watching."

He stepped over the threshold and the smell overwhelmed him, it welcomed him home. "What are you cooking, Mamma?" he asked.

"Pasta Fagioli but you're not getting any!" she replied, angrily, "because you break my heart over and over." As she followed him inside, she closed the front door and looking out onto the courtyard, she waved at her neighbours. She smiled to herself as she waved at them. She thought to herself, *Everything is going to be alright now because my boy's home* and closed the front door. I know precisely how she felt, because so is mine.

Printed in Great Britain
by Amazon